A Breath of Frost

ALSO BY ALYXANDRA HARVEY

THE
LOVEGROVE
LEGACY

A Breath of Frost

ALYXANDRA HARVEY

WALKER BOOKS
AN IMPRINT OF BLOOMSBURY
NEW YORK   LONDON   NEW DELHI   SYDNEY

First published in the United States of America in January 2014
by Walker Books for Young Readers, an imprint of Bloomsbury Publishing, Inc.
www.bloomsbury.com

For information about permission to reproduce selections from this book, write to
Permissions, Walker BFYR, 1385 Broadway, New York, New York 10018
Bloomsbury books may be purchased for business or promotional use. For information on bulk purchases
please contact Macmillan Corporate and Premium Sales Department at specialmarkets@macmillan.com

Library of Congress Cataloging-in-Publication Data
Harvey, Alyxandra.
A breath of frost / Alyxandra Harvey.
pages   cm.   (The Lovegrove legacy ; [1])
Summary: When three cousins in 1814 London discover their magical powers and family lineage of
witchcraft, they accidentally open the gates to the underworld, allowing the spirits of dark witches
known as the Greymalkin Sisters to hunt and kill young debutante witches for their powers.
ISBN 978-0-8027-3443-3 (hardcover)   •   ISBN 978-0-8027-3445-7 (e-book)
[1. Witches—Fiction. 2. Magic—Fiction. 3. Cousins—Fiction.
4. London (England)—History—19th century—Fiction.
5. Great Britain—History—George III, 1760–1820—Fiction.] I. Title.
PZ7.H267448Br 2014   [Fic]—dc23   2013028809

Book design by Amanda Bartlett
Typeset by Westchester Book Composition
Printed and bound in the U.S.A. by Thomson-Shore Inc., Dexter, Michigan
2 4 6 8 10 9 7 5 3 1

All papers used by Bloomsbury Publishing, Inc., are natural, recyclable products
made from wood grown in well-managed forests. The manufacturing processes
conform to the environmental regulations of the country of origin.

For my mother. *Je t'aime.*

A
Breath
of Frost

Part 1

UNTESTED

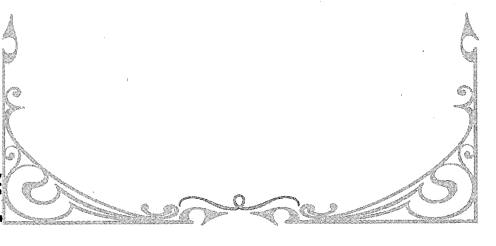

.Prologue

1814

Breaking into a dead woman's house was easy work since she rarely complained.

Breaking into a dead witch's house was a different matter altogether.

You were as likely to come across some bit of wandering magic as a weeping relative pacing the floor. When a witch died, many of her spells unraveled and the results were unpredictable at best. Moira might get lucky and the house wards would break first. On the other hand, Mrs. Lawton's ghost might push her down the stairs.

She'd have to risk it. One-Eyed Joe wanted what was inside, even if he didn't know it yet. And the old lady's body would be hauled off to the cemetery tomorrow. Moira had no intention of becoming a grave robber.

Moira stayed crouched on the roof next door for over an

hour, watching carefully as a household lamp was carried from room to room. The gargoyle on the corner of the Lawton house was draped in black bombazine, like the mirrors inside would be. Mourning extended to all parts of the house, and the ghost was expected to protect its family while the gargoyle slept.

Finally, the lamplight floated upstairs. She waited an hour after it was extinguished, just to be safe. She wished she had Strawberry with her, but her friend was off on another job. And if she took one of the boys they'd want the bigger cut just for being there. Even though Moira had been stealing things to sell at the market since she was nine years old, and some of those boys barely had a year under their belts.

She hopped over the gap between the roofs and slid down a drainpipe to the parlor window on the north side of the building. It was customary to leave it open for the spirit to pass through. Moira didn't mind sharing with a ghost; she was used to sharing the rooftops with vampire pigeons, rats the size of hedgehogs, and Nigel the snorer. She left a muffin on the sill as an offering. Mrs. Lawton might have preferred wine or sweets as many spirits did, but Moira only had one lemon-drop candy left and she wasn't about to give it up for a dead woman with no taste buds.

She wiggled inside, grateful poor girls didn't have to wear corsets, and Madcaps didn't even have to wear dresses. Her trousers were frayed in one knee and two sizes too big, but they were comfortable and allowed her to move in ways that would have snapped the spines of soft aristocratic girls.

The house smelled like whiskey, cheap lamp oil, and a dead body. There was no odor of lemon balm, which was a relief.

Warlocks smelled like lemon balm, so she knew for sure that she was stealing from a regular witch. Warlocks just weren't worth the risk. They were ruthless in life and worse in death.

Moira paused, waiting for her vision to adjust to the gloom and assessing her surroundings. The protective eyes painted on the thresholds and over the lintels were draped in black material, just like the gargoyle had been. There was the usual assortment of chairs and trinkets. She didn't know how people lived in such close quarters with so much clutter. She hated the feeling of being inside a building, without a view of the sky or seven different escape routes at all times. Moira's feet burned, the way they always did when she was courting trouble. She tried to ignore it, reminding herself the walls were soft enough to kick through, if worse came to worst.

She knew the upstairs had two rooms and the attic was full of mice. She'd sent her familiar inside earlier in the day, just to be sure. Having a cat as a fetch was infinitely more practical than the wolves and eagles the fancy witches coveted. They might be more romantic than an alley cat, but you couldn't exactly send your wolf-familiar into the body of a real wolf in London to any reasonable purpose, could you? Cats, on the other hand, were everywhere and rarely noticed.

A scrawny russet tabby with a bent ear leaped out of Moira's rib cage. The fiery pinpricks in her heels subsided to a low warning itch. The first time she'd felt Marmalade leave her body, Moira had thrown up. And then spent the night crying because she thought she was going crazy. One-Eyed Joe found her and fed her mint tea and told her stories about witches and magic.

He'd taught her to avoid the Order and never sell to a warlock without a disguise and that her familiar was her closest ally, literally created out of her own magic.

Marmalade swiped at her leg with a ghostly claw. Blood welled on the scratch.

"You know, Strawberry's familiar is a little white mouse. She brings her flowers." Marmalade knew full well that Strawberry's familiar was a mouse; keeping the two apart was a constant struggle.

Magic clung to the cupboard on the wall and billowed like pink steam out of a teapot. Old lady Lawton was a tea-leaf reader and she'd protected the tools of her trade and the magical artifacts in her home from tampering and theft. Luckily, Moira wasn't interested in those.

She crept forward to the dining table. It was covered in a white sheet on which Mrs. Lawton lay in her best dress. Her gray hair was curled and a silver brooch was pinned to her collar. Moira left the pin even though it would have fetched a decent price. It wasn't what she was after and it felt rather rude, considering.

She gently pried Mrs. Lawton's eyelids open. They felt like stiff paper. Her right eye was cloudy and vacant, her left perfectly clear and blue as cornflower petals.

The glass eye of a blind witch three days dead.

She popped it loose, trying very hard not to hear the vile popping sound it made when it came free. She tucked it into the pocket of her striped green waistcoat, refusing to gag.

She placed a coin over the eye socket, as payment. It wasn't

stealing if you paid for it. And, if you believed in the old stories, you had to have a coin to pay your way to the other side.
She hoped it would appease the ghost long enough for Moira
to slip out the window.

It wasn't enough.

Mrs. Lawton's spirit sat straight up out of her body and
screeched.

"Thief! Thief in the house!"

"Bollocks!" Moira jumped a good foot into the air and then
stumbled back against the wall, gasping. Bloody ghosts. Marmalade hissed, fur rising like a boot brush. When no one came
running to investigate, Moira released her breath.

Mrs. Lawton didn't drift forward like pollen or moonlight or
any of the things poets claimed. Ice skittered over the floorboards as she slammed into Moira, mouth opening wide to show
rotted teeth. Her breath was toads and mushrooms and mildew.

Moira clamped between her teeth an iron nail she'd dug out
of a rafter. The iron helped, but it didn't banish Mrs. Lawton
completely. The ghost's hand closed around Moira's throat. Her
touch burned even as frost filled the space between them.

Mrs. Lawton shouldn't have been able to do that, even as a
recent ghost. There were wards over London. Locks on mystical gates and portals. Binding spells. The Order.

Mrs. Lawton didn't seem to care for any of those fail-safes.

And for a dead old lady, she packed quite a punch.

Moira's feet felt branded, as if she didn't already know she
needed to get out of here. *Now.* She was weak as boiled turnips.
Her vision started to go gray and blotchy.

Marmalade knocked the teapot over. The handle cracked ominously.

Mrs. Lawton turned her phosphorescent head so quickly her neck snapped.

Marmalade batted the teapot as if it were Strawberry's mouse, rolling it closer and closer to the edge of the sideboard. Mrs. Lawton's grip loosened. She ground her teeth so savagely, one fell out and corporealized when it hit the ground.

Marmalade flicked the teapot once more and as it tumbled, Mrs. Lawton lunged for it, momentarily forgetting Moira. Moira scooped up the dead woman's tooth and tucked it next to her glass eyeball before diving out of the window. She scampered up the first drainpipe she found, flattening herself onto the roof to catch her breath. Her black hair tangled around her, catching in the shingles. A neighbor thundered out of his door in his nightshirt.

When Marmalade jumped up beside her, Moira rolled over onto her feet, brandishing a dagger. The cat calmly licked her paw. Moira let out a shaky laugh. "That did not go as planned, Marmalade," she said. "Let's go home."

She walked the ridge like a circus girl, balancing lightly and keeping her chin high. When she reached the edge she turned right, intending to head home.

Pain gnawed at her, as if her boots were full of angry bees.

She stumbled to a stop, cursing. She wanted to go to her favorite summer rooftop made of slate tiles that held the heat pleasantly. There was even a spot of thatch she'd used to plug up a hole that made for a fine pillow. She kept excellent care of the roofs, as all Madcaps did. A leak meant ladders and repairmen and sometimes the Order's Greybeards with their spells and pointy swords. But without a reason to look up, most shop owners didn't have the time to bother, at least in the East End.

It was different in Mayfair, where rooftops were spelled to keep Moira and her kind away and gargoyles crouched, stuffed with magic. Madcaps had long learned the trick of pacifying gargoyles, if nothing else. And anyway, Moira preferred the East End. Home was home, whatever it smelled like. And however many hungry, crazy ghosts roamed.

And it was safer here, so long as she kept to the chimney pots and the shingles. Mrs. Lawton couldn't follow, not while her body still lay in state. And the other Madcaps left symbols scratched into the tiles, warning of unsteady roof timbers, vermin, Greybeard patrols, and recruiting men. They were even worse than the ladies who came with baskets for the poor and pamphlets about the dangers of living on the street. As if any of the street urchins, Madcaps, or regular orphans ever chose St. Giles or Whitechapel because it was the better alternative. Just ask her brother.

Before the Order had caught him.

A flock of vampire pigeons circled overhead, sending children below shrieking for cover. Moira wasn't worried. Madcaps never fretted over the pigeons. They'd trained them with bloody leavings from the butcher stalls at Leadenhall market. It was one of their few weapons against the Greybeards and even occasionally, the ordinary night watchmen. London was not kind to the poor or the supernatural.

She preferred to control her own life even if it meant sleeping wrapped around a chimney pot for warmth. Dirt and cold rain didn't scare her, not like having her essence trapped in a Greybeard's bottle.

And she didn't particularly like Mayfair, which was fine since its inhabitants loved it enough for everyone.

Which made her wonder why she was now running *toward* it.

But she'd learned, even before Mrs. Lawton, that when the bottoms of her feet itched the way they did right now, she ignored them at her peril. The last time she'd ended up dodging the nightwatch for an hour and a half after she was caught with a handful of stolen pocket watches. The Order might claim you, but the nightwatch could clap you in irons and shuffle you into a poorhouse. She shuddered at the thought and kept running, her trousers rolled above her ankles and her boots marked with sigils for speed. She stayed well south of Newgate prison, raced past courtesans waiting outside the theater on Drury Lane and along the Strand to Pall Mall.

All because her toes itched.

The alleys between buildings widened. She left the shops that tilted together like dandies holding each other up after drinking themselves sick. She ran until the worn shingles turned to copper flashing and marble columns. The clubs and shops were made of white stone, gleaming like bones. She wanted to stop on one of the flat roofs to catch her breath, but pain stabbed up her ankles and all the way to her knees when she paused too long.

It only receded when she kept moving, kept running, and

only toward Grosvenor Square of all places, all mansions and columns and balconies. A single mansion could have taken up an entire block in Whitechapel. They were fit for aristocrats and royalty, not Madcap girls dressed as boys with pockets full of stolen goods. The gargoyles became elaborately carved art in rose-colored stone and marble, not river clay fired in a coal grate. They still stank of magic though, that curious mixture of fennel seeds and salt.

She kept running, though she didn't know why.

Until she turned around.

She slid down the pitched roof of a window overhang and dangled off the edge, her fingers cramping as she struggled to hold on. Not precisely an improvement.

But what could you expect from magic that made your feet itch?

The sigils painted on her boots gave her cat's feet on the rooftop, but they weren't enough to make her fly. Not only were her arms screaming, but if someone happened to look out of the window, she'd be hauled off to prison as a housebreaker. Gritting her teeth, she swung herself like a church bell, back and forth, back and forth, until she'd gained enough momentum to let go. Flying, it turned out, felt a lot like falling. She hit the steep roof of a stable, landing with a painful thud that made her wince. The neighbor's poodle began to bark.

All around her came the cracking of stone and the splintering of shingles. She heard it even over the clatter of carriage wheels on the street below, the restless horses in the stable, and an orchestra playing music for the fancy folk. They danced while overhead, the magic wards they didn't even know protected them, broke.

Gargoyles of all shapes and sizes, all sneers and smiles, deserted their posts. A few crumbled to dust but most—too many—launched off roof points, dormer windows, and rain spouts. They took to the air, the stretch and flap of their wings leathery and brittle. They cast off pieces of shingle and stone all over London. Moira had never seen anything like it.

With the gargoyles gone, the rooftops weren't safe.

London wasn't safe.

Chapter 1

It was the most boring event of the Season.

Emma was promised dashing young gentlemen in starched cravats dancing until dawn, and kisses in dark gardens. Instead, there were only whiskered old widowers in creaking stays who smelled like lavender water and arthritic cream, and more wallflowers than seats. As if being a wallflower wasn't bad enough, being forced to stand in uncomfortable shoes that pinched while debutantes cast her pitying glances—and the few young men cast her none at all—was so much worse.

She longed for the forests of Berkshire and the stars overhead. She stifled a yawn since her chaperone, Aunt Mildred, would lecture her all the way home that yawning was neither pretty nor polite behavior. Neither was tapping one's foot to the music, eating too many pastries off the buffet table, or laughing loudly. In short, anything remotely amusing. Worse yet, Gretchen was hiding in the library and Penelope was in the garden with the very handsome and muscular Mr. Cohen. Penelope somehow managed to consistently flirt with social scandal and skip away unscathed. But that left Emma alone, once again.

If only Lord Durntley would trip on his way to ogle Lady Angelique's bosom. If only he'd crash into the footman and toss the tray of custard tarts so it could land on Lord Beckett's abysmal toupee.

If only something *interesting* would happen.

She leaned against the wall, even though young ladies weren't supposed to lean, slouch, or otherwise bend. With nothing left to distract her, she took the small bottle out of her reticule, winding the ribbon around her finger and letting the candlelight shine through its murky depths. It was rather strange-looking to be jewelry and didn't appear to contain any kind of perfume Emma would ever want to smell, let alone smear on her wrists, but it was the only thing she had of her mother's. She carried it as a sort of talisman.

She'd only actually seen Theodora Day, Lady Hightower, three times in her entire life. Three identical Christmas mornings at their country estate, chaperoned by the housekeeper, five footmen, and a great-uncle she hadn't seen since. Each time, her mother sat in a chair by the window, staring at the woods, pale as the snow outside. She hadn't even blinked when Emma approached to sing her a carol. She never spoke, except to scream the one time Emma tried to hold her hand.

Four debutantes drifted Emma's way, giggling and trailing chaperones and admiring younger sons of earls and viscounts. "Lady Emma," Daphne Kent simpered formally, even though their families were friendly and they'd known each other since they were children. Now that they were out in society, they were meant to acknowledge each other with long boring titles and curtsy and talk about nothing at all. "What a unique bauble." Her eyes sharpened. Emma had no idea why. She'd never been interesting to Daphne, and likely never would be.

The other girls, Lady Lilybeth Jones, Lady Sophie Truwell, and Lady Julia Thorpe curtsied a greeting, perfectly in unison. They wore identical white dresses, ornamented with beaded ribbons and ostrich feathers in their hair. Emma curtsied back, barely stopping herself from rolling her eyes. Gretchen wouldn't have stopped herself at all.

"Isn't it just a lovely ball?" Sophie smiled. "I vow, I've never seen such beautiful roses." There were enough yellow roses in the ballroom to sink a ship. Their scent mingled with perfumes, hair pomades, and the melting beeswax from the candles.

Emma stifled a sneeze. "Lovely," she agreed.

"Did you hear? Belinda has had an offer already!" Lilybeth squealed as if she couldn't help herself. "From Lee Hartford!"

Julia glanced away, mouth tightening. "She's only sixteen."

"Don't be jealous," Daphne said. "You'll get your chance. Anyway, he's only a baron's second son. Your father should look higher."

Lilybeth tittered. Sophie looked sympathetic. Emma just blinked. It was as if they were speaking a foreign language.

"Pardon me," Julia murmured before walking away, the pearls in her hair gleaming. Her hands in their elbow-length gloves were fists at her sides.

"Never mind her," Daphne confided. "She's quite desperate.

She fancied herself in love with Lee. Worse, she fancied him in love with her."

"You're positively wicked," Lilybeth said.

"Hush," Sophie added. "We'll be overheard."

Daphne, for all her fluttering eyelashes and simpering smiles, looked smug. Until she realized the young men were watching, and then she blushed prettily. Emma felt bad for Julia. The other girls turned to look at her expectantly. She didn't know what to say. She didn't want to get married. She didn't want to poke fun at others to be noticed. She didn't want to wear white dresses, as expected of all debutantes in England. She simply didn't fit. She never had.

"I think Julia's very nice," Emma said finally, just to fill the silence.

Daphne shook her head on a sigh. "Let's go, girls," she added, pityingly. They moved off like a flock of geese, whispering and giggling. One of their beaus trod on Emma's foot as he hurried to follow and didn't notice enough to apologize. Emma gave serious consideration to tripping him. Especially when he jostled her hard enough to make the ribbon slip off her wrist.

The perfume bottle fell to the floor. It broke in half, leaking thick fluid that smelled like rot and roses. A crystal bead rolled out, coming to a stop against her foot. She stared down at it, annoyed. "That was my mother's," she snapped, but he was already gone.

She bent to gather the pieces. One of the shards sliced into her left thumb, drawing blood through the thin silk of her glove. Around her, a country dance was in full swing, polished shoes squeaking, and skirts flouncing. Aunt Mildred searched the floor for her and her cousins. If Emma crossed the room in order to make her way to the library to hide out with Gretchen, she'd be caught. She needed a quiet corner. For some reason, holding the broken pieces of her mother's perfume bottle made her want to cry.

She eased backward until she was mostly hidden by the potted palms. She slid along the wall until she came to the nearest doorway and then stepped into the relative peace of the hall. A silver candelabrum filled with beeswax candles burned on a marble table. The soft, humid scent of orchids and lilacs drifted out of the conservatory. She pulled off her stained glove so as not to instigate one of her aunt's mind-numbingly dull lectures, and practically dove into the indoor garden.

Extensive windows and a curved glass ceiling held in the warmth and moisture of hundreds of flowers. The marble pathway wound around pots of daffodils, lilac branches in glass vases, and banks of lilies pressing their white petals against the windows. She tried to see the stars through the ceiling but mist clung to the glass, obscuring the view. Instead, she contented herself with wandering through the miniature jungle, listening to the faint strains of a waltz playing from the ballroom.

It wasn't all she heard.

The soft scuff of a shoe had her turning around, frowning. "Is anyone there?"

She thought she caught a shadow, but it was gone before she could be sure. It wasn't the first time since her coming out that she'd thought someone was watching her. Only it didn't just feel like being spied on.

It felt like being hunted.

It made no sense. Who would bother to spy on her? She was the seventeen-year-old daughter of an earl. She was barely allowed to visit the chamber pot without a chaperone. Nothing interesting ever happened to her.

Shivering, she reminded herself not to be a goose. There were a hundred reasons why someone would walk through the garden room and not want to be seen. Like her, they might be hiding from a chaperone. Or more likely they were looking for a private place to steal a kiss. That was why there were so many strict and tiresome rules about proper behavior; no one wanted to follow them in the first place.

Thumb throbbing and still holding what was left of her mother's keepsake, Emma forced herself to go deeper into the scented shadows. If only to prove to herself that she wasn't one of those girls who were afraid of every little thing.

Although sometimes, fear was the only logical response.

And not only because the ground lurched under her feet, as if it had turned into the deck of a ship in a storm. She grabbed the nearest table to steady herself. Pots of orchids rattled together. The room lurched again, making her belly drop. Her ears popped. A vase of calla lilies tumbled to the polished floor and shattered. She felt as if there was ice melting off her, or invisible chains falling away. It was the strangest thing.

But still not as strange as a girl stumbling out of the leaves, covered in blood.

Chapter 2

She crumpled before Emma could reach her.

The girl's brown hair fell in ringlets out of its pins, dragging on the ground. Her eyelids fluttered. Emma thought her name was Margaret, but couldn't recall for certain. They'd made their curtsies to the queen together last month, wearing ostrich feathers and ridiculous court-ordained panniers.

Now she was wearing blood.

Emma dropped to her knees beside her. "Where are you hurt?"

Margaret moaned, managing to open her eyes. "I don't know." She jerked suddenly and began to weep. "Feels like the time I fell out of a tree when I was little. Broke my collarbone."

Emma gingerly pushed her hair off her shoulder, wincing at the bump protruding under Margaret's pale skin. "You've broken it again. The earthquake must have knocked you off your feet."

She shook her head. "No, there was . . . can you feel it? It's so cold."

Pain must be confusing the poor girl. And no wonder. Blood filled the hollow of her cracked collarbone and dripped down her arm, soaking into her gloves. It looked worse than it had just a second ago. "I'll get help." Emma leaped to her feet.

She rushed down the path, clutching the hem of her gown so it wouldn't trip her up. "I need a doctor," she called out, sliding the last few feet along the slippery flagstones. She could hear agitated voices in the ballroom. "Someone help—" She crashed into a man just inside the door, partially obscured by ferns. He caught her in his arms, steadying her.

"Not that way, love. The tremor knocked a candle into the curtains. Ballroom's on fire."

She recognized the voice and stifled a groan. "Not you," she muttered.

Anyone but Cormac Fairfax, Viscount Blackburn, heir to the Earl of Haworth.

They hadn't said more than a word to each other in months, not since that night in the gardens when he'd kissed her. The next week he'd gone away to school and refused her letters and turned away whenever she entered the room.

She still had a fierce desire to kick him.

He'd recently turned nineteen, and was tall with strong shoulders under his navy blue coat. His cravat was simply knotted and blindingly white under a severe jawline. His dark hair was tousled, and his eyes narrowed with disgust. She'd hoped he'd gotten ugly since she'd seen him last, at Lilybeth's dismally boring birthday celebration.

No such luck.

He was just as handsome, just as lean, but the edge of danger was new. She wished it was unattractive. He raised an eyebrow and looked ready to make some pithy comment when he noticed the blood on her thumb. He seized her wrists. "You're hurt."

She squirmed in his grasp. "I am now," she said, trying to break free. "Let go."

He was too busy staring in horror at the broken perfume bottle she was clutching. She had to admit the odor was unpleasant but it didn't deserve that kind of reaction, surely. Especially not with wisps of smoke starting to drift out of the ballroom behind him.

"Where did you get that?" he asked, oblivious to the danger.

"Never mind that," she snapped. Didn't he know how fast fires could spread? "There's an injured girl back here. We need to get her out." She yanked out of his hold, throwing him a dark glance over her shoulder. "Are you coming or not?"

He followed, grim-faced as the corridor filled steadily with smoke. The flickering of the fire in the ballroom seemed to have a curious violet hue. She thought she smelled lemon balm and fennel seeds.

Margaret had managed to push herself up into a half-sitting position. Her cheeks were clammy, her eyes red with tears. "I smell smoke," she said, coughing.

"It's all right," Emma said with more confidence than she felt. "We'll get you outside and with all the smoke someone's already fetching a doctor, I'm sure."

"What's your name?" Cormac asked.

"Margaret York."

"Gently then, Margaret," he murmured, bending to scoop her into his arms. She gasped when the movement jarred her collarbone. "Sorry, not far now." His comforting smile died when he glanced at Emma. "The door," he snapped.

She yanked it open, glaring back at him. If he hadn't been holding an injured girl, she might have thrown a potted orchid at his head. He carried Margaret outside, laying her carefully in the grass. He took off his coat and placed it over her for warmth.

Smoke crept out of the ballroom windows like dark snakes. The lawns were crowded with frantic guests. A gentleman in old-fashioned buckled shoes fainted. Footmen raced about, opening doors and sweating under their powdered wigs. The light was too bright at the windows, the smell of scorched silk wallpaper and paint wafting out. More footmen raced from the kitchens with buckets of water.

"I have to help with the fire," Cormac said to Margaret. "But you'll be fine." He turned to Emma. "Can I trust you not to get into any more trouble?" he asked acidly. She'd never seen him with a temper. He was usually draped over some girl or another, smirking.

They both watched him go, his white shirt tight over the muscles of his arms and back.

"He's divine," Margaret murmured.

"He's a prat," Emma returned. Margaret just smiled. "I have to make sure my cousins are out," Emma added. "And fetch that doctor for you. Will you be all right here?"

"As long as I don't move," she assured her through gritted teeth.

Emma went right through the hedge, not bothering to go around it. She found Penelope standing on a bench by the fountain looking disgruntled. Mr. Cohen was nowhere to be seen. "Have you seen Gretchen?"

Penelope shook her head. "I was looking for you."

"She's probably still in the library then." They went around the side of the house. Gretchen was always in the library. Not because she loved novels the way Penelope did, but because it was the only decent place to hide. She loathed these affairs and when she couldn't avoid them, she snuck away as soon as she could.

"I hate this ball," Penelope muttered, sounding more like Gretchen than herself.

Emma cupped her hands around her eyes, peering through her reflection into the shadowy rooms of the Pickford mansion. Penelope climbed into the bushes and did the same. The bite of smoke covered the usual smells of Mayfair: horses and roses. "I've found her." Emma tapped on the glass.

On the other side, Gretchen poked her head around a bookcase, frowning. She appeared to be holding a pink dog. She pulled open the window. "What on earth are you doing out there?"

"Didn't you feel the tremors?" Emma asked.

"A few tremors require you both to stand in the rosebushes?"

"The house is also on fire," Emma added. "You might have noticed?"

"It is?" Gretchen sniffed deeply. A warning bell rang from the front door, alerting the watch and the neighbors. If the wind picked up, the fire could spread throughout the city, ravenous and pitiless. Gretchen handed the dog to Emma, before hiking up the hem of her ball gown and sliding out of the window. Beside her, Penelope raised her eyebrows. "What is that? Candy?"

"It's a dog."

"If you say so."

Gretchen patted it absentmindedly. The dog licked her nose frantically. "I don't have biscuits," she said. "You look like a tea cake. Honestly, I'm embarrassed for you. And I hope you bit Lady Pickford for doing that to you," she said conversationally.

Smoke drifted between the trees. "If only it would rain," Emma said.

The sky opened overhead like a broken water jug. Rain pattered over the roof, soaked their dresses and tangled their hair like seaweed. In moments, the gardens were a maze of ruined silk, mud, and slippery stone. A balding duke slid on his perfectly polished shoes right past them and into a hedge. A dowager who usually limped on a diamond-studded cane gathered up her hem and darted over the lawn, her wrinkled knees bare. Prim Aunt Mildred was shouting something about the apocalypse. Footmen passed buckets to one another, emptying the ornamental pond.

"Doesn't this seem rather odd?" Emma asked, frowning. Earthquake, fire, Cormac. Something wasn't right. She worried at it like a loose tooth.

Gretchen snorted. "I'm holding a pink dog. Odd doesn't quite cover it."

"Daphne just fainted," Penelope pointed out, crossing her

arms so her dress wouldn't cling to her figure. Her grandmother
would never forgive her the impropriety. Her parents wouldn't
care; they rarely came out into society. The other fashionable
girls in their thin white gowns were soaked through, corsets,
ribbons, and legs outlined in great scandalous detail. A young
lord tripped over his own foot when he turned and saw through
Emma's wet dress. Penelope shifted to cover her, glowering at
him so fiercely he hid behind a tree.

Gretchen tilted her head as chaos continued to boil around
them. "Daphne is playacting," she said dismissively. "And not
very well, I might add. Who faints in such a comfortable position? Not to mention she ought to have toppled right into
those rosebushes if gravity was at all involved." She sighed.
"And that footman is barely strong enough to hold that kind of
bucket. He's doing it all wrong." She thrust the wet dog at
Penelope. "Here, take the tea cake, would you?" She dashed
away toward the struggling footman. "Lift with your knees,
not your back, muttonhead!"

Emma watched her go, resigned. Gretchen would now classify this as the best ball they'd ever attended since she'd avoided
the actual social gathering in favor of hauling buckets of water
and battling a fire. In the rain, no less. Gretchen loved the rain.
Emma was less enamored with it. She pushed her soggy hair
out of her face where it clung uncomfortably to her forehead.
At least it would help stop the fire from spreading. Already it
seemed less virulent, its burning jagged teeth easing from bite
to nibble.

"I suppose we ought to help," Penelope said dubiously. She

spotted Mr. Cohen cowering under the cover of an elm tree. "That tears it," she muttered. "Let's, shall we?"

Emma followed her gaze. "I thought you liked him."

Penelope glanced away, her cheeks red as berries. "Not anymore."

She scowled. "What did he do?"

"Nothing. It's not important."

"Penelope. I'm wet and cold and perfectly willing to shove him into the shrubbery."

"He called me fat."

Emma hissed out a breath. "I beg your pardon."

"It's nothing, really." She forced her voice not to wobble. "He embarrassed me, is all."

"Think how embarrassed he'll be when I wrap his smalls around his fat head."

Penelope, feeling decidedly more cheerful, had to drag Emma toward the burning house, where they stood uncertainly at the edge of a line of shouting men. Someone broke the window from inside the ballroom, glass cracking into the hollyhocks. Smoldering drapes followed, coiling like a smoke-breathing serpent.

"Why does Emma look like she's swallowed a bee?" Gretchen asked when her cousins pushed their way toward her.

"Mr. Cohen called Penelope fat," Emma replied.

Gretchen's smile died. "Did he, now?"

Penelope now felt perfectly vindicated and couldn't quite recall why she'd let Mr. Cohen hurt her feelings in the first place. "It's nothing."

"I hope he wakes up swollen like a balloon," Gretchen muttered.

While her cousins stewed and plotted painful vengeance involving Mr. Cohen swelling to such proportions that all the buttons popped off his evening wear and he ended up naked in the ballroom, Penelope couldn't help but admire the parade of half-dressed men under a flash of lightning. "Well, now," she grinned appreciatively, wounded pride utterly erased. "There should be more fires, don't you think?"

"What?" The sight of Cormac in his shirtsleeves, the wet fabric clinging to his muscles was particularly distracting. Emma felt compelled to stare, as if under some sort of spell. She blinked rain out of her eyelashes when Cormac went blurry. She had to remind herself that she'd sworn to hate him. She turned her attention back to the buckets sloshing from hand to hand, until her fingers cramped. Smoke stung her eyes and seared her throat.

"And I had no idea Tobias was so well-muscled, did you?" When the rain faded to a patter in the leaves, Penelope pouted. "Drat. What a shame. If we're not all going to die horribly in flames, I'd rather like to see more shirtsleeves."

Emma was still wondering why the sight of Cormac lifting heavy buckets and wiping mud off his face made her feel so peculiarly warm. Even her toes in her paper-thin dancing slippers were hot. She must be catching a fever from standing out in the storm. Cold water spilled down her dress but she barely noticed. The rest of her was burning with sweat and screaming muscles. She didn't look up from the endless parade of heavy buckets until Gretchen came out of a cloud of smoke, grinning and covered in soot and dirt. "Fire's nearly out."

The rain started to fall again, the wind pushing it mostly

toward the house. The cousins remained relatively untouched, darting under the widespread boughs of an oak tree.

"Should rain be able to do that?" Penelope asked, perplexed. "Not that I'm complaining but . . ." She shook her head. "Do you think someone slipped laudanum in the lemonade? Because this is turning out to be the strangest night."

The pink dog leaned against Gretchen's ankles, looking miserable. She bent to scoop him back up into her arms so they could shiver together. The guests became a river of silks and wilted cravats pushing toward the waiting carriages.

"I need to find the doctor," Emma remembered.

"Why?" Gretchen looked instantly concerned. "Did you burn yourself? You should have left the buckets to me."

"I didn't get near enough to burn myself," Emma assured her. "But a girl was hurt during the tremor. She's broken her collarbone."

"I thought I heard someone say the doctor was with the ladies near the hideous cherub statues," Gretchen said. "They sent someone to fetch him as soon as the curtains caught fire. I'll get this dog back to Lady Pickford, after I inform her the fire was no doubt penance for abusing this poor thing with pink fur and ridiculous ribbons," she added, spotting Lady Clara self-administering smelling salts.

"I'll get your Aunt Mildred to the carriage," Penelope added to Emma before picking her way through the wet grass.

Covered in mud and soot, Emma went in search of the doctor. She found him surrounded by pale ladies clutching smelling salts, and a footman with a nasty burn on his forearm.

His shirt was charred into tatters. She told the doctor where Margaret was waiting and then returned to join her so she wouldn't have to wait alone. The main path was currently congested with girls in various states of dismay, both feigned and unfeigned, surrounded by attentive young gentlemen eager to help. Cutting through the garden seemed the path of least resistance.

She really ought to have known better.

She'd already had every indication that the night was an unmitigated disaster. She wasn't sure what made her assume the worst was over. Chronic optimism, perhaps.

Or chronic madness.

It did run in the family, after all.

Chapter 3

Cormac stalked toward Emma, abandoning a group of soggy men congratulating one another. There was such dark intensity in his chiseled features that she instinctively backed up. She hit the tree behind her but Cormac didn't stop his advance. He was practically pressed against her.

She shifted to move away but he blocked her, wrapping his hand around the branch by her head. "Don't cast any more spells," he said ominously.

The smell of smoke clung to him, just like his soot-stained linen shirt. His cravat had been lost somewhere in the mud. She could see a tarnished silver chain around his neck, the pendant tucked under the folds of ruined fabric. She was suddenly viciously curious as to what it might be. She frowned at him. He didn't deserve her curiosity. She had to remind herself of that. Sternly. And repeatedly. "What on earth are you talking about?" she asked finally.

He leaned closer, so close she could see the amber in his dark brown eyes and the faint whisper of stubble on his cheeks. So close she couldn't help but remember the long, dark kiss they'd shared, not so long ago.

As if she could ever forget it.

And if he had, she'd smack him.

She might smack him anyway if he didn't stop looming. "Have you been practicing?" she asked with false sweetness. "You've improved."

"Practicing what?" he asked, momentarily distracted. His brow furrowed in confusion.

"Looming."

He muttered something under his breath. "That spell was powerful," he added tightly. The moonlight made his cheekbones sharp as knives. "You ought to show more care. Considering." There was a wealth of implication in that one single word.

Trouble was, she had no idea what he was implying.

"Considering what, exactly?" she asked.

He tossed his wet black hair off his forehead. A drop of rain ran slowly down his aristocratic nose. "Don't play me for a fool, madam."

"Then pray don't act like one," she shot back, thoroughly nettled.

"Remember what I said." He leaned closer still until she felt the brush of his arm on her shoulder. His shirt clung to muscles she tried very hard not to notice. "If you do not wish to be exposed to the Order, you'll take very great care, Lady Emma."

"Cormac?" she asked with exaggerated patience. "What the hell are you talking about?"

"Do you think this is a game?"

"No, I——" She had no idea what she'd been about to say. All thoughts were snatched away by a sudden gust of wind. It slapped at them with enough force to wrench them apart. Emma stumbled back onto the path, trying not to slide across the slick flagstones. Her dancing slippers may as well have been spun out of sugar for all the protection to the elements they offered. The wind was wrapping itself around her, and pushing at her like an invisible hand. She stumbled, trying to find purchase. Her right foot slipped and she flailed.

"What the hell?" Cormac had her by the elbow. The wind buffeted them both, forcing them away from the crowds. It was colder than any March wind had the right to be. The force of the gust pushed them through the grass and back to Margaret's side.

Frost clung to Margaret's hair and eyelashes and dripped off her fingertips in slender, delicate icicles.

"Why is she covered in frost?" Emma asked. Margaret twitched. Emma dashed forward, nausea roiling in the cauldron of her belly. "Lord, don't——"

She died before Emma finished her plea.

Stranger still, a small white creature made of mist and frost snuffled out of her chest. It was a star-nosed mole. It lifted its head before hopping down to the ground. Then it paused, flashed red, and darted into the shadows. The ice on the girl's body cracked.

Emma's brain felt like the honeybee trapped in amber that sat in her father's library. She eventually opened her mouth to shout for help, remembering how to breathe, and what one was supposed to do when faced with a dead body. Besides be ill all over one's shoes.

"You saw that, didn't you?" Cormac asked, his voice dark as the smoke billowing through the broken glass all around them. She could actually feel it, scraping lightly over the back of her neck, like teeth. Something deep inside her shivered.

She swallowed. "I think I must be ill." She hadn't just seen a star-nosed mole. She was in shock.

His gaze fastened on to hers, as if he'd read her thoughts. "You can tell me."

She'd forgotten just how persuasive he could be, his eyes fixed on her as if she was the only girl in the world. As if she mattered. He'd looked at her like that once before.

But she knew better now.

Let him think her mad. It was no doubt why he'd refused to renew his attentions. Someone must have found out about her mother and told him. She'd have suspected Daphne, knowing the other girl had chased after him for years now, but if Daphne had found out she'd have told everyone, including the Prince Regent. "A star-nosed mole climbed out of her chest."

He nodded, as if she'd confirmed something perfectly sensible.

She stared at him. "Did you hear me? A *mole,* made of *nothing,* climbed out of her *chest.* How is that even possible?" And why wasn't he more alarmed? Why was he so blasted calm, as if this sort of thing happened to him all the time?

That was not comforting, actually. Not in the least.

The sounds of the agitated guests seemed very far away all of a sudden. "Her parents . . . we should . . ." She trailed off. "Do something." Shouldn't they?

He approached the girl, his jaw clenching when he turned her hand over and saw the symbol. "The mark," he said softly, stunned. He turned on Emma. "How long did you leave her?"

"I helped with buckets and then went to fetch the doctor." She rubbed her arms, trying to get warm. "What does it mean?" she asked. "Do you recognize it?" It looked like a four-petal flower, with the tips unfolding into spirals.

"Yes," he said darkly. "Emma, this is very important. Forget what you've seen here."

A laugh burst out of her, startled and strange. "As if I could."

"Hell and damnation," he snapped when he spotted a footman gaping at the dead girl. It was only a matter of moments before the others came rushing at them out of the damp gardens.

Before she could make a sound, Cormac's hands clamped around her arms, keeping her still.

"What are you doing?"

"Trying to save you," he answered sharply. His eyes were intense, searching. "Though you seem determined to thwart my every attempt."

That seemed rather unfair, considering all he'd done so far was snap at her for no discernible reason.

"Now hide!" he hissed. "Before someone sees you."

She stared at him. "What are you talking about? I can't just leave." Though what she could do for the poor girl now, she had no idea.

"If you won't run for yourself, do it for your cousins. They can't be seen here any more than you can," he insisted.

She gaped at him.

And then he pushed her right into the bushes.

Chapter 4

Emma.

Of course, it *had* to be Emma.

People who didn't believe in luck had the luxury of not having decidedly *rotten* luck.

And it only proved what he'd been telling himself all along. He'd made the right decision. If she was going to hate him, at least it would be on his own terms. And if he craved glimpses of her the way the drunks in St. Giles craved cheap gin, she never had to know. It wasn't safe. Every day he served as a Keeper for the Order of the Iron Nail proved it to him.

The fire was out and smoke drifted in eye-stinging clouds, but it wouldn't be long now before someone else noticed the dead girl on the lawn. He pulled a snuffbox from his pocket. Regular gentlemen carried tobacco in them but his was filled with a fine powder of crushed apple seeds, quartz crystal, and

mugwort. It was spelled especially for him, to call in reinforce-
ments. When he threw a pinch up into the air, it hung there in
direct opposition to all laws of physics and gravity. A glitter of
pale-blue sparks arced up into the sky, like a string of stars.
They hovered above them, only visible to those who belonged
to the Order.

Luckily his partner and friend Tobias was also at the ball,
and the first to find him. He stared at the girl. "Who is she?"

"Margaret York. I thought she was injured in the tremor."

Tobias shook his head. "Earthquakes don't cover girls
in ice."

"Exactly." He crouched next to her body. "She's covered in
bruises. They weren't there half an hour ago. It doesn't make
sense."

"Whatever happened, it packs a powerful punch." Tobias
pinched the bridge of his nose, as if his head ached. He wouldn't
have shown even that hint of weakness to anyone but Cormac.
"The air is practically shivering."

He sounded disapproving. Tobias preferred order in all
things, and if he didn't become First Legate, if not the head
of the entire Order, Cormac would eat his hat. Tobias devoutly
believed in rules and regulations and strict guidelines for witches.
If he hadn't been born a witch himself, Tobias might have become
a Witchhunter instead of a Keeper.

Cormac, meanwhile, had joined the Order mostly to thumb
his nose at them all for not believing he could succeed.

"Did you see who did it?" Tobias asked. His usually fastidi-
ous clothing was marked with soot.

Cormac thought of Emma dropping a witch bottle. "No," he replied. He'd been right behind her when she'd been racing back to Margaret's side. The magical traces on her person wouldn't link her to the victim. Small mercies. He doubted the Order would think so, or even Tobias for that matter. They'd been to school together and Cormac considered him a brother, but there was no denying Tobias was a bit more starched than he was. He didn't have five sisters to plague him, to begin with.

He shook his head over Margaret's broken body. This might have been her very first ball. She certainly wasn't trained enough to use magic to protect herself. The Greymalkin family preferred to drain witches before they learned how to fight back. His fists clenched. "I thought the Greymalkin had gone into hiding," he said, glaring at the unfurled knot on the girl's palm. It was a scornful imitation of a regular witch knot, which could be drawn with a single unbroken line. The Greymalkin severed the pattern, deliberately unfurling the petal-like points into spirals. "Or were wiped out altogether."

"Greymalkin? Really?" Tobias took a closer look at her palm. There were few families who rivaled the bloodthirst of the Greymalkin. Stories were told about exploits hundreds of years old that still held the power to terrify. "They haven't done this sort of thing since my mother was a deb," he added. If Cormac recalled his history correctly, Tobias's mother also used to hunt them. Tobias swore briefly, tones clipped and icy.

"What do you see?" Cormac asked him. Cormac had charms that allowed him to discern hidden marks but his own magical lineage had skipped him entirely, choosing instead to concentrate its considerable power on each of his five younger sisters. That bad-luck problem again.

Still, clearly he had better luck than Margaret York.

Tobias's blue eyes narrowed to focus on magical residue Cormac couldn't see, even with his True Sight charm. "Blood curse, I think. It's hazy." Tobias was a brilliant tracker. If he couldn't pick out the magical traces with any certainty, there were few others in London who could.

Sweat curled Tobias's hair as he struggled to harness the dark magic swirling around them. Even ungifted as he was, Cormac felt it too. Anyone could. Murder left its own mark, even beyond blood and brutality.

"It was definitely someone at the ball," Tobias confirmed, leaning against the tree and panting as if he'd been chased down by rabid dogs. His voice was hoarse as he tugged at his cravat.

"That narrows it down to nearly three hundred guests," Cormac said. "Not to mention several dozen servants." He rose to his feet. "Some of which are coming this way, even now."

He jerked his head in the direction of three footmen heading back toward the kitchen with empty buckets. The smoke was no longer thick enough to hide Margaret's body, or either of them, for that matter. They couldn't afford to be caught in the web of questions that would inevitably result. They couldn't even wait for other Keepers to arrive. Once the girl's family descended, they wouldn't have the chance to do what needed doing. Magical trails went cold fast. Screaming mothers seemed to make them go even colder, faster.

"I can track it awhile yet," Tobias said grimly as they stepped back into the concealing shrubbery. By the time they made their way around several statues, a fountain, and clipped hedges, the first cry of alarm rang through the wet and smoky night. They slipped around the guests crowding together, and pressed against a row of harried footmen who were trying to keep them from disturbing the body. Whispers of murder caught faster than the fire in the brocade drapes.

The chatter faded in a wave, retreating like the tide, when the rumor of a dead girl was proven to be fact. Someone screamed. A decorated captain who had fought in the Battle of Trafalgar fainted. Cormac stayed near Tobias, all the while searching for anyone who might look guilty, and for Emma's distinctive red-brown hair.

"There's magic leading that way." Tobias nodded to the hydrangeas Cormac had tossed Emma into. "It's connected to the murder."

He went cold. "Are you sure?"

"It's not a clear read," he admitted, frustrated. "But it's there. It's connected magically somehow." Before Cormac could suggest it was a simple matter of magic attracting magic, Tobias turned his head sharply. "Ow, bloody hell." He massaged his temple. "It's over there as well. And there." He sighed. "It's bleeding into the general panic of the guests."

"Let's try past the gates," Cormac suggested. "If we're lucky, the murderer has already left the party."

"He has," Tobias confirmed. "He's just gorged on himself on someone else's power. He wouldn't be able to hide the effects, or the residue of violence. Not with so many witches in attendance, even if it is mostly debutantes. And he'd have to know the Order is on its way." By the time they'd reached the road, Tobias was stumbling. He paused to be sick behind a carriage painted like a peppermint bonbon.

"Magic leads that way," he said when he was well enough to lift his head. He pointed straight to a passing carriage. A familiar face stared at them through the window. "Isn't that Emma Day?"

Cormac clamped down on his expression, refusing to betray any emotion. The carriage rumbled by.

Tobias wiped his mouth with a pristine white handkerchief. "The bloodcurse trail goes that way," he pointed in the opposite direction, much to Cormac's relief. They followed it around the corner, past several mansions and over to the next street bordering the park. Tobias retched one more time.

"Blood curses are vile," he said wearily. "They taste like rotted leeks." He wiped his face with a grimace. "Nasty business."

"That's not all," Cormac said steadily, reaching for the dagger in his boot. "If I recall, Greymalkin magic of this kind always unleashes the Sisters."

"Bollocks."

"My sentiments exactly."

Chapter 5

Two hours later and the strange, peculiar night was no closer to making any sense at all.

Emma had leaped into the carriage and proceeded to stare so wide-eyed that Gretchen asked her if she'd had too much champagne. She desperately wanted to tell them what had happened but Aunt Mildred was dreadful at keeping secrets. So she could only sit against the cushions as the carriage rattled over the cobbles, the image of the mole clambering out of the dead girl's chest repeating in her mind.

It made no sense.

Not the first time she replayed it, and not the hundredth.

"Well, that was fun." Gretchen grinned, slouching back against the seats. The swinging lantern cast long fingers of light over her face. They'd been safely in the carriage and driving away before Margaret's body was found. Emma wasn't sure

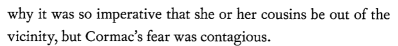

why it was so imperative that she or her cousins be out of the vicinity, but Cormac's fear was contagious.

"What have we learned from this, girls?" Mildred asked primly, as if she hadn't just been scrambling onto benches to watch the ballroom burn.

"Never attend a ball?" Gretchen guessed.

Mildred's nostrils flared. "Do I have to remind you, yet again, that you have a duty, Gretchen Thorn?"

Penelope groaned and kicked her cousin's ankle. "Now look what you've done."

"I don't see how marrying some balding old earl who smells like liniment paste is my duty to king and country," Gretchen replied mutinously. "Napoleon is out there and I'd rather be a spy against the French than a wife." She rubbed her hands together. "I think I'd make a dashing spy. Or I could dress as a boy and be a soldier."

Emma was barely listening. She'd just seen a girl die in front of her. She widened her eyes at Penelope. Misunderstanding, Penelope rolled hers in response. Mildred's speeches about duty and manners were only outnumbered by Gretchen's speeches about becoming a spy.

"Do you still think this is a game?" Mildred snapped, the mask of prudish and slightly befuddled maiden aunt slipping. "Even now, after your come-out? You have one duty and one duty only, to repay your parents' kindness by securing yourself an eligible bachelor to marry. Before they choose one for you, and they shall, if you don't smarten up."

Gretchen blinked, sitting up slowly. "Aunt Mildred," she

said, even though Mildred was only technically Emma's aunt through her father's side. "Why are you so upset? Did the fire frighten you? Do you need your smelling salts?"

When she reached for Mildred's reticule, Mildred rapped her across the knuckles with her fan. The delicate ivory sticks snapped. "You will all three of you listen to me most carefully," she said severely. "You have two options: find a gentleman with manners who will marry you, or wait for your father to find one for you. The first is preferable, though by no means guaranteed. The second is most likely, and most unpredictable. You may scoff at my methods, but I think you would prefer to choose your own husbands. Girls always do. And I suspect boys do as well, despite what earls and viscounts convince themselves once they have children of their own."

"Or we could not marry at all," Gretchen felt the need to point out, rubbing her pink knuckles. "Like you."

"And be a burden on your family instead? What happens when your father dies, Gretchen? Or your brother? Who will take care of you then?"

"I can take care of myself."

Mildred snorted. It was the most indelicate thing they'd ever seen her do, which only underscored her seriousness. "Do you not think I thought the same, when I was your age? I was going to be a novelist. I turned down a perfectly good offer of marriage, and by the time I realized my foolishness, there were no more to be had. Instead, I've had to live off my brother's largesse and endure the pity of my friends and the impertinence of my ungrateful nieces." Her eyes flashed. "Make no mistake.

Marry, or become a governess or a mistress. There is only one clear and acceptable choice." She turned to stare out of the window and did not speak again. Her cheeks were red with temper.

"Damn," Gretchen muttered to Emma under the cover of the creaking carriage wheels. Mildred was seriously put out to have mentioned the indecorous and invisible subject of mistresses. "What's got her skirt in a knot?"

Emma just shook her head, equally bewildered. Mildred was usually a faded, kindly woman who fussed over the right color gown and the proper way to pour tea. None of it seemed terribly important to Emma at the moment.

She could only take herself up the dry path to the front door after her cousins were dropped off and her aunt left for her own small house. The rain must have missed this part of London, even though the Pickfords only lived a few streets away. The house echoed around her as she let herself in. The butler, Jenkins; the housekeeper, Mrs. Hill; and all the other servants were asleep. Not that it would have mattered. Her father had strict rules that the family was never to encounter the maidservants in any of the rooms or even on the stairs. They had to scurry into empty corners whenever Emma passed by. It hardly encouraged a sociable household. Especially when Emma tried to befriend one of the housemaids when she was thirteen and the girl, just thirteen herself, was turned out. Her father was an unsympathetic man, made of rules and protocol and the august pride of the Hightower earldom.

He was dull as dishwater, really.

She went down the hall to the library, her wrap dripping

unpleasantly when the tassels dragged against her leg. Draping it over the grate to dry, she lit one of the candelabrums and lifted it high, casting a warm glow over gilded letters and leather spines. She rifled through them at random, hoping for a mention of moles, marks, or Orders. She wasn't surprised when her search proved futile; she hardly expected her father to have books of such a nature. He preferred political tracts, historical treatises, and plays in their original Latin. Even novels were too frivolous for Lord Hightower.

Too anxious to sleep, Emma did as she always did when she returned to an empty town house large enough to comfortably house a family of ten. She snuck down into the kitchens, skirting the maid asleep on a pallet by the empty grate, and helped herself to a handful of almond biscuits and a jar of blackberry jam. Then it was back up to her bedroom, the smallest in the house, awkwardly shaped and drafty in winter. But it had the benefit of a wide balcony that she'd converted into her very own observatory. She'd hung gilded stars strung from the ceiling on silk thread. They shimmered when the lantern light caught them. Emma had also dragged a chaise to the railing (scratching the floor in the process), and covered it with cushions and a blanket. Angled just right, she could see most of the sky.

She'd found comfort in looking up at the stars since she was a little girl. It was a shame the infamous London fog often covered them in a yellow veil, but on those rare nights when the lanterns were put out and the wind was brisk, the sky became a field of fireflies. Rain clouds hung in tatters over the river, but on her secret balcony, she was alone with a thousand stars and stolen sweets. It was as warm as the frigidly opulent house ever felt.

Before curling up on the balcony, Emma dragged her mother's box from under the bed. She'd found it in the attic when she was eleven years old and had been hiding from Penelope, Gretchen, and Gretchen's twin brother Godric, in a game of hide-and-seek. It was an old-fashioned patch box with one dusty heart-shaped patch left in one of the compartments. Ladies would have worn them to cover smallpox scars. Curiously, the compartment for the brush was filled instead with salt and wrinkled rowan berries. The third section had held the small green glass perfume, which was now mostly lying in shards on the Pickford ballroom floor. The last section was locked.

Gretchen once tried to pry the hinges of the locked compartment apart with a knife but with no success. Emma was relegated to shaking the box gently. It rattled enticingly but refused to give up its secrets, even now. There could be love letters in faded ribbons inside, dried roses from her first ball.

Or decapitated doll heads.

Emma had no idea how long her mother had been crazy, after all.

And it was no use asking her father about it. He never spoke of her mother. And when she asked questions, he merely left the room. Or the house. He'd once left the country entirely. So she was left with an old box that wouldn't open and the broken top of a mysterious glass bottle full of a questionable substance.

That wasn't quite right though, was it? Cormac had apparently deciphered the mystery of the bottle with ease. After which he proceeded to lose his composure and his good manners entirely. Curious, that. If she still knew anything about him it was his reputation for gallantry, top marks at Oxford when he wasn't down from school for the Season, and a secret duel at dawn that wasn't so secret. Such things never were. But even after he'd snubbed her, she'd only ever seen him being charming and handsome, ever dancing with wallflowers, which his friend Tobias disdained.

And smoldering.

There was no denying the man could smolder.

Still, he clearly knew more about her own family than she did, and whatever he knew disturbed him. Evidently, she brought out the very best in his character. He'd sent her home without answers, only more questions.

Despite herself, she missed him. She missed his crooked smile and the way he'd held her hand. She'd have thrown herself into the Thames in the middle of winter before admitting it to him. Naked. In broad daylight.

He'd been autocratic and cryptic, assuming he could intimidate her into silence or obedience, just like her father.

Worse, she'd let him.

She sat up.

Well, they'd just see about that, wouldn't they?

Chapter 6

The Greymalkin Sisters were notorious.

Of all the warlocks in London, they had been the worst.
They served only themselves. They weren't witches after all,
but warlocks. They admitted to no authority from the witching
society and therefore would not be regulated by the Order.

And even though they hadn't been seen since the French
Revolution, everyone knew their names. Magdalena, Rosmerta,
and Lark were spirits of past Greymalkin warlocks clinging to a
twilight life, long after their deaths. They weren't actual sisters,
merely female descendants from the same family lineage. There
had once been seven of them, before the Order managed to banish them.

Magdalena hovered off the pavement, so pale Cormac could
see right through her to the wet cobblestones of the street. She
was the eldest, wearing a medieval gown. It was long and blue,

ending in misty tatters that caused steam to rise off the puddles
under her bare feet. Her hair was loose, since knots and braids
bound power and caused spellwork to go awry. Through the long
thick tresses scurried all manner of insects: wasps, beetles, and
black spiders. Death's-head moths fluttered over her head. When
she smiled, a nearby gas lamp flickered frantically.

Behind her the other two Sisters waited, sinister in their still,
expectant patience.

Under his shirt, Cormac's charms and the silver chain they
hung on prickled painfully with warning. It stung hard enough
to scar the already satiny-worn skin it had branded with previ-
ous warnings. And he'd only been part of the Order since just
after Christmas. Tobias turned slowly, as if he could delay the
inevitable. He was still clammy and weaving on his feet from
the poisoning of tracking a blood curse.

The Sisters descended.

They moved so fast they blurred into nothing. There was a
heartbeat of unnatural silence, not quite long enough for Cormac to reach for his weapon, but just long enough for ice to form
on his fingertips. Tobias swore and his blistering words turned
to frost.

Rosmerta wore a Tudor-style dress over a whalebone corset,
and a choker encrusted with rubies and a pearl the size of a
quail's egg. A silver sickle knife hung from her waist, catching
the hazy yellow-tinged light. She was wreathed in poisonous
flowers: deadly nightshade vines for a crown, belladonna at her
wrists, red bryony berries in long loops around her neck and
white hemlock stalks woven into a belt. She stank of valerian
and bruised lilies.

Magdalena and Rosmerta reached out, touching fingertips around Tobias, as if circling him in a child's game. Every time a Greymalkin drained witches of their power, the Sisters were strengthened. They were currently gray-lavender shades, having been deprived of a witch's full power for decades. The Greymalkin family had been hiding too successfully to properly feed their dead ancestresses. But with enough power they could rematerialize.

Their hunger was sharp as badgers' teeth. Cormac could see the power gathering under Tobias's skin as he tried to shield himself. He managed to fight back, searing Rosmerta with a blast of sun-bright magic. She screeched, her hair singeing.

It wasn't enough.

Tobias made a choked sound of pain and slumped to the ground. The Sisters peered down at his fallen body. He twitched, teeth chattering. The color leached from his face, his hands, his eyes, even his clothes. Everything about him looked bleached and faded. Cormac lunged toward him, only to be stopped so abruptly by the third Sister, he felt he'd been thrown from a horse.

Lark wore the brown woolen dress of a peasant girl with a misty plaid shawl around her shoulders. She reached for Cormac, tears glistening in her eyes. She was said to have been quiet and kind, the rose among Greymalkin thorns, until her beloved died on the Culloden moors. The battle against the British had raged so desperately that nearly two thousand Scots were lost. She'd walked the fields of dead and butchered men until the hem of her gown was stained in blood, as it was still. She was silent, sad, and sweet.

She was the worst of them.

When she reached for Cormac, the air shattered. It froze in his nostrils, making it difficult to breathe. Frost clung to his eyelashes. He fumbled for the dagger in his boot with numb fingers even as the charms around his neck shot light through the buttonholes of his shirt. It was brief, like sunlight glinting on water or a sword's blade.

She stumbled back, holding a hand up to her eyes. "A trick," she sighed. Blood began to drip from the hem of her dress. Ice cracked under Cormac's boots. She dragged her hand across his chest, leaving fresh singes in his shirt. The material crackled as it burned under a sheen of ice. Ghosts pulled so much energy from the atmosphere around them that their touch scorched, even as everything else around them froze.

"You deceived me," Lark said so mournfully that he nearly apologized. He felt odd, as if he were under a frozen river. He was too cold to move, too cold to care. "You have no real power, only borrowed trinkets." Those trinkets would have made a meal for her, if there wasn't a witch to drain not three feet away.

She drifted away to join her sisters. They hunched over Tobias, scattering beetles, poisonous berries, and icicles. His patrician features were gray. The gas lamps went out, pulled by an invisible wind. The Sisters floated there, their edges growing sharper and more distinct. A bird fell dead from the sky, landing in the middle of the street.

Tobias didn't have much time.

But none of them wanted Cormac and so would not be distracted.

Cormac tossed another pinch of summoning powder, to warn the Order they were needed. The sparks cast a pale blue light over them, flickering and fading away. Magdalena was the first to look up, more satiated than her sisters. Her eyes glowed with an unnatural brightness. "The Order of the Iron Nail," she sneered. "Go away, little Greybeard, before I eat your spleen for your impertinence."

He'd once had a governess threaten the very same thing. He'd tossed a plum pudding at her head, if he recalled correctly. This time he chose salt and iron shavings, ground down from the horseshoe of a white horse with one blue eye.

He carried the banishing powder in a red pouch, sewn with magical runes by his youngest sister. It was a standard weapon of the Order, as useful as swords and pistols. More useful, truthfully. There were too many creatures that didn't fear bullets. But demons dreaded salt, curses broke under the gaze of a blue eye, and spirits feared horses and boats, both used to carry them off to the Underworld.

Cormac leaped into their circle, standing over his friend and tossing another handful of the banishing powder. Ice burned his exposed forearms, leaving angry white welts. Rosmerta shrieked as the powder formed into a white horse and galloped at her. She jumped out of the way, scurrying to hide behind her plaid-draped sister. Blood and ice hit the pavement. A large beetle was crushed to ash under a bright hoof. The horse tossed his mane, sending death's-head moths tumbling into one another, wings shredded.

Rosmerta's poisonous vines lifted in the air, as did her hair and the full bell of her skirt, all being towed toward the white horse. She grabbed a handful of her sister's bloody hem, fighting the inexorable pull, still shrieking. The other two stopped draining Tobias, turning to glower at Cormac, then at the horse.

"No!" Magdalena snapped viciously. "We've been too long denied."

"I can't hold on," Rosmerta shouted above the roar of the wind and the pounding of hooves like cannon shot as the white horse circled and circled. A strange honey-scented wind flattened Cormac's hair and tugged at his clothing. Tobias slid a few dangerous inches along the pavement. Cormac crouched to hold onto the back of his collar, securing him. Tobias was exhausted to the point that the white horse might accidentally take him as well.

Cormac had to lure the Sisters away. Where they went, the white horse would follow. He touched the amulets around his neck. They'd been a temptation for other creatures before, from revenants to necromancers to warlocks. He just had to make them more appealing than the last dregs of Tobias's magic. He slipped the chain off, unclasping it. Amulets clattered together.

Rosmerta turned to glance at him once. He dropped a charm for agility and stepped on it, shattering the glass bead. She licked her lips, but didn't leave her post.

"Don't you want it?" he asked. "Why fight over what little he has left in him?" He held up the chain, the amulets spinning together. "When I have all of these?"

He broke three wolves' teeth meant to guard him from a werewolf's bite.

Rosmerta abandoned Tobias first.

He took a few steps, cracking a memory charm like a hazelnut.

The horse nipped at Magdalena. She hollered a curse and his mane singed briefly. Ghostly smoke smelled like cold water and metal.

In unison, the Sisters turned to Cormac.

When he was certain they were following him, he crossed the street and headed to the seclusion of the park, dropping charms as he went. Curse-breakers, dream-shields, lock-singers. He kept the charm for True Sight, slipping it into his pocket. If he was going to distract the Sisters long enough for the Order to arrive, he had to be able to see them.

He broke his strongest shield-charm last, leaving him vulnerable. He knew it would be irresistible to the Sisters. It was the most powerful magic he carried on his person; it had taken three witches three long nights to forge it.

And he just had to distract them a little longer.

Long enough to survive.

And hopefully not get his own sisters killed.

Chapter 7

"Gretchen, your gown! It's positively ruined!"

Gretchen smiled brightly as she dropped onto a gold velvet chair. She was covered in soot and mud, and the ribbons on her dress had dye running all over the skirts. It blended to a virulent shade of purple where it met the pink smears left behind by Lady Pickford's ridiculous dog. She was rather proud of the effect. It looked a little like a sunset over the moors. "Best. Ball. Ever."

"Up, you savage!" Her mother very nearly shrieked, despite her daily assertions that ladies only spoke in pleasant whispers. A talent, it need not be said, that Gretchen did not possess. "You'll stain the fabric and I've just had that chair delivered."

Gretchen's father frowned at her over the rim of his scotch glass. The amber liquid glowed like honey in the firelight. "Darling, you might inquire as to her well-being. She's more feral looking than usual."

"Tut," Lady Cora Wyndham replied shortly as Gretchen abandoned her seat. It was uncomfortable anyway. Her mother had a tendency to purchase fashionable furniture without a single thought to comfort. "I can see very well that she is perfectly fine."

Gretchen refrained from comment, mostly because Godric burst into the drawing room, dragging in the scents of evening: rain, wine, and candles. "So it's true then," he said, sparing Gretchen a glance as he strode to the sideboard. He poured too much whiskey into a crystal tumbler and it sloshed at the rim. "There really was a fire at the Pickfords' ball?" he tossed over his shoulder.

"Yes." She beamed at him. "And an earthquake. It was all very exciting."

"And did *you* set the fire?" Godric teased, knowing her all too well.

She grinned back. "I'm afraid I didn't think of it."

Lady Wyndham made a sound in the back of her throat which she reserved entirely for her children—like a wet cat in winter. She would never deign to show anything but cool politeness in public. It was sometimes difficult to believe that she was sister to both Emma's mad mother and Penelope's wildly unconventional mother. "Did you pay our respects to the Pickfords?"

Gretchen paused. "Yes?"

"That's hardly convincing," Godric scolded her, laughing. "Try again."

"Whatever did I do to deserve such an uncouth daughter?" Lady Wyndham sighed.

"I was a little busy, *Maman*. I was hauling buckets of water and rescuing pink dogs."

"You hauled buckets?" her mother repeated, aghast. "Honestly, Gretchen. You do delight in vexing me."

"I fancied myself rather heroic," she returned, crossing her arms. "If it had been Godric you'd be fluttering about, full of ancestral pride."

"Twins or not, you are *not* Godric," Lady Wyndham pointed out crossly. "And now that you've had your come-out, recent as it may be, it's time you started to behave accordingly."

"Oh, *Maman*, honestly. It's nearly three in the morning."

"A lady is a lady, no matter the time," she sniffed.

Gretchen opened her mouth to retort but her father shot her one of his famous haughty glances before offering his wife his arm. "Let us retire. You know how quarreling is bad for the complexion. You might get wrinkles."

Lady Wyndham practically galloped from the room. Gretchen and Godric exchanged a speaking glance before breaking into laughter when their parents were safely out of earshot. Gretchen snatched the glass from her brother's hand to steal a sip.

"I hardly think that's what mother meant by proper behavior," he chuckled as she went cross eyed.

"That is horrid," she sputtered, wiping her mouth with the back of her hand. Her throat was on fire. "Why on earth would you drink that on purpose?"

"Serves you right. Ladies don't drink whiskey."

"Don't you start." She took another sip just to prove a point, as her brother knew full well she would. The taste didn't improve the second time around. She did feel a pleasant sort of warmth in her chest though, which took some of the sting away. "Why are you home anyway?" she asked, slumping back into a chair. The fire had turned to coal in the grate, glowing like red eyes. "I thought you were determined to keep to your bachelor apartments with the other lads." She was dreadfully jealous. She longed to live away from her mother's constant and unbearable speeches about proper behavior and proper manners and proper properness.

"I just came to fetch my old silver pocket watch," he replied, making a face. His blond hair tumbled into his eyes, scarcely shorter than her own. She approved of the new fashion of cropped hair for girls, it felt positively freeing not to have her head scratched by pins and weighed down with pearl brooches. "I lost it to Edward in a wager last night and he's already asking after it."

"I don't know why you insist on playing at cards," she said affectionately. "You're terrible at it."

"I suppose I am," he admitted amiably. "Horse racing, now that's a different matter."

"I haven't forgotten you said you'd take me—" she broke off when he froze, blinking rapidly. "Are you going to cast up your accounts?" she asked. "Mother will kill you if you're sick on her carpets, exalted heir or not."

Godric just shook his head, color draining from his cheeks.

"You're white as paste." Gretchen frowned, rising slowly and looking over her shoulder. She half expected to see her mother with another lecture on deportment. Instead, there was only the sofa, several potted ferns, and a table glittering with crystal bowls filled with sweets. The housekeeper had an occult sense as to when Godric might be stopping by, and she always kept his favorite candies on hand.

Godric swallowed. "Bollocks," he muttered.

"There's nothing there." She tilted her head. "How much of that vile drink have you had?"

"Just a sip," he replied hoarsely. "Don't you see her?"

"Who?" Gretchen reached out to touch her brother's sleeve. "I think you should stick to wine," she added, grinning.

But the moment her fingers pressed into his arm, Gretchen's smile died.

The sound of roaring wind and water was in her ears, making her feel as if she'd fallen into the Thames. Shivers raced up and down her arms. Her fingers tightened on Godric's sleeve. He stepped closer to her, mouth working but no sounds emerging. Gretchen felt the same way: stupefied and stunned speechless. Because she could see the girl now.

The very dead girl.

The sound stopped as suddenly as it had started.

But the girl remained. She was dressed for a ballroom, in white silk with a ribbon tied under her breasts. Her hair fell in disheveled curls and there was blood on her neck and down her arms. The rest of her was winter: the white of snow, the dark of bare branches, the indigo of storm clouds. The painting of some ancient Wyndham ancestor wearing a ridiculous ruffle was perfectly visible through her body. A star-nosed mole with red-tipped fur raced around her feet.

"Margaret York," Gretchen said, stunned. "But you were only hurt a little . . ." She stepped away from her brother, her eyes still so wide they were uncomfortably dry. When her hand fell away from his sleeve, Margaret's ghost vanished.

Swallowing, Gretchen raised her fingers again, slowly. The moment she touched her brother, Margaret reappeared. "That can't be good," Gretchen murmured.

Godric's laugh was strangled. "I should think not."

"No, I mean I can only see her when I touch you."

"I wish I could say the same." Sweat popped on his forehead. He wiped it away, tousling his curls, which made him look younger. "If I'm not foxed, I must be mad."

"Or you can see ghosts."

He slid her a glance. "That is not an option."

She tried to smile. "Well done. You sound just like Father."

"There's no need to descend into insults," he muttered. He lifted his chin, like a captain about to go down with the ship. "I don't see her anymore," he announced.

Gretchen heard a low buzzing, as if her ears were full of honeybees. She shook her head to clear it. "You're lying," she said.

"How do you know?"

"I just do." She paused. "I can hear it."

He blinked at her before tossing back the remainder of his drink. He hissed as he swallowed and Gretchen now perfectly understood why men did that. She'd hiss too if she had to drink something that tasted like a peat bog. Ignoring him, she looked at Margaret. "What happened to you?"

"You're talking to a ghost," he said.

"Well, we won't find anything out just standing here gaping," she replied reasonably. Margaret didn't so much as glance at Gretchen. "Can you talk to her?"

"How should I know? And why would I *want* to?"

"Godric, stop being such a goose."

He snorted. "As soon as you stop acting as if this is perfectly normal." He tensed when the girl took a step toward him. "Damn," he whispered. He nudged Gretchen with his elbow. "I wish I had a normal sister."

"You do not. Now, go on."

He met the girl's brown eyes, even though it turned the sweat to ice under his hair. There was something primal about talking to the dead. It was disconcerting in a way his bones objected to, turning cold and shivery. "Are you . . . dead?"

Gretchen was the one to reply. "Of course she's dead, you tosspot."

"They're here," Margaret said, only there was no sound. She mouthed the words.

"Who's here?" Gretchen looked around wildly. When the mole suddenly darted at them violently, Gretchen yelped. Godric swore, stepping in front of her protectively. The little mole kept attacking them, his teeth surprisingly sharp. Blood dimpled Gretchen's ankle. She made a dash for the fireplace, dragging Godric with her by the sleeve. He hunched over her, taking the brunt of the mole's anger. Margaret just hovered under the chandelier, looking wispy and wretched.

Gretchen pulled the iron poker from the firewood basket,

swinging it down so savagly, Godric nearly lost an eye. The curved pointed end of the poker sliced through the mole and it fell apart, like ashes and fire, dissipating into nothing. The girl followed, falling apart like burning paper. They left behind a cold draft and the faint smell of smoke.

And a single small paw print in the scattered ashes from the grate.

Panting, Gretchen lowered her makeshift weapon. "Is it gone?" she asked when Godric stepped away and she could see nothing but her mother's favorite ceiling frieze, the one with urns of flowers and Roman ladies eating grapes.

"They're both gone," her brother replied. Without another word, he left the drawing room.

"Wait!" Gretchen chased after him down the empty corridor. He paused briefly on the threshold of the open front door. A carriage rumbled down the street behind his shoulder. "Where are you going?"

"Where do you think?" He looked at her as if she was the mad one, seeing ghosts and rabid star-nosed moles. "To get very, very drunk."

Chapter 8

"What the hell are you doing here?" Cormac snapped as three of his sisters swarmed around him. "Go home! Now!"

Colette, Georgiana, and Primrose just stared at him as if he were a curious specimen of beetle pinned to a corkboard. "Certainly not," Georgiana said crisply. "We've come to save you."

Cormac groaned. "Georgiana, you're not a Keeper. You talk to *birds.*"

She narrowed her eyes at him behind her spectacles. A pigeon swooped down and yanked several hairs from his head. He grabbed at his stinging scalp with a muffled curse.

"You're just embarrassed," Colette pointed out, nodding with approval at her twin. "You don't want the Order of Iron Arses to know your baby sisters saved you." Reverence and refinement had escaped Colette's character entirely. Even as a baby, she insisted on spitting up on every duke that came to the house.

She'd have spat on the Order if she could. "They should be embarrassed. Since we got here first," she added proudly. "And we're girls."

"I'm aware," he said drily. He was also aware that the Grey-malkins would burst through the tree line at any moment. He had to get his own sisters safely away from here. Easier said than done, clearly.

Colette frowned at the quiet lawns, inhaling the sweet perfume of roses. They hadn't even bloomed yet, Colette just had that effect on plants. "What exactly are we saving you from?"

"Nothing," he said, trying to sound convincing. He'd convinced Emma he cared nothing for her. He'd convinced the spirits of ancient warlocks that he was dangerous. He'd even once convinced a river-demon to swim away without his decapitated head in its teeth.

But he had yet to convince any of his sisters into doing any blessed thing they didn't already want to do.

"How did you even find me?" he asked. "And *please* tell me Mother and Father aren't on their way too." If he was going to die, he'd rather not die mortified and coddled.

"They're not back yet from that tedious dinner party," Primrose assured him. "But Talia woke up screaming," she added quietly. They were all familiar with the sound of their baby sister's screams. No amount of herbal teas or medicines helped. "She said you were in trouble and sent us here."

"With this," Colette added, holding up a very pink hair ribbon longer than her arm. It was stitched with tiny seed pearls along the edges. She shrugged at his questioning glance.

"She was adamant," Primrose added.

Cormac took the delicate ribbon gingerly, shaking his head. "She probably just had a regular bad dream," he insisted.

"She also said to tell the Order to shove their iron nail up their—"

"She did not," Cormac sighed, interrupting Colette.

"Actually, she did this time," Primrose said. "In a way. She said to tell you: *Bottles break and knots undo but the only real binding is love that is true*."

"How very poetic." Cormac frowned. "Now *go home*. As you can see, I'm perfectly safe."

Primrose raised an eyebrow. "Cormac, you're covered in frostbite and soot."

"There was a fire in the Pickford ballroom," he said impatiently, herding them toward the street. "Talia must have dreamed of it and panicked. You know how she feels about fire."

"That doesn't explain the frostbite—argh!"

Colette had just caught sight of the first Sister. Cormac swore viciously and with great feeling. There was no getting them away now. Colette already had a knife in her hand and a mad smile on her pretty face. Birds woke squawking in the treetops as Georgiana spun around to see what everyone was gawking at.

His plan had worked. Problem was, he was no longer protected.

And neither were his sisters.

"Primrose," he snapped. Adrenaline sang through him, making the situation clear as a bell jar. He didn't have magic to rely on but he had the Order and their training. He hadn't had the chance to grow complacent, not like regular witches. "Tobias Lawless is wounded two streets east of the gate. Help him. All of you." Primrose had a particular talent for healing. Her interest in the Sisters evaporated. Even fear didn't have a chance to sneak under her determination to save a life. She took off running in the opposite direction. "Go with her!" Cormac told the others. "You can't leave her alone."

"And we can't leave you alone either!" Colette exclaimed. She met Georgiana's eyes. Georgiana nodded and ran after Primrose, trailing agitated robins, sparrows, and pigeons. The hawks remained, screeching at the Sisters. "I'm staying with you," Colette declared. "So save your breath, big brother."

And then there was really no more time left to argue.

Cormac stepped in front of her and lifted the ribbon, feeling ridiculous.

The Sisters swarmed, shrieking. The trees shivered, either from the unearthly sound, or Colette's reaction to it. A rain of acorns pelted them. The white horse glowed between the branches as it approached, neighing loudly. The ground trembled under its hooves.

"Where's your shield-charm?" Colette asked in a small voice.

"Gone," he said succinctly.

"Bollocks."

He half laughed despite himself. "Stay behind me." He shifted, blocking her although he knew it was futile.

"We might prefer witches," Magdalena spat at Cormac. The jewels on her crossed girdle glistened and her skin was brighter, more moonlight than lavender. She'd fed deeply on Tobias, and on Cormac's amulets. "But any life feeds us," she added silkily. "And I think yours will be sweetest if you die screaming."

Ice sheened the trees, the leaves, and individual blades of grass at their feet.

"Come on then," he called out, stalking toward them. They were so accustomed to people fleeing from them, both uninitiated and witches alike, that they hesitated, confused. Lark began to weep without a sound, her tears the most corporeal part of her, as if they were all she was made of. Cormac smiled his most condescending, taunting smile, the one that had once caused Georgiana to order a bird to mess on his shoulder.

It never failed.

They circled him counterclockwise, and he circled against them clockwise to undo their work. The horse approached, like the moon between the dark tree trunks. Moths, hawks, and roses battled in the air. The Sisters clawed at Cormac, cackling. He squinted through the debris of dead leaves and dust, disoriented. The True Sight amulet in his pocket glowed briefly, fighting to clear his sight. The Sisters keened like a winter storm.

He knew the exact moment they sensed Colette's power. She felt it too, and the wind raked at them, filled with flowers and shredded petals. The trees tossed back and forth, clawing at the Sisters. They abandoned Cormac for sweeter fruit.

He fell slowly, toppling like a ship's mast struck by lightning.

"Cormac!" Colette shouted.

He sprawled on the cold ground, ice blocking his nostrils

and sealing his eyes shut. He had to drag his fist across them to loosen the frost. He coughed, pushing himself up on one elbow. The world tilted and spun like a game of tops.

Colette stood tall, pale but determined. She pushed her magic out, taunting and tempting the Sisters. She focused on Rosmerta, feeding power at the poisonous flowers draped all over her. The nightshade vines tightened.

"What are you doing?" Rosmerta clawed at the green tendrils bruising her head and crawling down around her neck, choking her. Real plants couldn't do her harm, but these were connected to her magic, and the lives she'd taken when she'd been just another Greymalkin warlock. The bryony berries burst, leaking juices that seared through her dress, through her flesh and right down to ghostly bones.

Magdalena shimmered right behind Colette, touching her on the back of the head. Cormac smelled burning hair, just as Colette crumpled. Colette's hawk-familiar exploded out of her back, from between her shoulder blades, to peck viciously at the Sisters.

Cormac dragged himself through the grass. Gritting his teeth at the confounding weakness, he crawled inch by inch, the pink ribbon tucked in his pocket. Colette began to convulse, just as Tobias had.

The end of the ribbon unfurled.

At this proximity, he could see the tiny letters, hastily written in blurred ink. *The Greymalkin Sisters*, followed by a string of symbols.

Talia had sent him a binding spell.

Cormac fumbled for the iron nail all Keepers carried after their initiation into the Order. It was wrapped in black thread and tucked into a special pocket sewn inside all his jackets. He rolled the ribbon tightly into a little ball, holding Colette's gaze until he was sure she wasn't staring blankly through him. Then he flicked his wrist in one sharp motion and sent it unraveling to her hand. Her fingers twitched. The horse's back hoof slammed into the ground beside her head. Sweat melted the ice in her hair as she forced her arm to move. Finally, finally, she grasped the ribbon. Grass grew over her fist, securing it to the ground even as the tree beside her shed its leaves.

Cormac drove the nail through his end of the ribbon and into the earth. Colette's magic seeped through the roots of dandelions, oak trees, and rosebushes. The power of the iron nail shivered through the ribbon, unleashing the binding spell.

Magdalena and Rosmerta froze and Colette let out a long, ragged breath.

It wouldn't be strong enough to hold them there, but combined with the white horse it should be enough to send them away. If they tried to return to the area they'd be sucked into the binding, which was a painful affair.

Above him, the horse grabbed Lark's plaid, dragging her into the binding spell. Colette pushed herself up, teeth chattering. Relief flooded through Cormac. He pushed dizzily to his feet, still holding onto the ribbon.

Confined by iron and magic, the Sisters could only huddle together as the white horse trampled through them until they fell apart like moldy lace. Then it vanished as well, turning back into a handful of banishing powder.

Which was, of course, the precise moment the Order arrived, finding Cormac holding a pink hair ribbon, with flower petals in his hair.

Worse yet, Virgil was with them.

A murderer and three cannibal Sisters were no longer the worst thing he'd dealt with that night.

The older Keeper was a stranger, but the scars on his hands proved him to be a veteran of the Order. He took one look at Colette and the grass dying around her and her frantic hawk-familiar, and handed her a piece of jet dipped in rivulets of silver. It cracked to dust the minute she touched it, absorbing the residue of dark magic contaminating her.

"No need to worry," Virgil announced. "We'll take care of this for you. Unless you wanted to keep this for your hair?" He yanked the pink ribbon out of Cormac's hand before he could say anything.

Magic spent, the white horse had fallen apart, but the binding ribbon hadn't completed its work quite yet.

The Sisters whirled back into spirit form, blasting frigid air so sharp it left bloody nicks on exposed skin. Virgil stumbled back a step, knocking the third Keeper, Prescott, off his feet. Magdalena made a grab for him, singeing through the sleeve of his coat. The odor of charred wool mingled with the wet mist. Prescott's teeth chattered as his magic leeched from his body. Virgil looked ill. The older Keeper swore under his breath, shoving between the Sisters and the others. He tossed iron shavings into the air, muttering in Gaelic and resecuring the ribbon with a spelled dagger.

There was a crack of violet light and the Sisters were gone.

"Good thing your little sister was here to help you," Virgil said with the kind of sweet politeness that made old ladies seem downright rude. "Wouldn't you say, old chap? At least someone in your family has power."

Cormac didn't reply. It wasn't the first time Virgil had insulted him and it wouldn't be the last.

It might be the last time he had his own teeth though. The image of his fist plowing through Virgil's face was deeply satisfying.

"I came out looking for the Sisters," Colette declared, shielding him the way he'd tried to shield her from the Sisters. "I cast a spell to summon them. So actually, Cormac saved *me*." To underscore her point, an oak branch slapped Virgil across the face. He stumbled, letting out a thin shriek. Colette burst out laughing.

Cormac shook his head. "Never mind, Colette," he said gently. "You don't have to lie for me."

"But it's rather funny to hear him make that noise," she said. "And I do feel dreadful," she added. "I could probably throw up on his shoes. They look new."

Cormac only smiled and turned to the other Keepers. "Tobias is two streets over," Cormac said. "They nearly drained him."

"I'll go," the older man offered, loping away. Virgil and Prescott remained.

"Cormac saved Tobias's life." Colette taunted Virgil with all the maturity of a three-year-old after too many sugar biscuits. "What did *you* do tonight, you pompous ingrate?"

Cormac grabbed her arm when she wove on her feet, still exhausted despite her temper. He didn't bother to hide his grin when Virgil avoided Colette's glare the way he'd have avoided an escaped asylum patient.

"The Sisters," Prescott whistled through his teeth. "Rotten luck, Blackburn."

"We banished them," Colette pointed out crisply.

"They'll be back," he said, shrugging.

"Probably," Cormac agreed. "But not tonight. And that's good enough for me."

"The Order wants to talk to you."

"Yes," Cormac sighed, running his hand through his hair. "I imagine they do."

"They're waiting in the carriage around the corner."

"Of course they are."

Chapter 9

Emma knew full well that being caught sneaking into bachelor apartments in the middle of the night would ruin her utterly. She would be cast out of society, shunned, and very likely locked in the cellar by her very irate father. All that, without even taking into account the dangers that lay in the dark streets between here and there.

So she'd just have to make sure she wasn't caught.

She was wearing her most voluminous cloak, her face tucked back into the deep shadows of the hood. There wasn't enough money in the world to bribe her father's coachman to run her out in the family carriage, even if her father had owned an unmarked one, which he did not. He thought it only proper that he be recognized wherever he went. He could travel between gaming hells, Parliament, and brothels with impunity since earls were accorded special allowances.

Earls' daughters were not.

Emma stopped long enough to slip a small paring knife from the kitchen into her reticule. The newspapers were forever reporting on people getting robbed at night—even in the glittering neighborhood of Mayfair. Sometimes especially then.

Besides, she was enjoying the thought of brandishing it at Cormac.

She kept to the hedges, darting from cover to cover as she made her way down the street to the nearest ball. Luckily, she didn't have to go far to find the road clogged with carriages, ladies in diamonds, and men in crowned hats. She used the crowd as a shield, dashing between the horses until she found an empty hansom cab for hire.

She tossed the driver a coin and an address, slamming the door behind her. The seats were squashed and the dim interior smelled like rosewater and cabbages. She bounced along the worn cushions, holding onto the edge of the window when the carriage turned sharply. Peeking out between the curtains, she saw gentlemen laughing together outside a tavern, the windows of her father's club lit with oil lamps, and a woman wearing a very questionable gown standing inside a doorway. Torches and gas lamps gave everything a yellow glow, like gold coins at the bottom of a very deep wishing well.

The carriage stopped in front of a large house with a clean front step flanked with burning torches. She jumped out, unable to make the steps lower properly. The coachman was huddled in a greatcoat, yawning. "If you wait for me, I'll double your fee," she said.

He grinned. "Aye, miss."

She hovered on the pavement, trying not to imagine what he must be thinking of her and what she was doing here. She certainly had bigger problems than that. For one thing, this particular street was most disobliging. There wasn't shrubbery anywhere in which to hide; there were only lampposts and paving stones and the clatter of wheels on the cobblestones behind her, none of which were especially helpful. Also, a formidable butler now stood in the open doorway, eyeing her.

Blast.

She crossed behind the carriage, hiding behind its bulk. She hovered there uncertainly, running through curses under her breath. The coachman, overhearing her, gave a startled guffaw. "I didn't know goats could do that," he said.

She smiled at him weakly. Her mind raced as she tried to imagine a way past the butler. If he was anything like Jenkins she would need nothing short of magic.

A carriage pulled ahead of her hired cab and disgorged young gentlemen and ladies who should've known better. They were a riot of colorful silks, all hats askew and crooked cravats. They stumbled across the sidewalk, arm in arm. They headed toward the bachelor apartments like a flock of geese constantly changing leaders mid-flight.

Finally, a little luck.

Emma crept close enough to smell the port from the open bottle the young man with red hair swung negligently from his fingers. One of his friends was singing a song about a sailor and his sweetheart. It put her poor cursed goats to shame. She trailed after them, trying to appear part of the festivities without actually drawing their attention. The butler nodded to the gentlemen and politely refrained from noticing the women at all.

Oil lamps burned in the foyer, casting wavering light over the marble floor and doors opening onto rooms down the hall. The balustrade of the staircase was shaped like a buxom mermaid. She'd never drown with proportions such as those. The party trampled up the steps. Nerves had her palms tingling. She rubbed them on her dress.

That was when she noticed the light spilling out from the front opening of her cape.

Light spilling from *her*, in fact.

She gasped, holding up her hands. She squinted at the flare of light, as bright as the Pickfords' curtains when they caught fire.

Something was very wrong with her.

"What's that, eh?" Someone slurred at the top of the stairs, blinking owlishly. "Bloody girl's on fire."

Emma gasped and leaped into the potted ferns and ficus trees grouped together on the landing. It occurred to her that she was spending a lot of time hiding in shrubbery lately.

"You're foxed," one of his friends laughed, slapping him so hard on the shoulder they both nearly fell headfirst down the stairs. The mad flailing to regain their balance distracted them from Emma. She stayed huddled behind the leaves, trying not to hyperventilate.

Her left palm was *glowing*.

She rubbed it hard on her dress and the glow dimmed but didn't fade away completely. Her hands, all evidence to the contrary, felt perfectly normal. If her eyes had been closed, she'd never have guessed anything out of the ordinary was happening.

The glow weakened, the light like molten iron boiling in a blacksmith's shop. It poured and ran into new lines, like the blade of a newly forged sword under a hammer. The pattern was simple, curving into a four-leaf clover minus the stem.

Floorboards creaked as the party made its way into one of the rooms. A voice carried up the stairs from the back of the house. She couldn't stay here. She curled her fingers into a fist, trying to hide the strange glow. It made her feel vaguely sweaty to look at it, as if she'd climbed too high up a tall tree and couldn't find her way back down.

She forced herself up to the first floor, which was sectioned off into bedrooms with small attached private parlors. She knew Godric had a room overlooking the street, as he'd told them stories of hiding under the bed when he saw his parents' carriage pull up to the curb.

However she had no idea which room belonged to Cormac.

This seemed so much easier in novels. And the *Times* made it sound as if housebreaking were as easy as buying muffins from a cart.

She forced herself to stop sneaking glances at her palm and concentrate. The door at the end must be Godric's since it faced the street. The voices of the group she'd followed inside were a dull roar at the other end on the right. She moved slowly to the room beside her, listening at the door for a moment. When she reached for the doorknob, it turned easily. She craned her head inside.

And promptly slapped her hand over her own eyes, nearly blinding herself.

Subterfuge was a dangerous business.

And she could have lived a full, happy life without ever seeing William Purejoy's backside.

She pulled the door shut hastily with a smothered apology. Well, it was meant to be an apology. She couldn't help the laugh that choked out of her. Something thumped against the door and she leaped back. It sounded like a shoe. Or a chair. If he was that peevish about his privacy, he really ought to use the bedroom and not the parlor rug.

By process of elimination, Cormac had to be behind one of the other two doors, assuming he was at home. And unoccupied.

If he was with a girl, she really would have to stab him.

She pushed the next door open an inch, half-afraid of what she might see. She released the breath she hadn't realized she was holding when she saw nothing more exciting than embers in the fireplace grate and the outline of a chess set on one of several tables. The faint glow from the mark on her palm gave off just enough light that she could move about without running into the furniture. There were books, a tea tray, and a crystal on the windowsill. But no convenient letter addressed to him, or portrait of a family member on the desk.

As it turned out, subtle hints weren't necessary.

She was pushed against the door, secured by a steady iron grip.

"Well, now, what have we here?"

Chapter 10

The Chadwick town house was rather grand from the outside, boasting to Mayfair that a duke's granddaughter was in residence. The boast was deliberate, a poke at those who still whispered, nearly twenty years later, that said granddaughter had eloped with a man with no land and no title, and against her father's wishes at that. That he was wealthier than most of the aristocracy was both a balm and a sting.

Behind the white Grecian columns was a snug home with all the warmth of a country cottage. In fact, the Chadwicks vastly preferred their country house to living in London but had insisted on being in town for Penelope's first Season. They were a small family but a close one; case in point, Penelope went straight to her mother's upstairs parlor. It was a haven where corsets were denied, shoes kicked off, and the art on the wall was courtesy of her mother's own talent with absolutely no historical value whatsoever.

"*Maman*, you're still awake at this hour?"

"I was waiting up for you." Lady Bethany sat on a settee piled with embroidered cushions, the most prominent sporting a lopsided swan with three feet. It had been Penelope's first attempt and she'd been so proud of it, despite the crooked stitches. Her mother had never allowed it to be tucked away or replaced. She was currently drinking from a pot of chocolate and reading a salacious novel full of doomed maidens and ruined castles. Or was it doomed castles and ruined maidens? Penelope was desperate to find out. She leaned against her mother with a small sigh.

"Was it dreadful, my darling?" Bethany asked, slipping a ribbon into her book to mark the page. "Dancing debutantes and fortune hunters?"

"Worse."

She raised a dark eyebrow. "Worse? Goodness, how did you manage that? I remember those horrid balls."

"Mr. Cohen called me fat," she replied, wrinkling her nose. "I didn't even know I *was* fat until this wretched Season."

"Mr. Cohen is a sad young man who does not deserve you."

"That's what Emma and Gretchen said."

Bethany smiled her serene smile. "I assume they used more lurid language. But I did warn you, kitten. I don't see why you insist on having a Season. You don't need to marry. Your father has set you up with an inheritance to rival what mine would have been."

"If you hadn't married Papa."

"Yes."

"Do you regret it?"

"Not for a moment," she replied. "Friends who blow with the wind are not friends at all. I found a good man with a good heart. And he fills out his jacket rather nicely, if I do say so myself." She reached for her cup. "I love your father and I'd be happy to be Mrs. Chadwick instead of Lady Bethany, if your *grand-maman* wasn't so . . ."

"Invested?"

"I was going to say violent," she returned drily. "You know she loves my title, and your own, more than we ever shall. More than my own mother did."

"I know. That's part of the reason I agreed to this Season. It makes her so happy."

"She wouldn't want you to trade your happiness for hers, whatever she might have to say on earls' sons and vouchers to Almack's Assembly Rooms. She never had a Season. She can't understand."

Penelope stole a sip of rich melted chocolate from her mother's teacup. "I know. But I want what you and Papa have. I want love." She gave a dreamy sigh, perfectly able to picture it: a man with wide shoulders and tousled hair, reciting Shakespeare's sonnets as they rode through a summer storm.

"You've time enough for that, surely."

"I hope so. Because I also know perfectly well that I only receive the invitations I do because of my inheritance and my uncles' connections. Being the niece of two earls with impeccable reputations does wonders."

"Those men are pompous bores but I suppose they have their uses." She made a face. "Cora has outshone them in dull propriety, which is saying something. I never thought a sister of mine would turn out so bland. You never can tell, can you?"

Penelope knew perfectly well that Gretchen's mother had equally damning things to say about Bethany, though being boring was never one of her sins.

"Don't let them change you." Her mother stroked a hand over her hair. "Did you get caught in the rain?"

"You could say that."

"That sounds rather ominous," she teased. "Should I be shivering?"

"No, of course not. It's only . . ." She shook her head dismissively. "I'm sure it's nothing. Papa would say I've read too many novels."

"*Pish*, there's no such thing," her mother replied instantly. "As well he knows."

"I felt . . . odd. Too much excitement, I suppose."

Bethany looked at her. "Did you remember your rhymes?"

"*Salt for meat and salt for defeat*," Penelope recited obediently. She shook her head. "*Maman*, some of your rhymes have never made sense," she added with a kiss to her cheek. "Good night."

She was at the door when her mother spoke quietly. "Oh, before you go, hand me that ring, would you? The one in the dish just there."

"Of course, *Maman*." The little porcelain dish painted with violets had been there for as long as Penelope could remember. She'd played with its trinkets as a little girl. Her favorite was the small silver bell that tinkled merrily when she shook it. The ring was a simple pewter band, set with tiny seed pearls. She'd handled it before, wondering at the dark spots that never scrubbed clean and the one pearl on the edge, melted flat.

So there was no explaining what happened when she touched it.

The world tilted suddenly until she wasn't herself anymore.

She was the girl wearing the ring. Her hand seemed to glow briefly. She could see the ring gleaming on her finger by the lamplight. No, not lamplight.

Firelight.

She was dressed in a simple white shift and there was snow falling lightly. Rope tied her tightly to a wooden post, chafing her hands and neck raw as she struggled to free herself. Her hair was untied, long and blond, utterly unlike her regular dark curls. Smoke billowed thickly around her, choking her. It made her feel listless, drugged.

Not just snow, but thin white ash, drifting in the cold air.

She heard the snap of the flames as they ate through the hay packed between the logs, as they traveled mercilessly toward her, hungry and insatiable. The winter moon watched unblinking. People pressed closer in a circle around her, held back by fear, smoke in their lungs, and guards with spears. Ice and snow melted in the town square, running in rivulets on the cobblestones and catching the moonlight.

This isn't real, Penelope thought frantically, even as other alien thoughts braided with her own.

I won't let them hear me scream.

It was an empty vow of course. No one can hold back the

screams, not even girls who aren't really being burned at the stake.

The shriek ripped from her throat, echoing in the velvet-and-lace-trimmed room. The smoke made everything hard to see, the faces of the silent crowd, her own mother in her favorite yellow dressing gown. Penelope coughed, choking.

And then her mother had her tightly by the wrist, flinging the little pewter ring onto the carpet. It lay there looking innocuous and pretty, just another bauble. Penelope gasped for breath, sweat dampening her neck. It took a long, painful moment for her to realize she wasn't actually on fire. She was safe in her mother's parlor with the candles and the chocolate pot.

Her father burst into the room, sword in his hand. The door slammed into the wall, knocking a painting off its hook. The glass cracked, shooting shards at their feet.

"We're all right, Phillip." Her mother was white as the ashes from the pyre.

"What the devil happened?" he demanded, searching the shadows grimly.

"I . . . nothing," Penelope said hoarsely, her throat burning dry. "A dream . . . I must be more tired than I thought."

"I heard screaming." His sword point lowered to the floor. He used his other hand to tip her chin up. "Should I call for the doctor?"

His wife shook her head. "No, love. She's not ill."

Penelope wasn't sure she agreed with that assessment.

She suddenly felt exhausted, so tired she could barely focus on her parents' concerned faces. The idea of being burned at the stake seemed distant and ridiculous. She was too tired to care about anything but her bed. She yawned, eyes watering. "I just need sleep," she mumbled thickly. She trudged wearily through the small crowd of servants, hurrying down the stairs from the attic with candles and questions. The housekeeper was holding a boot like a war club. Penelope didn't see the look her parents exchanged behind her, resignation laced with something else, something close to fear.

Only worse.

Chapter 11

Emma froze.

This had seemed like a much better idea just a few minutes ago.

The mark on her hand flared so brightly the room was briefly gilded, like the tail of a comet. Cormac had her pinned to the door. He still smelled of smoke and his shirt was open at the throat.

"Who sent you?" he demanded. His hold tightened.

She kept her face down, hidden in the shadows of her cloak. Suddenly, she didn't want him to know it was her, even though it was her own stupid fault she was even here in the first place.

He gripped her wrist, forcing her palm back. The mark glowed. "I'll ask you one more time. *Who sent you?*"

There was nothing of the earl's son who'd carried an injured girl, or the young man who'd thrown buckets of water at a raging fire, and especially not the person who'd once asked her about the stars in a winter garden. This was a part of him she had never seen before, a cold gleam she'd only ever associated with the lords when they returned from a particularly bloody hunt.

She shivered. "No one sent me," she insisted, her voice barely a whisper. She stared at her palm, traced with bright, impossible lines. Cormac, instead, stared at her. She could feel it, and kept her face turned away.

"I don't believe you," he drawled, leaning so close that she felt the breath of his words on her cheek. There was nothing but darkness between them.

This wasn't going at all as planned.

She tried to yank free of his grasp. Her hood fell back. When she finally turned to look at him, his aristocratic profile was unyielding and frightening. Until he recognized her. His shock was palpable. He released her so quickly she stumbled.

"Emma!" He looked more flustered than she felt, which was saying something. "What the devil are you doing here?"

She caught herself on the edge of a bookshelf. "I was looking for you, actually."

"Were you now, love?" he purred, regaining his composure. He was probably used to finding girls in his chambers. He leaned one hand on the wall by her head, boxing her between his body and a table. "I had no idea. You should have said. I'd have been more welcoming."

"Not for that!" She absolutely refused to let on that her breath was suddenly hot in her chest.

"Are you sure?" he asked, running his lips along the side of her neck until her knees felt as if they were made of water. She shoved at his chest. He was laughing as he stumbled back. "If you're not here to kiss me, love, you should go home. I'm sure it's past your bedtime." He was speaking as though he wasn't covered in soot, blood, and bruises.

She narrowed her eyes. He thought he could distract her and embarrass her until she fled. "You have answers, Cormac. And I have a lot of questions."

"And no sense of self-preservation," he countered. "You can't just call on a gentleman. Alone. At night."

"Exactly," she agreed. "Which just proves my point. I'm desperate and I need your help."

"Believe me, you don't want my kind of help," he said quietly, with a small, self-deprecating smile.

"I agree," she said. "But surely, it's better than none at all."

He shook his head, his disheveled hair falling over his forehead. "The fact that you can say that proves how little you know of me."

"Yes, we established that a long time ago." His gaze snapped onto her. She lifted her chin, inwardly cursing herself. She'd sworn she'd never mention her silly daydreams of their courtship, or that stolen kiss under the mistletoe.

"You really want my help?" he asked, stepping close to her again, as if he was trying to intimidate her or impress upon her the seriousness of the situation. As if she didn't already know how serious it was that parts of her anatomy were glowing. "Then take my advice," he said. "Get back in your carriage and go home. Now."

"That's your advice?" she echoed. Truth be told, it was more of a squawk. "Not good enough," she added, flinging her hand up so that the light seared his pupils. "What the hell is happening to me?"

He pushed her arm away, blinking. "It's just a witch knot; it's nothing to fly into the boughs over."

"I AM GLOWING. Though I admit it's usually only a brief flash."

He winced, covering her mouth when her shout reverberated through the plush room. His other hand went around her waist, dragging her close.

"Whgtdfmll," she mumbled, glaring daggers at him. If there was any justice in the world, his eyeballs should have shriveled up and his hair fallen out under the fury of her glower. The entire parlor should have spontaneously combusted.

The wind slammed through the open window. An inkpot slid across a table. A candle fell over.

"Damnation," he cursed, annoyed. "Stop it. Isn't one fire a night enough?" He released her abruptly to toss the contents of the water jug on his washstand at the smoking curtains.

"That was the wind," she pointed out. "How could that be my fault?"

He just shook his head, disgusted. "Come on," he said, gripping her elbow and dragging her into the hall. She dug in her heels. He tugged harder. "I'd rather you didn't burn my house down around my ears."

She rolled her eyes. "Don't be ridiculous. And I won't be put off. What exactly is a witch knot? Is it contagious? What does it mean?"

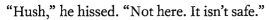

"Hush," he hissed. "Not here. It isn't safe."

"Where are we going?"

"I'm taking you home. You can't very well travel alone."

"I got here by myself, I'll have you know."

"And look what that got you."

She looked at him pointedly as he hauled her down the servant stairs and out onto the pavement outside the carriage house. "Point taken."

"Tell me you have a hack," he muttered, keeping to the shadows along the fence that bordered the house from the neighbors.

She sent him a smug smile and motioned to the waiting coachman out front. He tipped his hat at them. "There."

She climbed inside and waited for Cormac to do the same. He sat on the backward-facing seat, as all gentlemen did. He was silent for a long moment as the horses broke into a walk, pulling the carriage through the gathering fog. The stars were swallowed, one by one. It always made her feel lonelier when they went.

"I suppose this is better than the carriage ride I just took with several very disgruntled members of the Order." He looked at her pointedly, as if she ought to know what that meant. "If any other Keeper but myself had found you tonight, you'd be in chains."

She shivered. "Why didn't you do the same then?"

He didn't answer, instead looking out the window as London passed them by. The white columns made the houses look like a parade of ancient temples.

Emma swallowed, her mouth suddenly dry. She uncurled

her fingers, her palm open like a flower in her lap. "Please, explain this to me," she said simply.

"All witches have a witch knot." He shifted, his knee pressing against her. The dark confines felt suddenly intimate. "I should think as the daughter of one of the infamous Lovegroves you'd know that much, at least. You are descended from a long line of witches, it's no use trying to pretend otherwise."

She tilted her head, wondering when exactly he had decided she was gullible. Probably somewhere between the time she'd kissed him with embarrassing enthusiasm and before he'd jilted her. "I don't believe in witchcraft, Cormac. I'm not a child."

"Then perhaps you might explain to me why it's raining inside this carriage?"

He was right. A very fine rain was falling from the worn ceiling, misting on her cloak and in his dark hair. She jerked back and the rain stopped. "That's not possible."

"It is for a witch."

"Did I really make it rain?"

"Yes, of course," he said impatiently. "And you should know better."

"What about the earthquake?"

"The Order believes gates to the Underworld have been opened." He paused, frowning. "Possibly because of that witch bottle you broke."

"Well, I certainly didn't break it on purpose." She frowned back. "And what in the world is a witch bottle?"

"It keeps spells and sometimes other things. Worse things."

"And the Order?"

"They keep the peace between witches, and hunt warlocks."

She pinched her nose. "That's not actually helpful. And what's a warlock, then?"

"A dark witch, who uses magic for evil."

"Pretending for a moment that I believe you," she said, feeling chilled and awkward and ridiculous. Still, it was hard to argue with rain falling from the ceiling of the hackney cab. "How do you know so much?"

"My family is like yours."

She glanced curiously at his hands. "But you don't have a knot."

"No," he said, his voice emotionless. "I don't."

She considered pressing him for details but he looked away, his jaw clenched. "Though you haven't been tested," he added. "You appear to be a weather-witch."

She thought of the rain in the garden and had no counterargument to make. "At least I'm not glowing anymore." She should probably be terrified, but there was such a swirl of confusing thoughts in her head that she felt slightly numb. She wondered idly if her father knew anything about this.

"The knot is very faint at first, and it gets darker the more you use your magic. It only glows at birth and at death," he explained. "Though never quite as prolonged as yours."

Emma frowned. "But I've done neither today, thanks very much."

"Your powers were unbound. That is a kind of birth. Certainly to the councils."

"Councils?"

"Governing bodies of witches. There's the Council Arcanum for all magical creatures. And the Order of the Iron Nail who keep the peace, as I said. Magisters who make the judgments and The Weird Sisters who . . . keep to themselves."

"How very . . . parliamentary," she remarked. "And dull. My father sits in Parliament and gives long speeches about taxes and hedgerows," she pointed out. "If we're talking about witches, shouldn't it be more exciting? Flying on broomsticks and the like?" She paused, eyes wide. "Can I fly?"

"No," he said, half laughing. "And believe me," he continued drily. "The Order is more exciting than you care to know. And they'll be sending Keepers for you now."

She swallowed nervously. "Should I be afraid?"

"Yes," he said, sounding sad and resigned.

"Of you?"

He paused, his smile dark and mocking. "Perhaps."

She shivered, replaying the events of the night. The smell of smoke was still acrid in her nostrils. "Margaret . . . that was my fault? My mother's perfume bottle caused an earthquake?"

She couldn't help but stare at Margaret's blood on Cormac's collar from when he'd carried her. Her stomach roiled and her eyes stung. "I feel sick."

"Emma," Cormac said sharply. He grabbed her arms and gave her a little shake. "Listen to me very carefully. You are not to blame."

"How can you know that?" She didn't even kick him for shaking her. Mortified, she felt better when he was touching her.

"Because there were other marks on her body," he said quietly.

"Truly?" Relief had her teeth chattering. Little comfort to Margaret, though.

"Yes. And she set the fire herself."

"How is that possible? She was in the back of the garden room."

"I've just been told by the Order her magic gave her the ability to control fire. When she got hurt, it spiked and a candle set fire to the curtains. That part was an accident."

Relief was delicate and short-lived, like an eager moth drawn to a candle, moments before its wings caught fire. "Only that part?" She met his gaze. He looked grim. "Are you implying it was murder?"

"No. I'm not implying it." He let go of her. "I'm saying it outright."

Chapter 12

Emma spent most of the night pacing her bedroom floor, and listening for Keepers and God only knew who else to come for her. The witch knot was still on her palm, but at least it no longer glowed.

People didn't just start glowing. It simply wasn't done. Whatever Cormac might have to say on the matter.

His urgent warnings still rung in her head. She felt like a church bell, reverberating with iron aftershocks. She jumped at every sound. Fear made her feel like her mother's witch bottle, broken and jagged. She still had the paring knife she'd slipped into her reticule earlier. She wasn't entirely sure how useful it would be against magic.

Magic and witches and secret societies and murder.

It seemed too odd to be true, and too real to be a delusion. Her mother was clearly involved with some very peculiar things before she went mad. Emma couldn't help but wonder if it was the cause of her illness in the first place. She felt a little crazy herself at the moment. All of this over a broken perfume bottle.

Cormac's presence in the whole debacle was not helping.

Even remembering the nights she'd wept into her pillow over him, her heart still raced to see him. Clearly, there was something severely wrong with her. The proper reaction was anger and disdain. She ought to snub him.

Instead, she'd been caught prowling his rooms in the middle of the night.

No, she absolutely positively would not think about him now. Surely, she had priorities and they had nothing to do with the feel of his arms around her.

She stopped pacing long enough to press her hot cheek to the cool glass of the window. The light was turning pearly, mist curling through the gardens and over the cobblestones. The gas lamps flickered, barely piercing the pale gloom of London at dawn. Most of the Beau Monde wouldn't rise for hours yet; balls went so late into the night that Emma saw a few carriages emblazoned with family crests trundling home. Ladies in wilted finery and gentlemen in creased waistcoats slept inside, half-drunk.

In an hour, the house would be full of soft puttering, with footmen bringing in coal and setting the tables, and milk being brought to the back door. For now, she could have been entirely alone in the marble and stone house. Even the last star had faded.

It wasn't long before she saw one of the family carriages deposit her father at the front door. He'd spent the entire night at his club, as was his habit. She darted down the stairs to find him handing his hat and gloves to bleary-eyed Jenkins. The old man's wig was askew.

"You're up early," her father said to her as he passed her on the landing. He didn't stop.

"Wait," she said. She crossed her arms against the cold of the house. The maids weren't even down from their attic rooms yet to light the fires.

"Emma, I've yet to sleep. Make it quick." He looked down his nose at her. "You ought to be in bed."

"I know," she said carefully. If she was too direct, he'd snap at her and she'd never get any answers. She mustn't mention her mother. "Something happened last night."

He stifled a yawn. He smelled of port and smoke. "I'm really very tired, Emma. Talk to your aunt Mildred. That's why she's your chaperone."

"We were at the Pickford ball," she said hurriedly as he started to climb the steps. She tried to keep pace. "Where that girl was murdered."

He looked briefly taken aback. "I heard a fire broke out because of the tremors and she panicked. Murdered is a rather harsh word, surely." He patted her arm awkwardly. "No need to be frightened now."

"I'm not frightened."

"Oh. Well. Good night, then."

Frankly, it was the most he'd spoken to her in years.

But it wasn't nearly enough.

"Someone mentioned Mother," she blurted out, despite her best intentions to be subtle. "Something about the Lovegrove sisters . . ."

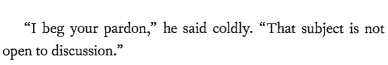

"I beg your pardon," he said coldly. "That subject is not open to discussion."

"But . . ."

"*Good night,* Emma." His frigid tone brooked no disagreement. He marched away without another word. Frustrated, she watched him go with narrowed eyes. When she heard his bedroom door shut firmly behind him, she hurried back down the stairs. She plucked her shawl from the parlor, scrawled a hasty note, and slipped out the front door.

If she had anything at all to do with that poor girl's death, even inadvertently, then she had a duty to find out what had happened to her. And to prevent any such thing from happening again.

Outside, the coachman had already taken the carriage around the side to the stables, but the horses were still harnessed. "I need you to take me to Berkshire," she told him.

"What, *now?*"

She nodded. "This very moment." Before she changed her mind. "To my mother's house."

He only sighed, opening the door for her and pulling the steps down. She handed him the folded note. "And please have this delivered to the Chadwick town house before we leave."

He called into the stables to arrange delivery, while she sat clutching her hands, the four-petaled mark on her palm hidden under her gloves. She didn't relax until the carriage rolled into the street and neither her father, nor Jenkins, chased her down to demand she return to the house or ask where she was going.

The sun was over the rooftops and the treetops by the time they reached the country house. She rarely visited, even though her father's estate was next door. He kept his wife, Theodora, here and only brought guests to his own manor. Penelope's mother, Bethany, had given up any claim to the Lovegrove family house once she saw that Theodora was only easy when she could stare at Windsor Forest, which pressed up against the old Tudor house. Gretchen's mother, Cora, distanced herself from the family entirely, barely acknowledging she had sisters at all.

A housekeeper opened the front door, blinking owlishly at Emma. It was early for visitors, even if they'd been accustomed to them in the first place. "Bless me, it's the mistress's daughter," she said with a bemused smile.

"Hello," Emma said politely. She had no idea what the housekeeper's name was. "I've come to see my mother."

"Of course you have." She beamed. "I'm Mrs. Peabody. You won't remember me after all these years." The housekeeper led Emma up to the second floor. The house was full of dark wood and white walls, and old paintings. She opened a door with a handle shaped like a drooping flower. "Here you are. Ring if you need anything." She hesitated as Emma stepped across the threshold. "Mind you don't stand between her and the window. She gets . . . agitated . . . when she can't see the forest."

Emma nodded to show she understood. She couldn't seem to speak the words that stuck in her throat like a too-large mouthful of honey cake.

The bedroom was large with no curtains on any of the windows, nor on the old-fashioned wooden bed. Every view showed the forest everywhere, even on the walls, which were painted with trees. Emma recognized her aunt Bethany's artwork. The branches were black silhouettes, reaching and tangling together like lovers' fingers. They arched up over the ceiling. A massive oak tree was also painted around the fireplace, stretching out branches in all directions. The sunlight caught the minutely detailed green leaves. The roots unfolded like the hem of a complicated dress. In a crude hand, a small red bird had been added to the crevice where a branch split off from the trunk.

Theodora Lovegrove Day reclined on a chaise longue, staring at the forest through the glass. Her hair was brushed and clean but loose and tangled at the ends. It was black like Penelope's and had none of the red sheen Emma's had, like deer fur. Her eyes though, were the same shape and her nose had the same tilt.

"*Maman?*" she said, and had to clear her throat and try again when her voice broke. It seemed odd to call this stranger "*Maman.*" She took a cautious step closer, watching her mother's face. She was still pretty, if pale. She was murmuring to herself, too softly for Emma to make out the words.

Emma crouched beside her. "*Maman?*"

Theodora glanced down and then back to the forest without a trace of recognition. Emma knew she shouldn't feel hurt, but she had to bite her lip to keep it from trembling regardless. She took a deep steadying breath. "Lady Theodora, I've come to ask you some questions."

Theodora shrugged. "Doctors ask too many questions." She cringed suddenly, clutching at her arms. "I don't want to be bled again. Slimy leeches." She scratched at the inside of her elbows until her skin welted and bled.

Emma tried to stop her. "Don't," she said, noticing a lattice-work of faded scars over her mother's witch knot. She'd clearly been scratching at it for years and it was still as dark as ink. "Please, I'm not a doctor." She held up her own palm, showing the symbol the color of weak tea. "See? I have one too."

A sweet bright smile changed Theodora's face entirely. She pressed her fingertips to the glass. "Do you see?" she asked. "He's watching."

Emma crossed to the window, looking out to the gardens below and the lawns stretching to the woods. "I don't see any-one," she said carefully, remembering feeling the same way at the ball the night before. "Who's watching you?"

Theodora only smiled dreamily. Emma swallowed back tears, feeling exhausted and helpless.

"They won't take me into the woods, but they can't stop me." She lowered her voice. "I can fly." She bounced a little in her chair. There were dried leaves under her feet and acorns cluttered on the windowsill and scattered on her lap. "And I don't even need a broom." Her eyes moved as if she was fol-lowing the circuit of something Emma could not see. "Pretty strawberry bird," Theodora giggled before turning to stare at her so abruptly and fiercely, Emma leaned back. "Are you the white stag?"

She rose to her feet. "No, I'm your daughter." Wind pressed at the glass and it shuddered. Windsor Forest remained still as a painting in the distance.

"What's your name?"

"Emma."

"I don't know anyone named Emma." She sniffed. "But you smell like trees. Sit next to me." She patted the cushion. "I like to watch the forest," she confessed quietly after Emma perched on the foot of the fainting couch.

Emma tried to smile, wishing her cousins were with her. "I like to watch the stars." Anxiety made her mouth dry and her lips stuck to her teeth. "Do you remember your perfume bottle?" she asked. She glanced over her shoulder to make sure the door was closed tightly. "The witch's bottle?"

Theodora blinked but didn't reply.

"It broke," Emma continued. "I wanted to know what it was." She paused. "What I am."

"You're a girl."

"Yes. But the Lovegrove girls are different, aren't they?" She pointed to the witch knot. "We can do things other people can't do, can't we?"

Theodora giggled again.

"What can you do, *Maman*?"

"Anything," she said happily. "Everything." She looked at the forest, then at Emma, dropping her voice to a loud conspiratorial whisper. "I'm still waiting," she sighed. "Always waiting."

And then no matter how Emma tried, she could not get her mother to say another word. She finally left, when Mrs. Peabody brought up her mother's tea tray.

If there were parents more frustrating than hers, she'd yet to hear of them.

Chapter 13

Hyde Park was the most privacy three girls accustomed to chaperones and a various assortment of maids and footmen were likely to get. Emma returned to London and waited for her cousins inside a small grove of oak trees, while seriously wondering if her mother's madness was contagious. She pulled a rolled-up scrap of parchment from the reticule dangling from her wrist. She'd made a list in the carriage on the way back from Berkshire. It was everything Cormac had told her and her own account of the night. If she was going to get to the bottom of this mess, she'd have to be practical. Gretchen would advise immediate, and preferably violent, action, and Penelope would quote some dead poet at her.

It was too late for poetry.

Though to be honest, the poets had as much chance as she did at figuring this out.

She rubbed her hand on the skirt of her walking dress until the skin chafed and went red. The knot looked angry but it didn't disappear. Emma sighed. Back to her list, then.

A deer poked her shy head between two low-hanging branches, chewing a mouthful of grass. Or whatever it was deer ate. She was delicate and strong, all muscled flesh under the red fur.

Emma held her breath, list forgotten.

The second deer was equally beautiful. She pushed farther into the grove, bluebell blossoms between her teeth. Her white-tipped tail flicked back and forth.

The third deer made Emma curious. She couldn't help a wide smile, even as her heart pounded in her chest. She was afraid the sound of it would startle them away. Herds of red deer weren't uncommon in the park, but they tended to run away from people and horses. They didn't gather next to them like guests at a tea party. And they didn't bring their families, all picking their way past the oaks. She felt as though she were in a painting, as if nothing around her was quite real.

One of them brushed past her and she smelled the musk and mud of its body. She stayed as still as she could even though some primal part of her wondered, quite loudly, if she shouldn't be running for her life right about now.

"I swear I don't hunt," she offered, her voice sounding odd in the stark peace of the grove. Several deer lifted their heads at the disturbance. Their hooves were powerful, and she remembered the stable boy who'd had his leg broken last week by a peevish pony. If a pony could be dangerous, what about wild deer? "And I don't eat venison." At least, not after today. "Anyway, I was here first."

She was reduced to false bravado in front of placid, grass-nibbling deer.

The moment stretched on, impossible and beautiful.

But by the time she counted thirteen deer, Emma was decidedly nervous.

Especially since the last to push past the oaks was a stag, with a huge rack of velvet antlers, like polished and gilded branches. His fur was thick, turning from winter gray to summer red. He towered over the rest, all muscle and primal power. Another deer shifted to brush past her, making room for the stag.

When he bellowed, Emma jumped, adrenaline tingling under her skin. The sound was loud and ancient, wild in a way London folk couldn't understand. This wasn't a wildness to do with too much champagne or dancing until dawn. This was cave paintings and stories told after dark. It was primitive and as old as the stars.

The stag turned his head to stare at her.

She wondered if anyone had ever been eaten alive by a herd of deer.

When his eyes met hers, she felt the connection in her bones. The trees shivered and flattened under a sudden gust of wind, showing their leafy underbellies. The birds fell silent. Fear fled, too wispy and unnecessary to hold onto. Something akin to joy bubbled through her, like hot springs coming out of barren rock. For the first time in her life, she didn't feel lonely.

She lifted her hand, the one with the painted witch knot. She moved slowly, so slowly it was like being underwater. Her fingers hovered over the stag. She paused. A red bird darted over her head. The stag stayed still, patient.

"Please don't bite me," she murmured, barely louder than a breath, as she stroked his shoulder. When he didn't snap at her, she dug her fingers into the thick fur. It was both rough and soft. She had the insane urge to lay her cheek on it. The knot on her hand felt warm.

And then her entire body felt warm. She could smell everything: the rich earth, the tender new grass, the crushed acorns, the faintly skunk-like odor of fox pups in a nearby den, the very sun on the hills. She felt different. Unconstrained.

Furry.

A quick, startled glance froze her breath in her throat and her every thought somewhere in the back of her head. She felt an urge to run, to bound through the forest. The wind tugged at the hem of her dress, revealing a leg now lengthening and narrowing and growing a sheen of red fur. Her bones shifted, not unpainfully, and bent at angles at odds with her body.

She'd traded an unearthly glow for fur. Not precisely an improvement.

Still, she abruptly and quite desperately wanted to believe in witchcraft. It was a far more beautiful justification than madness.

The deer around them continued to eat. A few stepped nearer, blinking those wide liquid eyes. Ears flickered. A head turned sharply. Several tails lifted, flashing white.

"What the bloody hell is—urk." Gretchen strangled her own words, snapping her jaw shut so fast she nearly bit off her tongue in the process.

The deer scattered, going off in every direction, like a storm of shooting stars. The stag bellowed and charged away, flinging clumps of dirt at them. Emma stumbled back, ducking to avoid being skewered by an antler. Under the privacy of her skirts, her leg turned back into ordinary flesh.

Gretchen goggled at her. Before she could say anything, Penelope joined them, squeaking as she stumbled into the grove. Her eyes were wide. "I was nearly trampled to death by a herd of deer!"

"Emma was petting a stag like it was Lady Pickford's pink poodle," Gretchen returned with a quick grin. "So you'll have to do better than that."

"Last night I was burned at the stake."

"You win," Gretchen said as Emma struggled against the desperate pull to follow the deer and run wild over the hills. "And . . . what?"

Penelope shook her head helplessly. "I don't know. I touched a ring and suddenly I wasn't myself anymore."

"You didn't think to choose to be someone who wasn't being murdered?" Gretchen asked.

"I didn't exactly have a choice in the matter, Gretchen," Penelope replied. "Believe me."

Gretchen rubbed her ears. "You needn't tell the truth so loudly."

Penelope looked at her oddly. "What are you talking about?"

"You don't hear that buzzing?"

"No," she said, glancing at Emma. "Do you?" They waited through a long pause, not receiving a reply from either a convenient swarm of honeybees or their cousin. "Emma?"

"Hmm?" Emma forced her attention back to the achingly empty grove and her very boring human self. "Sorry?"

"You ought to pay attention when your cousin tells you she was murdered."

Emma blinked. "Neither of you look particularly dead."

She snorted. "Perhaps not, but I did see Margaret's ghost last night." She shook her head sadly. "And then I read about it in the newspaper this morning."

Penelope sank down into the grass, looking tired and perplexed. Gretchen stretched out next to her, staring up into the complicated tangle of oak leaves. Emma was the last to sit, tracing her fingers in the print left by a deer hoof. "Let me see your palms," she said softly.

"Whatever for?" Penelope asked. "It was my legs the fire burned and I've already searched them for burns. It only *felt* as if it were happening to me." She shuddered.

"All the same," Emma insisted. Her cousins stripped off their gloves and held their hands out.

"What the blazes is that?" Gretchen burst out. Penelope snatched up a handful of grass and used it like a handkerchief, trying to rub the mark away.

"Don't bother," Emma told her. "It won't come off. It's called a witch knot. And at least they're not glowing."

"Is this some sort of prank?" Gretchen asked, tilting her

hand this way and that. The symbol was so pale, it was barely noticeable. "Because I don't understand it."

"Apparently, the Lovegrove sisters were witches. And since it runs in the family, we are too."

Gretchen broke out laughing. "You're not serious."

Penelope smiled. "That's something out of a gothic novel, Em. Well done. Are we tragic and misunderstood, doomed to wander unloved over the moors?"

"I'd prefer a moldering old castle," Gretchen put in. "Something with damp, dark dungeons."

"Unfortunately, I'm serious," Emma said, rolling a cracked acorn under her fingers. "And I didn't make it up."

Gretchen rolled over. "Well, who told you such a ridiculous thing then?"

She squirmed. Both Gretchen and Penelope raised their eyebrows at her.

"Cormac," she mumbled.

"Cormac?" Gretchen screeched. "That—"

"When did he tell you this?" Penelope interrupted before Gretchen could really get going. She'd happily eviscerate Cormac's character for the rest of the day, given half a chance.

"Last night," Emma admitted sheepishly. "When I snuck into his apartments."

Gretchen sat up slowly. "You snuck into *Cormac's* apartments?"

"Yes."

"Without *us?*" She pouted. "I thought we agreed he was to be loathed and insulted at every opportunity."

"He knew about the knot. And my mother's trinket bottle. About us."

"About us being witches," Gretchen returned doubtfully. "I think he's having a laugh at your expense. And I mean to make him suffer for it. As soon as possible."

Penelope shook her head. "I think he's right," she said. "I relived being burned at the stake as a witch," she said. "That can't be a coincidence."

"And rain inside a carriage is impossible," Emma added.

"Not if there's a leak," Gretchen grumbled. "And I'd like to know what else you did in the carriage."

"Nothing more interesting than making it rain."

Gretchen blew out a breath, ruffling the short hair at her temples. "You're both serious."

"You did just say you saw a ghost."

"After drinking whiskey. Which is vile, by the way. And I didn't see my hand glow."

Penelope frowned. "But think about it. My mother's always making us recite those silly rhymes. Perhaps they're spells. She was even burning feathers and lavender outside my door last night. It smelled like death. I was too tired to tell her to stop though. That sounds suitably witchy, don't you think?"

"No offense, but your mother's always been eccentric, Pen. I mean, she's an artist, after all." Gretchen rolled her eyes. "And can you imagine *my* mother prancing about reciting spells? That's where your theory falls apart. Rather spectacularly, I might add."

Emma couldn't help a chuckle. "The mind does boggle," she agreed. "Still. Cormac was serious. And he seems to think other Keepers from the Order will be coming for us."

"Who?"

"A kind of magical policing force."

Penelope's eyes widened with recognition. "That's why," she murmured, reaching into her reticule and pulling out two narrow iron hairpins set with tiny pearls. She wore one tucked into her curls. "Mother made me promise we'd wear these."

Gretchen took one, frowning at it. "Iron?"

"She said it would keep us safe. She was most adamant."

Emma slid the pin into her hair. Gretchen did the same with a disgruntled sigh. "Why hair bobs?"

"No one would suspect they were anything but decoration," Penelope guessed. "You know how my mother is always going on about using society's own preconceptions against them."

"They must be magical," Emma said slowly. "To keep us safe from the Order, I wonder?"

Gretchen glowered. "What do they want with us in the first place? We can't have broken the rules already. And if they want us so badly, why didn't Cormac take you away at the ball?"

Penelope smirked. "Because he's sweet on her."

Emma stared at her. "Don't be ridiculous."

"Well, he did kiss you."

"That was months ago. And he's kissed half the girls in London since then," she pointed out. "We should go talk to your mother, Pen," she added, changing the subject away from the very complicated Cormac.

"We'll go first thing in the morning."

"Why not right now?" Emma asked.

"Because my mother's not at home right now," Penelope said. "She's helping one of her friends prepare for a ball."

"And because *my* mother is having one of her supper parties." Gretchen grimaced. "And you both told her you'd be there. More importantly, you also promised you'd save me from the tedium since I can't escape to the library this time." Her expression hardened. "Anyway, if the Keepers really are after us, like Cormac said, then we're safer together. We'll cut through the crowds on Rotten Row right now and then you'll spend the night."

"*Witches*," Emma pointed out. "And *murderers*. Surely that's more important than dancing and tea cakes."

Gretchen didn't look convinced. "You'd think so, but you know my mother."

Chapter 14

After a long dinner of turtle soup, roast beef with stewed celery and asparagus, followed by syllabub decorated with fresh violets, the ladies retired to the drawing room. They sat demurely and chatted over champagne. Their daughters flipped through the latest issues of *La Belle Assemblee* for new dress patterns, wondering when the young men would join them again. There were twenty-four couples in attendance, with their various sons and daughters. Friendships were strengthened at such events, and matches considered. Accordingly, Lady Wyndham had invited mostly the parents of single young men and only a few girls so as not to appear too obvious.

Daphne and Lilybeth drifted toward the small card table in the corner that Gretchen, Emma, and Penelope had monopolized for their own purposes. The two girls' white dresses gleamed like moonlight. Emma's dark-green ribbons had already begun to unravel from her hem and Gretchen was picking the stitches of her left glove, as she always did when she was bored.

Daphne clucked her tongue. "Gretchen, that hair pin is dreadful. It's completely lost its shine."

Gretchen just looked at her steadily. She didn't blush or cringe, as most girls did when Daphne turned the sharp edge of her tongue on them. Lilybeth cringed beside her, even though she knew for a fact that her every hairpin and jewel was gleaming perfectly. She'd made sure of it.

"Daphne, go away," Gretchen said plainly and without rancor. Daphne sucked in an offended breath. Gretchen shooed her as though she were a bothersome fly. "Go on."

"Did you see how Daphne kept touching Cormac's sleeve?" Penelope whispered, once Daphne and Lilybeth had flounced off.

In fact, Emma *had* noticed.

"I'm sure I didn't," she replied instead.

Penelope snorted. "Right."

"I *told* you he wasn't interested in me."

"Then why did he keep staring at you?"

"He's a Keeper," she replied. "He was probably trying to figure out how to lock us all up before the tea is served." She snuck another glance at the window, wishing she could see more than just the reflection of the candles and the glowing glass globes of the lamps. As always, Aunt Cora had lit every beeswax candle she could find, just to prove she could afford it.

"I think the hairpins are working," Penelope assured her. "Anyway, no one would dare interrupt an Aunt Cora soiree, not even scary magical knight-types." Aunt Cora believed in the social graces of polite society and she expected her guests to do the same. The only ones who ever gave her trouble were her own family.

"No one's coming for us," Gretchen agreed. "Shame, really. I tied a small dagger above my knee, just in case. It took forever to secure it properly. Stocking ribbons aren't very practical."

"I'll remember that." Emma couldn't help a smile.

"I couldn't find anything about Keepers or ghosts in father's library," Gretchen added.

"Me neither," Penelope said. "Though I did notice all sorts of strange things I'd never seen before. Iron trinkets and the like. Even the potpourri *Maman* makes isn't like other potpourri. It's full of salt, for one thing." She tapped her left palm. "And this strange symbol. It's embroidered everywhere, now that I know what I'm looking at. I tried to see her palm as well for the knot, but she was wearing gloves this morning. And the only reason she let me come here at all is because she seems determined to keep me in crowds of people."

"Are we sure the Keepers are all that nasty?" Gretchen wondered.

Emma remembered the starkness in Cormac's eyes. "Yes."

"Well, I reckon they bleed like any other man. Oh Lord," she added, taking a fortifying sip of champagne. "Here comes my mother. Perhaps they could come take us away right now."

The cousins pasted identically innocent smiles on their faces as Lady Wyndham sailed gracefully in their direction. Only they could see the martial glint in her eye. It was nearly as sharp as the prisms shooting off the many ropes of diamonds around her neck. "You three ought to be mingling."

Gretchen rested her chin on her hand wearily. "I'll need some cake first to give me the strength. Why can't we sit around and drink port and tell bawdy stories like the men do?"

"Do not disgrace me," her mother said. "Many of these ladies have perfectly suitable sons."

"I'll need sweet ices and black coffee as well as that cake," Gretchen muttered.

"Aunt Cora, what lovely gloves," Penelope interrupted hastily before a proper row could ensue.

"Thank you." Aunt Cora was briefly distracted, though still clearly dubious.

"I adore the embroidery," Penelope continued. Since she was the only one who appreciated needlework, and did her own without whining about it, Aunt Cora was mollified. Her elbow-length gloves were edged with embroidery in a pale orange, to better match the striking tangerine walls of the drawing room. Black basalt urns decorated the tables and crowned the carved mantelpiece. "May I see them?" Penelope pressed. "I should dearly love to duplicate those doves."

"I suppose," Aunt Cora sniffed, reaching for the ribbon that secured her gloves. Emma leaned forward slightly to get a better look. It was clear Penelope was trying to see if their aunt had her own witch knot. Half the women in London could have them and they'd never know it beneath all those gloves.

The men chose that precise moment to rejoin the party, led by Gretchen's father. They certainly looked cheerful, with eyes slightly too bright. Cormac glanced at Emma but he chose to sit with Daphne and Lilybeth. The dove-gray of Cormac's waistcoat was arresting against the black of his jacket and his hair. Emma tried to pretend he clashed horribly with the tangerine walls. He didn't.

Lady Cora promptly forgot her gloves and turned a welcoming smile on the others. Within minutes the housekeeper had brought in a cart laden with tea, coffee, seedcakes, and jellies. Footmen circled with yet more glasses of champagne and claret.

"Now what?" Gretchen groaned when her mother came their way again. "I'll never get any cake."

"I've just had word that the opera singer's carriage broke a wheel and so she will be late. Penelope, you will favor us with your playing in the meantime." It was not a request. Penelope's talent at the pianoforte was already talked about.

Penelope crossed the room to the pianoforte, where two candles had already been lit on either side of the sheet music. She'd play for her aunt, but she'd choose her own music. These insipid songs would not do. She needed something with more fire. Her first selection had lumps forming in more than one throat, moody tragic passion trembling on every note. The second piece woke the inebriated old duke snoring in a gilded chair near the back door. He spilled his drink all over his silk pantaloons.

Since the ladies were all smiling, Lady Wyndham accepted her husband's hand to lead the first impromptu dance. There was, of course, nothing impromptu about it, but the innocent deception added to the mystique. Everyone would politely pretend the floor hadn't already been cleared to make space for the quadrille.

Cormac stood up with Daphne and a young man whose name Emma had forgotten led Lilybeth to the floor. At the end of the country dance, Daphne smirked at Emma over her shoulder.

Penelope's eyes narrowed before her fingers hit the keys again. Music swelled through the room, soft as water.

"She's playing a waltz." Gretchen grinned behind her plate of biscuits. "Mother will have fits."

Most of the young ladies of their acquaintance wouldn't be allowed to dance the waltz. It was considered risqué, to be held so close in a gentleman's arms. On the other hand, a hostess knew when a small scandal elevated the reputation of her soirees. Lady Cora inclined her head just barely, and couples began to gather.

"I didn't know my mother had it in her," Gretchen said with surprised approval. She closed her eyes briefly. "She's diabolical," she added as a gentleman, obviously prodded by Lady Wyndham, approached Gretchen. He bowed over her hand. "Oh, very well," Gretchen said, dragging him onto the floor. His new shoes slid on the perfectly polished parquet floor and she had to steady him.

"I say, your cousin is enthusiastic." The young gentleman had sidled up so quietly Emma didn't notice him until he was practically pressed to her side. His breath was pickled in brandy and he kept staring at her cleavage through his monocle. "Fancy a dance?"

She gritted her teeth. "No, thank you."

"Come on, what's the harm? Especially when the very proper Lady Wyndham approved it."

The very proper Lady Wyndham was also watching them carefully. She widened her eyes at Emma. Emma pretended not to notice. When her aunt set her glass down, Emma knew she was doomed. She couldn't turn down the dance if her aunt interfered. It would be considered rude. Though, for some reason, her companion's perusal of her décolletage wasn't held to the same standard.

"I . . ."

"I'm afraid Lady Emma promised this dance to me," Cormac cut in smoothly, claiming her hand and twirling her away before the other gentleman had a chance to protest. His palm was warm and gentle on her lower back. She felt the heat of it through his gloves and her thin dress. She had to hold onto his shoulders as the room spun around her. She'd never actually danced the waltz before. What if she trod on his foot?

Wait. It would serve him right.

She really *must* remember that.

"That one was a Keeper," he told her.

"So are you," she felt compelled to point out.

"Yes, but he's drunk and not very good. Your hairpin will keep him befuddled for now."

She nearly froze, but he kept his arms around her, leading her through the dance. She could smell his sandalwood soap. "Why doesn't it work on you?"

"I already know what I know," he said quietly. "Anyway,

they only work on a single Keeper at a time. It would never hide you from an entire unit."

"Then why haven't they come yet?"

His smile was crooked. "Because they've been distracted by a murder and opened gates to the Underworld. But you're being watched, even now. That opera singer's carriage wheel was no accident."

Emma frowned. "What do you mean?"

"She's not known to us. She could be a warlock, or someone you've hired to help you escape."

Emma grew cold, glancing again at the windows. "That's who's been watching me this whole time. The Order."

"Of course. You're wise to stay among other people. But I wouldn't let your guard down just yet." His voice was a whisper tickling her ear. She felt it in her knees. She hadn't noticed but he'd circled them around to the doors that opened into the garden. In the whirl of couples, he tugged her outside into the privacy of the shadowy patio.

"What are you doing?" she asked, instantly defensive. She glanced wildly about for other Keepers, half expecting him to turn her over to men with chains.

Instead, he only closed his hands around her shoulders and dragged her against his chest. His eyes burned with a dark emotion that made her mouth dry and her throat hot. She could only stare at him, eyes wide. "Emma, if only you knew."

She didn't even have a chance to ask him what it was she was supposed to know.

He bent his head and kissed her, his mouth sliding over hers until her lips tingled. He tasted like honey wine and she felt instantly drunk. Her head swam and her breaths were small burning embers in her chest. His hands roamed over her back, fingers gliding up to dig into her hair. When his tongue touched hers, she was sure his hands were the only thing holding her up. There was no thought, no past, no future, just his mouth.

The kiss was wild and desperate and more delicious than a hundred iced tea cakes.

Until he pulled roughly away. His hands were still gentle on the exposed skin of her arms between the top of her glove and her beaded sleeve, but his breath was violent.

"Damnation," he said, his voice dark and agitated. "I can't do this."

And then he was gone, leaping the stone balustrade and stalking across the dark lawns.

Chapter 15

Even without magical powers, mothers were terrifying creatures.

When Cormac stumbled home at four o'clock in the morning, his mother was waiting for him in the upstairs hall. The light of the lamp she held flickered on her face. "Cormac, you've mud in your hair. What on earth have you been doing?" She paused. "Never mind, I don't wish to know, actually."

He blinked at her owlishly. "How did you know I'd be here instead of my apartments?"

She smiled gently. "Talia told me, of course. She seemed to think you might be distressed."

He leaned against the newel at the staircase, suddenly exhausted. He'd done everything he could think of to forget about Emma.

Impossible.

He'd visited White's, his club, and gambled for hours. He'd

seen a country estate, luckily not his own, lost on one bet of cards. And then he'd walked all the way home from Covent Garden, half hoping a thief would be foolish enough to accost him. He could have used a spot of violence. He felt sure his sister Talia, in addition to knowing his whereabouts, also knew just how much of his brain was occupied with forbidden and dangerous thoughts of Emma.

Proving his point, and the general shrewdness of mothers, she smiled again. "There were some lovely girls at the soiree this evening. Before you disappeared."

He tried an air of nonchalance. "Is this one of those speeches about matrimony?"

"You've time enough for that, darling. You're still young yet."

"I'm telling Primrose you said that." Primrose was only a year younger and was feeling the pressure to find herself a husband.

"It's different for girls."

"And I'm telling Colette you said *that*," he teased.

"Emma is a lovely girl," was his mother's reply. She looked at him the same way she'd looked at him when he'd been four years old and had broken his favorite wooden shield.

And he was very much afraid he would end up breaking Emma as well.

He felt the color drain from his face. "What?"

She touched his cheek. "Don't fret."

He wanted to point out that he was a man of nineteen and men didn't fret, but she was right. "Does Father know? Or the Order?"

She pursed her lips. "Of course not. He wasn't there to see you tonight."

He sat on the top stair, leaning his head back wearily. "So it's obvious?"

"Only to me, dear," she assured him. "A mother knows these things."

"Then you also know it's impossible."

"Nothing's impossible when it comes to love."

She was a romantic, and she always had been. "This isn't one of your novels," he said.

She ignored him. "I looked her up in the *Witch's Debrett's*."

He groaned. The regular *Debrett's* was used to record the lineages and titles of the aristocratic families of Britain. It was the bible of matchmaking parents. And parents being parents, there was a secret version entirely dedicated to witching families.

"Her family is very powerful. The Lovegroves have been witches since the time of the Romans. I couldn't find very much recent information, however. Most of it's lost in scandal and rumor."

"You wouldn't, would you?" he said. "No one can remember anything about Emma's mother and she's too mad to tell us anything herself. The only thing anyone can say for certain is that her magic is very powerful and unpredictable. She apparently took out three Keepers, one of them her own father."

"Oh dear."

"Exactly. Which is part of the reason the Order wants Emma brought in." He felt bleak at the thought. A winter wind howled inside his chest. "Father might very well be following that command as we speak."

She set her lamp down. "Your father is currently snoring like one of those beasts at the zoological gardens. He came home an hour ago stinking of port and smoke. I can assure you he was in no condition to be attempting any Keeper duties."

That was something, at least. Some of the tension left him and he found he could unclench his jaw after all. Emma would be free for just a little longer. And that was just a little longer that she might not despise him.

"You've worked so hard to be part of the Order," his mother continued. "I worry you won't work as hard on your own personal happiness."

"Mother, I don't lack for companions." He tried not to blush. What a conversation to be having with his mother.

She waved that aside. "I saw the way you looked at her. And that kind of connection is precious, whatever the complications."

"More precious than my oaths? Than the safety of the witching families of London?"

"Yes."

He blinked at her savage tone. "You can't mean that."

"Let the witches look after themselves every so often. I'm far more concerned with your heart."

He groaned. "Don't be. As you said, I'm young. I've plenty of time."

Her smile was sad. "There's never enough time when it comes to matters of the heart." She ruffled his hair. "Try to get some sleep."

As if he could.

He didn't even bother getting up from his position on the step, only bent one knee and leaned back to get more comfortable.

He shouldn't have kissed Emma. He knew better. He just hadn't been able to stop himself, not when she'd kissed him back just as desperately. He remembered every moment of the time they'd spent together over Christmas, before he'd realized who she was and how little she knew of their world. She was surrounded by witching families and yet neither she nor her cousins knew a thing about it. And try as he might to broach the topic, she never quite understood what he was trying to say.

It hadn't mattered at the time. He'd been happy enough to sit in the garden under a thick sheepskin blanket while she pointed out the stars and the shapes they made. They'd drunk mulled wine and eaten oranges until she tasted of them when he kissed her.

And now everything was different.

Well, not everything.

He still wanted to kiss her.

He pulled an acorn from his pocket. It was painted with a miniscule pattern in white, spelling out Emma's name in a long-forgotten language that looked like nothing so much as bare branches in winter. He stared at it, hating his life, his lack of gifts. Himself.

He had to act now, before it was too late. If he didn't prove himself now, the Order wouldn't listen to him later, when it mattered.

He had duties, responsibilities. He'd taken a blood oath to protect witches from warlocks, and from one another if necessary.

He broke the acorn. The tracking spell activated immediately, linked to the fine powder of crushed horsehair and gargoyle dust he'd left in Emma's hair when he'd kissed her. Like tree roots, it would grow and spread, following her wherever she went.

The moment she left the relative security of her aunt's magic-protected house, as well as the public scrutiny of guests and bystanders, the Order would be able to find her.

She'd been marked.

Chapter 16

Emma and Gretchen descended on the Chadwicks' house after breakfast. Emma practically tripped the poor butler, trying to get the door open faster. "Our cousin's expecting us," she said. She peered up the massive marble staircase. A statue of a nymph stared down at them from the landing. "Penny, hurry up!"

"All right," Penelope grumbled, still pinning up her hair as she came down the stairs. "It's obscenely early."

"It's eight o'clock."

"As I said."

"Be grateful," Gretchen told Penelope. "She was knocking at my door before the maids were even finished lighting the fires."

Penelope shuddered.

"Where's your mother?" Emma asked, ignoring them both. She was already tired of feeling as though a Keeper lurked around every corner.

"She's in her stillroom," Penelope replied, leading them through the dining room so she could snatch a roll from the sideboard. Gretchen took two. They went down a hall decorated with Egyptian-style statues and out into the garden. Aunt Bethany distilled perfumes when she wasn't painting. Today the small shed was permeated with the thick scents of lilies and oranges.

"Girls, you're here early."

"That's what I said," Penelope agreed around a mouthful of bread. She dropped onto a wooden bench. Emma looked around the familiar room. Dried flowers and herbs hung from the ceiling and bottles filled with oils and tinctures lined the wall. Salt was scattered under the single window and the door was crowned with rowan branches.

Suddenly it didn't look like a stillroom for perfumes but a place to store strange ingredients for strange spells.

"You've known all along," Emma said quietly.

Bethany put down the bottle of limewater with a small sigh. "Yes, my darlings. Witchery is in the blood, after all." A badger spun from starlight and shadows emerged from the hem of her gown and snuffled past the cousins and through the partly opened door.

"What the bloody hell is *that*?" Penelope blurted out.

"My familiar," her mother explained calmly. "You'll find your own, soon enough. All witches have one. It's the shape your magic takes to protect you."

"But what does it all mean?" Emma asked. "Cormac was maddeningly cryptic. Even before I made it rain."

"I suppose we should be surprised your ignorance of magic lasted as long as it did," Bethany replied. "You'll see others with the knot now," she added, lifting her own palm. Her knot wasn't as dark as Emma's mother's had been. It was more like faded brown ink. It made Emma think of old pirate maps and cave paintings done in ocher.

"So Godric and I really saw a ghost covered in blood?" Gretchen asked. "Poor Godric, he's going to be right put out."

"Why didn't you ever tell me?" Penelope added.

"You wouldn't have believed me, kitten," she answered. "The spell my sister worked was powerful. Even if you had been inclined to believe me, it would have prevented you. Lord knows, the Order tried again and again. You're lucky the spell did what it did. Every time they tried to question you, you didn't understand what they were saying."

"I don't remember being asked about witchcraft," Gretchen pointed out. "I think we'd recall something like that."

"Not with Theodora's spell. She was always more powerful than the rest of us combined. She not only bound Emma's powers, but she accidentally bound all of you as well. Cora was about ready to deliver the twins but I didn't even know I was pregnant yet. Most people can't work that kind of spell on purpose, never mind as residue."

"Is that what made her mad?" Emma's voice felt scratchy in her throat.

"Yes, I'm afraid so. So she can only have done it to protect you."

Guilt made Emma feel sick to her stomach. First Margaret,

now this. Bethany squeezed her hand. "Your mother loved you. She wouldn't regret the cost, not when the spell worked so well for so long."

Emma regretted it enough for the both of them.

"But why?" she asked.

"I wish I knew."

"How can you *not* know why she bound us and bound herself?"

"Because my memory was altered too. I remember her coming out of the forest with blood on her dress, and the look on her face, and then nothing else. Except the knowledge that whatever I'd seen made me want to grab my happiness with both hands, no matter the consequences. I eloped with your father that very night." She smiled sadly at Penelope. "My mother sent me her mother's jewels. Father was distraught, especially when Theo's name was stricken from the *Witch's Debrett's*. Whatever magic she worked traveled on the power of her name, it must have. Even the Order can't quite remember what she did; they only know they fear her. Our own father wasn't able to recognize her after the spell was cast."

"But *why* would she cast a spell like that?" Emma had come for answers, not more questions. But her aunt didn't reply.

Instead, she stood up slowly, frowning at the rowan branches over the door. They shivered, dropping wrinkled red berries. Her luminescent badger-familiar darted back into the still-room, teeth bared. "Blast," she said sharply. "You're going to have to run."

She took a strip of cloth from her worktable and poured the

contents of the nearest bottle over it. Essence of lime stung the air. As soon as the material soaked up the limewater, mist curled out of it, rolling down the table and across the floor. It lifted like smoke off a bonfire, bringing the chill damp of sea air.

Gretchen clapped her hands over her ears. Bethany spared her a surprised look. "You're a Whisperer," she said.

"A what?"

"Never mind, there's no time. The Feth-Fiada spell might buy a few minutes at most, but it's better done with seawater," she muttered. "The Keepers are relentless." She kicked aside the small, colorful rug under the worktable to reveal a simple trapdoor set into the floorboards. "Go," she whispered to them urgently. "You'll end up in the goblin markets, but it's the best I can do."

The hole in the ground yawned and stank like a black mouth full of rotted teeth. A wooden ladder disappeared into its depths. "If they follow, remember your rhymes." She kissed Penelope's cheek before shoving her under the table. "Now go!"

The sound of footsteps echoed off the flagstone path leading to the stillroom.

Emma knotted her skirts between her knees and lowered herself down the ladder.

"Goblin markets?" Penelope asked above her as her foot touched the first rung. "I sincerely hope that's a metaphor, because it sounds . . . unhygienic."

The darkness below was palpable, as if Emma were climbing down into a pool of ink, or the ocean in the middle of a moonless night. It was cold, until she hit the third step and then a strange warmth snaked through the damp. Emma felt dizzy, and held on tight. Gretchen's boot came around the opening, lowering to the ladder. Her skirts swung like a bell, blocking some of the light. Dirt rained through the floorboards.

A man cursed just outside the stillroom. Penelope tried to climb back up the ladder.

"I'll be fine, they're not here for me," her mother snapped, pushing her back down into the cellar, and slamming the trap-door shut above them. Penelope fell onto Gretchen, and they both fell on Emma.

Emma decided she was getting rather tired of being pushed.

Being landed on wasn't much fun either.

Chapter 17

"Ooof," *Emma wheezed.* "Someone's elbow is taking liberties."

"Sorry, sorry." Gretchen shifted. "But if Penelope's left foot gets any closer to my cleavage we'll have to read the banns."

"Mmmgrllk."

Emma paused, mid-shift. The smell of damp and spices was curiously strong. "Pardon?"

Penelope squirmed and spat out what felt like a wad of lace. "I sincerely hope that was someone's petticoat and not a rat," she groaned, extricating herself from the tangle of flailing limbs. "Ouch, that was my nose!"

"Well, stop fussing about!"

"I have to get back up there! My mother's alone!"

"I don't hear any footsteps," Emma said, frowning up at the ceiling. Or what she assumed was the ceiling. She could have been frowning at the back of Penelope's head for all she knew. "Perhaps they've gone?"

They listened carefully, hearing only their own breaths echoing loudly in the dusty dark. Eventually Emma could make out a woman's voice but it didn't sound like Penelope's mother. Nor did it sound distressed.

"I'll just sneak up and have a look. Where's the ladder?" Penelope wondered, her shoes scraping the beaten earth floor.

Emma squeaked in response. "That was my backside," she added wryly.

Penelope shuffled around. "I can't find the ladder."

"Let me try," Emma said.

"No, you don't understand. I can't find the ladder because there is *no* ladder. There are four walls I can touch without barely a step from the middle of the cellar and nothing overhead."

"That's impossible," Gretchen said.

"There seems to be a lot of that going around," Emma said, waving her hands wildly over her head. No ladder. She waved harder, then jumped up and down as high as she could.

"My eye!"

"My foot!"

But still no ladder.

"Blast," she said. "Now that I could use a hand that glows, it's not glowing." She shook it, like a pocket watch she'd accidentally dropped and was hoping to reset. She swallowed thickly. "And do you know something?" she added in a strangled voice. "I don't think I care for the feeling of being buried alive." Cold sweat pinpricked her arms and the back of her neck. Her breathing felt shallow, rattling in her dry throat. She tried to picture the stars, the forests of Berkshire, the stag in the park . . . anything but the walls closing in on her. "We really need to get out of here."

"Let's make a careful search," Gretchen suggested. "In case there's a tunnel leading outside. Didn't the Catholics build escape routes when Henry the Eighth got all choppy and insane during the Reformation?" Gretchen spent so much time in libraries at balls that she'd developed very diverse reading habits.

Emma could barely remember her own name, never mind historical trivia. She counted her breaths the way she usually counted stars. Five for Cassiopeia, nine for Leo, seven for the Plough.

"Wait!" Penelope said. "Let's link fingers so we always know where each of us is. We can stretch to investigate the walls and the floor."

"It's not like we can get lost in here," Emma said tightly. "There's not enough room. There's not even enough air."

"Are you sure about that?"

She thought of dead girls, witch knots, and turning into a deer. "Good point."

It was slow, tedious work but the feel of cool stone and damp mud under her fingers was calming. The others didn't seem to be as affected as she was. She focused on dragging her nails between the stones to find a hidden latch or lock.

"Got it!" Gretchen called out just as Emma's hair started to fall out of its pin, slippery with sweat. "It feels like a regular doorknob but I don't feel a door."

"Turn it anyway," Emma said.

A door opened to sunlight so bright it blinded them for a long, disorienting moment. Emma took a deep steadying breath, glad for the feel of the breeze on her face, even though it smelled strange, like flowers and sea salt.

They were definitely not in Penelope's mother's stillroom.

They emerged into a narrow alley between two crooked shops that rose over three stories high, blotting out the sunlight. The cobbles under their feet were marked with symbols. Pomegranates were strung like lamps, crisscrossing over the bridge from rooftop to rooftop. They were peeled open in sections, revealing phosphorescent red seeds. Below the red fruit lanterns, the narrow bridge teemed with every creature imaginable, haggling over tables piled with curiosities.

There were bottles filled with graveyard dirt, lengths of cords in every color imaginable, jars filled with feathers, herbs, and iron nails, stones with holes in them strung on pieces of leather, tarot cards, baskets of fruits, and tiny birds in wire cages swinging between the pomegranates. Silver coins crossed palms, mandrake roots were carefully inspected and sorted according to some process Emma didn't recognize. A pack of white dogs with red ears slept in the shade. A little boy darted between passersby, chased by little shadows attached to some invisible creature.

Emma found her voice. "I guess we found the goblin markets."

Between the humans, creatures prowled. A naked woman with a lion's head padded by a man with ram's horns. A little girl with a bloody, gap-toothed grin walked a griffin on a silver chain. Three men circled a pegasus with blue-black wings, inspecting it as if it were a regular horse for purchase at Tatter-sall's. And through the open window of a nearby tavern, goblins in red caps sang about murderers and poets over tankards of black ale.

"Is that the Thames?" Penelope leaned over the side of the railing between two narrow shops tilting toward each other. "I don't live anywhere near the river."

"And I don't remember London Bridge looking quite like this, do you?" Emma shook her head, stunned.

"Not for nearly two hundred years," Gretchen agreed. She pointed to pikes over the main drawbridge gate. Long black hair hung with silver charms caught the light. "They haven't put heads on those pikes since then."

Emma took a step back. "I'm not sure those heads are even human."

"That doesn't make it any less revolting," Penelope said, sounding queasy. She turned back to the bustling market, watching a ghostly lady in a white dress drift by, icicles falling from her bell sleeves and breaking into pieces. The cousins stood and stared at the peculiar business of the bridge for longer than was probably wise.

Definitely longer than was wise.

Bells began to ring softly. Emma didn't notice them at first. They blended into the confusing swirl of colors and textures but now she could see them hanging from wooden signs, attached to posts, on cat collars and dog collars and strung on a necklace of beads wound around the pomegranate lanterns. The sound was gentle at first, like wind chimes on a summer day. The volume built and built, until the sound shivered through the air, turning summer day to autumn storm.

The street emptied.

Winged ladies took flight; hobs scurried up drainpipes to run across the roofs. Shop doors slammed shut and were bolted; hidden cellars opened and were locked just as quickly. A man with a mane of soft blue spikes like a hedgehog vanished entirely. A horse bolted down the way, hooves striking sparks.

"*Now* what?" Emma asked.

"The Order," an old man spat as he shoved past them to the black iron railing. "Hide yourselves!" He pulled a shawl over his head and leaped off the bridge, a long white feather in his hand.

"We could jump too," Penelope suggested, casting another dubious glance at the river. The old man had drifted easily down to a boat and he was now racing from deck to deck toward the shore.

"We'd break our heads on a boat," Gretchen said.

"Or get eaten by a kraken," Emma added.

"How do you know there are krakens in there?"

"How do you know there aren't?"

A man shot past the opening of the alley. Those who hadn't taken cover fled from him, including a beast with three rows of needle-teeth. The cousins crowded back into the alley. Emma peered through a clump of ivy trailing off the tavern sign. The man stopped at a stall across the street and spoke to a woman with long white hair. There was a black stone set into the top of his cane. "He's turning back this way," she warned, flattening herself against the wall. "Since everyone else is avoiding him, we should too. He's got to be a Keeper."

"*By footprint I mark you, by iron I bind you,*" Penelope blurted out.

Emma and Gretchen stared at her. "Come again?"

"I stab you . . . no, that's not right."

"I should hope not."

Penelope squeezed her eyes shut. Emma watched the man slide a coin to the white-haired lady. "*Struck through mud and struck through dirt, if you return, return to hurt.* That's it. One of my mother's rhymes," Penelope explained impatiently. "Now we just need an iron nail."

Gretchen pulled the hair bob Penelope's mother had made them from her hair. "Try this."

She tossed it at Emma, who watched the Keeper across the bridge turn around to face her way. He was momentarily distracted when two other men marched a woman with a bloody witch knot on her hand to a halt in front of him. She snapped something at them, sparks lifting the ends of her hair. The black stone set in the man's cane exploded. He stumbled back, his hat tumbling to the ground and rolling toward Emma. She edged away from it as if it was poisonous.

The witch screamed pitifully when the Keeper, ignoring his hat, slipped a chain around her neck. The pendant was made of iron nails, bent over each other like wheel spokes, all circling another black stone. She cringed when it touched her. The bridge stank of lemons and fennel.

Emma dropped to her knees, where the dirt of the alley

spilled out onto the cobbles. She searched for human footprints among the hooves and claw marks. Finding one, she drove the pin through it with as much force as she could. The iron bit into her fingertips, bruising them. Penelope gave Emma her hairpin as well.

The witch sagged between her captors.

Penelope glanced around desperately before she leaped at an empty ale barrel, scratching furiously at the iron studs until her nails tore. The bands were rusted to the thick wooden slats. "It's no use."

"Give me your brooch!" Gretchen told her. She used the pin to dig a nail out of the soft wood of a window frame, grown gray with the steady drip of rain down the uneven walls. "Got one!"

Emma pierced another shoe print, and assorted marks belonging to boots, birds, cats, and what she swore must have been a badger the size of a pony. A prisoner's cart with iron bars around the sides and across the ceiling rumbled into view. Inside, men and women sat with bound hands. One wore an iron collar attached to the bars. Even the other prisoners leaned away from her.

"This isn't happening," Emma whispered, feeling useless. She didn't notice the clouds gathering, like ripe plums on a branch. Rain pelted the bridge, pinging off rooftops and cobblestones. At the very border of the stones, she saw the unmistakable print of an expensive shoe.

"The rest of the nails are stuck," Gretchen replied, contemplating using her teeth. "Damn." She ducked down. "I think the innkeeper just saw me."

"But I need one more!"

"Use mine," Cormac said from behind Emma's shoulder. He wore breeches and a dark green cutaway coat. His cravat was spotless and the brim of his hat shadowed his face. She felt her cheeks flame just to hear his voice.

"You!" Gretchen hissed through the sudden rain. "What the hell are you doing here?"

Cormac didn't look away from Emma. He offered her the nail the way other men would have offered a posy of rosebuds. "It will help," he said. "But I'm afraid it won't be enough. Folk magic can't fool the Order. Not for long, anyway."

Emma snatched it from him, relief and suspicion drowning any response she could have made. Jagged light speared the sky. The bridge shook under the force of the thunder, chasing down the lightning. She jabbed the nail through the last clear footprint, using her shoe heel to add as much force as she possibly could. Gretchen slipped between her and Cormac, scowling.

The witch was hauled up into the cart, where she sprawled on the floor spitting curses. No one looked their way. "It's holding," Emma murmured.

"But we still don't know how to get home," Penelope said, pushing her thick wet hair off her face. "And I wish you'd stop making it rain."

"I can get you home," Cormac said quietly.

"And why should we believe you?" Gretchen asked. "You've broken our trust before."

"Stay here then, if you prefer." He said it like it made no difference to him either way, as he took a bundle wrapped in black velvet from the leather satchel he wore across his chest like a sword. Under the velvet was a doorknob made of cut glass and painted with a miniature map of London. "Or take this instead. It will take you back to London proper," he said.

"Why are you helping us?" Gretchen asked.

"Does it matter?" Cormac asked in return. His wet hair tumbled over his forehead. His smile was grim and enigmatic.

"You could have taken us in before," Emma said. "Several times in fact. Why didn't you?"

"Because I didn't have to," he said curtly. "But you can stay here, if you'd like. It's your choice, and I won't offer it again."

"Very well," she said reluctantly, raising her voice to be heard over the wind. She wasn't about to let her cousins be snatched away in an iron cart, or worse, just to save her pride.

"Just place the doorknob on any door and it will take you back," Cormac instructed, handing it to Gretchen. She snarled but took it.

"There's a cellar door over here." Penelope motioned them to the back corner of the shop sharing the alley with the tavern.

"Not another cellar," Emma muttered.

Gretchen crouched, gingerly setting the glass handle on the wooden door. Light filled the lines of the map like fire following a trail of lamp oil before it shone through, and stabbed out in all directions. Gretchen pulled and the door unlatched, opening so swiftly it slammed into the ground.

"How do we know he's not sending us off somewhere worse?" Gretchen asked, not moving to climb down into the dark hole. Dust wafted up, disturbed by the rain.

"Because there is no place worse right now," Penelope

squeaked, pointing at the mouth of the alley. Three men wearing badges with the iron wheel of the Order blocked any other hope of escape. "Emma, come on!" she added, trying to reach out, but Gretchen had already pushed her into the opening. Penelope grabbed Gretchen's hand as she fell. They both tumbled out of sight. Emma ran to join them.

Cormac jerked her back like a flyaway kite. He was stronger than she remembered. Of course, last time she'd fallen *into* his arms. He hadn't had to resort to snatching her against her will. She tugged back, trying to break his hold.

"I'm sorry, Emma," he said as the door slammed shut and the painted glass handle cracked in half. The cellar was just a cellar again. "Saving them was the best I could do for you."

Gretchen and Penelope were gone.

And she was stuck here.

With Cormac.

And the Order.

Chapter 18

One-Eyed Joe's tent was at the end of the bridge with one side catering to the regular folk of London wanting to purchase cameos, and the other side serving the goblin markets. Moira honestly wasn't sure which clientele was odder.

The tent was cramped and smelled of apples and smoke and frankincense. There was a table facing each opening displaying a dizzying array of cameos. Ladies sat with unicorns, danced with gentlemen, picked posies and poisons. Birds brought messages, babies rocked in cradles, lovers entwined. There were miniature vignettes, and those who knew how to look, knew that they came true if you had the courage to slip one under your pillow. And the coin to purchase it, of course.

An apothecary cabinet stuffed with shells, onyx, agate, and the other tools of his trade hulked behind One-Eyed Joe's stool. If anyone but he touched it, they came away with burning blisters on their fingers. Moira was no exception, as she'd discovered when she was eleven. She still had a scar under her thumbnail to remind her.

Tarnished silver butter knives and scissors hung on threads, spinning from the ceiling. It was the first magic One-Eyed Joe had taught her to make for herself. It was only good for keeping away the Wee Folk who liked to pilfer shiny objects, but she'd been so proud of it. The real wards were sewn into the inner tent walls, which were made from scraps of Persian rugs and tapestries. The heavy woven material was hung with silver amulets and cameos of griffins with sharp teeth and dragons. There were nearly as many cameos secured to his top hat. No creature, magical or otherwise, crossed One-Eyed Joe's wards easily. The same cameos that brought pretty dreams could bring nightmares. Most people were more keen on risking their limbs than a month's worth of bad dreams.

Most, but not all.

The wind-chime knives spun and spun, threads tangling. The ceramic figurine of a white bird, perched on a branch that served as a tent beam, chirped warningly. The bird over the goblin market entrance was red. It didn't move, staying as still as china figures ought to stay.

Moira turned sharply and caught the collar of a young boy as he dashed past behind her. When she swung him off the ground, he swung back with his fists. She dodged them easily, but her cap tumbled off, releasing her long hair. "Easy," she said sharply. "Before I call the Watch."

He stilled, eyeing her balefully through a mop of dirty hair. "Bless me." He blinked. "Yer a girl!"

"And you're a lousy pickpocket," she returned, shaking a

small cameo of a water nymph from his closed-up fist. "No one steals from One-Eyed Joe."

He gaped at her. "How'd you even know? I'm the fastest from 'ere to St. Giles."

She leaned in close. "You're not faster than me."

He gulped. "Sorry, miss."

When his lower lip trembled, Moira dropped him back to his feet. He ran away as if his backside were on fire. Moira glanced at One-Eyed Joe knowingly. He sat on his stool wearing his usual gray coat and purple cravat. He maintained the buttons were carved from the bones of a basilisk.

The smoke from his pipe drifted in shapes of griffins, pegasi, and very naked mermaids. The bowl looked as if it was stuffed with butterfly wings today. Marmalade prowled inside Moira's chest, hunting instincts awakened by the glitter of the wings and the swirl of magic, but when she leaped out, it was only to curl up at One-Eyed Joe's feet. She'd never forgotten the kitten-dreams he'd sent Moira to comfort her when she was little. Moira had never seen One-Eyed Joe's familiar and still had no idea as to what animal shape it took. Her latest guess was a ferret.

"What did you do this time?" she asked, knowing the boy hadn't gone white as boiled potatoes because of her. She hadn't even begun to threaten him.

"Made your hair turn to snakes," One-Eyed Joe chortled. He dealt in illusions, which was why his tent floated so easily between worlds. London never knew that the old man who sold cameos of roses and the Greek goddesses who were so fashionable, was anything but what he appeared to be. That he smelled like gin and old lettuce stopped them from getting close enough to get too curious. "Thought he was going to wet himself."

She ducked into the tent, feeling comfortable for the first time since her run-in with the gargoyles. She'd slept under the table facing the goblin markets for three years before she took to the roofs. She still slept there occasionally when the winter cold was too bitter to brave.

"There's my best girl." He coughed through the smoke, sounding as if his lungs had grown thorns and were scouring him from the inside out. The silver thread on his eye patch was embroidered in the shape of an eye. "What have you brought me, lovely?"

She handed him a slightly wrinkled lemon. It went straight into the pocket of his greatcoat. He loved lemons the way children loved sweets. She still wasn't sure if he actually ate them. You never could tell with witches. He sniffed. "What else have you been doing? You stink of the dead."

"That's a fine thank-you," she said wryly.

"Out with it, Moira."

She pulled the silk-wrapped eyeball from her waistcoat. She presented it to him with a bow and a flourish best suited to the dandies of the Mad King decades earlier. One-Eyed Joe unwrapped it carefully.

Mrs. Lawton's glass eye stared up at him, covered in the salt grains Moira had rolled it in after the gargoyles left. Salt was the most basic protection magic there was and she'd pickled herself like cured beef. It was still falling out of her pockets and the collar of her coat.

"Ah, lassie." The smoke from One-Eyed Joe's pipe turned into floating eyes, all blinking at her. She poked her finger through one and it fell apart. "You didn't."

"You need it." She shrugged. "Don't pretend you don't. And there's not enough blunt in London to buy it, even on the other side of the bridge."

"Stealing from dead witches is dangerous business."

She grinned. "I was taught by the best."

"Toad-eater." He grinned back, his teeth very white in his dark face. "Are you dealing in flattery now? And what will they call me, lassie? Two-Eyed Joe doesn't quite have the same ring to it."

"You'll still be the dream-bringer, old man."

"Who you calling old?"

She heard the bells as soon as she stepped behind the table and closed the curtain to London behind her. "It's the Order." She frowned at him when he just sat there, rolling the glass eyeball between his scarred fingers. "Aren't you going to hide?"

He just grumbled and refused to move from his stool. Moira reached for the fastenings of the brocade curtain that would close off the stall to the goblin markets. She'd stolen the material for him from the back of a cart with a broken wheel just last year. "Leave it," he barked.

She stared at him. "Are you mad? Do you want them tramping through here like the gits they are?"

"I'm not scared of no Greybeard."

"You taught *me* to be, just like you taught me the rest." She kicked the leg of his chair. "Come on."

"I'm comfortable. Let them come," he snorted. "They're not here for me and they won't risk the nightmares. Not again and not so soon."

"It's bad out there, Joe," Moira argued. "I was in Mayfair and all the gargoyles have fled."

He patted the small gargoyle statue on the table beside him. "Not this one."

"That's because you feed him a lot of milk and whiskey."

"And the fancy can afford to do the same." He shrugged. "What do I care if they're too stupid to do it?"

"No," Moira said quietly. "You don't understand. *All* the gargoyles fled."

"Bad luck."

"Bad luck? That's all you have to say?" Marmalade stretched and then leaped back onto Moira's chest as she flapped her hands in agitation. She could feel the Greybeards out there on the bridge. Doors and shutters were slammed shut. Witches scattered, even the ones with nothing to hide. "I can't stay, Joe. I won't be press-ganged into the Order."

"I bloody well think not," he harrumphed. "As if my girl couldn't outrun a bunch of fat Greybeards."

"So what are you saying?" She rubbed her forehead. When One-Eyed Joe got into one of his moods, it was difficult to keep up. "I should run?"

"Of course you should run, are you bacon-brained all of a sudden?"

If she'd been a cat like Marmalade, she might have hissed.

"Get yourself to the park. I hear the Serpentine is lovely this time of year."

"I've had my fill of the fancy," she muttered. He just scowled at her stubbornly until she sighed. "Why am I off to Hyde Park exactly?"

"You'll know when you get there."

Chapter 19

For some reason, Cormac kept turning her into an idiot.

And at some point, preferably before it killed her, she would have to remember that he was only kind to her for his own secret, and clearly nefarious, purposes. Her only comfort was that Gretchen and Penelope were safely away.

There she went again, trusting in his kindness. The door he was so eager to send them through could have dropped them anywhere. She swallowed, rage and fear making her feel as if she'd eaten lightning.

Keepers blocked the bruise-tinted light at the mouth of the alley. One carried a sword and they all had iron-spoke pendants dangling from their hands. "Is this her?" one of them barked.

Emma took a hasty step backward, then another. Her heart hammered in her chest, echoing in the sky. As they continued to advance, she backed up farther and farther until there was nowhere left to go. She half expected to topple over the side of the bridge. Instead, she collided with Cormac's chest.

Falling into the cold, garbage-choked Thames would have been preferable.

His hands closed around her upper arms before she could dart away, as if he was steadying her. But she knew it was actually to restrain her. He bent his head, his lips brushing her ear. She jerked away, her hands clenching into fists. "Don't fight," he whispered, his breath warm on her neck.

She suppressed a shiver. The snarl was impossible to repress. "Where are my cousins?"

"Safe," he replied softly. "As you will be, if you don't fight."

"That's the worst advice I've ever heard." She stood as stiff as a fireplace poker in his arms, too aware of the strength in him and of the warmth of his body blocking the cold wet wind. She was a thousand times a fool.

"Trust me."

She laughed, although there was nothing humorous about her situation. "I was wrong. *That's* the worst advice I've ever heard."

His fingers tightened. "Then hear this, at the very least, Emma. Don't lie. The Order will know and it will go badly for you."

"Lie about what?" She struggled but he stood firm and unyielding behind her. She twisted, trying to see if she could break his foot or some other more vulnerable portion of his anatomy.

"Don't even try it," he advised quietly.

"I haven't done anything wrong!" she insisted, raising her voice so the others would hear her. "I don't even know what the bloody hell the bloody Order is bloody about!"

"The mouth on her." One of the Keepers blinked. "Are you sure she's a bleedin' lady?"

"Yes," Cormac answered coldly. "And you'll treat her as such."

"Why? Because you're the only one who can insult and manhandle me?" she retorted hotly. "My father's an earl! My mother is granddaughter to a duke!"

"Oh, we know who your mother is, lovey," came the reply. "So don't make us bind you to the wheel."

"What does that even mean?"

"The pendant," Cormac explained dispassionately. She couldn't see his eyes, couldn't tell if he was truly as cold as he sounded. There was nothing cold about the way he kissed. "The wheel with the black stone will bind your powers like the cage, and it's far less comfortable."

"Comfortable" and "cage" weren't words she would have used together in the same sentence.

Her mouth went dry. "You're not putting me in that thing."

"Come on." A Keeper yanked her out of Cormac's arms. She dug in her heels but it made no difference. "We haven't got all day to coddle a murderer."

"Murderer!" she squawked, shoving back at him. "I didn't kill anyone!" But hadn't she told Cormac that Margaret's death was her fault? Wasn't she the one who'd broken her mother's spell bottle? Even unwittingly, had she opened the way for a murder? Did that make her culpable?

The cage loomed, lightning flashing off the hinges. Three shackled witches huddled near the door, hissing at her.

Not culpable enough to let herself be dragged away in chains, she decided.

She looked over her shoulder at Cormac, who stalked behind Emma and the Keeper. The rain fell in shining gray sheets, like windowpanes falling from the sky and shattering on the stones. "Cormac, please."

"Don't make me ask you again." The man gripped the back of her head, fingers knotting in her rain-tangled hair. She cursed and elbowed him in the nose. He let go, howling as his blood dripped onto the ground. She'd never admit she'd hit him accidentally. And when he grabbed for her, she decided that while she didn't have Gretchen's skills with a sword, she might just be a biter. Her teeth scraped deeply enough to draw blood. One of the witches slapped her iron manacle to the bars like iron applause.

Cormac stepped in front of her, knocking the other Keeper aside. "Mind yourself, Orson."

"She broke my ruddy nose! And then she bit me! Bind her!"

"No hope for it now," Cormac told her quietly. He was gentle but unyielding. He might not let her be hurt or insulted.

But he also wouldn't save her.

He forced her up the steps and into the cart, the gate clanging shut. She felt it in her teeth. The rain stopped. "Told you she was making it rain," one of the women muttered.

A man reclined in the back corner as if he was at his club. Water ran off the brim of his beaver hat. "It's useless to fight the Greybeards on the bridge, lass," he said.

Emma shivered, curling into herself. "I thought they were Keepers?"

"Greybeard's a nickname," he explained. "After the gray witch bottles they use to trap us."

Emma swallowed. That didn't sound encouraging. "Where are they taking us?" she asked as the cart rumbled into motion, clattering down the lane. Cormac kept pace on a huge brown horse. Behind them the bridge filled with people again, emerging warily from shops and alleys. Goblins ran behind, tossing rotten fruit at the cart. Sweet moldy pulp burst under the wheels.

"To the ship, where else?" one of the women snapped. She was barefoot and there were little silver bells on a chain around her ankle. They sang out when she moved and when she noticed Emma looking, she snarled. "Mind yourself, morsel."

Emma drew back. She could have sworn she felt lightning crown her head like the antlers of the stag in the park. The cage pressed on her, as if she was wearing manacles and a collar like some of the other prisoners. Faces watched them pass through shop windows. She thought she saw a gargoyle crouched over a gutter move.

When they reached the end of the bridge, the air shimmered. As the horses pulled them between the carved gateposts, Emma felt a strange pressure in her head. Behind her, London Bridge looked the same as it always did, crowded with fine carriages, farmers' carts coming into the city with baskets of early onions, radishes, and strawberries, and boatmen shouting insults at one another on the river below. The smell of strange flowers and fruits and wild creatures became ordinary water, fish, and horse droppings. It was like any other late morning, rain clouds breaking apart and crowds coming together.

Just as Emma was hoping a passerby on the street would come to the aid of people locked in a cage, the Keeper sitting next to the driver draped them in thick gray wool. The last thing she saw was Cormac's dark, inscrutable gaze. He seemed to be trying to tell her something, but she was encased in stuffy shadows before she could figure it out. They rattled back and forth on the hard wooden benches as the horses moved onto rougher roads. She tried to wriggle her hand through the bars to catch the end of the heavy material. She only managed to force two fingers out and they cramped as she contorted them. The edge of the drape fluttered just out of reach.

"It's no use," the man said again, his Scottish brogue thick and unconcerned. "We've been charmed. Even if you managed to uncover us, all they'd see is a cart full of goats."

"Goats?" she echoed. She couldn't help but feel insulted.

"And the road under our wheels is jinxed. Any witch who knows what we are would find himself having all manner of accidents if he tried to reach us. Didn't your mam teach you anything, lass?"

The cart came to a stop, the wheels groaning like old men on a cold winter's night. The witch in the collar began to weep and claw at her throat, wailing. Emma clutched the edge of the bench, anxiety burning in her belly. She could smell dead fish and muck, and from the sheer volume of voices and screeching gulls, she assumed they were at the docks. The stifling curtain fell off the bars and the sunlight pierced between the captives. She felt it.

But she couldn't see it.

The quality of the light changed, making the inside of her eyelids pink as a seashell. No matter how hard she tried, they wouldn't open. The rose-petal darkness was inescapable.

"I can't see," she squeaked. Her lids were sewn shut. She could feel the tiny stitches between her lashes with her fingertips. They didn't hurt but panic shivered through her. Shallow breaths were torn from her like autumn leaves in a storm.

"It's a blinding spell," someone told her, as if she were a child fretting over imaginary monsters under the bed. "It'll fade when they want it to."

She bit down hard on her lower lip when it threatened to wobble. She wouldn't show them an ounce of weakness. They wouldn't feed on her fear and confusion like beasts. She wouldn't be a feast. They'd choke on her first. She'd see to it.

Just as soon as she could actually *see* again.

Lifting her chin and wrapping herself in hundreds of years of aristocratic upbringing, she shuffled forward toward the cart steps. A hand closed around her elbow, guiding her to the ground.

Without warning, the blinding spell fell away.

Sunlight stabbed at her. Emma blinked back tears, waiting for her sight to readjust. The stark whiteness faded until only the edges of the river caught the light and magnified it. The

Thames was sluggish in its banks, pushing listless brown water between fine ships and tiny rowboats. Mud larks gathered on the banks, scavenging for lost shipments, coins, or the teeth of abandoned bodies.

She stood on the edge of a gangplank pressed into service as a bridge to a huge ship waiting in the middle of the river. She didn't need to be told the ship and the gangplank were both spelled, since no one noticed them at all, except for one scrawny dog barking at them from a rowboat. The ship drifted quietly, undisturbed. It was painted dark blue and white, with floral ornamentation wrapped around scowling gargoyles. Knotted ropes of every color dangled from the rails. The sails were stitched and marked with symbols. The mermaid figure-head was carved out of mahogany and painted in painstaking detail.

"Is that a p-prison hulk?" she stammered, her throat seizing. She'd read about them in the newspaper. They were decommissioned ships used as prison facilities for criminals. Murderers. She thought of Margaret again.

"On with ye," Orson barked, nudging her in the small of her back with the tip of a dagger. One of the witches was already crossing to the ship.

Emma stepped carefully, the wooden boards bending under her weight. It wasn't much wider than a bench and felt considerably less sturdy. Far below, the river teemed with activity. She considered jumping into the dirty water and swimming to safety. The moment her foot touched the gangplank, her eyes snapped shut of their own accord.

It was so violent and unexpected, she jerked back and nearly toppled off. Adrenaline raced through her, making her dizzy. The sudden darkness was disorienting and she froze, swearing until she ran out of words. Orson laughed harshly before his dagger poked her again.

"Thought about jumping, didn't you?" He chortled. "Now you'll walk blind."

The walk was longer and more excruciating than she could have imagined. Her steps were tiny, dragging inch by careful inch across the wooden planks. A gull's piercing cry startled her and she slipped. The sound of water lapping at the ship's decorated hull seemed very close. The dog was still barking. She forced herself forward, muscles tensing so hard her legs felt as if they were made of bricks. She could very well imagine the hundred ways she could die horribly by falling off the gangplank.

And the thousands of ways she could die horribly if she made it to the ship.

Ursa Major, the Plough, Orion the Hunter, Hydra. She recited star constellations to herself until her heart didn't feel quite so much like a ripe strawberry about to burst on the vine. She was afraid she'd run out of stars.

Sweat curled her hair by the time she reached the ship and blinked her sight back. The first thing she saw were clear glass wine bottles set close together like fence posts. Each held a floating eyeball that bobbed in seawater, always watching.

Keepers waited on the deck, stern-faced and armed with swords, pistols, and strange silver nets. Green glass balls filled with bits of colored string and herbs hung overhead. The wind snapped the sails like dragons' wings. The other captives were led away into the shadows of the deck.

She never thought she'd miss their company until she was marched down a set of steps into the dark heart of the ship, alone.

Chapter 20

She was taken to a room lit with oil lamps glinting off bottles of
every size and description. Elegant wine bottles, squat jam jars,
and lamp globes hung from hooks, interspersed with hundreds of
clay jugs with long necks and curved handles. They were locked
in birdcages, wooden chests, and baskets, and secured to the
wall in box-like shelves. They were filled with bird bones, hair,
brightly colored threads, rowan berries, silver needles, what
looked like tiny withered hearts, and iron nails. When the lamplight flickered, she could have sworn she saw ghostly faces pressing against the glass from inside the clear bottles. One jar was
packed with teeth, floating in some kind of green liquid. The clay
bottles shook and trembled when she stared at them too hard.

Orson gave the bottles a wide berth as he stepped up to bow
at three men waiting behind a carved mahogany screen. They
were hidden in a shallow alcove and she could only see enough

of them through the openings in the carving to know they were old, with white hair, except for the one in the middle, who didn't have any hair at all. Orson shoved her roughly to the middle of the room. "Kneel in front of the magisters."

"I think not," Emma burst out. Kneeling was the last straw. You could only steep in fear so long before you began to feel numb to it.

He forced her down until her knees hit the witch knot painted in white on the floor. Iron shavings stood in mounds around her, like glittering ant hills. She felt weighed down, with a pressure in her head, the way she did before a particularly vicious storm.

The magisters were stern and silent until Emma couldn't help but shift from one knee to the other. Her hair was damp and stuck to her neck, her walking dress streaked with mud and stained with fruit pulp. She'd never felt less like an earl's daughter.

"Emma Charlotte Day, daughter of Theodora Lovegrove." They used her mother's maiden name and didn't mention her father at all. They also hadn't technically asked her a question so she stayed stubbornly silent. Sometimes fighting petty was better than not fighting at all, whatever Cormac might have to say about it.

The magisters exchanged disapproving glances. The bald one drummed his fingers on the table in front of them behind the screen; another made notes on a sheet of parchment. She heard the scratch of the quill. She knew what they were doing. They wanted to intimidate her into babbling like a child or dissolving into tears. But she'd made her curtsy to the queen in a ballroom full of pompous courtiers. She faced debutantes on a daily basis. She'd even sat through a three-hour supper with her father once. She wouldn't crack so easily.

"You flout our rules. You would be an oathbreaker like your mother?"

"My mother's ill, not an oathbreaker." She frowned. "And what rules?"

Cormac's warnings sounded in her head again. *Don't lie. Don't fight.*

Her own warning battled his: *Don't trust Cormac.*

Someone in the confines of the ship screamed. The bottles shivered at the sound. She cleared her throat so her voice would sound stronger than she felt. "I don't know your rules enough to break them." But she was feeling decidedly in favor of learning them for the express purpose of demolishing them.

Fear, apparently, made her contrary.

"Then know this." The magisters were still lecturing her. She probably ought to pay attention. "Ignorance will not save you from the consequence of the witch bottle if you do not answer truthfully."

It was clearly a threat, even if it didn't make sense to her.

"She doesn't know what that is." Cormac spoke quietly from the shadows. He was leaning in the doorway, looking faintly bored. His white cravat glowed in the half-light. She hadn't even known he was there, watching her being interrogated. If fear made her feel contrary, Cormac was making her feel downright feral. "You'll have to do better if you want to frighten her into obedience."

She turned her back on him on principle, even though her

nape tingled, feeling exposed and vulnerable. Pain flared in her bruised kneecaps. "Why is he here?" she snapped.

"As he was there when the spell was cast and the body found, he stands as your intermediary. He accuses or supports as he sees fit."

She was doomed.

"The Lacrimarium are witches who can bottle familiars. They're named after a type of jar the ancient Romans used to collect the tears of mourners at funerals," Cormac explained to her, avoiding the actual question of whether or not he was going to support or accuse her. As if there was any doubt. "Their victims survive, but without their magic, most go mad."

"It's an unfortunate side effect," a magister agreed.

"An unfortunate side effect," Emma echoed. She thought of Aunt Bethany's magical badger and about her mother, and glanced at the bottles again. The faces were even worse, now that she knew she wasn't imagining them. A person's essence shouldn't be trapped like a mouse in the pantry. She leaned away. The magic in the symbol under her feet slapped at her. Her nose began to bleed.

"Your mother's isn't here," Cormac answered quietly. "She trapped herself so we couldn't do it for her. It's a rare gift. The Lacrimarium are few and their magic hard to navigate."

She wiped her face, blood streaking her sleeve. "Good."

"Did you or did you not break a binding spell, causing irreparable damage?" one of the magisters demanded.

Emma lifted her chin. "I didn't even believe in spells until two nights ago."

"That is not an answer, Lady Emma."

"I don't even know *how* to cast a spell," she insisted. "Never mind *un*cast one."

"You opened gates we haven't mapped yet, random gates that might take weeks, even months to locate. The Greymalkin family walk free in London along with all manner of hungry spirits."

"My mother's perfume bottle broke accidentally. That's *all*."

One of the magisters sucked in a startled breath. "The bottle."

"As I said," Cormac pointed out smoothly.

"She'd have to be enormously powerful to manage that unintentionally," his companion returned doubtfully.

"Think of her mother."

Emma felt the moment they all turned to stare at her again. "Your mother defied the Order," a magister said sharply.

"Did she?" Emma retorted, remembering what her aunt Bethany had said. "How?"

The magisters paused.

"You don't know, do you?" she pressed. "So how dare you call her an oathbreaker?"

"We know when magic has been worked against us, little girl," he said sternly. "And you have no notion of how many witches died to keep the Greymalkin Sisters locked out of London. Even before Margaret York's untimely demise."

"Magisters, I do not believe that Lady Emma had anything to do with her death," Cormac said deftly. "Tobias and I followed the trail of the blood curse and it did not lead us to her." He stepped fully out of the shadows. "But she did see Margaret's familiar in the form of a star-nosed mole. And it turned red, as expected."

"As if the Greymalkin mark wasn't proof enough of murder," a magister muttered.

"Lady Emma's witch knot didn't appear until afterward. And you know she doesn't belong to us until it appears."

"I don't belong to you *now*," Emma said defiantly.

"In fact you do," was the magister's reply. "We claim all those who bear the knot." She opened her mouth to protest but he cut her off. "We will deliberate." They began to talk lowly among themselves.

"What part of 'don't fight' gave you pause?" Cormac asked harshly.

"Does it even matter?" Emma asked, suddenly exhausted. She stood up just because she could. She wove on her feet. "How would I know? None of this should even be real."

"The Order is real," he said. "And the ruling witching Families. And they can have you bound or broken, Emma."

"Perhaps you should have thought of that before you brought me here."

"I gave you as much time as I possibly could. You could have spent the last day and night in the brig, awaiting questioning." She couldn't read his expression; it was both too complicated and guarded. She wished, irrationally, that he wasn't quite so striking. It wasn't just being handsome; anyone could be that. His nose was a tad too long . . . but there was something in him that drew the eye and held it. "I've taken oaths to protect the witching Families and society at large."

"From me?" she asked, spreading her arms mockingly. She knew she looked as bedraggled as she felt. "How brave you are."

"Emma."

Whatever he'd been about to say was lost in the shuffle of movement as the magisters rose from their seats behind the screen. "We have decided." A cold voice filled the crowded space. "We will accept Cormac's testimony." He paused. "For now."

Emma bristled at his tone. Orson paled. She blinked, confused. She was fairly certain she wasn't as scary as all that.

"Mrs. Sparrow," another magister spoke, this time uneasily. A woman had joined them. She looked haughty and calm; tall and thin with black hair. The others watched her as though she were made of spiders and thorns.

She glanced at Emma. "So you're the Lovegrove girl then, are you?"

Emma nodded, mouth dry. Mrs. Sparrow narrowed her eyes, then sighed. "You've scared her half to death," she muttered, before blinking long and slow, like a cat.

Cormac swore under his breath. Everything went gray, like Aunt Bethany calling up the mists again. Emma felt soft as water. The gray brightened unbearably to a searing white, then went black.

Cormac caught her as she crumpled.

Chapter 21

Penelope and Gretchen landed in the Serpentine River.

Penelope's long hair wrapped itself around her throat into a rope that threatened to choke her. Gretchen surfaced next to her, sputtering. She treaded water, scowling at Penelope. "I *really* don't like him."

Penelope was too tired to reply. She swam until she could feel the bottom of the pond under her toes. Magical travel left one feeling disoriented and drained, with all the vigor of a wet washcloth. She coughed to clear her lungs of water as she waited for Emma to land, shouting her usual creative curses.

"Gretchen," she finally said, slowly, warily, when nothing happened. "Where's Emma?"

Gretchen's eyes widened and she spun in a circle, treading frantically. "Did she land before us?"

"I was the first one through," Penelope said. "Wasn't I?"

Gretchen took a breath and dove deep down beneath the surface. The water churned under the force of her kicking. Ducks scattered indignantly. Penelope realized she had no idea how deep the pond was. Gretchen popped back up, took a deeper breath and disappeared again. Penelope lowered herself under the water and opened her eyes. Everything was murky and faintly green. She went as deep as she could, trying to see Emma's red-brown hair, or the sway of her gown.

Nothing.

After several burning breaths, Gretchen swam closer, shaking her head. They both kicked up to the surface. "I can't see her," Gretchen said, gasping. "I don't think she's down there."

"That's good, isn't it?" Penelope asked, eyes red. "It means she hasn't drowned."

They dragged their weary bodies back to the bank. "But it also means she never made it through the doorway." She snarled. "Now I *really* hate Cormac."

Penelope hauled herself out of the cool water, shivering. Her dress weighed more than she did, dragging her down. Her muscles ached and worry gnawed at her with dull, rusty teeth.

"We have to find her."

Gretchen was already on the grass, reaching down to help her up. "Just as soon as we figure out how to find those bloody goblin markets again."

"We'll just have to go back to my mother's stillroom," Penelope said, twisting water out of her hem. "And go through the cellar door again."

"You might want to get away from there," a girl interrupted.

"You're starting to draw attention." She wore patched breeches and a striped waistcoat. She wasn't wrong. People riding by were pausing to watch, a few even pointing. Hyde Park was accustomed to horses and rowboats, not swimmers.

"Want the Order to find you?" the girl asked acidly. "Your choice. But I'm not hanging around waiting for that lot." She darted into a copse of trees.

Gretchen and Penelope exchanged a startled glance before Gretchen shrugged and took Penelope's hand, yanking her after the girl. They found her sitting on a low branch, swinging her feet carelessly. She grinned. "Good choice."

"Who are you?" Gretchen demanded.

"Moira's the name," she answered, hopping down to the ground.

"Gretchen Thorn," Penelope introduced them. "And I'm Penelope Chadwick."

Moira tilted her head. "Penelope, you say?"

"Do I know you?" she asked quizzically. She felt certain she'd remember meeting a girl who went about dressed like a boy. Even Gretchen hid her identity when she followed Godric about, wearing his borrowed breeches.

She raised her eyebrows. "I doubt that, don't you? I'm not exactly a debutante." She smirked.

"How do you know about the Order?" Gretchen asked.

"I know things about the Order that would make your hair curl," Moira added darkly. "Bound my brother to the wheel, didn't they? Before they bottled him and made him mad."

Gretchen blinked at Penelope. "Was that even English?"

Penelope shook her head. "I can decipher Shakespeare in my sleep, but I have no idea what she just said."

Moira rolled her eyes. "Why would One-Eyed Joe send me to help you two?" she muttered. "After I gave him presents and everything." She pushed her long, unbound hair off her face. "The Order traps the familiars of witches they don't like or binds their powers when they've been troublesome. Unfortunately, the prats think everyone who doesn't do exactly as they say is troublesome."

"They were on the bridge," Penelope said. "With a cart."

Moira sucked in a breath. "Brought the iron cart, did they? Bloody bad luck."

"Our cousin was left behind," Gretchen added. "We need to get back there to find her."

"It's too late for her." Moira shrugged. "When the Order takes the bridge, there's no one safe. They'll have her already."

Penelope felt herself blanching. "Where would they take her?"

"To the ship."

"Then let's go," Gretchen said. She paused at the edge of the trees when Moira didn't move. "What?"

"You'll never find it. It's cloaked with invisibility spells."

"I thought you said you were sent to help us?" she retorted. "Not that we even know you to trust you."

Moira lifted one shoulder and let it fall. "One-Eyed Joe knows things, he does. He wanted me here and that's good enough for me."

"So help us find the ship!"

"They won't keep her there long," she said. "If they plan to keep her, they'll send her to Rowanstone."

"Is that . . ." Penelope paused. "A prison?"

"May as well be," Moira snorted. "But no, not exactly. I can tell you how to get there but I'm not going near the place myself. Too many bloody fancy folk about."

"Thank you," Penelope said.

"Always ready to cause the Keepers some trouble. Now, keep up." She tossed them an unrepentant grin over her shoulder. "Because if the Order tracks you, you're on your own."

Chapter 22

Emma woke up confused and disoriented. She couldn't figure out where she was, beyond a comfortable feather mattress in a warm room that smelled of fennel and beeswax. Her mouth tasted like fennel as well. It made her tongue itch. She sat up slowly, pushing her hair off her face. The light outside the window was golden and crossed with long shadows.

She swung her feet over the edge of the bed to survey the rest of the room. She could have been in any fine house in London. There was a wide mahogany bed with brocade curtains, two stuffed chairs by the fireplace, a desk with a plain writing table, and an armoire for clothing.

It was only when she stood up for a closer look that the chamber showed its strange underbelly. A small red bundle hung from a ribbon on one of the clothes-pegs. A large blue bead in the shape of an eye was fixed to the wall above the door, and the door itself was painted with gilt knot work so complicated it hurt her head to follow its pattern.

It all came crashing back.

Witchery.

The Order of the Iron Nail.

Cormac.

She indulged in a most therapeutic and ill-mannered tirade of curses, in several languages. Her Latin was better than her French, but she fancied anyone listening would understand her meaning well enough.

Trouble was, Emma had no idea if anyone *was* listening.

A quick peek under the bed and in the empty armoire proved she was alone. She tried the door, without much hope that it was unlocked. When it swung open easily she jumped back warily. Relief and suspicion warred within her. She eased carefully out of the room, but only after she'd grabbed the nearest candle-stick as a weapon. Holding it up threateningly, she stepped farther out in the hall. The walls were papered in burgundy paisley and they stretched on and on in both directions. There were no other doors.

Frowning, she quickened her pace. The hallway didn't change. Even when she broke into a run there was only the silk paisley paper and the occasional sconce and decorative ceiling molding. There wasn't even a staircase or a front door to hint at where she might be. And since she'd fallen unconscious on a ship, she might not even still be in London. How would Gretchen and Penelope find her? And how would she find them if they were in trouble?

She was well and truly a prisoner of madmen.

She ran back to the bedroom because it was the only other place available to her and the unending hallway was proving surprisingly unnerving. She recalled the feel of the earth pressing down on her in the cellar and choked. She wouldn't panic. She was a witch, wasn't she? She had options she'd never dreamed of.

And a window.

Never mind witchery—this was far more practical.

There was a bowl of salt and rowan berries on the sill which she flung aside impatiently. The window opened, letting in a rush of cool air that cleared the strange taste out of her mouth. She was three stories up, overlooking a pretty London garden and carriage lane. The lane was bordered with a high wooden fence and flowering lilac. She released a breath she hadn't realized she was holding. Everything outside her window looked perfectly ordinary not only to London, but also to the neighborhoods she was familiar with. She might even be able to walk home.

The sky was darkening quickly, revealing the first star of the evening. The smog was too thick to see Sirius, but Venus twinkled through the haze. The trees shook their branches at her, but they were too far away to touch. She'd never be able to swing onto one without breaking her neck. She may as well have tried to reach for Venus herself.

She heard a whisper and leaned as far out of the window as she dared. Surely if she yelled for help someone would hear her and call the constables, at the very least. "Hello down there!"

There was another muffled voice and a cry of "Bollocks!"

Emma blinked. "Gretchen?" She could scarcely believe it when both her cousins emerged from the lilac bushes. "Thank God."

"Never mind God," Gretchen muttered. "I'm the one with leaves up her nose."

"How did you even find me?"

"Long story," Penelope called up in a loud whisper. "Are you hurt?"

"Not a bit. You?"

"I'll be better when I've planted my boot up Cormac's backside," Gretchen grumbled.

"Never mind that now." Penelope nudged her. "Get Emma down from there."

Gretchen surveyed the side of the house carefully. She finally chose a trellis on the left and scampered up, a length of rope coiled around her shoulder like a sleeping snake. When she reached the top of the trellis she was still only at the second story and too far from Emma's window. She shifted, securing one arm through the grid of the iron trellis. "Ready?"

Emma hooked her own foot around the leg of the desk and leaned out another few precious inches. "Ready."

Gretchen threw the end of the rope as hard as she could. It missed by several feet and nearly toppled her off her perch when it whipped past her. Penelope tossed it back up and Gretchen tried again. It came closer, but still not quite close enough.

"Third time's the charm," she huffed with grim determination. Her forehead was shiny with perspiration.

The rope flew up and Emma caught it. Gretchen's laugh was infectious. Emma was grinning in response as she darted back into the bedroom and tied the rope tightly around one of the bedposts. She tested with a few hard tugs to satisfy herself that it would hold her weight.

Climbing down a rope seemed simple enough in theory but it was a rather awkward affair in practice. Her long skirts got in the way, tangling and catching the sill as she swung one leg over. It took a surprising amount of courage to leave her perch, one leg dangling precipitously over the edge. Her hands were damp with nerves. The ground was a very long way down. Surely the house was taller than a regular house.

And it was probably packed with witches, magic, and kidnappers. A broken leg seemed a small enough price to pay for her freedom.

She closed her eyes and dropped over the edge, sliding down the rope. She hung there for a moment, the bricks cool on her hot cheek, while Penelope gasped and shouted poetical rhymes at her. She rhymed when she was nervous. Emma's arms screamed with the effort of supporting her entire weight as she inched down slowly, carefully, painfully.

She stretched out a leg, trying to reach the top of the trellis with her toe. Her leg cramped and her knee throbbed and she stretched and stretched and still could not reach it. "Bloody hell," she gasped. "It's too far."

"Nearly there!" Gretchen said encouragingly. "Try again."

"But don't look down," Penelope said, less encouragingly. "You might fall off and break your head open."

"Yes, let's avoid that, shall we?" Mrs. Sparrow said calmly from an open window next to Emma. She was close enough that Emma could see the moonstones on her necklace. "It sounds rather messy."

"Run!" Emma shouted down to her cousins.

Unfortunately, Gretchen and Penelope didn't have time to even turn around, let alone run. Footmen emerged from the stables at the end of the lane and more blocked the way out to the road. Mrs. Sparrow clucked her tongue. "My dears, there's no need for dramatics."

A fatalistic sort of calm had come over Emma as she dangled uselessly on her rope.

"Show the ladies into the drawing room, if you please," Mrs. Sparrow continued, as if it was all very normal. "And have someone fetch a ladder for Lady Emma. She doesn't look at all comfortable."

Emma considered screaming for help but Gretchen and Penelope were already being marched inside the magic house. The footman who brought the ladder was so young he still had spots. He didn't say a word to her, not even when he reached out to steady her by touching her hip. He flushed bright red. Emma was quite beyond embarrassment.

She was shown back into the house, which now appeared to have a normal number of doors and stairs. There were portraits of formidable-looking women on the walls and the sound of girls chattering came from the closed ballroom. Mrs. Sparrow, Gretchen, and Penelope waited in a spacious drawing room with enough chairs to seat dozens of guests. Emma sat between her cousins on a settee meant for two. They clung to one another, perfectly willing to be squashed uncomfortably. Mrs. Sparrow poured tea from a silver pot next to a plate piled with biscuits and cakes. "I expect you're wondering where you are," she said.

"And why I was abducted," Emma returned with remarkable calm, all things considered.

"Abducted?" Mrs. Sparrow raised an eyebrow. "Don't be silly. You were brought here for your own good."

"Against my will."

"Sounds like abduction to me," Gretchen added.

"I could have left you to the Order," Mrs. Sparrow said sharply. "Especially after what happened to poor Mr. Cohen."

Penelope looked startled. "Mr. Cohen? What happened to him?"

"He was taken ill. His head swelled up," Mrs. Sparrow elaborated, watching them carefully. "Luckily their family doctor also happens to be a witch or the poor fellow might have died."

"Is he all right?" Penelope asked.

"He'll recover. He and his family were told it was an exotic sickness that traveled here on one of the ships."

Gretchen frowned. "I hardly see how that's our fault."

But Emma did see. All too clearly. "I said he had a fat head," she said slowly, trying to recall the exact details. "We were angry because he was unkind to Penny. Gretchen, you said something too but I don't recall what it was."

"I said I hoped he swelled up like a balloon." She blinked. "Blast."

Penelope frowned. "How were they to know?" she demanded. "You can't very well blame them for speaking out loud."

"I do not," Mrs. Sparrow replied. "Others would. Especially given your family connections. These things happen rather frequently, only most witches come into their powers much younger and the damage is less severe. They have had some training and knowledge, at least enough not to set this sort of thing in motion." She shook her head. "Nothing for it now, I'm afraid. Have one of the strawberry tarts. They are divine."

They accepted tea and tarts because they didn't know what else to do. Etiquette didn't cover taking tea with witches and kidnappers.

"What is this place?" Emma asked finally. "And why didn't it have any doors earlier?"

"It was spelled," Mrs. Sparrow replied. "You could do yourself harm wandering aimlessly in these corridors." She smiled. "I'm the headmistress here. Welcome to the Rowanstone Academy for Young Ladies."

Emma set her teacup down with a jostle. Tea sloshed over the rim. "I was kidnapped by a *finishing* school?"

Gretchen scowled. "Did my mother put you up to this?"

"This is hardly a regular school. We don't teach mathematics or languages and we only take in the daughters of certain families."

Emma's mouth went dry. "Witching families."

"Exactly. Witches ought to be well versed and well trained in all the magical arts."

"What if we don't want to join witching society?" Gretchen asked. "I don't like the rules I've already got, thanks very much. I'm not keen on learning new ones."

"We definitely don't want to join them," Emma confirmed. "I've met their magisters. And I didn't care for them."

"I'm afraid they will insist," Mrs. Sparrow said. "In any case, it is not a suggestion. Especially for you, Lady Emma."

"Why me?"

"Because of your mother, of course."

Penelope linked her arm through Emma's. "What about her mother, exactly?"

"That is a rather long tale," Mrs. Sparrow replied smoothly. "One that is shrouded in mystery, even to me. Regardless, there are things you must learn."

"Here."

"Here. Lady Gretchen and Lady Penelope, you may attend day classes, but it would be best if Lady Emma boarded with us for a while."

Gretchen crossed her arms. "If Emma stays, we stay."

Mrs. Sparrow inclined her head. "If your parents agree, you may of course board here."

Emma shook her head. "I'm certain my father didn't give his permission," she said. She couldn't have imagined his reaction to a request that his only daughter live in a boarding school run by witches.

"Actually, we sent for your belongings while you slept. He was most obliging."

Her jaw dropped. "My father knows about witchery?"

"Certainly not," Mrs. Sparrow replied. "But he was told by my very great friend the Duchess of Whitefield that a spot had been offered to his daughter at the best finishing school in Britain."

"But why isn't he here then? Why wouldn't he at least say good-bye?" Penelope squeezed her hand. Emma squeezed back but lifted her chin and refused to betray any other reaction.

"That cold fish," Gretchen muttered.

"I couldn't say," Mrs. Sparrow replied.

"And hang on a minute!" Gretchen blurted out. "What about my brother then?"

"He will be attending the Ironstone Academy for Young Men next door. It is more secretive than our school, of course, as it doesn't have the option of passing as an exclusive finishing school. Pity. They could use some manners." She shook her head. "He will retain his current lodgings as they are only rented out to witching families in any case. Your mother knows that." She refilled their forgotten cups. "I know you must have a lot of questions. You'll be given a guidebook and a history primer and I daresay after a good night's rest, everything will look better."

"We can't just leave Emma here alone," Penelope protested.

"I'm afraid you must." Mrs. Sparrow rang a silver bell. "The carriage will take you home now."

Gretchen shot to her feet. "I don't think so. Who are you exactly? And why should the Order get to decide our fates? And why are you picking on Emma?" She paused to yawn, despite her agitation. "Why am I so sleepy all of a sudden?"

"Don't look at her!" Emma tugged Gretchen's arm. "She can bewitch you to sleep."

Mrs. Sparrow just smiled. "I don't need eye contact for that, dear."

Penelope's eyes were already half-closed. Emma pinched her and turned to glare at the headmistress. "Stop it! Please, I'll stay here if you stop."

"A little rest wouldn't do them any harm."

"But it's unnerving." She understood now why the men on the ship had been afraid of her and wouldn't meet her gaze. "Please leave them be."

"If they go quietly," she allowed. "And do as they're told."

"Don't fight her," Emma pleaded with her cousins, annoyed to be echoing Cormac's bad advice. "Yet," she added in a whisper.

Gretchen scowled. "I don't like it."

"I know." Emma tried to smile. "But if you both go then I'll know at least someone out there knows where I am."

"Your father knows."

"Someone who cares, then," she amended. "And I'll know where you are too. Or should be," she added warily. "How do we know you'll take them back and not to the ship or some other horrid place?" They clasped hands tightly.

"This school isn't a punishment," Mrs. Sparrow assured them. "It's an honor and a privilege. You ought to consider yourselves very lucky indeed."

"Lucky?" Emma echoed. "I've been chased through goblin markets, caged, forced to walk a gangplank blind, and threatened at every turn. You'll forgive me if 'lucky' isn't quite the word I'd choose."

Mrs. Sparrow clucked her tongue. "That's quite enough of that." She gave them each a silver ring set with a miniature painting of a blue eye surrounded with pearls. "To avert the evil eye," she explained. "We find they go a long way in preventing accidents. You are required to wear them while at school."

"I've seen these before," Penelope said.

"They were a fashion in polite society several years ago. They serve the same purpose as the more traditional beads from Greece, but we find them less conspicuous."

The doors to the drawing room were opened by a footman. "The carriage is ready, ma'am," he announced, bowing.

Behind him the hall filled with girls streaming out of the ballroom and up the stairs out into the courtyard. They seemed perfectly healthy and happy. One girl had smoke rising from her hair, but she didn't seem too upset about it.

"You see?" Mrs. Sparrow said gently. "There's nothing to fear." She waved her hand at the footman. "Show her in." To the cousins she added, "You even know some of our students."

Lady Daphne Kent entered the room, her white dress spotless and her blue ribbons perfectly in place. "You asked to see me, headmistress?"

"I did, yes. You know these young ladies, do you not?"

Daphne looked at the cousins. Something flickered in her face. "I do."

"Excellent," Mrs. Sparrow said briskly. "Doesn't that put your mind at ease? I'll leave you to reacquaint yourselves while

I give Thomas the carriage directions." She left to talk to the footman.

"You're a witch?" Penelope blurted out. "Is *everyone* a witch now?"

"Don't be absurd," she said dismissively. "Our families know each other because of our shared magical blood. It's why we all grew up together. And also because your families needed to be watched, for all our sakes." She sniffed. "You look dreadful, by the way. Did you fall in the Thames?"

"Hello to you too," Penelope muttered.

"What's your familiar then?"

"I don't know," Penelope replied. "Perhaps I don't have one."

"All witches have one," Daphne said impatiently. "And some are more acceptable than others."

Emma thought back to the afternoon in Hyde Park. "Deer," she declared with a great deal of certainty.

"Passable," Daphne said, with obvious reluctance. She turned to Gretchen.

Gretchen shrugged. "Don't know. Maybe Penelope's right."

"It would be an animal you see in spirit-form or as a real creature who is drawn to you and has been since you were little."

"Dog." Gretchen smiled slowly, winking at her cousins. "The pink kind."

"Dog. Common," she declared. "As expected."

Gretchen's smile died. "Is that so? And what's your familiar then? A shrew?" She was tired, frustrated, and nettled beyond good sense. "And your talent? Ringlets so tight they stunt your brain?" She didn't admit that her own talent amounted to honeybees buzzing in her brain.

Daphne's eyes narrowed. "You would benefit from a proper finishing school, Gretchen Thorn."

Penelope held Gretchen back as she tended to answer remarks with her fists if she wasn't stopped. Emma just rubbed her face wearily. Mrs. Sparrow approached them with a pointed smile. "There now. I'm sure you'll all get along splendidly, won't you?"

They looked at one another with resigned distaste, evil-eye rings glinting in the light.

"Yes, Mrs. Sparrow."

Chapter 23

When Emma was shown back to her rooms, there were three new trunks stacked by the door as promised. She was so exhausted she felt as though she were floating inside her own head. She wanted nothing more than to sleep, but she knew if she lay down her mind would only continue to race in circles. She went to the window and stared up at the sky to count the stars and had to crane her neck at an awkward angle to see anything at all. She felt bruised all over; one more ache hardly signified.

Cassiopeia, Libra, Orion.

With every constellation and every star, her chest felt less compressed, her mind less like a thread pulled too tight and about to snap. She rifled through her trunks until she found a nightgown and then contorted herself like the acrobats who balanced on horseback at Astley's Amphitheater in order to undo her corset by herself. She found her mother's box packed with her books, jewelry, and a miniature of her, Gretchen, and Penelope that Aunt Bethany painted last summer.

Her life suddenly resembled one of those swoony gothic novels Penelope loved so much. Which was all very well and good in literature but rather a different matter in real life.

For one thing, in a novel surely Cormac would have rescued her instead of handing her over to his unpleasant brethren.

And yet, he had seemed to genuinely want to help her when he'd forced her to hide at the ball and again with the iron nail in the goblin markets. Popular opinion claimed women were mercurial and difficult to understand. Clearly, they had never met Cormac.

She was sure it said nothing particularly complimentary about her character that she found herself thinking about him at all. And to think, he'd been a witch all this time. And Daphne! She couldn't imagine anyone less likely to be involved in witchery. Daphne acted as though she didn't have a thought in her silly little head beyond the next soiree and the state of her silk slippers. And here she was carrying an immense secret her entire life.

Emma fiddled with her mother's patch box. She'd tried hairpins, brooch pins, and the tip of a sharp knife, but the last compartment simply would not yield. She was determined to try again and decided on the letter opener from the writing desk. She tried delicate maneuvers, finally giving up and jamming the tip in and wrenching it back and forth. Her finger slipped and slid along the edge of the blade. The force of her grip sliced her skin open, blood welling to the surface.

She sucked at the cut instinctively, glaring at the box, then her small wound. It wasn't deep, merely insult added to injury. The copper taste of blood on her tongue made her think of Aunt Bethany explaining that witchery was in the blood. Feeling foolish but with her heart thundering in her ears, Emma squeezed the cut until a drop of blood fell onto the lock.

When she tried lifting the lid this time, it opened easily.

Inside was a small piece of antler lying on a bed of salt and rowan berries. She lifted it gently, the antler soft as velvet. It was wrapped in black thread and struck through with an iron nail. The tip of the nail was bent double around a strip of leather on which were knotted two rings, one silver, one gold. The antler was small and light and didn't seem to particularly warrant as much fuss as the locked box suggested.

Until her blood smeared against it.

Warmth tingled through her, starting at her heels and traveling up her legs, spreading through her stomach and chest and up her arms, gathering at the crown of her head. It felt as though her head had suddenly caught fire.

She felt her eyes roll back as the darkness claimed her.

Chapter 24

1796

Theodora wore her red cloak because her father hated it so much.

She paused for effect in the doorway to the breakfast room.

"Theodora Ophelia."

She doubled back and poked her head into the room to flash a grin at her father's disapproving face. "Yes, Papa?"

Her sister Bethany smiled into the jam pot. Her other sister Cora just sighed.

"You know I don't like you wearing that cloak," her father said.

Theodora fluttered her eyelashes innocently. "You don't?"

"It's common," Cora sniffed.

She rolled her eyes. "You're just pouting because whenever you try to wear this color it makes you look like a boiled potato."

"Theo, it's not safe to draw attention," her father insisted.

She leaned against the doorjamb impatiently. "It's just a cloak. And I'm only going to the woods," Theodora huffed. "Honestly, why must you be so dramatic?"

"The Greymalkin are out there still. Do you want them to find you?"

Superstition held that the Greymalkin were drawn to bright color and bold people. Theodora couldn't figure out why they'd care if her clothes were drab or if she dressed like a peacock—so long as her magic was strong enough to feed them. But she knew better than to ask her father. He still woke screaming, remembering the deaths he'd seen at their hands when he was a boy. She'd only meant to tease him with the cloak, to prove she was too old to be told what to wear.

"Oh, Papa," she said. "The Greymalkin haven't been seen for years. They were banished by the Order. And anyway, everyone wears bright colors now. You've seen Lord Babbington's frock coat. I defy you to find a brighter rainbow."

"It's hideous," Cora agreed.

"Lord Babbington isn't a Lovegrove. None of them are. And anyway, he's proving to the Families that he's not afraid."

"Well, I'm not afraid either."

"But we're an ancient family, Theo. Far older than the Babbingtons. That requires certain sacrifices and precautions. You know this." He pushed his half-eaten breakfast plate away. Her mother passed him a cup of fresh tea. "The Sisters killed seven people that one night alone."

"In Windsor Forest?" she asked gently.

"Well, no."

"There, you see? And everyone knows Greymalkins prefer town to nature. There's nothing to worry about." She pressed a loud kiss on the top of his head. "I'm only going for a little while. It's been raining for days and days and I can't bear to be cooped up a minute longer."

She bolted from the house before he could order her to change or stay behind altogether. She wouldn't obey, of course. She couldn't set that kind of precedence, not now that there were murmurs of a marriage contract being brokered for her with either the boy next door, Alphonse Day, or one of the sons of the Order. The son of Lord Babbington, to be exact. He wanted the prestige and power of the Lovegrove witches and the Hightowers, knowing nothing about witchery, wanted the Lovegrove country estate.

She had absolutely no intention of being known as Lady Babbington for the rest of her life. Alphonse wasn't much better though. He had the advantage of not being a witch and so hadn't been raised on a steady diet of fear and secrecy like the Keepers' children. But he had all the warmth of a Greek marble statue.

Besides, she was nearly seventeen years old—she fully intended to have a proper coming-out ball and her own Season in London to dance and flirt before she was sold off. Cora was visiting, having just returned from her honeymoon and she was only eighteen; but she'd at least had half a Season. And she seemed happy enough, blushing and asking Bethany to paint a miniature of her husband.

Theodora couldn't imagine ever asking anyone to paint a portrait of Alphonse Hightower. Or anyone by the name of Babbington.

And just as if he'd read her thoughts and wanted to curtail her fun already, there he was. Alphonse rode a beautiful horse and sat with the proper, rigid posture usually reserved for soldiers and spinsters.

"Blast," she muttered, diving behind one of the two giant gargoyles flanking the front door. She waited until he was occupied with swinging out of the saddle, the stableboy holding the reins and blocking

his view somewhat. She darted to the yew hedge, which was accented with trees trimmed into pyramids and perfect circles. She hopped from tree to tree, tucking her bright red cloak close to her body. Her magic worked best when it had a focus. It was especially good at augmenting spells. It was absolutely no use at all in hiding from unwanted suitors.

She ran full tilt across the lawns and through the fields to the forest. Birds squawked, erupting out of the long grass. Her familiar fluttered in her chest, before winging free to follow. She ran until her lungs burned and she was laughing for no reason at all. It felt glorious to be in the cool shadows of the forest, without any expectations made of her either as a girl or a witch.

She walked for a long time in the dappled light, under oaks and pines and ash trees with lightning scars. The spring rains had given way to more flowers than there were stars in the sky. She walked for a long time, twilight-colored blossoms pressing against her ankles. They caught on her cloak and the hem of her dress. She lay down in the bluebells for a rest, pretending she was floating in a pond.

By the time she was ready to return home, she was utterly lost.

She usually rode her horse through the woods, sticking to the well-worn path. She'd never realized how easy it was to get turned around inside the forest where all the trees looked the same. The bluebells mocked her, covering her footprints and confounding her further. She stumbled between the trees, tying knots in the soft green branches to mark her way. It took her another quarter of an hour to stop walking in circles.

Finally she saw a narrow trail, barely used, and seriously considered kissing it. It wasn't the Great Walk or even the path she was *used to, but surely it would lead her to one of them. The sun slanted lower through the trees. At least Alphonse would be long gone.*

She followed the trail as it curved to accommodate a meandering river. She stopped to have a drink and it tasted like the wild mint growing on the banks. She was feeling cheerful again when a man dropped out of a tree right in front of her.

Before she could even react she was flat on her back with a hand clamped hard over her mouth. He was only a few years older than she was but he was wind-worn. His eyes burned green as sunlight through the leaves. His brown hair was long enough to fall past his collar and was caught back with a strip of leather away from his temples to keep it out of his face. His body touched hers from throat to toes.

Her father was right. She was going to come to a bad end because she'd defied him and worn a red cloak.

She pushed as much magic as she could, until she felt hollow. Her captor's magic pushed back and where they collided, there was a spark of pale blue fireworks between them. Her familiar possessed the nearest crow and dove down at his head, cawing and pecking ferociously.

He jerked back just enough for her to bring her knee up viciously. She missed her target but at least jabbed him in the stomach, knocking the air out of him.

"You're a witch!" they accused each other at the same time.

He crouched warily, only rising when she scrambled to her feet. He was handsome in a way that none of the boys she knew would ever be. He was rugged from living outdoors, while they were soft and pampered. His hair was unpowdered and had obviously never been shorn to accommodate a wig. He wore a brown leather coat over a linen shirt with no cravat, embroidery, or ornamentation of any kind. She couldn't help but think of Lord Babbington's multicolored coat. There was a quiver of arrows strapped to his back and at least a dozen knives scattered over his person. She looked for his witch knot but he wore leather archers' bracers and the left one covered his palm.

Energy thrummed through her, making her pulse race and her fingertips tingle. It wasn't fear, exactly.

"That's no way to treat a lady," she said frostily, to hide the fact that she was still gasping nervously.

"Ladies don't walk here alone," he pointed out. She noticed one of his daggers was actually a piece of sharpened deer antler, the blunt end wrapped in leather. "Don't you know what happens to girls in red cloaks who get lost in the woods?" He moved as if hunting her. He was quiet and predatory, sure of his every movement.

She stumbled back and hit a willow. She froze. "I'm not lost."

He didn't smile, just kept crowding her against the tree. The long, feathery leaves shivered in the wind. The familiar-possessed crow landed on a branch, watching them with a suspicious yellow eye.

"And you're not the wolf," she added. The crow cackled.

"You have no idea what I am."

"I think—"

"Quiet." He cut her off grimly. Instead of saying anything else, he grabbed her arm and hauled her through the ferns. "You do exactly as I say, do you understand?"

He dragged her to an oak tree by the side of the river, even as she was trying to decide if she should struggle or cry out for help. His hands closed around her waist and he tossed her up onto a thick branch. "Climb," he said.

"Why should I trust you?"

"If you want to wait around and meet the real wolves, that's your choice. If you don't, then climb, Princess." He turned to peer through the undergrowth as if her decision made no difference to him. She couldn't hear anything but her own ragged breaths. She stood carefully, climbing from branch to branch until she found a safe spot to perch.

He looked so grim and fierce, she couldn't help but think of the stories of Herne, the huntsman who haunted Windsor Forest. Surely ghosts didn't have such interesting arm muscles. He shifted to reach into a bush and pulled out a bow. He nocked an arrow and hid behind the oak tree, waiting. Brown leather blended into trunk, green eyes into leaves. If she hadn't known he was there she would have walked right past him.

It was another long, tense moment before she heard anything to warrant his caution. A tree branch snapped, someone cursed. There was a laugh and the splash of a body falling into the river. "Oi!" The man in the river slipped as he struggled to get to his feet. He went under again and resurfaced sputtering. He lifted the jug of cider. "Look what I found. Must be Ewan's."

"Might be his father's. Best not cross him so give it here," one of his companions said.

"Not likely," he shot back, tipping the jug back for a long drink. Theodora could only see parts of them, an arm, an ax, the jug as the sun hit it. She assumed they were poachers by the collection of horns, feathers, and foxtails on their belts.

"What's this?" She saw movement as one of the poachers bent to pick something out of the grass. "Looks like a pearl button."

A poacher stepped closer and she could see blackened teeth and bristle on his cheeks. He sniffed the air again. "And I smell perfume, lads." He grinned. Theodora froze, pressing back against the oak. "Perfume and a pearl button. Looks like we'll be poaching more than deer today."

Below her, her huntsman cursed under his breath before putting his arrow away and sauntering toward the river. "I didn't think your lot came this far south."

"Ewan," the poacher said, not exactly pleased. "What are you doing here?"

"Supplying you with cider, it seems," he replied.

"Know anything about this?" The pearl shone prettily against his muddy fingers.

Ewan shrugged. "It's a button."

The poacher narrowed his eyes. "It's too fancy for the girls we know."

He shrugged again, looking bored. The poacher flipped the button in his hand like a coin. He snatched it out of the air and paused. "What's that?" He squinted at the oak tree. "Bit of red velvet, I reckon."

Theodora swore and wondered if she should climb higher or leap out. She didn't fancy being treed like a cat. She climbed down a few branches and hesitated.

"You've been holding out on us," the poacher said. His companions jostled closer, peering up into the leaves. "I knew you were a good huntsman, Ewan, despite your father, but I had no idea how good." He leered. "She'll fetch us a pretty price. I bet someone's missing you, love."

Ewan reached out and pulled her out of the oak. She landed hard, stumbling against him. There was no use in pretending she wasn't a lord's daughter. She'd mocked the boys she knew for being soft but she was no better than they were, in her gold-thread dress and velvet cloak. She was worse actually, since they were still safely at home being brought pots of chocolate and coffee.

Ewan's grip was like iron. He tugged her roughly but she noticed he was actually shielding her from the others with his body. Between them, she'd take her chances with her silent huntsman.

"She's mine," he said.

"O-ho, lads," the main poacher laughed. "Is it true love, Ewan?"

"Doesn't matter," he replied calmly. "I found her, I'm keeping her." His antler dagger was in his hand. She felt the strength and magic coiled inside of him.

"We'll see, won't we, mate?"

Fear made Theodora's breath rattle in her throat like bones. She'd pushed too much of her magic at Ewan earlier and now there was only a little left, like the dregs at the bottom of a wine bottle. Her bird-familiar kept hold of the crow's body and circled overhead, caw-ing furiously.

Violence simmered in the quiet grove, by the pretty river. Theodora did the only thing she could think to do. She pulled out her gold earrings and removed the garnet beads from her neck. "Here." She thrust it all at the poachers. "Take them."

"Lovely," the poacher said, sucking his rotted teeth, big fingers reaching for the jewelry. "But not enough, I'm thinking. Not nearly enough."

He crushed her fingers, grinding them together until she squeaked.

Ewan didn't yell a warning of any kind and his expression didn't change. He brought the end of his antler dagger down on the poacher's arm with enough force to snap it like a rusty hinge. Theodora yanked herself free even as he spun, and she dove into the safety of the ferns. Ewan smashed his bent elbow into the poacher's face, breaking his nose. The garnet beads fell into the grass, slick with blood. The others closed in, armed with ax and club. Ewan was light and quick on his feet for someone so obviously muscled. He dodged a blow aimed at his ear and leaped over the swinging arc of the club.

The wounded poacher was on his knees now, grunting in pain and using his uninjured hand to stuff the necklace and earrings into his vest. He pulled out a long, pitted knife from his belt and stabbed at Ewan's feet.

Ewan was a good fighter, strong and sure, but he had honor where his opponents did not. Theodora didn't have the luxury of the rules of duels and battles. She'd fight dirty because it was all she had.

The crow shrieked and dove down, pecking at the poachers. They tried to cover their faces, fingers coming away with blood. The crow attacked again, yanking out tufts of hair and slicing through skin. Since she didn't have any other weapons, she slid down the bank into the river to claim the discarded jug. It was made of thick clay and it was heavy even though drained of its contents.

"Run!" Ewan shouted at her when he realized she was doubling back. He looked as stunned as she felt.

She ran through the shallow water, coming up behind the lead poacher. As he stabbed at Ewan again and sliced through the top of his boot and along his shin, Theodora smashed the jug down on the back of his head. He made a strange sound and teetered for a moment before toppling over, covered in shards of crockery and the sticky residue of cider. The crow laughed like an old woman after too much whiskey.

The other two poachers howled and doubled their efforts. The club grazed Ewan's side and he twisted away. The arrows in his quiver snapped under the impact of the blow. He leaned into the momentum of his twist and turned all the way around, coming up on his attacker's opposite side. The handle of his antler dagger caught the other man in the sternum and again on the back of the neck when he doubled over in pain. Ewan drove his fist into the third poacher's throat, leaving him gagging and staggering into the river.

"Time to go," Ewan said to Theodora.

He took her hand and pulled her along through the undergrowth. He didn't need to knot branches or leave markings to find his way. He wound around trees and through meadows, and they ran until her shoes rubbed blisters onto her toes. He didn't speak, not even when they burst out into the path and the trees thinned to show the green and gold fields between the forest and the Lovegrove manor house.

"They'll come after you now," she panted.

"I can handle the likes of them." He shrugged.

"But . . ." She bit her lower lip.

He stared at her. "You're truly worried for a woodcutter's son?"

She stared back at him. "Of course I am! You saved my life!"

His smile was rare, she knew it without having to be told. It was a weapon in itself. It made her feel warmer than their mad run through the forest. She blushed and didn't know why.

He stepped back, melting into the ferns.

"*Wait,*" she said, still trying to catch her breath. "*You saved me. My father would reward you.*"

"*What do I need money for, Princess?*"

She truly had never met anyone like him.

She stopped on the edge of the forest, still in the cool, concealing shadows. "*Thank you, Ewan.*" His name was sweet on her tongue, sweeter than cakes and sugared violets.

He inclined his head in reply. The branches behind him looked like antlers. He took another step back and was gone.

That night, as the sun set, she stood at her bedroom window and watched the light turn the color of smoke between the trees. For a brief moment she thought she saw Ewan at the edge of the woods, watching her.

The next morning she found strawberries in a small basket on the garden wall.

Chapter 25

Emma didn't know how long she'd been unconscious, but it wasn't long enough for the candles to have burned out. Had it been a dream? Or some kind of memory? She had no way of knowing and no way of asking her mother at the moment.

She only knew her head still ached like the devil. She must have hit it on the floor when she fell. She clutched it, wincing at the pain. There was no blood in her hair, or wound to account for it.

Only antlers.

There were *antlers* growing out of her *head*.

She felt the soft, velvet-covered tines, like branches of a tree. She wondered, stifling a hysterical giggle, if Mrs. Sparrow had slipped laudanum into the strawberry tarts. Emma knocked over a small table in her haste to get to the looking glass by the armoire.

She really did have antlers.

They curved gracefully out of her hair, three amber-colored tines on each side. They were thick at the base, dimpled like raindrops on a calm lake. They slanted back slightly and were no longer than the span of her hand. They didn't hurt exactly, but they were heavy and unwieldy.

She pulled and pushed at them but they didn't move, any more than a real stag's would. She remembered touching the deer and feeling her foot turning into a hoof, her leg covered in thick russet fur.

Witchery was one thing. An earl's daughter with antlers was something else altogether.

Feeling rather wild, she sank onto the edge of the bed.

Mrs. Sparrow was right. She should be grateful to be at the academy.

Because now she truly had nowhere else to go.

Part 2

UNBOUND

Chapter 26

Emma had been at the Rowanstone Academy for two weeks. In those two weeks, she learned a great many things.

She learned that the gates to the Underworld still needed to be located. They opened randomly from dusk to dawn and then sealed themselves shut. Restless spirits paced on the other side, just waiting for such an opportunity.

She learned that rumors of her mother followed her everywhere like a torn hem dragging along behind her, catching up dust and detritus.

She learned that someone had already sent the evil eye against her, shattering her school charm so that it had to be replaced.

She learned that burning rowan twigs called the dead, salt worked best against spirits and evil, and iron stopped everything in its tracks, at least temporarily.

She even learned that staring into her looking glass for hours on end did not make her antlers any less surprising.

Neither did poking them.

She had *not* learned, however, how to make them disappear.

Mrs. Sparrow assured her that though there was no way to remove them completely, she would eventually be able to glamour them away and venture back out into society once more.

She had also not yet learned who Ewan was, and why she had hallucinated his meeting with her mother. She could only assume it had been a hallucination, a memory stored in her mother's magical charm. Emma was reading her way through the library, trying to understand this new world in which she found herself. Magic was tricky; apparently even dedicated and educated scholars couldn't agree on how to classify it. Some called it divine interaction, others a kind of new science. The best they could agree on was that it was a mystical energy, invisible and unbreakable, such as what made plants grow and stars stay up in the sky.

Emma could have asked one of her teachers about the strange dream, but she didn't want anyone knowing more than they already did about her mother. She'd gone to great lengths to hide herself away from the witching world, and until Emma knew the reason why, she felt it safer to keep the experience to herself.

She was surprised to find she rather enjoyed boarding at the school, though being restricted to the grounds because she had antlers was becoming tiresome. So she would master this spell everyone insisted was beyond her current capabilities. And she would master it between the rosebushes and the marble statue of

Hecate, with her fellow students pressing their noses to the windows behind her despite the early hour.

Emma turned her back on them and took a deep breath. Mrs. Sparrow insisted a calm mind and calm body increased success. She took another breath. Calm body was considerably easier than calm mind. See how calm they would be, with antlers sprouting from *their* heads. They were *heavy*. And cumbersome. And they made brushing her hair awkward.

A small bird descended from a nearby oak tree and Emma flapped her arms warningly.

Quite aside from anything else, having birds perch on one's head was vexing.

Another deep breath.

She turned clockwise three times, her thumb instinctively seeking the poison ring on her right hand. It was silver and dated back to Tudor times. It was filled with dried fern dust, crushed crystal, and bilberries. She whispered the words she'd been taught. It could be done without the prayer but only by far more experienced witches. *"A magic cloud I put on thee; from dog, from cat; from cow, from horse, from man, from woman; from young man, from maiden; and from little child. Till I again return."*

The rain started almost immediately.

The Fith-Fath spell was used by those who wished to be invisible or shape-shift into the form of an animal, usually a deer. That she was working it backward was no surprise. Everything felt backward these days. She spent most evenings in front of her looking glass, trying to work glamour. She usually gave up for the night when her face disappeared but her antlers glowed green. And after several soggy carpets and hail in the ballroom, her magical attempts were banished to the walled gardens.

They were quite large with white pebbled paths, groves, fountains, and extensive herb gardens for spellcraft ingredients. As she understood it, natural magic, such as her ability to work the weather, was innate. Spells channeled that magic but required specific incantations and ingredients, such as herbs and special stones. Cunning-men and weird-wives weren't natural witches, but they'd learned to harness that same magic for healing and love charms and other assorted spells. Emma fully intended to seek one out if she couldn't get the hang of this blasted glamour by the end of the week.

She tried the spell again, spinning and spinning until she was dizzy. The rain continued to pelt her until she sneezed. She wished she could at least learn to make it rain *warmly*. It would be a great improvement. Her dress clung in damp, cold folds to her legs, and her hair curled against her neck. Thunder shook the sky. When it cracked again, close enough to the school to rattle windows and cause a few startled shrieks, Emma smiled to herself.

A girl meandered out of the shrubbery, her long, pale hair falling like shining swan feathers to her waist. She was all moonbeams and mist, delicate as pearls and orchids, except for the wickedly jagged knife at her belt. It looked to be made of a kind of white horn, spiraling tightly to a point. Emma thought her name was Olwen. She didn't board at the school and mostly seemed to spend her time wandering about.

"Oh." Olwen blinked at Emma and then at the sky, as if

she'd just realized it was raining and she was soaked through. "Good morning. Are you real?"

"Um . . . yes?" Emma wasn't entirely sure why it had come out as a question.

Olwen's smile was bright as a harvest moon. "Oh, good. I must be back then." Despite what Emma had been learning, most conversations still didn't make sense at the school. "Is it teatime? I'm famished."

"Tea sounds like a lovely idea," Emma agreed. They were hurrying down the path toward the house when the garden gate opened. Well, Emma was hurrying, Olwen had stopped to smell some kind of a tree.

"Olwen! There you are, finally!" Cormac didn't even see Emma. She stepped back into the prickly embrace of a hawthorn tree, feeling trapped.

The last thing she wanted was for him to see her like this. She was wet and pale with cold. And there were *antlers* on her *head*. She tipped them back slightly, hoping they'd blend into the branches. He looked as sinful as ever, decadent and handsome; the way chocolate would look if it were transformed into a person.

He'd helped put her in a cage and left her to the Order.

After kissing her senseless.

Why did she keep forgetting that? What was *wrong* with her? Besides the obvious. Maybe that was it, the weight of the antlers was addling her brain.

"Here I am," Olwen agreed. "I've only been gone a few hours."

"Olwen, you've been missing for three days," Cormac said to his sister. "Again." The rain tapered off, reduced to dripping off leaves and petals. "Mother has been reading tarot cards all morning to find out if you were all right."

"I'm always all right." Olwen smiled serenely.

"Let's go before you catch your death. Isn't rain wet in the Faery lands too?" He sounded just like a big brother should: annoyed, impatient, and affectionate. Emma hadn't even realized Olwen was his sister; the younger girl wasn't out yet so their paths had never crossed. Though it became abundantly clear that she possessed the same inclination to utterly ruin Emma's chance of a getaway, dignified or otherwise.

"Why are you hiding in the thorn tree?" She turned to look at Emma curiously. "The rain off a hawthorn is only lucky on May Day and we've weeks yet before that."

Emma stifled a groan as Cormac snapped his head around to watch her emerge from the tree, leaves in her hair and thorn scratches on her arms. He didn't say anything for a full minute, his dark eyes widening when he realized her antlers weren't tree branches after all. He took off his hat, as if it interfered with his ability to stare. "You have . . . antlers."

She lifted her chin. "Obviously."

"They're new." She wished the sound of his voice didn't remind her so much of the rain, touching her all over. Even stunned, it sounded smoky and dark and delicious.

Olwen tilted her head consideringly. "I think they're lovely."

Emma's brittle smile warmed considerably. "Thank you."

"What happened to you?" Cormac asked sharply.

"That's not your concern," she replied stiffly.

"Olwen." Catriona interrupted them from the other end of the path, near the dining room doors. "Cook's made her currant buns." Her hair was even paler than Olwen's, so blond it was nearly white. Emma hadn't yet been introduced; she only knew the other girls whispered about Catriona and dared one another to approach her. Apparently, Catriona could look at you and see your death. Olwen didn't seem bothered, only looped her arm through her friend's and threw a smile over her shoulder at her brother. "I'll meet you in the carriage once I've eaten, Cormac."

Cormac shot her a crooked grin. "That could take days. I've seen you eat."

Olwen's laugh trilled behind her like a bird darting between the leaves. Emma turned to go. Cormac stopped her with a simple question no one had thought to ask her. "Is it painful?"

"Not exactly," she replied. "At least not anymore."

He stepped closer to her and she couldn't help but notice that he was looking into her eyes and nowhere else. No one had looked her in the eye for days and days, aside from her cousins. "When did it happen? Who did this to you?"

Emma sighed. "My own mother, it would seem." She shook her head. "Never mind, it's not important."

"I beg to differ." Cormac's fingers slipped around hers to keep her from bolting. "It's very important."

"Stop it," she said quietly. His eyebrows raised in question. "I'm not a fool, you know. Despite all evidence to the contrary," she added with a self-deprecating smile. "I know you don't care for me and never did. You trifle with girls for your own purposes. And I won't be trifled with, not anymore. If you want information for your precious Order, gather it in some other way."

"You *are* a fool," he whispered, his hand tightening around hers. He leaned in until his mouth was barely inches from hers. He smiled crookedly, wickedly. "If you think that."

She wasn't entirely sure what part of her speech he was referring to. It was surprisingly hard to think when he was so close. Her blood raced through her veins, pooling warmth in the oddest places, like the back of her knees and behind her ears. He was going to kiss her again.

"My lord Blackburn."

Or not.

Daphne stood not three feet away, batting her lashes demurely; so demurely Emma had the urge to poke her in the eye with one of her antlers. Girls trailed after her, giggling and sighing over Cormac. He blinked, looking a little like a trapped animal. "Emma is shockingly remiss in not inviting you in for tea. She's positively wild now, is she not?"

"Positively," he agreed, regaining his customary lazy smile, the one that hinted at the kind of boredom that produced delicious mischief. He glanced at Emma. "But I find myself thinking society manners deadly dull all of a sudden."

Daphne's expression froze. Sophie and Lilybeth's mouths dropped open. The combined force of the other girls sneaking jealous glares her way made the evil eye charm heat up, as if she'd been too long in the sun.

"The girls are swooning," she said with a soft, sad smile. She knew she'd never be one of those girls now, artlessly flirting with a handsome gentleman. Girls wearing antlers instead of bonnets probably didn't get many chances to flirt.

Cormac made a move to follow her, but it would take a stronger man than he to forge through half a dozen debutantes intent on talking to him.

Just as well.

She had her own mischief.

Chapter 27

Moira didn't need magical itchy feet to know she was in trouble.

She was always in trouble on this end of the bridge, ever since Atticus claimed it for his gang of Madcaps. She'd flattened him once on principle. He'd been pestering her to join them and hand over her exclusive connection to One-Eyed Joe. She'd refused.

Somewhat violently, it had to be said.

Atticus held a grudge nearly as deeply as Piper. She fancied herself his sweetheart but he loved himself more than she ever could. Somehow, that had become Moira's fault. And they hated that she wouldn't be cowed. It didn't help that she was faster than they were and that One-Eyed Joe wouldn't deal with them, only her. They'd chased her with a hellhound once and he'd cursed them with nightmares for a full month.

When they were at the markets at the same time, she kept to

her end of the bridge, but with all the gargoyles being trapped and hunted by the Order, that was becoming more and more difficult. And when she saw the rickety wheelbarrow of onions abandoned at the mouth of the alley, she'd known she had no choice. The wheelbarrow was actually full of small gargoyles that Moira and Strawberry collected on their nightly rounds. One-Eyed Joe gave them a charm to make them look like pungent, slightly spoiled onions.

The Order paid for every surrendered gargoyle, no questions asked. One-Eyed Joe did a brisk trade for a week or so, but most of them had either already been found by Keepers, or were now too far out of London to bother with. The fewer gargoyles there were left, the more vicious the competition became. Strawberry wasn't up for it and never had been.

And seeing the bruises on her face, Moira was suddenly keen to compete.

They had Strawberry cornered behind a shop that mostly sold grimoires—magicians' manuals—and dragon's-blood inks. The building leaned at a sharp angle toward the water and was so close to the wards, the back alley tended to shift in and out of view. Atticus preferred it for his nastier business and when the bookseller tried to chase him off, his customers were pelted with stones and slimy ropes of seaweed.

Currently, Atticus had turned a pile of broken crates into a throne. His hat was the same virulent violet as his eyes. He liked to claim he was the descendant of a Faery prince but Moira knew it was an illusion. She'd been the one to steal the ingredients for the glamour charm he wore under his collar. One-Eyed

Joe made it for the innkeeper's daughter and she'd traded it to Atticus for a kiss.

Three of his boys surrounded Strawberry, who was on her knees and weeping silently. She couldn't handle conflict, not since she'd escaped her mother's house in Paris. Piper loomed over her, laughing. They hated her for being French, and for being Moira's friend.

"Oi." Moira made sure her voice carried and that it dripped with as much derision as she could muster. She knew it infuriated Atticus. Right on cue, he stood up, sneering. His lavender eyes were smug and arrogant. She fully intended to smash her fist into one of them before the day was done. She leaned on the broom handle she'd taken from the wheelbarrow. It made a decent staff.

"Moira," Strawberry sniffled, still wrapped around a sleeping gargoyle with a chipped nose. Piper sneered, stepping cruelly on Strawberry's long hair.

"Keep smiling," Moira told Piper. "While you still have teeth."

"Girls, girls, fighting over me again?" Atticus laughed, still perched safely out of reach on his dais. "Moira, you know you can join us. All you have to do is apologize. And obey."

She blinked innocently. "Is that all?"

He preened, proud of his blond beauty, his reputation for cruelty, and his devoted gang. "Aye, my beauty."

Moira tilted her head, considering the offer. The lads shifted nervously, self-preservation instincts honed to a point. Atticus rarely fought his own battles. "Nah," she said finally, with mock regret. "I'd rather do this."

She smashed the end of the staff into Piper's foot, the one pinning Strawberry to the ground with her own hair. Piper howled and fell back against the wall. Moira spun, lifting the staff and walloping the three boys, one after the other. The first fell down, blacking out before he hit the dirt. The second, John, got a bloody nose, but the last, Rod, managed to duck out of the way just in time.

Atticus climbed higher on his crates. Strawberry dragged the heavy gargoyle down the alley. She was holding her arm at an awkward angle, teeth clenched. Piper launched herself at Moira, clawed hands going for her eyes. Moira swung the staff again, going low this time. She swept it behind the other girl's knees and knocked her flat on her backside. Marmalade streaked up the crates, hissing at Atticus.

Rod got in a good hit, cracking the breath out of Moira's chest with a flat-palmed strike. She gagged and tumbled into more crates piled in a kind of protective gateway. She crashed through them, scattering their makeshift fortifications. She kept hold of the broom handle, using it to help her back up to her feet. She jabbed out, aiming for eyes and noses and other vulnerable areas. John, Rod, and Piper dodged, unable to get closer. John's nose was crooked and already swelling.

Moira swung the staff over her head like a slingshot and they scattered. She climbed the boxes, the charms on her boots making her especially agile. She grinned, closing in on Atticus. Too late he realized his precious gang wasn't standing between them anymore.

"You'll leave Strawberry alone, you tosspot," Moira said

darkly, jabbing at him with the end of the staff, just enough to make him sweat. She knocked his hat off just because she could. It tumbled down into the alley, spattered in mud.

"Why you—"

He didn't have a chance to finish his threat. Moira slammed the staff into his stomach, knocking him backward. He sailed off his throne, hit the fence, and tumbled over. There was a shout and a distant splash as he landed in the Thames.

His gang froze, shocked. Moira hopped back down to the ground. "You can come at me again or you can go fish him out," she said. "Your choice."

"This isn't over," Piper hissed at her before they broke into a run to find Atticus. She was the first to jump off the fence in a show of heroism. Moira wasn't sure how getting herself immersed in the dirty water of the river was going to help and she didn't much care.

She darted down the alley to the wheelbarrow where Strawberry slumped, the gargoyle at her feet. She was cradling her wrist. "I think it's broken," she said. Her spirit-mouse was curled up on her shoulder looking mournful.

Moira swore. "Get in," she added, nodding to the wheelbarrow. She dragged the gargoyle by the ears, keeping a wary eye on the curious passersby. The glamour only worked once the gargoyle was inside the wheelbarrow. She could smell salt and flowers, as usual. "You had to get a beast of a blighter," she huffed, straining until she thought her eyeballs might explode.

"I wanted to do my part for once."

"You always do your part."

Strawberry sighed. "Not like you do."

"Just watch out for warlocks and Rovers," she muttered, sweat dripping into her ears. The bridge wasn't crowded yet and the pomegranate lanterns hadn't even been lit, but the ends were always a bit suspect, no matter the time of day. She got the gargoyle to the cart and hopped up beside Strawberry.

"Now comes the hard part," she said. Her arms felt like jelly. She grabbed the stone ears and hauled. The gargoyle tipped back and crashed into the wheelbarrow, tipping them both precariously. Moira scooted over, crushing Strawberry. A gargoyle's wing tip gouged painfully into her tailbone but the wheelbarrow righted itself. Strawberry's eyes were tightly shut and the lines around her mouth were white with pain. Her wrist was swollen and mottled with bruises.

"Well, so much for that idea," Moira wheezed. She shoved damp hair off her face. "We might have to leave it behind." A witch's ladder made of painted crow feathers worked into a braided cord hung from a signpost overhead. She flicked it idly, going through her options. A jar of blue evil-eye beads watched her from the nearest window. One of them blinked. She took another cautious glance up and down the bridge. They were starting to attract attention. "Blast."

She leaped off the wheelbarrow. "Right. Let's go." She skirted around the front to pull Strawberry to One-Eyed Joe's tent. She was reaching for the handle when the first familiar arrived, a fox with pointed ears who sniffed around the gargoyle. Three cats, a crow, and a swan with a vicious beak followed. Moira yanked on the wheelbarrow. One-Eyed Joe's illusion charms were strong, but she didn't know if they could hold if too many witches grew nosy. The goblin markets could turn volatile without warning.

When a Rover sauntered out of the shadows between the buildings, Moira swore. She couldn't keep this one at bay with a broom handle and a handful of illusion charms. She felt the menace rolling off him. The Order mostly kept them in check, but trust the bleeding Greybeards to be nowhere around when they might actually be useful for once.

"What have we here, my dears?" he asked unctuously.

Strawberry slid off the end of the wheelbarrow, covering the gargoyle with her skirts. She smiled sweetly, despite her wrist. "We've heard onions left in the sun for three days in horse urine increases magical power." She reached back for the pretend-onions, slimy with rot. "Would you like to try one?"

He looked suspicious but he stepped back nonetheless. It afforded just the distraction needed for Cedric to walk up behind him and cosh him. The Rover gurgled and fell in a heap. Cedric didn't even pause, he just went straight for the gargoyle and hefted it into the wheelbarrow.

"Cedric." Moira grinned at him. "Brilliant timing as always."

Strawberry clambered back onto the uncomfortable heap of gargoyles, patting her hair into place. Cedric grabbed the handles and pushed the wheelbarrow. "What happened to you two?" he asked. "Or do I even want to know?"

"Atticus."

Cedric's jaw tightened. "Of course."

She shrugged, grinning despite her aching arms and the splinters in her palms. "I pushed him into the river."

Cedric's smile was brief. "Again?" He readjusted his grip as the wheelbarrow thudded over the uneven cobbles. "What's in here? Rocks?"

"Pretty much," she said. "Gargoyles," she added in a whisper.

He scowled. "Why didn't you send word? It's not safe to be hauling this much magic around alone right now."

They stopped in front of One-Eyed Joe's striped tent. Cedric helped Strawberry off the back as Moira poked her head in the doorway. No customers. "Wheelbarrow's back," she announced.

"Onions?" he asked, looking up from a small shell he was carving into a cameo.

"Good crop," she assured him. She jerked her head toward Strawberry, who followed Cedric inside meekly. "Atticus's boys roughed her up."

"Did they now?" One-Eyed Joe asked mildly, lighting his pipe with a smoldering lily stalk. The embers smelled like wine and sugar. "Doesn't look broken. Just a sprain."

With her hair pushed back tidily, the bruises in Strawberry's face were stark. Cedric's eyebrows lowered. The smoke from the pipe formed into wasps. They hovered for a moment before shooting off down the bridge. "Let's just see how he sleeps this week," One-Eyed Joe added with a chilling smile.

Moira was already rummaging through the trunk under the table. She pulled out a length of torn fabric and wound it gently around Strawberry's wrist. Cedric stood back patiently, his hands in his pockets.

"Tuck a sprig of lavender in the wrappings," One-Eyed Joe said, pulling a handful from a jar.

"I didn't know lavender worked healing magic," Strawberry said.

"It doesn't. But the scent is soothing." He glanced at Cedric. "And you?"

"Dropping off a list for Mandala," Cedric replied. Mandala owned an apothecary shop on New Bond Street. He passed over a roll of parchment to One-Eyed Joe. He glanced at it, the smoke from his pipe turning into beautiful dancing girls with peacock tails.

"I'll need a few days."

"She reckoned as much."

One-Eyed Joe nodded. "Right then, it's getting crowded here and none of you are buying. So off you go."

They stepped outside, back into the sunlight. Cedric tipped his head. "Don't take any chances tonight, Moira. Atticus will be looking for you."

"I'll be fine." She shrugged. "Aren't you staying? The Cursed Fiddlers are playing at the Three Goblins. You love them."

"Have to head home," he called over his shoulder, already walking away.

Strawberry sighed, watching him. "Do you think he'll ever notice me?"

Moira shook her head. "That boy works for the fancy. He doesn't have time for a sweetheart."

"Haven't you ever wondered what would make him stay?"

Moira smiled. "Not me, Strawberry. He's like a brother to me." And he'd been her brother for a lot longer than her actual family. He'd been right there next to her when her older brother was carted away by the Order. "And not you either, I'm sorry to say. I reckon he's after a girl who will break his heart."

Chapter 28

"Duck!"

Emma didn't duck so much as sprawl ungracefully on the scuffed parquet floor. Someone giggled. She felt sure it was Daphne. She rolled over onto her back, huffing a sigh. "Somehow, I'd assumed magic would be more glamorous."

Gretchen's face was the first to peer over her. "I'm sorry," she said sheepishly. "I really thought I had it that time."

Emma stayed where she was. The floor was hard and uncomfortable but it was a great deal more uncomfortable to have broken glass, pendants, and chandeliers flying at your head. Which had been happening all morning.

Clearly, the famous Lovegrove magic needed work.

Gretchen was attempting to harness and focus her natural abilities, which was resulting mostly in any charms in the vicinity exploding. The ballroom ceiling was damaged with scorch marks and various substances she had no wish to investigate more thoroughly. The mural depicting the story of Medea was definitely the worse for wear, but that was only partially their fault.

The ballroom was converted into a training space when the schools were first established. The two buildings mirrored each other inside and rumor had it that there were doors leading between them. Needless to say, students searched on a regular basis and tried to blast them with spells on the rare occasions when they were found. Apparently a great many closet doors had fallen victim.

"Don't worry." Catriona drifted by. "This isn't how you die."

Emma rubbed her face, feeling only a little reassured. Gretchen helped her to her feet as she still tended to wobble, either under- or overcompensating for the weight of her antlers. Penelope was picking crystal beads from the chandelier out of her hair.

Miss Hopewell, one of the teachers, shook her head. "Let's try another demonstration," she said. "Lady Daphne, if you would?"

The rest of the girls were safely huddled on the other side of the ballroom, except for Daphne, who was smirking. She'd been sneering since she'd found Cormac in the garden with Emma, so Emma supposed a smirk might be considered an improvement.

Despite the fact that it was deeply unfair, Daphne was not only a favorite of the teachers, but she was also the most gifted in the school when it came to offensive spells. Her natural talent guaranteed that any magic would find its target. If she'd applied her aim to pistols or longbows, she'd have been a crack shot. It drove Gretchen to distraction.

Daphne preened as she sauntered up beside the cousins. "Of course, Miss Hopewell." She tossed her perfect ringlets before lifting her chin. Her expression changed, went from smug to focused as she faced the targets. Whatever else the cousins might think of her, there was no denying she was serious about her skills and the Order. Her father was the First Legate, which made him even more powerful than the magisters.

The targets were a line of large haystacks along the back wall. Some were painted with regular bull's-eye circles, but most were far harder to negotiate. Charms, amulets, and various magical triggers were hidden inside the hay. This morning alone, Gretchen had released a swarm of bees, made a turnip talk, and set all the dogs in the neighborhood howling. Even now her wolfhound-familiar pranced up and down the street. He'd first emerged when Emma and Penelope had to pull Gretchen off Daphne for the second time.

"Begin," Miss Hopewell instructed.

Penelope went first. Her natural magic had less chance of interfering, especially if she wasn't physically touching any of the charms.

"Shield," Miss Hopewell told her.

Elf-bolts of gray-green energy ejected from the haystack, seeking Penelope out like little arrows. They were fast and vicious. Penelope's hair lifted into the air, full of static. Emma and Gretchen stood beside her even though Miss Hopewell waved them away. Penelope flung the first few aside, muttering bits of Shakespeare under her breath, not because it helped her magic in any way, but because it calmed her.

"You'd do well to learn Latin," Miss Hopewell muttered. She seemed to find Shakespeare too wild for her classes. Especially when Penelope yelled: *Ass head and a coxcomb and a knave!* and some of the girls started to giggle uncontrollably.

The elf-bolts came faster and thicker, like a volley of arrows from the battlement of a besieged castle. There were too many to stop individually. Penelope had to create an energy shield, the way they'd been taught that morning. It was made of blue light and looked like a lopsided, old-fashioned wooden shield. It wasn't quite strong enough. The first bolt went through her hair, the second pierced her shoulder. It didn't draw blood or leave an obvious mark, but Penelope wilted, turning as green as stewed celery.

Emma and Gretchen both placed a hand on each of her shoulders, without comment. They pushed magic at her shield until it glowed brighter, purer. The elf-bolts disintegrated on impact.

"And attack," Miss Hopewell ordered.

The elf-bolts stopped, replaced by bats.

Penelope threw salt. Gretchen added a handful of iron nails. Emma cursed.

Nothing happened.

"Salt and iron aren't enough," Miss Hopewell remarked, which would have been more helpful before the bats began closing in. "They are only a vehicle for your magic in this case." She paused disapprovingly. "And that language is certainly not acceptable, Lady Emma."

With the three of them working together, it became

easier. They found a rhythm that allowed them better control than they had on their own. The bats transformed to hornets and then back to elf-bolts.

Emma caught the flick of Daphne's fingers but too late.

Much too late.

Her aim was so true that each bolt was hit and turned into a boiled beet that exploded all over the cousins. Red pulp splatted into their faces, hung from their hair, and stained their dresses. The other girls couldn't help but laugh.

"I may actually kill her," Gretchen said, pulling a mangled beet out of her ear.

"Honestly, girls." Miss Hopewell sighed. "You're going to have to practice far more often if you want to catch up." She left to summon a scullery maid.

"I thought the Lovegroves' magic went back for centuries," Daphne said, all false innocence.

"And I thought your family's charm went back that long," Gretchen shot back. "Guess it skipped a generation."

"The sooner you realize you're embarrassing yourselves and the school, the better," Daphne said darkly. "The academy has a reputation to uphold." She smiled archly before flouncing away, too fast for Gretchen to fling handfuls of mashed beets at her face.

The cousins stood in the middle of the ballroom, dripping vegetable matter and wondering why anyone would want to be a witch in the first place.

Chapter 29

Penelope was walking down the lane to the side door of the town house when Cedric rushed out of the stables. He was wearing his customary trousers and white shirt, his dark hair falling into his face. He didn't say a word, just swung her up in his arms, wild-eyed.

She held on to his shoulder, fully expecting to be dropped on her backside. Her hem caught the breeze, ruffling up over his arm. He rushed inside to the nearest bench, setting her down carefully and crouching next to her. The horses lifted their heads curiously in their pens.

"I'll get a doctor," he said, frantically.

She blinked at him, dazed from being grabbed so suddenly and then carried about. She hadn't realized he was so strong. Or that he'd gone mad since breakfast. "*I* am fine," she said, when he looked like he was going to be sick on her shoes. "I suspect you might be coming down with something though."

"You're covered in blood," he babbled. "You're in shock. Where are you hurt? We need a doctor!" His babbling turned rapidly to bellowing. Penelope glanced down at her red-stained dress, chest, and arms. Comprehension dawned.

"It's beets," she assured him quickly. "It's beet juice!" she yelled louder in case anyone had heard him shouting for a doctor. When her parents didn't come flying through the stable doors, she relaxed.

Cedric sat back on his heels, befuddled. "Beets."

She wrinkled her nose sheepishly. "From the academy."

"Beets," he echoed, rising slowly to his feet. "From the academy."

She tilted her head back to look at him. "Are you going to repeat everything I say? It doesn't make for very stimulating conversation."

He jerked his hand through his hair. "I thought you were hurt."

She popped up to kiss his cheek. "You're a darling," she said. He turned red. She assumed he was finally feeling the effects of carrying her weight around as if she was one of those bird-boned girls. "I'm perfectly well. Although slightly mortified and definitely vowing vengeance."

"So just another day then," he said.

"Precisely," she agreed cheerfully. She didn't take offense at his teasing, though in regular houses the coachman's grandson was not encouraged to chat up the master's daughter. Most coachmen and most horses weren't serenaded by piano music either. When her pianoforte was replaced she'd had the old one delivered down to the stables. She was convinced it made the horses happy and since Cedric loved music, she was determined that he shouldn't be deprived. It was a testament to her parent's unique ideas that they'd allowed her free rein with pianofortes and lessons in general.

She'd been playing with Cedric since they were children and when she was banished inside to be tutored, she insisted Cedric be allowed to join her. He grumbled about it, but all of her teachers were impressed with his capacity to learn, even with their prejudice against his Gypsy blood. She was less impressed with their knowledge of poetry. All her mother had cared about was that they study Mary Wollstonecraft's *A Vindication on the Rights of Women*.

Regular houses sounded terribly dull. And her father wasn't a lord anyway, despite her mother's aristocratic connections. He was wealthier than most earls and viscounts but he was in trade, having taken over his mother's brewery. Some of the titled families were perfectly willing to overlook his pedestrian bloodlines in favor of his wealth, though they loved to whisper about it behind their fans and brandy glasses. They'd have a fit of the vapors if they knew how friendly his daughter was with the coachman's Gypsy grandson.

Penelope didn't begrudge Cedric anything. Except for the fact that he'd known about witchery all his life and had never said a word. She didn't care what her mother said about her aunt's spell. "I still can't believe you knew," she muttered.

"So you decided to scare me to death?" He raised an eyebrow at her.

"That was just a side benefit," she replied. "But you were very heroic."

"Give over, I apologized a hundred times. And I was witched, as you well know."

"I guess," she pretended to grumble. "You should be at the academy too."

Cedric picked up a brush to groom a waiting horse. One of the stable boys could have done it but she knew he enjoyed the work. "You know I can't," he said mildly.

"But you're powerful," she exclaimed, grumbling in earnest now. "You could be a Keeper, if you wanted to. Though Emma says they're a shifty lot."

"Can't say I much care for them either," he agreed. "But it doesn't matter, Pen. The academies only take high-born witches."

"That's so unfair," Penelope said, scrubbing the beet stains off her hands in a bucket of water with more force than was strictly necessary. She went to sit at the dusty, hay-strewn pianoforte to work off her temper. "And if the Greymalkin Sisters are as horrid as everyone says they are, the Order should be glad of all the help they can get."

He wasn't the type to sit back where there was work to be done. He'd told her that before but had always refused to elaborate. She was used to his long silences, but not his evasions. She banged at the keys, playing a piece so menacing one of the mares kicked at her stall. "Mind the horses," Cedric told her, amused. "You're spooking them."

Penelope sent him a sheepish smile, the tune instantly

changing from sinister to soothing, with all the ferocity of a sleeping kitten.

"How are you getting on at Rowanstone then?" he asked.

She shrugged one shoulder. "All right, I suppose. Until the beets, anyway. I still can't find my familiar, though. I think it must have lost its way." She tapped a few keys lazily. "What's yours?" She'd forgotten to ask him before.

"Horse."

She smirked. He raised an eyebrow in question.

"I like the irony of it," she explained. "Daphne keeps going on about the hierarchy of familiars. And horse is one of the top. Not like hers." She positively beamed. "It's a toad."

Cedric snorted. "The witching families do like their hierarchies."

"Exactly." She rolled her eyes. "Which is why I intend to rub it in her face that the coachman's grandson, who isn't good enough for her precious academy, outranks her in the world of familiars."

He shook his head, well used to her grudges. "I'm not too concerned with what they think of me."

"I know." Penelope abandoned the pianoforte to stroke the horse's nose while Cedric kept brushing. "But I am."

"They love you, Pen. Why wouldn't they?"

She made a face. "Not me, you dolt. You. I care what they think of *you*."

"What for?" He looked surprised.

"Because." She waved her hand as if it made it all clearer. *Because you're clever and honest and brave,* she thought. If she said it out loud he'd only tease her. As it was, he wouldn't meet her eyes. She'd embarrassed him. He didn't want some plump, spoiled girl mooning at him.

"Anyway, I'd rather fetch and carry for Mandala than work for their lot," he said.

Penelope rested her brow on the horse's neck, tangling her fingers through his mane. "I still can't believe that spell was so strong it silenced you all. I don't even remember anyone trying to talk to me about witchery." She shivered. "It's disconcerting to know we were played with like paper dolls."

"Your mother did the rest in this house," he said half smiling. "She's right scary when she's a mind to be."

They stood by the horse in companionable silence for a long while. Penelope enjoyed the smell of hay and the stray cats who continuously wound around Cedric's ankles, begging for scraps. Every hungry animal for miles, even the cranky badger who lumbered out of the Park sometimes, knew him for a soft heart. She loved that about him.

He was such a gentle soul under all those muscles and serious expressions. When she was younger she'd told him her theory that she'd know her true love by a magical kiss, like all the girls in the stories did. He threatened to push her in the mud if she tried to practice on him. She'd had to settle for the next-door neighbor's son, and he kissed like a landed trout.

"Here's my little lady." Cedric's grandfather limped in, leaning heavily on his cane.

"Hamish." She greeted him with a big smile.

He nodded to the red beet stains. "Are you walloping my grandson again?"

"One time," Cedric muttered. "She broke my nose *one* time falling off a horse."

"I didn't fall off that horse," Penelope protested. "He was stung by a bee and threw me." She looped her arm through Hamish's, trying to steady him without being obvious about it. "Anyway, no changing the subject, old man. Where's my candy?"

"Sweets for the sweet," he chuckled. She couldn't remember a time when he hadn't said that to her, or slipped candy in his pockets for her to find. He patted them one by one. Penelope and Cedric waited patiently, exchanging a laughing glance. Hamish finally located the candy and pressed one into her hand. She popped it immediately into her mouth. She never actually cared for peppermints but it made him so happy to treat her.

"I'm going to lie down a little while," he said, shuffling off toward his room. "Storm's coming and I can feel it in these old bones. Wake me when the carriage needs driving, lad."

Penelope waited until he was out of earshot. "You're worried about him," she said, reading Cedric's expression. The housemaids always whispered that he was so stoic but Penelope knew where to look. His eyes narrowed slightly when he was worried and he tugged his hand through his hair when he didn't know how to react to something.

"He's hurting," he admitted.

She squeezed his hand. "I'll have Mrs. Brandon make up a poultice for his joints. And I'll stay in tonight," she added impulsively. "So you can drive my parents around and Hamish can rest."

"Thank you," he said quietly. His smile was crooked as he handed her a handkerchief. "Spit that candy out."

Penelope traded her candy for a brush and set to helping Cedric with the grooming. The horse nipped at her hair. She laughed and ducked out of the way. She caught Cedric looking at her. "What?" she said. "Do I have hay all over me? On top of the beets? I'd make a fine salad." She grimaced down at herself.

He shook his head, the glint in his eye changing. "Pen?"

"Yes?"

He nodded to the ground behind her. There were spiders crawling through the hay and mud, all in a perfect line toward her, like soldiers to a general. She leaped onto the rickety bench, clutching the brush like it was an ax. "Blargh!" It was the only sound she could form.

Cedric watched their careful and particular path. When she moved, they shifted course. "I think you've found your familiar."

Penelope stared at him, horrified. Her wail could be heard down the street. "Noooo!"

Chapter 30

"I never thought I could be so happy to be shopping for ribbons and dresses," Emma said, practically skipping into the shop. Large bolts of fabrics were piled to the ceiling. Printed muslins fluttered like moth wings and silks and satins caught the light. Ribbons, trimmings, and baskets of spangles were displayed on a wide table. Salesclerks circulated through the crowds to assist shoppers.

"I'm already bored," Gretchen said. "I don't see why Godric gets to learn how to patrol and fight the undead creatures coming through the gates but we still have to practice our curtsy." She gave a mock demonstration, her yellow dress billowing around her.

"Mrs. Sparrow says we must act like normal girls," Emma reminded her, "so that no one suspects Rowanstone to be anything but another finishing school."

"This *is* me acting like a normal girl," Gretchen pointed out.

"She's got you there," Penelope tossed a grin over her shoulder before going back to examining the bolt of pink brocade that had caught her eye. "Don't you think Madame Anisette could do something wonderful with this?"

"Not the dressmaker's too," Gretchen groaned, dropping her head in her hands. Alarmed, a salesclerk rushed forward with smelling salts.

"I'm just happy to finally be allowed off the school grounds," Emma brushed her fingers over a roll of green velvet ribbon as the salesclerk retreated from Gretchen's exclamation of "For God's sake, I'm not going to faint!"

"Even if concentrating so hard on this Fith-Fath spell is giving me a headache," Emma added when they were alone once more.

"It's holding very well," Penelope assured her. "You only look a little ill."

They turned the conversation to more mundane matters as the crowds inside the shop swelled. Ladies bumped against one another, murmuring about gowns, and drapes, and trimmings for bonnets. Penelope purchased enough fabric to outfit a troupe of Shakespearean actors.

The attending footman from Rowanstone followed behind them, carrying the heavy wrapped packages. The sun was bright, flashing off carriage wheels and copper drainpipes.

Godric slouched against a nearby lamppost, looking for all the world as though he was being rained on miserably. Even his hat looked depressed. "What's the matter with you?" Gretchen demanded, marching up to him. "You look wretched."

He shook his head, squinting at her. "Just sober."

Gretchen rolled her eyes. "About time."

"It wasn't my idea," he muttered.

Penelope touched his arm. He'd been her second true kiss and she remembered it fondly, even if it hadn't been remotely passionate. They'd both burst out laughing halfway through and decided to go to Gunter's for lemon ices instead. "Why are you drinking so much?" she asked, forehead wrinkling. "It's not like you."

"I can see the dead."

"I know," she said. "Gretchen told us. I can see them too, in a way. Only I can feel what they feel, if I touch something that belonged to them. And not just the dead, either."

"Bollocks," he said, drawing away slightly.

She snorted. "Like I want to know what you get up to."

He chuckled briefly. "Fair enough. Though it's not much fun lately, not with the blasted bone-whispering. If I'm drunk I don't see them nearly as much and people don't assume I'm insane when I talk to invisible people. They just assume it's the gin." He rubbed his eyes. "And let's just say with the gates opening all over the damn place, there seem to be more dead people than live ones."

Emma winced. That was her doing. "Why don't you walk with us?" she suggested, hoping to distract him.

"Where are you going?"

"To the modiste," Gretchen said. "So Penelope can have another dress made."

"I'm not going to the dressmaker's," Godric protested.

"Of course you are." Penelope slid her arm through his. Emma did the same on the other side. "We have you captive."

Gretchen snickered. "And if I have to suffer, so do you. That ought to teach you to skip out on your lessons."

He slanted her a glance, letting himself be dragged down the street. "How did you know?"

"Please," she scoffed. "As if you can hide anything from me. I know perfectly well you should be doing something interesting, mostly because we're not allowed. You've got the Order, if you want to train to be a Keeper. We have deportment lessons." The sarcasm dripping from her tone was sharp as needles.

"I'm not all that keen to become a Keeper," he said. "Our professors had us fight some kind of a goblin. It ruined my favorite hat. Do you know how corrosive their blood is?"

From the longing on Gretchen's face, he might have been talking about a visit to the confectioner's shop for iced cakes. "I hate you."

He grinned for the first time, looking like his old self. "Never mind, little sister."

"Tell the truth, they sent you away to sober you up."

He looked sheepish.

"Ha!" Gretchen exclaimed. "I knew it! Being a boy is *wasted* on you."

"Hey now, not so loud! There might be ladies about."

"Might be?" Emma teased him. "What are *we* then?"

"Unique."

Walking to a dressmaker's shop on a fine London morning ought to have been uneventful.

Emma really needed to remember how deeply her life had changed.

A man cantered down the middle of the street on a giant black horse, holding his own head under his arm. The eyes were staring balefully. His cloak billowed from his shoulders and the stump of a neck shadowed the collar of an old-fashioned frock coat. A whip hung from his belt, knotted and white, and made from a length of human spine. More bones were knotted into the horse's mane. The other coachmen didn't notice his grisly approach, but all of the other horses on the road began to pull at their harnesses. Panicked whinnies traveled like waves breaking on the sand.

"Can anyone else see him?" Godric stumbled, sounding strangled.

"Hard to miss," Penelope squeaked.

"So he's not a ghost?" He rubbed his face. "Just when I thought it was safe to quit drinking."

The road was descending into mayhem, carriages rolling this way and that. Pedestrians leaped away from the curb with angry shouts. Others stopped to watch curiously.

"It's a dullahan." The footman gaped.

"What do they do?" Emma asked.

"They carry people off to the Underworld, miss," he replied, his voice shaking slightly.

The massive black horse reared, sparks shooting off its hooves. The carriage beside them toppled sideways, jerked from its harness. There was a scream from inside.

Gretchen grabbed a pot of daffodils from in front of a shop

and heaved it at the dullahan. It nicked his side, crashing to the ground and shattering.

Both body and decapitated head turned in their direction.

The dullahan lashed the spine-whip at them, so close the tip snapped the air right in front of their eyes. Godric knocked his cousins out of the way. They tumbled to the ground, ducking their heads.

"They don't like being watched," the footman said needlessly, now pressed against the wall. Emma called up storm clouds, magic tingling and burning through her witch knot. Rain spattered the pavement. The onlookers hurried to hide under awnings and umbrellas.

The dullahan laughed and it was the sound of rusty iron wheels grinding together. Hearing it, the nearest coachman suddenly keeled over, dead. The horseman reached forward and snagged his spirit, yanking it savagely out of the fallen body. The coachman's luminescent essence screamed silently, trapped to the horse by the bone whip.

Horrified, Emma turned to the footman. "How do we stop him?" He just shook his head, pale as boiled leeks.

The rain fell harder, making everything dark and hazy. The cobblestones turned to ink, the stone pillars to gray shadows. Emma tried to push the wind between the gruesome horseman as he bore down on his next victim: a gentleman leaning out of his carriage window, his beaver hat snatched away by the whirling storm. He squinted into the rain, confused.

Emma shoved more magic into the weather. Lightning struck a lamppost. The wind tore at the dullahan's ragged cloak but it didn't stop his progress. His eyes pinned her through the sheets of rain. "It's not working," she said, shivering down to her very marrow.

"What do we do?" Gretchen turned on the footman. He looked ill. He didn't answer, didn't even blink when she shook his shoulder. He was too intent on the dullahan. Gretchen slapped the footman as hard as she could. His head hit the stones behind him. He blinked at her, no longer shaking. "How do we stop him?" Gretchen repeated.

"Gold," he croaked, shocked out of his panic. "They can't abide gold of any kind."

Gretchen looked taken aback for a brief moment before she and her cousins leaped upon Godric. "Oi," he said as they batted at him. Gretchen slipped his gold cravat pin free and darted forward to fling it at the dullahan. The pin scratched his leg, singeing his pants. The smell of scorched flesh touched the rain.

Penelope fumbled for Godric's gold cuff links and Emma dashed into the snuff shop behind them. Snuffboxes lined the shelves: enameled, bronzed, silver, and painted mahogany. The proprietor stared at Emma, unused to female clients, and certainly unused to having them paw through his merchandise. She grabbed all the gold-accented snuffboxes she could see and hurried back outside while he hollered for her to stop. Gretchen had liberated gold candlesticks from a coffeehouse. They stood beside one another, throwing their arsenal at the enraged dullahan.

The gold infuriated him, searing his hair and hands, and his horse. The burns were violent, acting like poison more than simply painful welts. His eyes rolled in his head, dark and malevolent.

Cuffs fluttering, Godric liberated a sturdy cane from a passing gentleman and used it to hack at the bone-whip as it lashed at his cousins. The rain shielded them from most of the onlookers, who only wondered if some prank was afoot. They had yet to notice the dead coachman. His terrified spirit was pinned to the dullahan's saddle with a rope made of violet light.

The horseman thundered toward the cousins, cobblestones cracking under the force of his horse's hooves. Gretchen ducked under her brother's cane and the savage whip, brandishing the last gold candlestick like a sword. She aimed for his eyes and he screamed. The sound was so vicious and inhuman that several people fainted, without knowing what it was they had just heard. The dullahan turned his horse around and galloped away, dragging the poor coachman's spirit behind him.

The rain lightened. The horses calmed. The cousins stared at one another. Emma shook her head.

"And to think I *wanted* to leave the school."

Chapter 31

Emma waited until everyone was asleep. There was a Keeper posted in the garden but he was there to worry about outside threats, not what was going on inside. And technically, Emma wasn't sure she was even breaking any rules. It was probably frowned upon to be out of her room after hours, but there was nothing in the rule book about it specifically. It wasn't her fault if those pages had inexplicably disappeared. And after facing a dullahan, everything else seemed a minor infraction.

She moved carefully down the hall. The teachers had long since retired and the few fires burning in the grates were crumbling to embers. She made it down the stairs without incident, but had to dive into a potted plant when Mrs. Sparrow's cat-familiar prowled toward the kitchen. She waited until the glowing swish of his tail had faded before climbing out of the dusty ferns and darting into the library. Most girls would sneak out to meet a handsome lad. Emma just wanted books.

She didn't know how else to get information on her mother. Lady Theodora hadn't attended Rowanstone since it had closed briefly when the Sisters were at their worst, but her defection from the witching society and her defiance of the rules was legendary. Surely someone somewhere had jotted down a few notes.

The library was extensive and immaculately kept. There were two stories of leather-bound books and folios, with a curving wooden staircase leading to a balcony that ran around the second floor. Rowan branches curved around the railing, with perfect slender leaves and tiny red berries of garnets. There was a large fireplace, several benches, and wide tables for studying. Bell jars and the glass doors of cabinets protected collections of amulets, crystals, and ancient grimoires from fingerprints and coal dust.

She went straight to the second floor, where there were locked doors and the journals of famous witching families. She found a small section on a bottom shelf with three Lovegrove journals. The first was written by Egremont Lovegrove, who had spent all of his time cataloguing the fungi of Berkshire in great and tedious detail. She didn't notice he was born two hundred years before her mother until she was half asleep over a description of ruined mushrooms. He'd even met Anne Boleyn and all he could talk about was the fact that she'd accidentally trod on a collection of toadstools he was keen to study.

The second journal was no more helpful, but at least it was exciting. Oona Lovegrove had dressed as a boy and snuck onto a ship to sail around looking for pirates, before turning into a pirate herself. She was a wind-witch, like Emma. Oona lived to be a hundred and three and mentioned the birth of her great-grandnieces Cora, Theodora, and Bethany, but she died before she ever met them. She did mention that Emma's grandfather was a Keeper, but that was all.

The third journal was written entirely in Latin. Upside down. And backward.

Emma skimmed for any mention of Theodora or Ewan but only got a headache behind her right eye for her troubles. She decided that since her own family was proving to be so vexingly enigmatic, she'd simply have to look elsewhere. She made a satisfying large pile of books on one of the tables and lit one of the oil lamps. There were worse ways to spend a few sleepless hours. For one thing, she could be sneezing in the bushes with her teeth chattering from cold like the Keeper outside.

She looked for mention of witch bottles and the Lacrimarium Cormac had told her about. Their spells required a great deal of time and concentration and the bottle had to be prepared under certain phases of the moon. Families of the Lacrimarium disowned them with elaborate unbinding rituals. Witch or warlock, no one wanted to be vulnerable to the bottle spell. Smaller traps were set by regular witches, if they could get the hair or blood of their victim, but the Lacrimarium needed no such thing. They didn't even need threshold days, which were times of power like solstices or May Day and midnight. And they didn't suffer the dangerous repercussions of being drained, blocked, or running mad. But they were rare and temperamental.

And none of them had a thing to say about Emma's mother.

Frustrated, she took her oil lamp and wandered through the library again, looking for hidden books or locked shelves. She didn't find either, but she did find the *Witch's Debrett's*. As expected, there were no Days listed but she found an impressive section on the Lovegroves. Her mother was listed, as were her aunts, along with their familiars. Theodora had claimed a red bird for her magical creature.

On the shelf below, Emma noticed large, thick leather-bound journals without titles. The only marking on the spines were dates in gilt paint. Out of curiosity, she reached for the year of her mother's birth: 1780.

The cream-colored pages were covered in simple faded ink, noting births, deaths, marriages, and other important magical events all over Britain. According to the records, a three-headed calf was born in Scotland who produced healing milk. In Cornwall, a mermaid was spotted off Land's End whose hair gave water-witches the ability to breathe underwater. And there, in April: Theodora Ophelia Lovegrove was born to George Lovegrove, the Earl of Whickam, and his wife Marianne Lovegrove, Countess Whickam.

Emma reached for the volume marked 1797. As far as she'd been able to infer, her mother was perfectly sane until after she'd given birth to Emma. It gave her a jolt to see her own name and birthday written in the precise handwriting: the seventh day of January, Emma Jane Day, born to Alphonse Day, heir to the Earl of Hightower and his wife, Lady Theodora Ophelia Day. It was faded more than any of the other writing, but still faintly legible, if she squinted hard enough.

She went back nine months, to when her parents were married and she was conceived. She didn't recognize any names until the end of August. Theodora Ophelia Day was faded even more than Emma's birth announcement had been, until it looked as though it was written in milk. Whatever else was recorded after her name was now gone entirely. The ink had faded away so that even when Emma held the oil light behind the thin parchment, she couldn't make out the haziest trace of what had been written.

Burning with curiosity, Emma checked every entry for 1796 and 1797 but couldn't find anything remotely enlightening. She finally put the books away and climbed down the stairs, chewing on her lower lip. She felt as though she was on the verge of discovering a new constellation, if only she could connect the stars together in their proper shape. At the moment she was confronted with a chaotic sky with no story to tell.

Also, very cold toes.

Rowanstone Academy was decidedly chilly once the fires went out in the grates. She slipped out of the library to seek the warmth of her own bed, and crashed right into another student. They both squeaked in alarm and Emma's lamp dipped dangerously low, nearly falling out of her grasp. The light slanted.

Sophie was pressed against the wall, her hand on her heart. She looked vaguely guilty. "You scared me to death."

"Likewise," Emma said through the beat of her pulse hammering in her throat.

"I thought you were Mrs. Sparrow." Sophie paused. "What are you doing down here?"

"I was in the library," she replied, also pausing. The door to the apothecary pantry was half-open behind her. The room inside had herbs and oils, jars filled with stones, ash, and water labeled with river names, huge barrels of salt, rope, and thread in every color, feathers, butterfly wings, dried rowan berries, and several strange things lurking in glass bottles. It was a witch's pantry, filled with ingredients for spells and charms. "Isn't that usually locked?"

Sophie glanced away. "Yes." When Emma just waited, she sighed. "I needed a few items." She pulled her other hand from behind her back. Emma's lamplight fell across a basket filled with toffees, salves in enameled boxes, and candied rose petals. From Sophie's red cheeks she'd expected stranger things, bat wings perhaps, or the eyes of toads. Two things, it should be said, she sincerely hoped never to have to touch. "We've gathered in the yellow parlor. Why don't you join us?"

Emma followed Sophie up the stairs, the wooden floorboards creaking under their slippers. The yellow parlor was a small, rarely used room tucked away at the end of the hall, near the servant stairs. It was also the farthest from any of the teachers' bedrooms. And it was filled with girls, some in nightgowns and others in ball gowns. She knew only a few of them by name. They were sitting around Jane Callendish, who was slumped on a settee under layers of shawls and wet handkerchiefs. She looked as though she'd been crying for hours. Her eyes were bloodshot and swollen, and the tip of her nose was red.

Daphne was the first to notice Emma. She, of course, was wearing a white silk gown trimmed with silver beads. Sapphires glittered in her hair. "What's she doing here?"

"I invited her," Sophie replied with her gentle smile, setting the basket on a side table. "We ran into each other in the hall. Quite literally."

"I'm not convinced we can trust her. She's a Lovegrove, after all," Daphne said. "And everyone knows their magic doesn't work quite right."

"Oh, Daphne." Sophie winced. "Don't be rude."

"Let her stay," Jane sniffled. "I need all the magic I can get."

"Jane's father sent word earlier this evening that he's officially signed her betrothal contract to Charles Fulcrum," Sophie explained as Emma sat on the rug, tucking her toes under the hem of her nightdress. Someone's familiar, a tiny burrowing owl, hopped across the rug to stare at her.

"And you don't care for him?" She hazarded a guess, considering the state of Jane's handkerchief and the piles of half-eaten sweets in front of her.

"I don't know!" Jane wailed. "I've never even met him!" Her blond hair was damp on her cheeks. She ate another handful of toffees. "My life is over!"

"I think you're lucky." Lilybeth fluttered. "Your Season has barely begun and you've already had an offer of marriage! My oldest sister had four Seasons and not a single offer. She's twenty-two now and my mother's given up hope for her altogether."

Emma remembered her Aunt Mildred's incensed speech about being unmarried and dependent on her brother's goodwill. Was it any better to be dependent on a stranger one's parents had picked out? A husband controlled his wife's property, her access to her own dowry, and even what she could buy in the shops if he wished it. Emma shifted uncomfortably. Her own father would be hoping to do exactly as Jane's had.

"My parents knew each other for years," Catriona said. "And my mother still throws the dinner plates at his head." She shrugged. "Anyway, you won't die at his hand." The girls sitting around her edged away. She just smiled benignly and helped herself to one of the stolen cakes.

"She's right," someone else said. "There are no guarantees either way."

"And would you rather become an ape leader?" Lilybeth shuddered.

"I don't like that term." Another student frowned at her. "We shouldn't call one another names."

Daphne rolled her eyes. "Spinster then, whatever. The reality is the same. Women who don't get married are ridiculed and pitied, unless they have wealth or power." Her expression hardened. "And I have no intention of being pitied."

Lilybeth shook her head. "I want to get married."

Jane wept harder. Sophie patted her shoulder. "Let's begin the ceremony," she suggested. "It will make you feel better."

"What ceremony?" Emma asked as the other girls slid off their seats to sit cross-legged on the floor.

"There's a secret tradition for girls about to be married," Sophie explained as she helped Jane sit on an embroidered cushion in the center of the circle. "Rose-petal candies for beauty, and other little charms to help her in her new life."

"So she'll know true love," one of the girls sighed. "The

rose petals will make certain Charles finds her the most beautiful of all. It's so romantic."

"It's about power," Daphne said firmly. "Just as I said before."

The ritual was simple but it seemed to give Jane comfort. The air smelled like sugar and beeswax and the candlelight was so soft it looked like honey. Lilybeth smeared rose oil on Jane's forehead and hands, saying, "So that Charles always looks on you and smiles."

Sophie fed her a spoonful of honey. "So he speaks of you sweetly."

Daphne held up a small hand mirror painted with an image of Artemis holding a bow with a nocked arrow. "So that you remember who you are," Daphne said. Jane looked at her own reflection silently.

"Did you bring the portrait?" Daphne asked.

Jane pulled the gold chain she wore over her head, revealing the small cameo on the end. "I had that strange old man at the goblin markets carve it for me last month when my father first brought up the possibility of Charles Fulcrum."

"Good," Daphne approved. "My father says his work is uncanny."

Jane ran her thumb over the cameo. The white shell gleamed on a smooth background painted red. Charles had a long nose, tousled hair, and a shy smile, if the carving was anything to go on. "I suppose he's handsome enough. I might grow to love him, if he's kind."

"He'll be kind," Daphne said forcefully. "We'll make sure of it."

Emma watched as Jane pulled a hair from her head and wrapped it tightly around the cameo. She added a length of red thread. "She'll soak it in honey and bury it under a rosebush," Sophie whispered to her. "It's supposed to ensure that she has a happy marriage."

"We have little enough say over our own lives," Daphne pointed out, as if she thought Emma would protest. "And even less once we become wives. This way, at least, we can protect ourselves, just a little bit."

The strangest part of the evening so far was that she actually agreed with Daphne on something. Gretchen would fly into a black mood if she ever found out.

"Is it time yet?" Lilybeth asked in a breathless voice, as though she'd been patiently waiting for a Christmas present.

Jane wiped the salt from her tears off her cheeks with the back of her hand. "I suppose so."

The silence the girls had held during the small ceremony shattered. They whispered and giggled and shifted excitedly. "Now what's happening?" Emma asked Sophie uneasily. She wasn't used to so many girls in the first place, never mind when they all giggled together. It was slightly disconcerting.

"They say a woman on her betrothal night and on the night before her wedding is especially able to predict the future husbands of unmarried girls."

The other students painstakingly wrote names on scraps of parchment and folded them up. They were dropped onto a silver tray, the kind butlers used to bring the calling cards of visitors to the lady of the house. Everyone stood up. Emma did the same, feeling decidedly nervous.

Jane pulled a folded square of parchment from the platter. "Percival MacTavish."

She spun on her heel, the way Emma and her cousins had done when they were little to make themselves dizzy. She stopped without opening her eyes and pointed to a girl with long brown hair and freckles on her nose. She gasped, clutching her fingers in excitement. Her friends hugged her as if she'd just received an actual proposal of marriage.

"Tobias Lawless."

She turned and turned, but when she stopped, her hands remained at her side. She opened her eyes, shaking her head. "No one here."

Several girls sighed, disappointed. Tobias was handsome for all that he rarely smiled. And he would be an earl one day. "He's frightfully choosy anyway," someone said, consoling herself out loud.

Jane read out another name. "Simon Watkin." She turned again, eventually pointing to Catriona. The white of her cheeks, her hair, and her nightdress made her look like moonlight. She blinked. "But I didn't even put a name in."

"All the same." Jane shrugged.

"I've seen his death," Catriona murmured. The girl next to her stepped away, wrapping her shawl tighter around her shoulders, as if Catriona's gift was contagious.

Jane just reached for another piece of parchment. She giggled. "This is the name of one of the footmen."

"Yes, but a handsome one," someone replied with a smug smile.

Jane closed her eyes and dutifully spun around again. Emma wondered if she was getting nauseated. She stopped and shrugged. "No one's going to marry the footman."

"That's all right." The girl who'd put in his name grinned wickedly. "I actually only want him to kiss me."

"There's a spell for that," someone else suggested, grinning just as wickedly.

"One more circle, Jane," Daphne interrupted, watching her carefully, like a hawk circling over a field. Emma wondered whose name she'd put in. Jane reached for the last three pieces of parchment.

"Cormac Fairfax." She flicked open the other two and laughed. "They all say Cormac Fairfax."

Emma hadn't written down a name. Three other students had entered Cormac into the pile. For some reason, the thought made her cheeks flames and her back teeth grind. Which was ridiculous. He wasn't the one for her, he'd made that plain. And he'd obviously been kissing as many girls as the gossips claimed, to have his name written down three times.

Jane twirled and twirled. The candles flickered. Emma's breath clogged in her throat.

Jane stumbled to a stop.

Slowly, so slowly, she raised her arm. Her finger extended, pointing to Daphne.

Daphne smirked, catching Emma's eye.

Jane, however, kept turning.

She pointed again, this time to two girls Emma didn't know. After one last circle, she pointed again.

This time, it was directly at Emma. She jumped, as though she'd been physically prodded. Her witch knot tingled.

"I'm sorry," Jane said finally, opening her eyes. "I just don't know who will marry Cormac."

Chapter 32

Emma went from learning to maneuver with antlers on her head to maneuvering the social pitfalls of a betrothal supper attended entirely by witches.

Since both Jane and Charles were from witching families, this first celebration had a very select list of guests: the kind of people who wouldn't faint if Emma's glamour accidentally slipped and she took a turn about the room wearing antlers. And to think, not so long ago she'd worried about being a wallflower.

"Quit fidgeting," Daphne snapped when they paused, waiting to be announced. They'd ridden together in the school carriage, equipped with more outriders armed with muskets and swords than a group of schoolgirls usually warranted. Daphne lost no time in telling them it was because she was the daughter of the First Legate of the Order and her father always saw to her safety. "Mind you don't tread on my hem when we go in."

"How about your head?" Gretchen shot back. "Can I tread on that?"

The butler, luckily, chose that moment to interrupt.

"Lady Daphne Kent, daughter of the First Legate."

Daphne's entrance was graceful and well rehearsed. The candlelight gleamed on the silver beaded flowers on the hem of her gown and the pearls woven into her hair. She glided between rows of orange trees decorated with crystal teardrops. An orchestra played softly on an upstairs balcony. The ballroom was beautiful, filled with silk gowns and diamond necklaces and cravat pins.

But now that Emma could see past the magical glamours, she noticed details she was amazed had remained hidden for so long. How did one not notice a glowing turquoise-and-green peacock, for instance? Even if it was someone's familiar and made mostly of magic. Above, several glowing doves circled the room between the glittering candelabras. A cat, two hedgehogs, and the sound of a horse outside in the rosebushes weren't the only indication that this was no ordinary event.

For one thing, a waterfall of sparkling water cascaded from the railings of the gallery, dissipating into sparkles and tendrils of mist where it braided into rivers of fire from a glittering candelabra, spelling out Jane's name. She stood below, smiling prettily, and looking nothing like a girl who'd recently eaten three handfuls of toffee while weeping that her life was over.

Daphne greeted her with a curtsy, before she and Sophie

and Lilybeth smiled at a group of Ironstone students, drawing their attention. Some of the focus was pulled away again, however, when the cousins were announced.

"Lady Penelope Chadwick, Lady Gretchen Thorn, and Lady Emma Day."

By the time Emma's name reverberated through the ballroom, everyone had turned to stare.

"Are my antlers showing?" Emma whispered, turning her Fith-Fath ring frantically on her finger. It was the first time she'd been out in such a crowd with her antlers.

"No," Penelope assured her out of the corner of her mouth.

"Blast," she said. "So it's just me?"

"Mother warned me this might happen." Penelope winced. "Witches or not, it's still polite society. And they love a good scandal. You've seen how they still look at Mother."

"This doesn't feel particularly polite," Emma muttered, lifting her chin. Still, she'd faced the magisters on the ship, she could face this. She couldn't help but scan the guests for Cormac but didn't see him anywhere. She wondered who else was searching the crowd, hoping for a glimpse of those dark eyes and that wicked smile.

"Well, come on," Gretchen said, marching them forward as though they were about to take on Napoleon's army. "Let's get this over with."

"Is that them?"

"Which one's the mad witch's daughter?"

"The red-haired one, has to be."

"Oh yes," Emma said drily, as gossips tracked their progress around the edges of the room. "This is so much better than being ignored as a wallflower."

Penelope grinned. "I'm half-afraid Gretchen is going to stab that old man with his own cane. You just know she's picturing it as a sword."

Emma had to grin back. Let them stare and whisper behind their hands. She could only feel sorry for them, without friends such as her cousins. They made their curtsies to Jane, who studiously avoided meeting Emma's eyes, and then hurried off to the refreshment table.

"I wonder where the library is," Gretchen said.

"I wonder if there are any handsome young men willing to dance a waltz?" Penelope added hopefully.

"I wonder if we can hide under the tablecloth," Emma put in.

Their hiding spot was slowly but surely encroached upon, until they stood with their backs against the turquoise silk-papered walls, surrounded by curious guests. Gretchen snarled and Penelope smiled at all of the young men. Emma held up her painted fan to cover as much of her face as possible. It helped her feel less exposed. As the questions grew more numerous and less polite, Gretchen eased along the wall, shoving Emma gently, who in turn had to press against Penelope or risk toppling over. Daphne was pouting on the edge of the crowd, narrowing her eyes as the young men abandoned her and her friends to catch a glimpse of the daughters of the Lovegrove sisters.

"Tell me," an elderly duchess asked Penelope, "will your mother be making an appearance?"

"No, I'm afraid not, Your Grace."

The duchess sniffed. Penelope's smile slipped, turning slightly feral at the edges. By the time the duchess turned to Emma, there were silvery spiders crawling up Penelope's dress. She squeaked when she saw them, smacking at herself with her fan.

"They're not real," Emma reminded her gently.

"They're still spiders."

It took another three quarters of an hour before Gretchen found an opportunity to save them all. "Quickly!" She shoved her cousins through the French doors and into the gardens.

"Why did you do that?" Penelope asked, stumbling against the stone balustrade. "I was finally talking to someone I was hoping would ask me to dance. He looked sturdy."

Gretchen rolled her eyes. "You don't need a sturdy dance partner," she said. "You need one with a brain in his head."

They went down the steps, crossing into the formal gardens. The stone paths wound around yew hedges whose shapes changed from swans to unicorns. "Illusion charm," Gretchen said, touching her ear with a wince. "Though it would work better with fewer poppy petals in it."

"Is your head hurting?" Emma asked, concerned.

"Not hurting, exactly. But there's a strange buzz when I'm around magic that isn't quite right. It stops when the magic clicks together properly like a puzzle. Apparently as a Whisperer, I can create new spells and fix old ones so they work better."

"Like a doctor of magic?" Penelope asked.

"I suppose." She wrinkled her nose. "According to Mrs. Sparrow it's very rare."

"Does she shout 'Control!' at you until you go cross-eyed?"

Emma asked sympathetically. "I swear she starts and ends every sentence she says to me with that caution."

"She'd make a decent general in the army," Gretchen agreed. "I vow, we haven't had a moment to ourselves since we were tossed into the academy. Have you burned at the stake lately, Penelope?"

"Happily, no. But I don't take off my gloves anymore if I can help it. I accidentally brushed against the edge of a painting in the gold parlor at Rowanstone and I was suddenly a footman with blisters on his heels and a bad belly from Stilton cheese." She sighed. "I was hoping to see something more romantic."

"Have you heard from your father, Emma?" Gretchen asked.

She shook her head. "No."

"Blighter."

She choked out a laugh. "I don't think you're allowed to call earls names."

"Bah. Godric will be earl one day and I fully intend to keep calling him names. Especially now." She lowered her voice, sounding worried. "He's drinking rather a lot."

"He's seventeen and home from Eton," Penelope pointed out. "It's expected."

"Even so." She worried at her lower lip. "It's different. He's not as cheerful and you know Godric, he's always cheerful, even when *Maman* is flitting about him. This ghost thing has him discombobulated." She absentmindedly tugged on one of the hedges. A green leafy swan nipped at her fingers. She pulled back sharply. "Ow, that's rude. Even for a magic bird."

"I'm sure he'll get used to it," Emma said. "After all, I'm

getting used to the antlers." She froze, groaning. "Daphne's on her way over here. That can't be good."

"Into the hedges!" Gretchen exclaimed.

"No use, she's just spotted us."

"At least she looks like a cat on bath day," Gretchen added smugly. "She can't stand sharing the attention of all those people."

"She can have it," Emma snorted.

"There you are," Daphne announced. Sophie and Lilybeth trailed behind her. "Everyone's talking about you. I supposed no one's asked you to dance though."

"Nor you," Penelope pointed out, nettled because it was the truth. "Or else you wouldn't be out here bothering us, would you?" Sophie, safely behind Daphne, hid a smile.

"We've decided it's time you proved yourselves to us," Daphne said.

Emma rolled her eyes. "As if we care about that."

"All the Rowanstone girls have to prove themselves," Lilybeth said, sounding shocked that the cousins weren't leaping to do their bidding. "I had to eat spelled iced cakes and they gave me feathers instead of hair for an entire week! And Sophie had to sneak down into the apothecary pantries to steal the rose-petal candies for Jane."

"And now it's your turn," Daphne declared with a brittle smile. "Unless you're too scared."

"Scared is it?" Gretchen snapped, instantly defensive. Emma and Penelope exchanged glances.

"If you're not scared, then you'll sneak out right now and

visit the House." When they didn't react, Daphne sighed. "The Greymalkin House. Really, where did you three even grow up?"

"You want us to leave the ball altogether?" Penelope said blandly. "How surprising."

"The house is near the Park. Turn left, then right. It won't take you long. Simply pick a flower from the other side of the gate."

"After which you send Keepers to chase us down?" Emma asked. "No, thank you."

"We'll tell them you're in the ladies parlor, fixing Penelope's hem," Sophie assured them, looking uncomfortable. Emma really couldn't figure out why she'd chosen Daphne and Lilybeth as friends. She seemed far too amiable for their schemes. "This isn't about getting you into trouble, truly. It's tradition, that's all."

"It's tradition that Daphne is put out because no one is paying her any attention." Penelope rolled her eyes.

Daphne tossed a curl over her shoulder. Her emerald earrings glittered. "I told you they wouldn't have the courage."

"Is that so?" Gretchen asked tightly. She nodded once, with military precision. "Right. Let's go." And then she vanished through the shrubbery, slapping at the mercurial hedges as she went.

"Oh honestly," Emma muttered as she and Penelope followed her. "I wish, just for once, she could let a dare pass her by."

Chapter 33

It was strange to be walking out at night, even in Mayfair. Girls were only allowed to shop, or walk in Hyde Park, during the day and always while trailing footmen or maids. Even distrusting Daphne's motives, there was something freeing about the feel of the wind on Emma's arms and the sturdy pavement under her shoes. The gas lamps flickered above, half shrouded in the thick clinging London mist.

"Where do we turn right, do you think?" Emma wondered. The lanes between the houses were private mews for stabling horses and the first street led to a cul-de-sac. They kept walking.

"I think we've arrived," Penelope finally said, sounding strangled. She stopped to stare down the street. "What's that?" She shivered. Emma and Gretchen also stopped to stare.

The house was faded, with peeling gray paint and a broken

shutter that stuttered loudly against the wall. A black iron gate heavily decorated with scrollwork and a magpie design in the center enclosed the wilted garden. Even the shadows were gray, clinging like mold to every surface. "Why haven't we ever noticed that house before?" she wondered. "It's positively dismal."

They waited for a lone carriage to pass before stepping off the curb to cross the street. This had been the fashionable neighborhood before Mayfair. The houses had a certain faded elegance, still beautiful in a way the Greymalkin House wasn't. It had been lovely once, when it was full of warlocks, but now only the bones remained along with the taint of neglected spells. Wilted and scrubby plants pushed through the fence.

"Let's get it over with then," Emma said, reaching for a vine of green leaves with curling tendrils and red berries. It was covered in a fine layer of dust or mold, she couldn't be sure. She was just glad she was wearing gloves, even if they would be ruined. She'd barely brushed against it when some kind of dark energy traveled through the fence. She could have sworn that a ghostly hand clamped around her wrist. It seared through her, bruising and burning through her gloves.

It wouldn't let her go.

It pulled until she was slammed painfully against the iron scrollwork.

"Something's got me!" Emma squawked. Gretchen and Penelope tried to drag her away. The push and pull made her bones hurt. She felt some insidious magic traveling up her arms, weakening her. Her visions went gray.

Gretchen and Penelope gave such a mighty pull, she was ripped away. It was exactly like an arrow being pulled out of her, sharp and scorching in its agony. The momentum flung her back and she stumbled off the sidewalk onto the uneven cobblestones. A carriage bore down on her, horses whinnying shrilly. The coachman yelled. But even with such brief contact, the magic of the house had sapped her. She couldn't seem to react quickly enough. Gretchen was sprinting toward her, looking terrified.

Someone yanked her out of the way.

Cormac glowered down at her, his dark hair falling over one eye. One very infuriated eye.

"Thank you," Emma said as the last of the draining magic faded. She shivered, feeling ill.

"Are you crazy?" he demanded. "It's not safe out here. Shouldn't you be at the academy?"

"We were at a nearby betrothal ball actually," she replied as Gretchen and Penelope swarmed around her. "What are you doing here?"

"Patroling for the Order," Cormac replied.

Gretchen frowned, half stepping in front of Emma. "You're not hauling her off again. Even if you did just save her life." Her familiar walked out of her body, a massive wolfhound with fur like hoarfrost and teeth like icicles. It growled.

Cormac only shook his head, disgusted. "Did no one tell you?"

"Tell us what?" she asked.

"The Greymalkin Sisters are roaming London and there are

still too many unmarked gates to the Underworld unleashing all manner of undead creatures."

"If it's so dangerous why wouldn't they say so?" Though now she wondered if the armed outriders on that carriage had less to do with Daphne's father's station and more to do with all the magic apparently whipping around London.

"They probably didn't want to worry you, seeing as the first victim was a debutante."

"Daphne didn't seem too worried when she dared us to come out here," Gretchen pointed out.

Cormac shook his head. "Are students still daring each other to come here? I was egged on to scale the gate when I was fifteen."

"What happened?" Emma asked.

"Virgil Clarkson broke my True Sight charm as I was climbing it. I couldn't see the gate anymore and I got disoriented and fell and cracked my head. He probably saved my life, in the end. Witches have died trying to break the wards." He ran a hand over his face. "You were bloody lucky all you got was a shove."

Penelope was still staring at the house. "I still don't understand how we never saw it before."

"It's cloaked and shielded under several layers of strong magic. Both inside and outside," Cormac replied. "Regular people only see a patch of weedy lawn or a house they don't care to approach. I'd forgotten you'd have been like them all this time." He cast the house a wary glance, searching for danger. "No one can get any closer than those gates."

"I don't think I'd *want* to get any closer."

"And the Greymalkin just live here in the open?" Emma asked, stunned. "And no one's done anything about it?"

"Of course they have. The house was abandoned some years back when the last known Greymalkin lived in London. The Order tried everything they could to get inside, or at least bring it down. Fires won't catch. Someone tried a cannon once but that only took out two carriages on the road. The house wards are too strong, even now."

"Wouldn't the Sisters use the house?"

"There are Keepers on watch, of course, but they haven't been spotted here." He shrugged. "Regardless, we've been at a standstill for decades. The wards prevent Keepers from getting in to dismantle the place, but because of the Order's own wards, the Sisters can't either. It's mostly just left to rot now."

The sky broke in half with a clap of thunder. Emma paused. "That wasn't me."

"No, it's fireworks," Gretchen said, looking down the street. The sky over the Callendish house was full of colors. Vibrant purples and reds and a silvery white streaked across the stars. The fog parted, going pink at the edges.

"I've never seen fireworks like those," Penelope breathed, as the sparks formed into the shape of two doves, chasing each other over the rooftops. "Even after the victory at Trafalgar."

Red bursts of light turned into hearts, shooting arrows off in every direction.

"Magic," Cormac said as strange-smelling smoke wafted toward them, like fennel and burning salt. He turned deliberately away from the miserable house. His arm brushed Emma's.

Gargoyles stared down from corners and towers. "Let me escort you back."

Once they'd left the oppressive atmosphere of the Greymalkin House, the tension left his shoulders and his gaze stopped snapping onto every shadow. "Shouldn't you at least be clutching me out of fear?"

She turned to look at him. "Why?"

"It's terribly dark, even with the fireworks."

She tilted her head. "I'm not afraid of the dark, Cormac."

He sighed theatrically. "But girls clutch at me out of fear all the time. Apparently I am a great defender against bees, spiders, moths, and suspicious-looking scones."

"They just want you to kiss them," she pointed out practically.

"Don't you want me to kiss you?" he asked, too softly for the others to hear.

Her cheeks burned. She hoped the glamour hid them as well as her antlers. "You've already kissed me," she said.

"Yes." He slanted her a sidelong glance, some of the teasing flirtation fading. The fireworks flashed above them, gilding his beautiful and inscrutable face. "I have, haven't I?"

She wasn't sure how to respond.

Instead, she hurried ahead to walk with her cousins. The pale columns and tall lampposts of Mayfair loomed around them, and music and candlelight poured out into the street.

"He likes you," Penelope remarked softly.

"Don't be ridiculous," Emma scoffed though the idea warmed her belly in a way she'd never admit out loud. She remembered Jane pointing at her. She bit down on the inside of her cheek hard to curtail her wild and inappropriate thoughts. Jane had pointed at a lot of other girls as well. "My own father doesn't care for me, Penny," she added quietly. "So why should Cormac?"

"Because your father is an ass," Gretchen put in firmly.

"And because I can tell that he does," Penelope said.

"You don't have any more experience with boys than I do, a few stolen kisses notwithstanding," Emma pointed out.

"I read books," Penelope said, matter-of-factly. There was no better argument in her mind. "So I can tell." She nodded to where Daphne was scowling at them from the garden as they turned down the Callendishes' lane. "And she can too."

Chapter 34

Later that night, Emma found herself in the library again.

She wandered along the shelves and the upper balcony, searching out mentions of her mother and the elusive Ewan. Whoever the man in Windsor Forest had been, he was important to her mother. He had to have been for her to store her memory of him inside a charm. Perhaps he had been her first love. Emma thought of Cormac because she couldn't help herself. She simply had to stop wondering if he felt the same tingling awareness of her as she did with him.

He'd kissed her.

He'd also run away through the dark garden cursing under his breath.

But the kiss had been worth it.

She really had to concentrate on something other than the way he smiled at her when no one else was looking. She frowned.

Maybe he was ashamed of her. After all, she did have antlers in her hair instead of diamond pins.

She was doing it again. Thinking about Cormac was not helpful.

Mind you, sorting through volumes and volumes on the history of witching families, divination, and old spells involving beetle parts wasn't particularly helpful either.

Still, Emma read until she was yawning wide enough to make her eyes water.

And until she heard a soft sound, a combination between a hiss and a draft of frigid air. She drew her feet up and peeked under the table for a wandering snake-familiar. There was nothing. She uncrossed her legs. If she was tired enough to be hearing noises then she was too tired to be making any sense of the books in front of her. Best to put them away and try again tomorrow.

It wasn't until she'd blown out the lamp that she heard it again.

Shivering, she stood slowly, trying to see into the shadows. She could smell the smoke off the lamp's extinguished wick. It would take too long to light it again. Her neck prickled, feeling vulnerable. Rain and mist pressed at the nearest window.

And the Keeper's face.

His cheek pushed painfully against the glass, his eye rolling with panic. His fingers scrabbled at the pane, leaving streaks in the fog. Emma shoved open the windows and rushed to drag him inside. He fell over the sill, sprawling on the carpet. There was sand on his cracked, sunburned lips and in his eyelashes, but his clothes were wet with rain.

"Ghoul," he croaked. "Get help."

She hovered indecisively. "I can't just leave you alone."

"It won't want me anymore," he wheezed. His iron-wheel pendant was burned black. "It'll want you now."

The ghoul slipped in through the open window. He was gray as old ashes. Sand scattered from the hem of his black robes. His hands were coated in grave dirt and when he smiled at Emma, his teeth were dark with congealed blood. Severed fingers were tied on a string around his neck.

"Bollocks to that," she squeaked, leaping over one of the tables. She crashed into a chair, sending it falling against another chair. They both clattered loudly to the ground as she leaped into the dark hall. The ghoul drifted through them, licking his rotted lips. Mrs. Sparrow's cat wandered off the servant stairs, saw the ghoul and hissed, every hair on end like needles. It vanished instantly.

Emma skidded on her bare feet as she bolted down the hall toward the ballroom. It was full of weapons and she needed something sharp and pointy. Anything sharp and pointy. She stumbled toward the broken targets and grabbed the first thing she found. An arrow, a handful of evil-eye rings, and a jar of salt on the floor. She threw the jar, scattering salt and broken glass. The ghoul's lips lifted off his teeth in a snarl. The smell of burning ghoul was no more pleasant than the smell of wet ghoul.

And from the bloodcurdling scream upstairs, she guessed he wasn't alone.

But Emma was.

He closed in, eyes crusted with dirt. A maggot crawled out of his ear. Emma gagged. She waved the arrow, feeling foolish. She'd need something considerably more impressive to scare him off. Especially when three more ghouls joined him, coming in from the window, their eyes a sickly, jaundiced yellow. A sudden wind whipped through the room, shaking the mirrors and the weapons in the racks. Hail pelted off Emma, stinging her bare arms. Lightning seared the sky, flashing off ghoul eyes and teeth.

Emma harnessed the fear curdling inside her, and pushed it out, turning it into rain, hail, snow, more wind. She focused until the storm shook the chandeliers, pulled sconces from their fastenings, and scattered the assorted debris of magical charms. She forced it to spin, pointing her finger and twirling it. She visualized the whirlwind with such certainty there was no room for failure.

Lightning hit the house so violently Emma was tossed into the wall. She slumped to the ground, breathless.

The ghouls continued to advance even though the storm tossed every available object at them. First salt, then the iron wall sconces, rowan berries, daggers, and then an entire tea cart full of china cups. The weapons clanked together uselessly, one of the bows on the wall snapping. An arrow finally found a target, piercing one in the eye. The other ghouls hissed and snarled, desert heat blasting off them. Their teeth were sharp and rust-colored, stained with old blood.

Emma was growing tired. The hail had long since stopped. She tried for snow and it made them hiss louder but she couldn't sustain it. Keeping her back to the wall, Emma tried to run for the nearest window. She knew she couldn't reach the door.

Just as she was beginning to think she wouldn't make it, Mrs. Sparrow rushed into the ballroom, looking like a proper storybook witch with her white-streaked black hair loose and wild, and waving an iron poker like a spear. There was blood on her nightdress. She narrowed her eyes and the ghouls shrieked, grabbing at each other. They stumbled together drunkenly and then fell together in a heap, asleep. There was the snap of a leg bone.

The winds died so abruptly, it rained sand, iron nails, and daggers. Emma's harsh gasps echoed loudly.

"Were you bitten?" Mrs. Sparrow asked sharply.

"No." Emma blinked rapidly. "Is that what they do? That's vile."

"They're cannibals," Mrs. Sparrow said, brisk headmistress again. "Fascinating, really. Though I prefer to study them far from my school. One of the open gates must have been near a graveyard. They don't usually stray too far." She looked at them with distaste. "We haven't much time. Ghouls don't sleep naturally so my magic won't hold them for very long." One of them was already twitching, thick fingernails tapping the floor. The sound sent shivers down Emma's spine.

"I thought this school had protective wards."

"It does," Mrs. Sparrow replied grimly. Emma decided that she would not like to be on the receiving end of whatever punishment her headmistress was devising. The glint in her eye alone was enough to draw blood.

A Keeper marched into the ballroom, followed by a student from the Ironstone school. His knuckles were white around the handle of the sword he held. "We'll take it from here, Mrs. Sparrow," the Keeper announced.

"You will not," she said mildly but implacably.

He blinked. "Pardon?"

"Fat lot of good you were tonight," she said. "One of my girls was bitten."

"We'll have her restrained." He paled. "There's no cure."

"I am aware. We'll take care of her. As we'll take care of this." She speared the young man with a look that had him gulping. Emma had no doubt he was remembering every scolding he'd ever received from governesses, grandmothers, and nursemaids. "You'll stay and watch. You might learn something." She turned to Emma. "You'll destroy the ghouls."

"What?" If that crazy old woman thought she was going to hack and stab at three twitching ghouls, she was dead wrong. She'd never seen or smelled anything more disgusting.

"Ghouls can only be killed with fire," Mrs. Sparrow said. She could have been lecturing a class for all the anxiety in her tone and posture.

"I don't have matchsticks," Emma replied.

"I can set a fire," the young man said helpfully.

"You'll stay where you are," Mrs. Sparrow told him. The Keeper grabbed his arm, shaking his head. "Do you think I want you burning the whole place down?" She pointed to Emma. "You have lightning."

She stared. "Only sometimes."

"And this is one of those times. Go on."

"Can't we just cut off their heads?" she asked, reevaluating her earlier opinions on the matter.

"Certainly not. Think of the mess."

Emma rubbed her suddenly damp palms on her nightdress. She had a feeling she was about to disappoint her headmistress horribly and embarrass herself in the process. Having a Keeper watching her did not help matters. It was hard to forget the feeling of that cage pressing down on her.

"Focus and breathe," Mrs. Sparrow advised, as she had with the Fith-Fath spell; which was an easier spell to cast and Emma still hadn't managed reliable results. "This is using your natural magic. There's nothing to do but be at one with yourself."

Which would have been remarkably easier before she'd learned about witchery.

And grown antlers.

The ghouls stirred, sand falling out of their mouths. The Keeper reached for his sword. Emma went to the window and lifted the glass to look up at the sky. She couldn't focus with monsters at her feet.

The clouds raced across the moon. She couldn't see any stars, but there was faint lightning in the belly of the darkest cloud. She stared at it, willing it to brighten and flash. Thunder rumbled.

"Now, Emma."

The lightning seared the clouds but stayed in the sky. Emma tried again, smelling the ozone and remembering the way it had hit the school earlier, shaking the walls. She'd managed it then, she could do it again. She took a deep breath.

A ghoul hissed behind her.

"*Now*, Emma!"

Lightning streaked, cracking tree limbs and setting leaves to smoldering. She leaped out of the way just as it flashed through the open window. It struck the ghouls and they hissed and twitched, robes and hair on fire. The smoke was oily and noxious. The lightning shattered the rest of the windows and burned their eyes. When their vision cleared, all that was left of the ghouls was a pile of sand turned to twisted glass and a proud headmistress.

"There are four more ghouls secured upstairs," she said to the Keeper. "You can bring them out into the garden. No sense in striking the house again if we can help it."

"Did that girl have horns?" Emma heard the student whisper as they rushed out.

"You did well," Mrs. Sparrow approved. "You didn't faint. And you're not hysterical. All in all, I'm rather impressed, even before you called the lightning." She nodded as they left the smoky ballroom for the gardens. "You might be as good as Daphne someday."

"I can't wait," Emma muttered.

Chapter 35

"The witching families of England have been holding the reins of power for centuries, though few know it, of course. Each family will have their own boasts, some of which must remain unsubstantiated and even more of which contradict each other. For instance, William Wallace's defeat of the English at the Battle of Stirling Bridge in 1297 was claimed by an ancient witching family of the Highlands. Conversely, Wallace's consequent capture and execution in 1305 was claimed by a family here in London. So you see . . ."

Mrs. Fergus was a very dull teacher, despite her rather eccentric appearance. She wore only green from the emeralds in her necklace to the ribbons on her shoes. Her morning dress was a dark forest green over a pale underdress in a more minty shade. She claimed to have had a dream on the night of her thirteenth birthday instructing her to wear only green for good luck and she had followed it to the letter these past thirty-two years. It did not signify that green did not flatter her in the least.

She droned on for another half an hour, until the door to the drawing room opened. The housekeeper poked her head in. "Mrs. Sparrow would like the girls who are attending the dancing lesson to know the carriages are ready."

The younger girls looked in awe as Emma, Gretchen, and Penelope gathered their belongings and left. Four carriages rolled away from the school, crowded with chattering students. The Duchess of Watford was hosting a morning dance lesson to give the girls a chance to practice before the annual Watford ball.

"Oh, blast," Gretchen muttered, spotting her mother in the ballroom, wearing an impressive day dress trimmed with French lace. Lady Wyndham's advice on etiquette was eagerly sought out by hostesses. Even Daphne looked impressed that she was present. Not for the first time, Gretchen wondered if she'd been accidentally switched at birth.

Lady Wyndham descended on them immediately, crossing the black-and-white checkerboard marble floor. The other students stayed together, staring at the footmen and maidservants working on the decorations. Baskets of greenery and pots of orchids waited to be distributed and the giant chandelier in the center of the ceiling had been lowered to replace the old candles. A dancing master stood at the very end of the enormous room, waving his hands at the man sitting at the pianoforte.

"Good morning, *Maman*." Gretchen sounded resigned.

"Good morning, girls. I trust you are ready to make me proud?"

"Only if Godric is learning to dance as well," Gretchen said, only half joking.

"All of the boys are," her mother said. "And they never give me half as much trouble as you do. I cannot understand why you insist on being contrary. You cannot possibly object to dancing."

"It's not the dancing, *Maman*. It's the boys with sweaty palms looking down my dress."

Lady Wyndham sucked in an offended breath. "You will keep your conversation pretty and polite." She looked at Penelope. "None of your gothic novels tonight, and none of your stars, Emma." She pointed at Gretchen, though the motion was not genteel. "And you will not set one foot inside the library, young lady."

"Oh, *Maman*."

She clapped her hands imperiously and the girls rushed to stand at attention. "Girls, the duchess has very kindly invited you here to practice your dancing. I trust I do not need to remind you to be discreet."

More girls arrived, none of them from Rowanstone. "Remember, girls," Lady Wyndham was saying. "You must show yourself to your best advantage at all times. You must be decorative and elegant and pleasant. Do not monopolize the conversation." She glanced pointedly at her nieces. "And do not display your intelligence too obviously, lest it intimidate your dance partner. You must have a care. Men are not as confident as they appear to be."

Gretchen rolled her eyes. "Then why aren't they working as hard to impress us? Why should it always fall to us?"

Lady Wyndham's nostrils flared. It was the only indication

that she was about to lose her temper. Her voice was cold and calm. "Napoleon has taken all of our young men, both proud and poor. They fight against him to keep us safe. The sad fact is, many will not return. They deserve our respect." She looked at each girl directly. "To put it plainly, there are more girls looking for husbands than there are men left to become husbands. Therefore, you must all be the prettiest and the most accomplished if you are to have any hope of success."

Daphne stood so straight, Lady Wyndham might as well have been a general in the army.

"I trust you do not need to be reminded that it is not acceptable to dance more than two dances with the same gentleman, however handsome he might be."

"Not even Cormac Fairfax." Someone giggled but Emma couldn't see who it was. Daphne's head turned sharply.

"Not even Lord Blackburn," Lady Wyndham corrected. "You may mark the following dances on your fan for this evening: the cotillion, the reel, and *la boulangere*."

"May we also practice the waltz, Lady Wyndham?" Lilybeth asked breathlessly.

"Certainly not," she replied. "Take your positions." She nodded curtly at the dancing master. "Begin."

The lessons went on for two hours, with Lady Wyndham interrupting the dance master with helpful proclamation such as: "We do not gallop, ladies. We *skip*." Even Gretchen found herself enjoying the exertion, though she never would have admitted it to her mother.

"The dancing master will be on hand to assist you," Lady

Wyndham announced when they stopped for lemonade. "And if you should feel lost during the ball, listen for him calling out the steps. He is there to make you look good." She nodded graciously. "You are dismissed."

"Quickly," Gretchen whispered to her cousins. "Let's make our escape before she notices."

They were near the doors when Lady Wyndham spoke again. "Gretchen a moment, if you please."

She froze, very much like a rabbit under the shadow of a hunter's hound.

"I am sending the dressmaker to you later this week, Gretchen. Don't forget."

Gretchen fancied she knew exactly how the rabbit felt just before it was eaten.

Chapter 36

The next day, Emma and Penelope went to Hyde Park. It was a rare bright London day without fog or the foul smell from the Thames tainting the air. Rotten Row was packed as always, with ladies in fine riding habits on horseback and gentlemen in cutaway coats and brimmed hats. On the other side of the riding track, painted and gilded carriages trundled by, filled with countesses and duchesses and their bored daughters eager to see and be seen. Emma and Penelope preferred to stay on foot, strolling over the lawns as the wind tossed the canopy of leaves, letting in more sunlight. They stopped to watch two carriages going far too fast in a race to see who would reach the oak tree around the corner. Just last year two people had died from a collision during such a race. Riders moved aside, grumbling. Money changed hands as bets were made as to the outcome.

"He's quite handsome," Penelope said, making a subtle motion with her head to point out the young man in question. He was leaning on the railing, watching the race. His pocket watch caught the sunlight. "Maybe he's my true love."

"Perhaps your true love is a portly old man with no hair on his head," Emma teased.

"Perhaps," Penelope replied, cheerfully. "So long as he doesn't mind an equally portly girl with a father in trade."

They meandered down the path, cutting away from the crowds and stopping to watch the ducks floating in the Serpentine. "I think we're being followed," Penelope muttered. "I was hoping that gentleman was eager to make our acquaintance, but now I think it's a Keeper. As if the footman wasn't enough."

Emma sighed, following her cousin's gaze. Behind their very polite footman a young man was walking toward them, looking nonchalant. It wasn't his pocket watch that had been gleaming but the chain of an iron-wheel pendant. "I suppose I shouldn't be surprised."

Penelope grinned mischievously. "He looks so severe. Shall we take him on a merry chase? And our very bored footman as well?"

"Let's."

They kept their pace steady and slow until they reached a curve in the walkway. Where it turned away from the water, disappearing into several small groves, they exchanged a quick grin and burst into a run. They flew through the grass, trailing bright laughter. Emma left behind ghouls and secrets and opened gates to the Underworld. There was only Penelope's hand in hers and the press of wind in their hair.

"Here he comes," Penelope exclaimed. "Oh, look at his face!"

They jumped over plants, nearly bowled down an elderly couple out for a stroll, and then ducked into the trees. Birds flew off their perches in a flurry of agitated feathers. They collapsed under a willow tree, giggling. Emma tucked a lock of hair back into the knot at her nape, listening for pounding footsteps or a warning shout. It was silly, but it made her feel better to have outrun a Keeper.

Not all of them were as easy to escape.

"Well, well."

Emma froze, shutting her eyes for a long moment. Penelope was grinning at her when she opened them again. "Lord Blackburn, how do you do?" her cousin asked, cheerfully unrepentant.

Emma turned around to face him. "Did the Order send you to follow us too?"

"You gave that poor man palpitations when you ran away," he answered, smiling easily. His navy coat perfectly set off the rich darkness of his hair and eyes. "I have to say, my Keeper duties rarely involve escorting two such lovely ladies as yourselves."

Emma lifted her eyes skyward. "Do stop flirting. You might hurt yourself."

"I am well practiced." He caught her hand in his, pressing a kiss to the back of her knuckles.

"I am aware," she said, her mouth quirking as she fought a smile. Even through her gloves she could feel the warmth of his lips. Penelope watched them as if they were a particularly fascinating play.

"It's never a hardship to escort two of the Lovegrove cousins," Cormac continued, still holding her hand. His thumb stroked the inside of her wrist, his left eyebrow rising in a perfect arch as he waited for her reaction.

"I need my concentration to hold the Fith-Fath spell," she said, snatching her hand back. Her fingers tingled. "If the glamour fades you'll be wandering the park with a wild deer-girl. Think of what it would do to your reputation."

"I can take it," he assured her. He glanced at Penelope who looked smug. "Aren't there always three of you?"

"Gretchen had to stay behind to learn embroidery," she explained, laughing out loud. "She was very seriously put out."

"She hates embroidery," Emma elaborated. "With a passion usually reserved for ball gowns and calves' foot jelly."

"Is there anyone who doesn't hate calves' foot jelly?"

"True. But apparently she needs embroidery skill for charms and spell bundles."

"While calves' foot jelly is good for nothing at all," Penelope added.

"I heard your cousin was a Whisperer."

"Yes. Are there male Whisperers as well?" Emma asked curiously.

"Certainly," he replied as they began to walk.

"And do *they* embroider?"

"Yes." He flashed a grin. "Yes, but only in secret."

"As long as it's fair and equal torture," Emma approved.

"I like embroidery," Penelope pointed out. "More's the pity."

Emma looped her arm through Penelope's. "Don't think for a moment Gretchen won't be needling you to do it for her."

"I know," she replied. "I don't mind."

They ducked out from the feathery branches and headed back to the path. The Keeper was red-cheeked and frantic, next to an equally concerned footman. "Easy, Thaddeus. I'll see the ladies safely home," Cormac told him.

He bowed stiffly at them and then stalked away. Penelope's lips quirked. "I don't suppose he'll ask me to dance now."

Cormac dismissed the panting footman as well, who left with a relieved smile.

"I *am* allowed off the grounds," Emma felt compelled to say.

"I know," Cormac returned easily. She'd noticed he always seemed more comfortable when there was no one else around. At the moment there was no one in sight. They were alone save for a rabbit eating dandelion leaves. "With the Sisters and the gates and now the ghouls, the Order is concerned for everyone's safety. They especially want Rowanstone students to be escorted."

At the mention of the gates, Emma felt another stab of guilt. She hadn't broken her mother's bottle on purpose, but she felt the weight of the ramifications all the same.

"I am but a glorified footman," he said with a twinge of bitterness. "But God and Country and all that rot."

"You sound rather cynical for a Keeper," Emma noted, intrigued despite her constant resolve to resist him. He shrugged one shoulder and let it fall, his easy smile returning. She was learning to recognize which of his charming smiles hid darker secrets and that was definitely one of them. His fingers brushed her as he walked beside her. The wind kicked up.

She glanced around, mortified. Did he know she was causing

the wind because she was nervous around him? Dust snapped the hem of her dress. The wind pushed harder. She frowned.

She wasn't *that* nervous.

The wind wrapped around her and gave her a great shove.

She remembered the last time she'd felt it do that.

"Oh no," she said, digging her heels into the grass. "Not again!"

There was no fighting the inexorable wind. Cormac and Penelope each took one of her arms but it only served to wrench them in their sockets. Cormac and Penelope let her go, doing their best to keep up. The trees tossed back and forth and the grass flattened around her, but the water of the Serpentine in the distance was still as a glass mirror.

Emma tripped over the foot of a girl half draped over the lower branch of an oak tree. Tiny icicles dripped from the bottom of her sleeve. Her lips were dusky blue with cold. She was utterly still, her eyes frozen wide open.

The wind died. Emma scrabbled backward. She met Cormac's eyes wildly, remembering vividly the last time she'd been dragged to a dead girl by a strange storm. Unlike Margaret York, this girl was dead before they found her.

And they weren't alone any longer in a wild corner of the park. They had an audience.

Worse still, it was Daphne.

Chapter 37

Daphne, Sophie, and Lilybeth hurried toward them, the flowers on their matching bonnets trembling with their shock. "We were waiting for our footman to secure us a boat when we heard someone shout," Daphne said, staring at the body in the tree.

A Keeper chased them from the path on the other side of the shrubbery. "Lady Daphne, wait!"

"Damn it," Cormac swore, stepping away from Emma so abruptly she stumbled. He wouldn't even look at her, when a few moments ago, she'd been sure he was about to hold her hand. "Virgil." He greeted the other Keeper with a stiff nod.

Virgil whistled through his teeth when he saw the body. He proceeded to puff up his chest and step in front of Daphne and her friends. "Nothing to be afraid of," he said pompously. "Your father himself asked me to protect you."

"Why do I keep stumbling over dead girls?" Emma asked

bleakly, her teeth chattering. She felt cold all over, like there was ice under her skin. Penelope rubbed her arms, trying to warm her.

"Yes, why is that exactly?" Daphne asked sharply.

Cormac took a pinch of the crushed apple seeds, quartz crystal, and mugwort herb he kept in his snuffbox and tossed it up. It hung suspended for a brief moment, before glittering into an arc of sparks to guide nearby Keepers to the spot.

"Oi, I can handle this," Virgil complained, though he'd yet to do more than glance at the body.

"You don't have the authority," Cormac relied blandly.

"And you don't have the magic."

Cormac's jaw clenched.

"And I see that though your sisters aren't here to save you this time, you're still hiding behind skirts," Virgil added with a sneer.

Emma decided right then and there that she didn't care for Virgil one bit. Thunder growled in the distance. Cormac shot her a quick, startled glance, before resuming his formal polite posture.

"Poor girl. Should we call for a doctor?" Sophie asked softly, her eyes very bright.

"It's too late for that, I'm afraid."

"Did she fall out of the tree?"

"I don't think so," Cormac said. "Do you recognize her? Is she Rowanstone?"

"She doesn't look familiar so I don't think she's a fellow student," Daphne replied. Shock made her skin shine like a pearl, sweat dampening her hair so that it slipped from its complicated updo. "And she's not dressed like society."

He crouched next to the body, frowning. She wore a simple dress in washed-out brown muslin and no jewelry. Her bonnet was made of straw with a few faded silk leaves. Her limp hand dropped, fingers uncurling. He stripped off her left glove while the others waited, breaths held.

The girl had a witch knot and it was altered, the ends unraveling.

"Greymalkin," Cormac confirmed. "What are these pin-pricks on her fingertips?"

Penelope leaned over gingerly for a closer look. "Those are from an embroidery needle," she said. "But to have that many? Even as a dressmaker's assistant, that's a lot."

"Are you sure that's what she is?"

"With those particular calluses and those pinpricks? Yes."

"You have the same marks when you embroider?"

"Not that many," Penelope shook her head. "Not all at once."

Daphne stepped closer to Cormac, glaring at Emma. "You found Margaret York as well, didn't you? Did you have some-thing to do with this as well?"

"I tripped over her." Emma replied, fuzzy with shock.

"I don't believe you," she said. "You're a *Lovegrove*. My father warned me about your family."

"Emma's not a murderer," Penelope said, incensed. "*We* just got here! It could just as easily have been your fault!"

Virgil looked as though Penelope had just slapped him. "I

was escorting these ladies and I can assure you they are most proper, gentle girls."

Daphne sucked in a breath. "And I'm telling my father you said that. He's the First Legate."

"We *know.*" Penelope shot back, unimpressed. "My father runs a brewery. So what? Emma still didn't do it. It's absurd for you to accuse her. And we just arrived," she added acidly. "With a *Keeper.* Don't you think if she *was* to blame, Lord Blackburn would have already secured her?"

"Blackburn's not much of a Keeper," Virgil put in, eyeing Emma suspiciously.

She narrowed her eyes at him. Lightning flashed in the perfectly clear spring sky. The crack of it hitting a tree made him jerk so violently he dropped his iron-wheel pendant. Daphne also jumped, looking pale. When Cormac offered her his arm, she took it with a grateful smile. He still wouldn't look in Emma's direction. She strongly considered bringing the lightning a little closer.

"Until the investigators arrive, we need to follow the trail before it grows cold."

"The Order has investigators?" Penelope asked.

"The Order has everything," Cormac replied without inflection.

"I can follow the blood curse," Daphne said briskly. "Lilybeth, stop *crying.*"

"But she's *dead.*" Lilybeth was moaning and squeezing Sophie's hand so tightly the other girl winced.

"Yes, and unless your tears have healing powers, they won't help. Now hush."

Daphne squinted at the girl and then at the ground all around them. She pointed her finger, following the trail.

The residue of magic traveled over the stones straight to Emma.

"I told you she was involved," Daphne said. Lilybeth looked like she might faint. Virgil stepped forward, reaching for Emma. Cormac shifted to stop him but Penelope was faster. She kicked him in the shin. Virgil squawked in pain, clutching his leg. Keeper or not, he wasn't sure how to proceed now. He was accustomed to girls who swooned and fluttered. Though, to be fair, Daphne was doing neither.

Penelope took off her glove, swallowing thickly. "Are you sure?" Emma asked her when she realized what she was doing.

She only nodded and reached out to touch the girl's arm. Penelope went faintly green.

"What do you see?" Emma whispered.

"Not her murder," Penelope assured her, sweat beading under her hair. "I can't control the flashes I get. I can only tell you that her name is Alice and she worked as a seamstress, as we thought. She sewed out in the street under the gas lamps at night." She shivered and opened her eyes. "That's all." She blinked several times. "Why do I taste leeks?"

Daphne was trying not to gag behind her gloved hand. "Blood curse."

"Oh. I can see it now too," she added, grimacing. "It does lead to you, Emma," she said apologetically. "But *also*," she said sharply before Virgil could react, "to Sophie and Lilybeth." She rubbed the spot between her eyes. "To all of us, actually."

Daphne's lips pursed. "It's everywhere," she admitted sourly, wiping her hands on her gown, as though the residue had left traces on her skin.

"How dreadful," Sophie murmured, just before her eyes rolled back in her head. Cormac caught her before she hit the ground. Lilybeth started to weep again. The investigator finally arrived, ducking under the concealing branches. He saw the body and cursed under his breath.

"Not another one," he said, looking sad and exhausted under the scars on his face. He snapped his gaze onto Cormac and Virgil before examining the girl. "Report."

"She's been marked," Cormac confirmed.

He sighed. "Damn." He paused, eyebrows lifting. "Lady Daphne. Are you hurt?"

"Not at all. Lord Blackburn has been with us the entire time. And Virgil, of course," she added when he went beet red with the need to be noticed.

"Good, good. How's your father?"

"Very well, thank you, Sir Reginald." She shot Emma and Penelope a smug glance.

Reginald squinted at Emma and Penelope. "I don't know you two."

"They're *Lovegroves*," Virgil said as though he were confessing that they were spies for Napoleon.

"Is that so?"

Emma and Penelope stepped closer to each other. Emma had no desire to be reacquainted with the magisters. "Actually, it's Lady Penelope *Chadwick*," Emma pointed out.

"And Lady Emma *Day*," Penelope added.

"I was with both these ladies and I can assure you they were not involved," Cormac said.

"How did you come to find the body?"

Emma swallowed. "A wind pushed me."

"A wind?" Reginald frowned at Cormac. "A harpy? No one mentioned any sightings recently." Harpies were strange bird-women who attacked with all the force of storm winds. They were local to Greece but occasionally traveled farther.

"No, sir. We detected no other creatures in the area. Lady Emma is a weather-witch."

"That still doesn't explain why the wind brought her here." He rubbed his chin, watching her thoughtfully. She tried not to squirm.

"I don't understand it either," she finally offered.

"Perhaps it's a simple matter of magic reacting to magic?" Cormac suggested. "After all, Lady Emma comes from a very powerful and ancient family. She may be more sensitive to magical undercurrents than we are."

"Than *you* are, certainly," Virgil snickered.

"That is not helpful," Reginald snapped.

"My apologies, sir."

"Hmm. See all the ladies home, would you, Blackburn?" Reginald ordered. "I'll speak to them again after I've had time to investigate the matter further."

"Certainly. We'll have to go on foot though."

Lilybeth shook her head frantically. "It's not safe. I'm not going. He doesn't even have any magic."

There was a strangled silence. Daphne nudged her hard. "I'm not afraid," she said.

"We have a carriage waiting at the end of Rotten Row," Virgil interrupted smoothly. "I can see Lady Daphne, Lady Lilybeth, and Lady Sophie back to the academy, but I'm afraid there isn't space for everyone else."

"Actually, we prefer Lord Blackburn's protection," Emma announced in ringing tones she hadn't quite meant to carry so far.

"Fine." He dismissed them curtly and turned to assess the victim.

Cormac, Emma, and Penelope began the walk through the park and back to the school. "What did she mean you don't have any magic?" Emma finally asked him, burning with curiosity. "You're a Keeper."

He didn't look at her but his expression was faintly mocking, almost bored. She knew he was hiding some darker emotion. "The Fairfax family has been a witching family since before the Battle of Hastings." The corner of his mouth lifted wryly. "Nearly as long as the Lovegroves." He shrugged. "But magic can skip generations, or individuals." He turned his left hand over to show her his bare unmarked palm.

"You don't have a knot."

"No. I joined the Order anyway, like every other Fairfax male. I had to train harder than everyone else. I still do. And I have to prove myself worthy every single day."

Emma made a face. "I'm beginning to know how that feels."

He snorted. "Sometimes magic's a harsh mistress."

"It's funny, isn't it?" she asked quietly.

"How do you mean?"

"Well, you were prepared for it and it skipped you. I had no idea it existed and I grew antlers."

"I think you're fetching with antlers."

She ducked her head slightly, blushing. When they reached the schools, Cormac bowed over their hands. "Ladies. It's been interesting." He waited until they were inside before he hopped over the decorative fence separating the two buildings and went up the path to Ironstone's front doors.

When Penelope followed Emma up the stairs, she paused. "What are you doing?"

"Do you really think I'm going to let you spend the night alone after what just happened?" Penelope shook her head. "Honestly, I'm insulted." She nudged Emma to keep climbing. "Come on, we can make a Greek temple out of our pillows like we used to when we were little. And chocolate," she asked from the maid they passed on the landing. "We're going to need a pot of chocolate." She tilted her head, considering. "Make that two."

"I wonder if magic is always like this," Emma said wryly. "Full of murders and ghouls and mean girls, and rules that don't make any sense."

"You know what my mother says about rules," Penelope replied, dragging her swiftly down the hall. "They only benefit the few with the power to make them in the first place."

"How is it that your artistic mother and Gretchen's proper mother are even related, never mind sisters?" Emma shook her head. She dropped into a chair. "Thank you, Pen. You were right. I don't want to be alone tonight."

"At least you don't kick like Gretchen."

"Or snore like you do," she teased.

"I don't snore!"

Chapter 38

"Pardon me, miss," a footman spoke from the doorway of the parlor. "A message has just come for you."

"For me?" Emma set down her book and took the hastily folded paper. It was ripped unevenly, and the message had been written crosswise against what appeared to be a recipe for lavender water. Definitely not from her father. Not that she'd expected him to write, but if he had it would have been on pristine parchment with a red wax wafer to seal his letter. "Who sent this?"

"Some boy who tried to nick a bag of potatoes from the kitchen. Cook was not pleased. He asked that it be taken to either you or your cousins." The footman bowed and left.

Emma held the paper up to the window where the sun was setting in a sky the color of tangerines. *"Hogarth's Print Shop off Piccadilly. Find Cormac. Hurry. Moira."*

She didn't know anyone named Moira. She stuffed the note in the pocket of her dress, mind racing. The name sounded familiar. Hadn't Gretchen and Penelope mentioned a girl named Moira from the day Cormac had sent them through the cellar door into the Serpentine?

Emma pounced on the first person she saw outside the library. "Have you seen Olwen?"

Daphne disengaged her sleeve from Emma's grasp, smoothing out the wrinkles she'd created. "I beg your pardon."

"Olwen," Emma repeated impatiently. "Have you seen her?"

"I believe she's in the garden, as usual," Daphne replied. "Why do you want to see Cormac's flighty little sister?"

Emma didn't reply, she was already bolting down the hall and into the gardens. She found Olwen tucked in a circle of lilac bushes. Her long pale hair was unbound as usual, reaching past her elbows. She was braiding daisies into a crown.

"Oh hello," she said to Emma. She had none of the insecurities and drama of the other girls; instead she seemed to float like a sleek ship between jagged icebergs.

Emma smiled a distracted greeting. "I need to find your brother. Do you know where he is?"

Olwen blinked. "Why?" Emma showed her the note. Olwen rose to her feet, her gentle eyes hardening. "Talia had a nightmare last night."

"Who's Talia?" Emma asked.

"One of our sisters," she replied. "She has premonitions. She said Cormac would need help before the moon rose." She dropped the circlet of flowers to take a scrap of parchment out of one of the many pouches on her belt. It was rolled into a little scroll. Opened, it was blank except for a few bits of periwinkle petals and stems.

"We don't have time to send a messenger to all of his usual haunts," Emma interjected.

"I know. This is a *tabula*." When Emma didn't look any more informed, she continued. "Most families make their own paper with a secret blend of ingredients. We can then use it to communicate with each other. There are magic mirrors too, but they are cumbersome." She pulled a stub of charcoal from another pouch and used it to scrawl Cormac's name plus the print shop. "Come with me."

Emma followed her out of the bushes and into the formal garden, along the box hedges and white gravel paths. Olwen stopped at one of the torches the footmen were lighting as the sun took the last of the honey-and tangerine-colored light with it. She held the end of the parchment into the flame and watched it burn, black smoke curling over their heads. "And now we wait for a reply," she said, pulling a larger scroll out of the first pouch. "The fire sends the message so it burns into the recipient's paper, or clothing." She made a face. "Occasionally into our skin as well," she admitted, rolling up her sleeve. On the inside of her elbow were faint scars, spelling out the words "*Where are you?*" "I walk the gates. Trouble is, I don't always know when or where I'm going yet. It takes a while to learn how to control it."

Emma thought of the rain that soaked her every time she became slightly emotional. "Yes," she agreed. "It certainly does."

She glanced at the spiraled horn dagger on Olwen's belt. "Is that why you wear that dagger?" She'd never seen the younger girl without it. She even wore it strapped to her ankle during comportment lessons when all they did was climb in and out of carriages, trying not to flash a glimpse those same ankles. It was the most tedious class by far, but their teacher insisted that witches were ladies too and needed to retain their place in polite society.

"It's made from unicorn horn," she explained. "Mostly, I'm welcome in the Faery lands." She shrugged. "But sometimes I'm not. And this is one of the only weapons that can be used against the Fae and dark magics . . . here we go," she interrupted herself, and lifted the underside of her hem. Fascinated, Emma watched words burning into the thin fabric. They wrote themselves as though Cormac was right there holding the quill. "*On my way.*"

"Thank you!" Emma squeezed her hand and pivoted around to dash back into the house. She needed her pelisse—a thick, fur-lined coat—for the cool air, a dagger of her own, and a way to sneak out without being caught. She didn't have time to trail footmen or maidservants, especially if Cormac was in trouble. She didn't even know how to summon the Order.

"I'll go with—blast." Olwen shimmered and disappeared entirely, looking annoyed as she faded.

Emma didn't have time to wait and see if she would find her way back quickly. She gathered her things and wrote a note on an ordinary piece of parchment. She shoved it into the butler's hands yelling, "Call the Order!" before tearing down the front walkway. She raced down the streets, dodging around surprised gentlemen, street sweepers, and wary milkmaids making their way back to the bridge to their farms. The black iron lampposts were like bare trees in winter, silhouetted against a darkening sky. Emma passed by confectioners, dressmaker shops, and haberdasheries, before finding a closed print shop. Her lungs were searing the inside of her chest and her legs had all the steadiness of marmalade.

Cormac was talking to a girl peering over the edge of the roof above, her long black hair streaming over her shoulders. "Thank God, it's you," she said to him before pausing. "Never thought I'd say that."

"What's happened?" He frowned up at her. "I just got your message. I thought you hated this part of town."

"I do," she said with great feeling. "Now more than ever. And I'm not keen on going to the Order for any reason, but you don't seem quite as bad as the rest."

"You don't know him very well, do you?" Emma interrupted but there was no real heat to it. She ducked into the alley, still catching her breath.

Cormac's expression was thunderous. "Emma! What are you doing here?"

"How do you think I found you?" Moira asked. "I'm Moira," she added to Emma. "Fast work. Can you climb? I'll put down a ladder around the side of the shop."

"Why?"

"I've found a bloody gate, haven't I?"

"Show me." Cormac's eyes shone. He glanced at Emma. "Stay here."

"Not likely," she replied, darting around him, racing farther

down to the alley and vanishing into the shadows. Cursing, he
bolted after her. She was already a third of the way up the ladder.
Her antlers shimmered in and out of sight. He could reach her
foot from the first rung. She pointed at him. "I'll kick you if you
even try it."

"Be reasonable. You're not trained for this."

"I'm not leaving you alone," she returned, as if he'd suggested she kick a kitten instead of him.

"This is what I do."

"Well, technically, I may have accidentally opened the gates
so I should learn how to close them, wouldn't you say? And
anyway, I was invited."

"This isn't tea. And Emma," he said, trying another tack.
"Your antlers are showing."

"Then better I stay out of sight, don't you think?" she retorted
reasonably as she slipped onto the roof.

Grumbling, he climbed up after her, cautiously slipping an
iron-wheel binding pendant out of his cuff. "I thought Madcaps
disdained ladders?"

Moira shrugged. "They're necessary in some parts so we
hide them on the roofs." She broke into a trot, confident of her
footing despite the height. "The gate's fairly small but I can't be
sure nothing's come through. I don't want my rooftops overrun
with ghouls. But I don't know how to close it either," she admitted grudgingly. She led them over to the next shop and over a
makeshift bridge that reminded Emma of walking the gangplank.
"It's actually over the bakery here, but you can't get up that
building because of the ovens."

She stopped on the corner of the bakery, which was emitting

a strange soft lavender light. There was a broken gargoyle statue and shattered shingles around a fissure of light. It burned violet, expanding to create a door of darkness in the shape of a reptile's pupil. Something leaked out, sliding and oozing over the roof toward them. It was a deep slimy green, like bracken and blackwater. Emma backed up, feeling nauseated just seeing it.

"That's magical residue. Something's definitely been through here," Cormac said. "Don't let it get on you."

"I wasn't planning on it," Emma said. Clouds began to gather overhead, eating up the stars.

"Rain would not be helpful right now," Cormac told her as he pulled various items out of his pockets. Emma's antlers shimmered into full view as she focused all of her concentration on keeping both the rain and the ooze away.

Cormac tossed a large handful of salt in front of the gate. The purple hue of the light turned violent and seared the eyes. The edges were like paper burning.

"Torch it," he ordered. Moira crouched down and immediately began to strike sparks with her flint. "Use this one." He handed her a crystal flint and three twists of hay braided with dried lavender and lily stalks.

"What can I do?" Emma asked.

"I need nine rowan berries and nine iron nails," he said, tossing her leather pouches. "And a drop of witch's blood. Moira?"

"She's busy." Emma rushed forward, already using the pin of her brooch to stab herself in the thumb. Blood welled to the surface.

"Not yet," Cormac said, scowling at her small wound. "Stay well back until I say so. Gates don't like being closed."

Moira struck the flint against the steel again, methodically and sharply. A spark ignited and blew out before it touched the hay-twists tinder. She swore and tried again, the cameo around her neck swinging back and forth.

A hound's head emerged from the gate. It was roughly the size of a pony, with eyes that glowed red and malicious. Saliva looped in ropes off its jaws, sizzling when it hit the ground. It had teeth as sharp as stone arrowheads. It was only vaguely canine, more like some twisted mutant combination of pony, dog, and gargoyle.

Emma tripped on her hem, falling onto her backside. She kept counting berries, scooting out of the way of the thick residue even as blood dripped down her palm, over her witch knot.

"Ghost dogs?" Moira leaped out of the way. "Aren't they usually friendly?"

"You're thinking spectral dogs." Cormac dodged a string of saliva. It seared through the broken wing of the gargoyle. "That's a hellhound. Don't look it in the eye!"

As the hellhound pushed through the small gate, black fur tinged with violet fire, Cormac gathered the berries and the nails and set them onto the salt. Moira was several paces away, still striking with the flint. "Nearly there," she panted.

Cormac pulled a slender iron dagger from his boot. It looked heavy and old and was inscribed all over with runes and symbols. A glass vial filled with salt was set into the hilt. He stabbed at the hellhound, jerking back to avoid its clamping jaws. The smell of sulfur overpowered them, worse even than the smell of the Thames on a hot day. It snaked out of the gate, practically visible in its stench. Moira tucked her face into her loose cravat and Emma now understood why she wore one. It was a smell she sincerely hoped never to experience again.

Another hellhound pushed out beside the first, tearing the gate wider.

"You girls should run," Cormac ordered, slashing with his dagger.

"You need us!" Emma argued.

"Idiot," Moira added, muffled through her cravat.

"Just like my bloody sisters," Cormac muttered back. "Take the rest of the nails from that pouch and throw them if the hounds get loose—argh!" A tooth scraped through the sleeve of his coat, the saliva burning the material, the tooth drawing blood. He stumbled back.

"Cormac!" Emma began to throw nails as fast as she could.

The first hound pushed through and darted past him, the second gurgled, Cormac's iron dagger in its throat. The hellhound fell apart like smoke and was sucked back in through the gate. The dagger clattered to the shingles. Cormac reached for another.

"Got fire!" Moira yelled, her cravat now around her neck as she puffed frantically at the small spark burning in the hay twist. She slid under the hellhound as it leaped for Emma, tossing the hay twist with the others. The spark caught. But the roof was angled down slightly and still slippery from the rain and Moira kept sliding. Emma grabbed for her but missed.

Moira tumbled over the edge.

Emma was running out of nails and the hellhound was between her and Moira. She looked around frantically. Cormac was too far away and fighting hellhounds. Emma threw her last iron nail and it cut through the beast, burning through him so he yelped. His body, being made of smoke and magic, re-formed instantly.

Emma tried a bolt of lightning. It blinded her momentarily, lifting her hair up and shooting sparks off the ends. The shingles melted at her feet.

The hellhound didn't seem to mind in the least.

"Emma, don't move!" Cormac threw himself forward, catching the beast by the tail. He pulled, dragging it backward, even as it snapped its jaws at Emma. Its claws left deep burning grooves in the shingles. Cormac's sleeves were smoking.

Emma launched herself at the end of the roof, practically toppling over herself. Moira dangled, fingers tightly clenched around the cornice, her hair billowing around her.

"I'm slipping," she grunted, digging her nails into the wood until they broke and bled.

"Hold on." Emma leaned down to grip Moira's wrist. She inched back, wrapping her ankles around a gargoyle's toppled head to steady herself. She hauled with all her might, pulling until her arms felt as if they would snap. Moira scrabbled for a foothold, finally finding enough to brace herself for a launch. She pushed off, flipped sideways, and rolled back onto the roof.

"You'd make a decent Madcap," she told Emma, wiping sweat out of her eyes.

Behind them Cormac was still battling the gate. The small fire burning on the salt would soon go out. Emma met Cormac's eye and he nodded, even as he reclaimed his dagger and stabbed the air in front of the hellhound's nose. The beast reared back, closer to the gate. Another swipe and it had backed right into the violet-edged opening.

"Now!" Cormac yelled, tossing a red bundle into the flames.

Emma jumped forward, squeezing her thumb and flinging a drop of blood at the fire. The fire shot up briefly, like a faulty gas lamp. The gate shimmered, burning edges peeling wider, shooting out vicious light and the gagging stench of sulfur. The gate pulsed, growing bigger and bigger.

"I think we've made it angry," she said, unable to look away.

"That's never happened before," Cormac said grimly.

A whip of magic, shining with all the colors of twilight, snapped out of the gate and wrapped around Emma's ankle, yanking her off her feet. She landed hard on her hip. She clutched at the roof frantically as her body was dragged inch by inch, closer and closer to the burning gate. She leaned back, trying to fight it. Moira pulled on Emma's arm but it only made pain shoot through her shoulder. The magical tether didn't snap.

Cormac stepped in front of her, trying to break the magical connection with his body, but the power of it flung him away. The charms around his neck slipped free of his shirt, burning brightly. He landed hard, breaking shingles. He was already struggling to get back to his feet, blood at the corner of his mouth, before Emma had moved another step. He tossed salt and flower petals and nails and anything else he could find in his charm bags.

Emma continued to be dragged over the shingles toward the maw of the gate. The tether of magic burned through her stockings. The portal ripped open farther and a man was suddenly there, wearing a sweep of antlers far wider and more magnificent than Emma's. His eyes were green as dandelion leaves in spring.

"You," he said softly, gently, as if he knew her. Emma didn't have time to wonder why he looked familiar. She kicked at the rope of light singeing her dress and crushing the delicate bones in her ankle together.

"Not her!" The horned man shouted into the portal behind him. "Close the gate!" he ordered Cormac, who was already bounding forward, iron dagger in his hand.

Greenish-black smoke shot out of the portal, wrapping around the man's throat, and strangling him. He toppled back into the shadows on the other side of the gate. The magical whip loosened around Emma and fell away. "Now!"

Cormac slammed his dagger down in front of the gate, driving it through the fire, the salt, and the roof. The portal edges singed and scorched, making the sound of hot water hitting cold metal. The violet light flared with unbearable brightness, forcing them all to drop down and cover their faces. There was silence for a long stunned heartbeat.

Cormac was the first to speak, pulling his arm away from his face. "Is anyone hurt?" he demanded, getting to his feet and pulling Emma up. She shook her head mutely, eyes wide. "Who was that man?" he asked. His sleeve was shredded, blood seeping through the linen shirt underneath. There were scratches on his hands and dirt on his face. His hat was long gone, his hair tousled and dusty.

"I have no idea," Emma replied.

"He seemed to know you." He cast a speculative look at the smoke lingering over the remains of the burned salt. "I'll have to call in the Order to seal that up properly."

"I already summoned them," Emma said. "Before I left."

Moira shook her head. "I knew I should have stayed clear of Mayfair."

Cormac's mouth quirked in a brief smile as he handed her a red bundle like the one he'd thrown into the fire earlier. "Take this."

"What's in it?"

"Powdered bones of dead witches, graveyard dirt, pepper, and other secret ingredients the Order uses against dark magic."

"The Order doesn't share with Madcaps," Moira said doubtfully, tucking the pouch in her belt.

"You're quite right, so I'd appreciate it if you kept it to yourself. But if you find another gate, use that." He handed her a calling card. "And send word direct next time, if you would."

"I'm not getting involved."

"It's too late for that it seems," he returned lightly.

She frowned over the edge of the rooftop. "Here come the rest of the Greybeards," she said. "If it's all the same, I'd rather not be here."

"Go on," Cormac said. "And take Emma with you. She can't afford to be further associated with the gates."

Moira was already running back along the gangplank. Emma had just enough energy left to keep tatters of a glamour on her antlers but she knew it was thin and transparent in spots. Not to mention that they were all covered in soot and blood. But Cormac still bowed over her hand as though they were back in Gretchen's mother's parlor, dancing a forbidden waltz. He kissed the back of her knuckles. When he straightened, he was a Keeper again, dark-eyed and stern-mouthed. "Go."

As she limped along the plank bridge, Emma finally realized why the horned man had looked familiar.

It was Ewan, the man from her mother's spelled memory.

Chapter 39

Emma went straight to the academy roof.

She cleared the clouds away until the bowl of the sky was painted with swirling masses of stars. They twinkled down at her, constant and familiar. She found she could breathe again. Nothing compared to their sheer number. She was tiny and insignificant and so were her problems.

Well, maybe not *all* of them.

Margaret and Alice likely didn't feel it insignificant that they'd been murdered.

Emma went back to counting stars. Just last month she'd have been wrapped in shawls on her balcony, eating biscuits and jam and watching the same stars through her telescope. She'd have spent the evening at some ball or soiree, trying to pretend that she wasn't bored and lonely. Her father would have ignored her. She'd have danced, drunk tea, and read novels while Penelope practiced on her pianoforte. They'd have shopped on Bond Street and Piccadilly, and gone to the theater. It would have been pleasant enough, on the surface. But she found she didn't miss it, not nearly as much as she'd have expected. Especially factoring in all the ways she had nearly died horribly.

She liked the bustle of the house around her, even with the suspicious whispers. She liked learning and pushing herself to explore different ideas. She was even getting accustomed to the antlers. She had a new life now and she'd best get about sorting it out.

One: her mother had defied the Order and no one seemed to know why. At least no one likely to speak to Emma. She felt certain Daphne wasn't about to invite her to tea with her Legate father, and he likely wouldn't know anything anyway. Her mother, by all accounts, had been a remarkably powerful witch, as evidenced by the smudged journal entries. How was the mysterious Ewan involved? Who was he, besides her mother's first love? He'd clearly died, or else he wouldn't have been on the other side of the gate.

Two: her mother had felt the need to bind her daughter for her own protection. So whatever it was she was hiding, she knew it would be a threat, even decades later. And again, it had to involve Ewan. Why else would a memory of his have been spelled into the antler charm?

Three: the spell had broken her mind and she no longer recognized Emma, never mind any complicated witch bottle she had worked eighteen years ago.

Four: her father was no help at all.

Five: she'd grown antlers.

Six: the gates between the living and the dead had been opened.

Seven: which was her fault.

Eight: they needed to be located and locked.

Nine: they'd already released ghouls, vengeful ghosts, hell-hounds, and who knew what other kind of creature.

Ten: witches were being murdered. Girls specifically, if the two so far created any kind of pattern.

Eleven: for some unknown reason, Emma kept finding their bodies.

Twelve: an antlered dead man recognized her.

Thirteen: Cormac. Just Cormac.

And she had absolutely no idea what to do about any of it.

Was it any wonder she was overwhelmed and had to resort to counting stars to calm her whirling mind?

"*I think she's up here,*" someone whispered loudly.

And that, she felt sure, was not going to help matters.

She stayed very still, hoping she looked like just another shadow. Footsteps padded cautiously out onto the shingles.

"*Why would she be up here?*"

"*Shh, you'll wake the gargoyles.*"

"*I don't see her. Are you sure about this?*"

"*I used a pendulum. I'm sure. Did you look—ooof.*"

One of the girls stepped on Emma's foot and they both yelped. One of her friends yelped even louder, and nearly fell off the roof altogether. Emma sighed, rubbing her ankle bone, already bruised from the tussle on the roof with the gate. Five students stood in a clump, staring at her. They were all in their night-gowns, hair twisted in rags or hopelessly sleep-tangled.

"Is it true?" asked the girl who had stepped on her.

"Is what true?" she asked, seeing the girls' gazes drawn toward her antlers.

"That another girl's been murdered! And you found her!"

Emma drew her knees up to her chest. "Yes. It's true."

"Truly?" There was an odd kind of awe in her tone. "Was there much blood—?"

"Grace, let some of us get a word in."

"I can't help it if you're too slow."

Emma groaned, dropping her forehead onto her knees.

"Get away from her," Daphne interrupted angrily, striding across the roof.

The girls shifted guiltily. Two of them moved away. "Why?" Grace asked. "We want to know what happened."

"I can tell you," Daphne replied. "Since I saw *her* with the body."

"Yes, you saw me," Emma retaliated, getting to her feet. "Because *you* were there too. And don't you think if I'd killed her I'd have had the foresight not to fall on her?"

The gawking looks swung back to Daphne. She crossed her arms. "I still don't trust you."

Sophie joined them. "Girls are dying, Daphne. We shouldn't be fighting among ourselves."

"You're too soft."

"Or you're too hard," Emma pointed out, grateful to have someone speaking up for her, even though she didn't know

Sophie very well. Daphne just glared at her again, spun on her heel, and stalked away. The others drifted after her, still whispering.

Sophie sat next to Emma. "I can heal those if you like," she said nodding to the bruises on Emma's arms and ankle.

"You can?"

"Yes, it's my magic." She stretched out her left palm, witch knot facing down over Emma's bruises. Emma noticed her knot was considerably darker than other girls'.

"You must heal a lot of people," she pointed out. Sophie didn't reply. She was too busy concentrating, sending a pulse of warmth through Emma's arms. It felt like sunlight. There was a flash of pain, like a burn, and then the bruises faded.

"Thanks for that." Emma ran her fingers over the unmarked skin. It didn't hurt at all.

"Daphne's not as hard as you think," Sophie said apologetically, shaking her hands out. The bruises had transferred to her but only to drip off like ink being washed away. "It's only that she prizes control and independence over all else. Her father is——"

"First Legate," Emma supplied. "Believe me, I know."

"It's a lot of pressure." She shrugged one shoulder. "Or so I gather."

"What about your parents?" Emma asked. "Do they think you're at a finishing school, or do they know the truth?"

"I don't have parents," she replied very softly. "They died a long time ago. Surely you've heard the gossip about my being an orphan?"

"I've heard a lot of gossip recently. Most of it is ridiculous."

"Well, in my case, it's true. I used to come up here all the time when I felt lonely, or the others were teasing me about being an orphan. Daphne is the one who made them stop."

"Daphne?"

"You sound surprised. If she counts you as a friend, she'll do anything for you."

"Oh." It didn't quite sound like the Daphne she knew. But then again, they certainly couldn't be counted as friends. And that was true even before Cormac was a factor.

"That poor seamstress. I keep seeing her face. Do you think they know who the murderer is yet?"

Emma shook her head. "I don't know. But I hear the Bow Street Runners are looking into it as well. They might not know about witchery, but it was still murder."

"And Margaret." Sophie shivered. "Did she not say anything? Give you even the smallest clues as to who attacked her?"

"I'm afraid not. With the chaos of the fire and everything . . . she died before she could say anything."

Sophie rubbed her arms as though she was chilled. "It's not safe anywhere, is it?"

Chapter 40

Emma snuck out just before dawn, when the darkness was thick as dust in an abandoned cottage, covering every surface and hidden corner. Even the stars had faded, now too few to count. The school was quiet, the windows reflecting only faint moonlight and fog. No one raised a cry or chased her down the lane with more questions. She wore a dark-brown cloak over her dress and kept her face hidden until she climbed inside the waiting hackney. She sat back against the cushions and breathed a sigh of relief.

"I knew you were up to something."

Cormac's voice made her yelp. Her heart thumped, shaking her bones from the inside out. Thunder shook the sky.

"You kicked me!" Cormac yelped back.

"What are you *doing* here?" she demanded, catching her breath. Rain pattered upon the roof of the carriage, then stopped.

"When I saw the unmarked hackney pull up to the school, I knew you must be involved," he explained drily, rubbing his shin. "I know how you like sneaking about in rented carriages."

She made a face. "Very funny."

He stretched his legs, making himself comfortable. "Where are you going?" His lazy gaze wasn't quite so comfortable. It seared the space between them. "Who are you visiting in the middle of the night, Emma?"

"Not that it's any of your business, but I'm going to Berkshire."

He blinked slowly, having expected a different answer. "Pardon?"

"I'm going to visit my mother," she said, irritably. "Now go away."

"You're going *now*? Alone? With a murderer at large? Not to mention ghouls and hellhounds?" He sounded so aghast, she nearly offered him smelling salts.

"I'm involved in these murders somehow, and it's more than just accidentally opening the gates. I need to know what's really going on before the Order binds me up like they tried to do to my mother, like they did to Moira's brother."

"Moira's brother broke the law," Cormac pointed out. "Several in fact. It was the Order or the mundane law, and the law would have hanged him as a thief."

"Perhaps. Still, I need to know why my mother cast so many spells, including one she *knew* would drive her mad."

"I can understand that," he said calmly.

She stared at him. He raised an eyebrow. "Cormac, go home. If I don't want to be caught, I need to go *now*."

"I'm going with you."

"You are not," she blurted out. "Why would you?"

He leaned forward so suddenly she edged back. "Emma, don't be obtuse. I'm not about to let you do this alone. You don't have to do everything by yourself, you know."

She tilted her head. "You could get into trouble."

"I've been in trouble since the day I met you," he replied, banging on the ceiling with the flat of his hand. The coachman responded immediately and the carriage lurched into motion.

The clip-clop of the horses' hooves echoed around them. Emma couldn't look away from his shadowed face, his cheekbones sharp in the very faint lantern light. He wasn't smiling one of his usual smiles, only watching her as if she was a mystery, as if she was precious. The memory of their last kiss burned between them. Emma shifted, suddenly feeling nervous. What was it about him that made the world narrow to a pinpoint?

He reached out, his hand sliding along her arm. She shivered and he grasped her elbow and tugged her forward so she was sitting next to him on the seat. The carriage rolled on, jostling them together. "What are you doing?" she whispered.

"We may as well pass the time," he whispered back, his voice husky and sweet. His eyes were dark as a moonless night, dark as a midnight lake closing over her head. She could drown and not care. She'd have suspected him of using some sort of magic if she didn't know better. He leaned closer, glancing at her mouth with a ghost of a smile.

"What's changed?" she asked, before his lips touched hers.

He froze there for a moment and her breath was hot in her throat. Her mouth tingled as if he'd already kissed her.

"What do you mean?" he murmured.

"You kissed me at Christmas."

"Yes," he whispered, tracing her lower lip with his thumb. Her breath trembled.

"And then you acted as if you barely knew me." She was embarrassed to bring it up but she couldn't go on thinking all these confusing thoughts about him and feeling these confusing feelings. He'd protected her and betrayed her too often. She had to take responsibility for her own heart, before it was too late. She forced herself to keep speaking, even though her voice felt too loud and too real in the soft warmth of the carriage. "Is this just a game to you then? Another girl on your list?"

"You're not just another girl." He didn't pull away from her, only leaned over onto the cushion.

"Aren't I?" She touched her antlers lightly. "I suppose not."

He sighed, jerking his hand through his hair. "Last Christmas, when I kissed you, I didn't know you were a Lovegrove. I only knew you as Emma Day."

She frowned. "So?"

"So then I joined the Order. If I stayed with you and they saw we had a connection, they would have ordered me to exploit it."

She bit her lower lip. "Even then? Before the gates? Before everything else?"

"Yes."

"And in the goblin markets? When you let them cage me?"

"Especially then. They would have sent someone else, someone a lot less gentle. People are afraid of your mother and her power, and so they're afraid of you. She defied the Order. You don't know how rare that is."

"I'm beginning to think she was right."

"Maybe she was. But if the Order knew I had any sympathy at all that night on the ship, they would have suspected *you* of that murder. You don't want to end up in Percival House on the moors—a kind of magical prison," he explained before she could ask.

"Or bottled and bound," she added.

"Yes," he replied grimly. "They've been watching you since you were born. The only thing that shielded you and your cousins was your mother's spell. Not only did it bind your powers so you couldn't be hunted, but it made it so no one could talk to you about witching families with any kind of sense. You simply didn't understand. She was clever, your mother."

"She's not like that now," she said in a small voice.

"She paid the price willingly," he said, digging his fingers in her hair and tilting her head back so she had to meet the full force of his gaze. "I would too."

She smiled sadly. "Don't say that."

"Why not? You won't forgive me? Even knowing why I did what I did?" His fingers tightened.

"I won't have anyone else hurt because of me," she told him.

"Not even a Keeper?"

"Not even a Keeper."

He closed the distance between them slowly, his eyes never

leaving hers. She had every opportunity to stop him, to move away, to break the moment. Instead she leaned in as well, until his mouth was on hers, or her mouth was on his, it hardly signified so long as they were together, breathing the same air, sinking into the same moment, closing any gap that might lay between them. His arms went around her, crushing her to his chest. Her hands slid around his neck. His tongue touched hers and for a blessed brief moment it no longer mattered where they had been or where they were going. There was only his mouth, his hands, and the way they fit together.

Outside the carriage, the roads slowly changed as they left the city for the outskirts. Dawn turned the sky pink and glittered on the dew. The mist was soft and birds sang from the hedgerows. The air changed, blowing crisp and clean into the open window. It smelled like leaves and damp earth and home.

When the carriage rolled to a stop, the thump of the coachman as he vaulted off the seat jerked Emma back to reality. "Wait." Cormac caught her hand. "There might be Keepers watching the house."

"But I'm allowed to visit my own mother, surely."

"Yes, but we need to keep up the deception that we are nothing to each other."

She took a deep breath, willing away the nervous twitch of her scalp around her antlers. He curled his forefinger under her chin briefly. "Forgive me?"

She nodded once. They didn't speak as the footman opened the door and lowered the steps. Cormac stepped down first and then motioned sharply for her to do the same. He scanned the area warily.

She descended into the courtyard. Emma looked at the house, turning her Fith-Fath ring around her finger nervously. Her mother's spellbox was tucked under one arm. Cormac closed his hand around her elbow, propelling her forward as though she were his prisoner. He looked as he had when he'd turned on her over Margaret's body. She lifted her chin and shot him a rebellious look. He winked at her from under the brim of his hat.

Mrs. Peabody answered the door with her bright smile. "Bless me, back again so soon? What a good girl you are." She moved aside to let them in. "Lady Hightower is still abovestairs, but she's awake. She had a bit of a wild night, I'm afraid, but she's calm now. No doubt seeing you will be a balm."

Emma swallowed, not as sure about that as the housekeeper seemed to be. In the privacy of the house, Cormac's hand slipped reassuringly into hers. He squeezed her hand hard and she glanced at him. He was looking at her antlers. She winced and shoved so much power into her glamour that the clouds raced over the sun for a moment, darkening the stairs. Mrs. Peabody blinked. "Strange weather today."

Theodora was curled up on the same fainting couch where she'd reclined the last time Emma had visited. Her hair was neatly brushed this time, but her eyes were slightly feverish.

"Is she ill?" Emma whispered.

"No, just a bad night," Mrs. Peabody assured her. "She'll be right as rain, don't you worry."

Emma approached cautiously as the housekeeper shut the door behind her. "*Maman?*"

Theodora didn't look away from the window and the woods beyond.

"I want to ask you about your spellbox," Emma continued carefully. She held it out and Theodora finally glanced at her.

"It's pretty." She stroked it like a pet bunny, before flipping the lid open. She recoiled. "Smells like iron." She stuck her tongue out. "But I like this," she added in a reverent whisper, lifting the antler charm bound in black thread. The rings clinked together. She slipped the silver one over her finger, heedless of the cumbersome charm.

"Why did you bind my cousins and me?" Emma asked, watching her carefully. "Can you remember?"

Theodora blinked. "I like to keep things in bottles."

Emma froze, looking at Cormac. "What kind of things?" She tried to keep her tone light, not wanting to scare her mother with her impatience.

"All kinds of things."

"Like magic?"

"People go in bottles. So does dirt. And teeth. And medicine." Theodora nodded proudly. "I collect them."

Triumph surged through Emma. "Can you show me?"

Theodora looked out the window longingly. Emma followed her gaze. "If you tell me where they are, I can get them for you," she suggested. "You don't have to leave the window."

Theodora nodded, then frowned sternly. "Don't break them."

"I won't."

Theodora looked right through her for a moment. "It's under the bed," she whispered loudly.

Her pulse pounding in her ears, Emma knelt by the bed. She lifted the blankets and peered underneath. Hundreds of acorns were hidden in piles underneath and, if the lumps were anything to go by, between the feather mattresses. There was a small trunk set precisely in the center. It bristled with dust, puffing up in little clouds as she dragged it out. Theodora didn't leave her couch.

The trunk was brown leather with brass hinges. It didn't look special in any way. There were no magical markings to hint at its contents. She opened it, half-afraid of what she was going to find inside. The clink of glass against glass had Theodora turning her head sharply. Emma smiled weakly in apology.

There were bottles of varying sizes and shapes, just like the ones that crowded the shelves in Aunt Bethany's stillroom and the school apothecary. They were mostly clear glass, though a few were warped and green and clearly much older. Some were filled with nothing but acorns or seeds. One held rosebuds, another salt and red thread, another yet was a mixture of earth, pearls, and a bent iron nail suspended in rusty liquid. Three held water, and one was clearly just a discarded perfume bottle. Emma had no way of knowing what spells were trapped inside and which should be released.

Or if any of them was the bottle that had made her mother mad.

"Did you trap your magic in one of these?" Emma asked.

Theodora's only answer was to hum to herself.

"This is important," Emma said, sharper than she'd intended. "I need to know how you defied the Order. Why you bound us and yourself. And I need to know why I keep finding the Greymalkin victims."

Theodora put her hands over her ears and shook her head, humming louder. Most of the words were garbled, only a few were clear: gold, door, oak.

Emma rubbed her face, the weight of the antlers making the back of her neck ache. The bottles were useless without an explanation. And clearly, none was forthcoming. The whole trip was useless. Her mother didn't know her. Her mother didn't know anyone or anything anymore. She was a broken doll and Emma didn't know how to fix her.

Cormac strode over the faded rugs toward her. "Your mother's bottle wouldn't be in there," he said. "If that's what you're searching for."

"How do you know?"

"You'd be able to see her familiar inside. Not to mention the Order has been through this house already. They'd have found that trunk ages ago."

Emma let the lid slam shut. "Blast." She pushed to her feet. "*Maman*, can you tell me who Ewan is?"

Theodora's head whipped around so fast, Emma actually took a step back. "Ewan? Where is he?"

"I don't know," she answered. "I thought you might."

Theodora's lower lip trembled. "I miss him."

"Is he the reason you did what you did?" Theodora only

shrugged bad-temperedly. "He saved you in the forest, didn't he?" Emma continued. "And you fell in love with him. But you married my father instead."

"I had to."

"Why? Why, *Maman*? How did Ewan die?"

Theodora shook her head violently from side to side, covering her ears with her hands like a child. Emma's shoulder slumped as she bit back angry tears. Cormac went to the tea tray and brought Emma's mother a plate. He waited until she'd noticed it before smiling his charming smile. "Lady Theodora, would you like some cake?"

Her hands lowered away from her ears. Cormac offered her the generous slice of gingerbread with a bow, as if earls' sons were accustomed to fetching and carrying every day. And Emma would have bet Keepers definitely didn't usually fetch and carry for mad witches who defied the Order. She wanted to kiss him all over again.

Theodora reached for the cake, now giggling happily. "*Gold is good but silver's better*," she sang. Cormac's chain of charms fell out of his shirt, poking through the buttons. The iron-spoke of the Order clinked against the plate.

Theodora screeched.

Cormac drew back but she'd already knocked the plate from her hand. It shattered on the floor. Theodora pointed at his pendant, still screaming and baring her teeth savagely. Cormac hurried to slip it back under his cravat. Theodora went silent but she followed him with a hateful gaze. It all happened so fast, Emma had barely moved from the side of the bed.

Mrs. Peabody burst into the room, taking a small bottle and a spoon from her apron. "What's all the fuss, poppet?" she asked briskly as she poured laudanum into the spoon. Emma used the side of her foot to slide the trunk back under the bed, just in case. "Carrying on in front of your nice guests here. Not polite, is it?"

Theodora spat on the floor. Mrs. Peabody sighed. "Time for your medicine." She slid the spoon into Theodora's mouth before she could move, holding her mouth and nose firmly clamped until she swallowed. Mrs. Peabody patted her hand. "There, poppet. All better."

"*Gold is good, silver's better.*" She drifted off, her head falling forward as the laudanum took effect. "*The lion stalks the maiden fair when the bear leaves his lair.*" She smiled. "*But where the hunter goes, only the serpent knows.*"

"What does that mean?" Emma asked, wide-eyed.

"Lord, I don't know. She's been singing it for years now, ever since she fell ill." Mrs. Peabody blew hair off her face. "I was the head housemaid when your mother was little. She and her sisters were such pretty little things. And your mother had wit and courage such as you've never seen." She shook her head sadly.

"Will she be all right?" Emma asked.

"Sleep will do her good, it always does. I expect the excitement of visitors was too much for her. Your father hasn't been here in years." She pursed her lips, clearly stopping herself from offering her opinion. "Still, he did her a kindness keeping her here. Could have had her in Bedlam Hospital, couldn't he? But only the woods from her childhood calms her." She paused. "It was good of you to visit again," she said to Emma.

"I should have come more often," she admitted, feeling like a horrible daughter.

"She wouldn't have remembered," Mrs. Peabody said. "The first time your aunt came Lady Hightower threw porridge at her. Didn't stop until Lady Chadwick started painting those trees on the wall, and then she was full of orders and advice. They seemed to help a little. So does the laudanum."

"I'll visit again," Emma promised even though all she wanted was to be out of the house and into the sunshine. The clouds raced away from the sun and fell apart like cobwebs.

"Don't fret, child. Your mother, as I knew her before, wouldn't have wanted you to see her like this in any case. I'll have your carriage brought back around, shall I?" Mrs. Peabody left the room.

Emma watched her mother's eyes move frantically beneath her lids. "That rhyme she was singing, about bears and lions. Do you think they're familiars?"

"They could be," Cormac replied.

"So it was a spell?" she asked.

"Perhaps."

She paced the room. "We're not any closer to an answer, are we?"

"I'm afraid not."

She stopped in front of the crudely painted red bird. "This was her familiar," she said softly. "I found it in the *Witch's Debrett's*." She ran her fingertips over the bumpy paint. "She misses it, even if she doesn't know why." She traced the swoop of the bird's wing. "It's a strange room, isn't it? With all these trees. And this one—ow!"

She drew her hand back. The red paint had chipped off, revealing a rusty nail still stuck in the plaster and she'd scraped herself. There was a tiny fleck of red on her finger, and she wasn't sure if it was paint or blood. She felt her eyes roll back in her head.

Definitely blood.

Chapter 41

1796

Theodora went back into the forest.

She didn't wear her red cloak.

She walked down the path, peering hopefully into the leaves. She didn't know what she'd even say to Ewan if she saw him, only that she couldn't stop thinking about him. She spent an embarrassing amount of time at the window staring at the last spot she'd seen him. She saw rabbits, a fox, and once, a white stag. But no Ewan.

So she decided to seek him out, despite what her parents would say, or her sisters, or society in general. She didn't care that he was a woodcutter's son. She only cared that he had saved her life, that he was strong and handsome and solitary. She'd even asked her father if he knew any local families with a son named Ewan. Bethany looked at her curiously but she just laughed and said she heard the village girls talking. She understood now why Cora would ask Bethany to paint her husband's portrait. She almost suspected a love charm but she'd checked herself thoroughly for magical residue and could find none.

And she couldn't find Ewan either. There were no more strawberries, no shadow of a man under the trees.

So she'd brave the woods to see him again.

She'd do it armed this time, at least. There was a dagger on her belt and she found a thick branch to serve as a staff. The bluebells had wilted away and there was nothing but green light and green shadows all around her. She was excited and nervous and apprehensive of running into the poachers again. She sent her familiar on ahead and kept to the road.

"Princess."

She knew that voice. It was the summer solstice, dark rich earth, cool forest shadow.

Ewan.

She stopped, her heart beating loudly in her chest. She turned slowly, hoping she didn't look as eager as she felt. She had no idea, after all, if he'd care to see her again. He wore the same brown leather coat, stitched at the seams with thick laces. His breeches had been mended under the knee, where the poacher's knife had caught him. His eyes were pale and green, even from a distance. She could almost believe that he wasn't real, that she'd dreamed him up.

"It's Theodora, actually."

"Princess suits you better."

She tilted her head. "I'm not sure that's a compliment."

He flashed his rare smile. "You think too much."

And then his fingers were tangled in hers and they were moving through the woods, Theodora's cardinal-familiar was a streak of red between the leaves. Somewhere along the way she lost her staff and tucked her hem up into the belt she'd stolen from her father, which she'd hung with pouches of things she thought she might need in the woods. She'd brought a hunk of bread and cheese, salt and rowan berries, an empty spell bottle, and amber beads. She didn't need any of them, just Ewan.

He brought her to a small grove on the other side of the wilted bluebell wood. "Step where I step," he murmured and she watched his feet carefully, matching his stride. There was no snapping of twigs or crunching of acorns, just two shadows moving between the trees, stopping in a patch of sunlight. He was still holding her hand when he showed her the deer, lying together in the grass, ears twitching. They lifted their heads at once, white tails flicking. Theodora froze, holding her breath. The deer were beautiful, with rough fur and wide dark eyes. The sun caught the pollen drifting over them.

They met every day that summer, sneaking off into sunlit meadows and exploring. The endless round of balls and parties, the new gowns and the politics of the Order ceased to matter. They just kept her from where she wanted to be. She ignored her parents and her sisters, and was downright rude to Alphonse when he called.

One afternoon in the garden, a white stag leaped the hedge and chased him right off the estate. Theodora knew she should be more careful and circumspect but she was filled up with joy and longing, and there was no space left in her for anything else. She was a tapestry already embroidered, a story already told.

She grew tan and lithe from running in the woods. He washed his hair in the river every morning before he found her. And he always found her.

It was madness to feel so much so soon. It tingled through her and made her head swim like champagne.

He took her to his house once, when fat rain pattered through the branches and the wind nibbled at them. It was a small hut made of wattle and daub, tucked between two oak trees. The branches were woven together to create the support for the roof. A circle of stones held the remains of a cooking fire near the front door, which was hand-carved willow wood. A small clay gargoyle perched protectively in a tree.

"Is this where you live?" she asked curiously.

"It's not much," he said softly, sounding as uncertain as she'd ever heard him. "It's not good enough for you."

She speared him with a direct gaze. "I'll decide what's good enough for me, thank you very much."

He stood, rain dripping from the ends of his hair as she ducked inside the small hut. It was dark and smoky and smelled like apples. There were two pallets on wooden boards, one in each corner. A table with two chairs sat between them. The floor was covered in wood shavings and dried flowers.

"Who are you really?"

He filled the doorway. "Just a woodcutter's son."

"You're more than that," Theodora returned evenly. "What's your last name?"

"Greenwood."

"The Greenwoods of the greenwood?" she echoed with a smile.

"Aye."

She rose on her tiptoes to kiss his cheek. At first he didn't move, afraid she'd bolt the way a rabbit bolted when there was movement nearby. She kissed his left cheek, then his right. Her lips were damp and cool. He could see rain beading her eyelashes.

His arms slid around her, hands cradling her hip bones. She'd taken to wearing the simple dresses the village girls wore while in the forest. There were no petticoats or pads between his callused fingertips and the curve of her body. She leaned into him, heat racing along her, starting at the point where his lips touched hers. She traced the muscles on his arms, down to his strong wrists. His palms stroked up her side. His tongue touched hers and her thoughts fled until she was nothing but flesh and nerve endings.

When she kissed him back, he spun her around, pressing her against the wall. The moment went primal and sharp, like pink summer lightning.

Just when she wondered how much more she could possibly withstand, he pulled away. She tightened her fists in his shirt, gasping.

He frowned. "My father's coming."

"How do you do that?" she asked, bewildered. "I can't hear anything but the rain." Not to mention it was difficult to concentrate on anything but his mouth, the way he moved, the smell of rain and smoke in his hair.

He pulled her behind him. "We can't be seen."

She raised her eyebrows. "Are you ashamed of me, Ewan Greenwood?"

"Don't be daft, Princess," he said as they darted behind the hut and continued deeper into the woods. "But my father isn't fond of witches."

"Isn't he one himself?"

"Why do you think he's not fond of them?" he returned drily.

She picked her way through the undergrowth. She was learning to move softly. She'd probably never be as quiet as Ewan but she was proud of her progress. It was proving useful in helping her sneak out of the house at night as well.

"Is he so fearsome then?" she asked, knotting her damp hair up at the nape of her neck. "Your father?"

Ewan's smile was brief and crooked. "Not in the way you think."

"Is he a poacher?" she asked carefully, not wanting to insult him. The sun peeked through the clouds. Mists snaked between the tree trunks.

"He'll only eat fish and the plants he finds in the forest," Ewan replied. "He won't eat animals at all."

"Truly?" She'd been expecting a wild man of a woodcutter, such as the one from the story of the girl in the red cloak.

"He's a gentle sort but he's the size of an ogre," he continued. She could tell by the way he spoke that he loved his father very much. "The poachers stay away because they're afraid of him. We've just enough magic between the two of us to convince them our grove is cursed. They say Herne hanged himself from one of our trees."

"Clever. Aren't you afraid of the Greymalkin?"

He snorted. "Here? Why should they bother with us?"

"I know," she agreed sheepishly. "Papa is obsessed with them," she admitted. "He thinks they wait around every corner."

"Maybe they do, in your world." He slanted her a glance. "I expect he only wants to keep you safe. I would too, if you were mine."

"I am yours."

He stopped walking. "You don't know what you're saying."

She narrowed her eyes. "Don't I, you great baboon?"

He laughed and the sound seem to startle them both. She'd never heard him laugh before. "Trust you to find joy in being called a baboon," she muttered, still cross that he hadn't immediately declared his undying love. He went serious, turning her to face him when she tried to stomp away.

"I only meant I have nothing to offer you," he said, stroking her cheekbone with his thumb. "Theodora, I live in a hut in the woods. It's charming to you now but when winter comes, you'd sing a different tune."

"Winter is cold?" she said witheringly. "I had no idea."

"Society's cold too when you cross it, or so I've heard."

"Hang society." She tossed her hair over her shoulder, every inch the noblewoman. "I have a generous dowry," she added proudly. "Enough to buy as much firewood as we'd ever need."

"Firewood's free to the ax here, Princess."

"Don't do that," she said quietly. She had to tilt her head back to meet his eyes. They were green and mysterious, and as indecipherable as the forest. "I'm not a fool, Ewan. I'm trying to tell you that I have money enough for the both of us."

"I know what I am." The corner of his mouth quirked. "Do you really think your father would give you that dowry if you married me? I'm poor and wild, even for a woodcutter."

"I have jewels," she insisted. "I could sell them, if that's what you're worried about."

His calm demeanor changed and she saw the wildness in him, the dark fierceness that ran through him like a river. "I want you," he told her harshly. "Just you."

He kissed her again, deeply and darkly until she shivered with it. "I only have secrets," he said huskily. "And it's not enough."

"Secrets?" She raised an eyebrow. "I love secrets."

"I knew you would." He grinned suddenly, looking younger. He looked around carefully before pulling off his coat. His shirt followed, exposing tanned muscles and narrow hips. Theodora swallowed, unable to look away. Lightning could have struck her blind and she'd still have looked. "What are you doing?"

His hand went to his belt. Her eyes widened. "Seriously, what are you doing?"

He turned his back, chuckling, and kicking his boots off along with every last stitch of clothes he had on, until he was standing in the dappled sunlight naked except for the scars on his arms. "I want to show you something," he said, over his shoulder. She bit back several inappropriate remarks.

And just when she thought he couldn't get more beautiful, she was proven wrong. He shimmered with the sunlight until she blinked, wondering if she was getting silly and swoony like girls in sensation novels. His muscles strained and moved, skin rippling as it turned to white fur. He fell to his hands, only they'd already transformed into hooves. He tossed his head showing off a massive rack of antlers. The tines curved up to the sky.

Ewan was the white stag.

His eyes were wide and green, and reflected his keen perception, his composure.

The white stag was Ewan.

"You're a shape-shifter," she said reverently.

He took a step toward her, so huge the ground trembled slightly underfoot. His ears flickered. Her familiar flew out to perch on his antlers, glowing as red as the strawberries he'd once left her. She *reached out to stroke one of his tines. He snorted out a breath and she jumped, startled. She laughed, shaking her head. "I love you, Ewan."*

And then he was himself again, clothed in nothing but the sun and shadows.

When he reached for her, she was already reaching for him.

Chapter 42

Emma woke up in a painted forest, cradled in Cormac's arms.

"You fainted," he said, stroking a lock of hair off her cheek. "I'll fetch a doctor."

"I don't need a doctor," she assured him, trying to sit up. Her head spun. Cormac shifted to let her move, but he didn't take his arm away from her waist. "I didn't faint."

"Sure looked like it to me. Scared me half to death."

"You fight warlocks," she half smiled. "An unconscious girl is nothing to that."

"But *you* are everything." She blushed as he met her eyes. "What happened?" he asked.

"Another one of my mother's memories," she replied, glancing at the settee. Theodora was still asleep, her hair tangled over pale cheeks. "She must have put it in the painting of the bird. Is that even possible?"

Cormac looked thoughtful. "She's been in this room for a very long time and magic tends to like patterns and repetition. So yes, I suppose it's possible. And the bird would have been a comforting symbol to her, as you've said." His hand was warm on her lower back, stroking her spine. "What did you see?"

"My father." She tilted her head to look at him. Her eyes were wide. "I think I saw my father." You could ignore the same green eyes but there was no denying antlers. They weren't exactly a common hereditary trait. And she'd been born almost exactly nine months after her mother wed Alphonse Hightower. She wasn't Emma Day, child of Lord Hightower. She was illegitimate.

"Lord Hightower?" Cormac said. "Why is that? He's not from one of the families."

"I don't think he's my real father."

"Who then? Butcher? Baker? Candlestick maker?"

"The man with the antlers."

"From the rooftop?"

"Yes." She pointed to her antlers.

"I suppose it makes a strange sort of sense," Cormac allowed. "And he did save your life."

"You both did."

"You saved yourself just as much." He shrugged, as if embarrassed by the compliment. She had to grin. It was so unlike him to squirm like that. "But it's a memory your mother would definitely have felt she needed to hide."

"That I'm a bastard?" she asked wryly. "Yes."

He took her by the shoulders, willing her to believe in what he was saying. "And I was born without magic. Do you think less of me?"

"Of course not!"

"Then why should you imagine I would think less of you because of something you have no control over?" He didn't say anything about society; they both knew the aristocracy would care very much indeed.

She waited. He waited. Finally, she blinked. "And that's all you have to say about it?" Most people of her acquaintance would shun her company if they found out. She might even be expelled from Rowanstone.

"You're hardly the first baby to be born on the wrong side of the blanket," he replied calmly. "And if no one knows about it by now, no one ever needs to know." He raised his eyebrows. "I assume Hightower *doesn't* know?" She shook her head. He didn't think she realized how tightly she was squeezing his fingers. "Then I'd leave it be."

The door opened before she could say anything else. "The carriage is ready . . . oh, dear. What's happened?" Mrs. Peabody blinked at both of them sitting together against the wall.

Cormac helped Emma to her feet while she tried not to flush bright red. "Lady Emma fainted."

Mrs. Peabody pulled a silver vinaigrette out of her apron. "Do you need smelling salts?"

"No, I'm fine, thank you," Emma assured her, more than glad not to have to inhale the sharp stench of whatever concoction Mrs. Peabody had in her vinaigrette. Gretchen's mother favored a vile combination of vinegar, ammonia, and rosemary.

"It's the shock of seeing your mother in one of her black moods, I expect," she said with a comforting smile as they descended the stairs. "Go on, now. It's too nice a day to spend worrying. Have your young man take you out for some ices."

"He's not . . . ," Emma broke off. "That is . . ."

Cormac winked at the housekeeper. "I most certainly am her young man."

Chapter 43

By the time Cormac caught up to the ship the next day, it was floating near Blackfriars Bridge. He'd had to double back twice to lose Colette, who had been following him all day. She was determined to find the famous Greybeard ship. It was cloaked from warlocks, Madcaps, thieves, and oathbreakers but he wasn't entirely convinced it would be enough to keep his sister out.

And he had enough to worry about with keeping Emma from the Order and the Order from Emma, never mind his five wild sisters. Emma couldn't have killed those girls. He knew it in his bones. But that wasn't nearly good enough for the Order or the magisters. They'd had fits over the name of Lovegrove and yet he still couldn't find anyone with any relevant details. The return of the Greymalkin family certainly wasn't encouraging them to be more forthcoming. And if the Order ever realized the Greymalkin had showed any interest at all in Emma, she'd be bound and her spirit-deer trapped in a bottle before she could blink.

He'd seen what happened to witches when their familiars were bound. Her mother was proof enough of the danger.

The hell he was going to let that happen to Emma.

He would be banished. They couldn't bind him, not like the others. But he'd sworn to serve the Order above all else and the magisters would punish him severely if they discovered his weakness. He was risking bringing dishonor on his family, on his forefathers who had served for centuries.

All for her.

They'd think him bewitched. There was no denying she was somehow connected to the murders. He'd seen how she was dragged to the victims and only magic could accomplish that. So for all their sakes they had to figure it out—and soon. He knew the Order and for all their sterling qualities, they were traditional to the point of blindness. They held to the sins of the fathers, and they didn't forgive. If the Sisters ever broke their pattern, the Order would be irrevocably lost about how to stop them.

Cormac hurried down the gangplank to the dark blue hull. The white scrollwork glowed and the bottled eyes watched his every step, finally glancing away when they recognized him. The colorful blown glass witch balls clinked together overhead like icicles. He didn't go toward the ladder to the magister's hall where Emma had been dragged. The meetings were held in the captain's quarters on deck. A wind-witch winked at him as he passed, the wind-knots at her belt and in her hair floating in a breeze that never seemed to abandon her completely. He winked back. He might be distracted, but pretty girls should never be ignored.

"Cormac." Ian, a fellow Keeper, was leaning against the wall just inside the door. "Thought you'd forgotten about us, mate."

"Sisters," he replied. "Mine, that is."

The cabin was polished oak from ceiling to floor and every piece of furniture in between. Iron nails gleamed, as much to secure the tables and chairs to the floor in a storm as for the metal's magical qualities. The iron wheel was painted on the ceiling, surrounded by stars. Rum bottles filled with salt sat in every corner. The sideboard was covered with platters of cheese, dark bread, currant tarts, meat pies, and fresh strawberries next to decanters of wine. Silver urns filled with tea and coffee, with spouts shaped into open-mouthed gargoyles, hulked on either end.

On the main table was a large painted map of London. Cormac had a similar one hidden inside his coat pocket. He'd have to memorize the Order's additions to keep his up to date. He wasn't as inflexible as they were, and perfectly willing to accept the help of girls, Madcaps, and witches without a penny or a pedigree.

There were a dozen Keepers scattered around Lord Mabon, the current head of the Order. Directly beneath him in power was Daphne's father, the First Legate. "Doesn't his daughter fancy you?" Ian asked nodding to him.

"All the girls fancy Cormac," Oliver Blake interrupted amiably. "Damn your eyes."

Cormac just shrugged. He knew better than to say that he found Daphne boring. In fact, he was finding every girl he met who wasn't Emma, boring. He'd never live it down if word got out. Never mind his friends, his sisters would be merciless. "Any news?" he asked.

Ian shook his head. "They still can't figure out what the Sisters are keeping the stolen magic for. It's making them down-right vulgar."

"Ho, Cormac." Virgil smiled snidely. "Taking up with a Lovegrove now. She seems just your type. Like her mother, she's too crazy to care that you haven't got an ounce of magic."

Cormac wasn't even aware of moving. Anger propelled him and suddenly Oliver was holding him back and Virgil was wiping blood off his nose. His own cravat was loose and he was breathing roughly, fists clenched. Virgil took a swing in retaliation but Cormac moved aside, still vibrating with adren-aline. The simple evasion infuriated Virgil more than the punch had.

"She's got bad blood, just like you," he spat.

This time it took both Ian and Oliver to hold Cormac back. The other Keepers turned to them, disapprovingly. Magic slammed the door shut and flung Virgil and Cormac apart.

"I thought you were men, not little boys," one of the older Keepers snapped. "You should have outgrown this childish behavior by now."

"And we have more serious problems," Daphne's father added sternly. Cormac and Virgil bowed to him in mute apology.

"Cross me again and I'll call you out, whatever the rules say about it," Cormac promised Virgil silkily, smiling a mad kind of smile. Keepers were forbidden from dueling each other on the ship and while out on any official business of the Order. Virgil stomped off to the other side of the cabin. The ship rolled soothingly beneath their feet. "I'm pretty sure I'm going to have to punch him again," Cormac said. At least Virgil would assume Cormac had reacted to the accusation of having bad blood, instead of the slight on Emma's name, which was the real reason his temper had snapped.

"I'd bet on it," Ian agreed.

"We've had good progress in reclaiming and reanimating the gargoyles," Lord Mabon was saying. "The gates are trickier. We've closed five of them so far. They appear at random and only stay open until the next sunrise or sunset." A scribe took notes at his left elbow, the scratch of his quill somnolent and steady. "We are, however, no closer to determining *why* the Sisters are back and to what purpose they are killing."

"For the pleasure of it?" someone suggested. "Do they need another reason?"

"For this many murders, and of young witches in particular, there is most definitely another reason," the First Legate said. "They are stooping to stealing the life force of rats and birds and people already dying. They clearly want to recorporealize and quickly." He sounded frustrated. Cormac realized how afraid he must be for his own daughter. "We've been through the Greymalkin family tree exhaustively and we can find no record of a son born to the line since the Revolution in France. They cut off that one's head and then the Sisters were banished to the Underworld. Whoever this new descendant is, he's fiend-ishly clever. But none of our soothsayers can locate him."

"We've bound the tombs and the witch bottles of the old Greymalkin witches we already know about," Lord Mabon explained. "But we can't know how many were buried secretly. As you know, they say the cellar of the Greymalkin House is built with the bones of their dead." He pushed his wine glass away in disgust.

"And though we're doing the best we can, it's not good enough. Not nearly good enough."

Chapter 44

The next evening Emma went back home when her father was out at his club. It gave her the opportunity to rifle through his desk and sort through boxes. She told Jenkins she needed to pack extra items for school. He complimented her on her curtsy, having no idea she was learning to fry ghouls with lightning and duck boiled beets.

She searched everywhere, trying to find hidden journals or mentions of any scandal involving a man named Ewan. All to no avail. She found boring speeches her father was writing for Parliament, household accounts, and a list of sheep-shearers to be hired for the country estate, but nothing remotely magical, and nothing about an antlered man.

On her way back to the academy, she ran through everything she knew, which admittedly wasn't much. She hadn't been able to decipher her mother's rhymes, and though the *Witch's*

Debrett's listed every witch's familiar along with their title, there were simply too many bears and serpents, and no lions at all. She felt as though there was something important hovering just out of reach. Something important that she already knew but didn't *know* she knew. It nagged at her like a splinter.

Gold is good, silver's better. The lion stalks the maiden fair, when the bear leaves his lair. But where the hunter goes, only the serpent knows.

It sounded like a country song one might hear at a fair. She'd read enough books in the school library to understand that gold represented the sun and silver the moon, but it didn't explain her mother's rhyme. Oak trees were dedicated to Thor the thunder god and Brigid the Irish goddess of poetry; they were also sacred to the druids. Emma was fairly certain her mother wasn't a druid. Did druids even exist anymore? She tried to recall if any of the doors in the Berkshire house were made of oak.

Ten minutes later, as the carriage drew near a clogged road full of other carriages waiting for guests at a ball, Emma was no nearer to figuring anything out. And she had a headache for her troubles.

Although, come to think of it, the tree in her dream was an oak. And she'd already noticed that it looked like the one painted on her mother's bedroom wall. To which her mother had added a red bird just like her bound familiar.

Surely that meant something.

But if her mother had hidden her bottle in one of the thousands of oak trees in Windsor Forest alone, never mind Britain, it was hopeless.

The carriage tilted dangerously, wheels creaking. Emma had to brace herself on the wall as the lantern swung, black smoke staining the curtains. She could hear the coachman shouting to the horses and then the wind was too loud to hear anything else. It rocked the carriage back and forth, whirling inside and pulling at her. The tassels on the cushions whipped her legs.

When the coachman stopped, she stumbled outside. The wind went with her and the sudden gust knocked him right off his seat. He sprawled on the sidewalk, his greatcoat flapping like wings. He was hidden in the shadows, other drivers had no reason to look back this way. The wind clung to Emma alone. It was still a calm spring evening around the house with the music and candlelight and girls in pretty dresses.

The coachman was breathing normally, though he was unconscious. Try as she might, she could not reach him. The wind was determined to shove her down the alley, to where a rickety ladder waited.

"Moira?" she called up, squinting through the whirling dust. "Is that you?" She didn't know anyone else who might be on the roof of a Mayfair town house.

Moira immediately looked over the edge. Her face was so pale she looked like the moon on the horizon of the ledge. "Emma?"

"Yes, are you hurt? Ow." The wind had tripped her and she cracked her elbow and the inside of her ankle on the ladder.

"It's not safe!" she said frantically. "Get back!"

The night air clearly had other plans. A wooden crate used to deliver bottles skidded across the ground, slamming into the wall beside Emma. It splintered into pieces.

When she put her foot on the lowest rung, the storm calmed down.

The inside of her mouth felt gritty with dirt and her hair was tangled around her antlers. Muttering, she climbed the ladder, casting another concerned glance at the coachman. He hadn't moved but he didn't look hurt, even from this vantage point. Moira however, looked dreadful. She waved her hands desperately. "Stay down there!"

Emma only climbed faster, finally pulling herself over the side. Moira crouched by the body of a girl with reddish-blond hair. A small mouse-familiar raced in circles, flaring red. "Strawberry," she said dully.

Emma exhaled slowly. "What happened? Let me fetch a doctor."

"It's too late for that," Moira said as Strawberry's eyes rolled back in her head. "She didn't want to be alone," she added, tears running down her cheeks and into her mouth. "I couldn't save her."

"Who did this?" Emma asked. "All the way up here?"

"I only saw her running away but it was definitely a girl," she replied, stroking Strawberry's forehead. Blood dripped onto the shingles. "Shh, shh. You're all right, 'Berry."

"A girl?" Emma murmured as she took her cloak off and bunched it under Strawberry's head.

Strawberry's breaths trembled pitifully. "Not your fine cloak, miss. I'm all over with blood."

"I'm going to find who did this to you," Moira promised fiercely. "Do you hear me, Strawberry?"

"Never mind," she replied. "I'll be a spirit soon and maybe I'll finally be able to protect *you*, instead of you always protecting me."

"I couldn't protect you from this," Moira said, still stroking her bloodstained hair. "I'm so sorry." Bruises rose on Strawberry's neck. Her wrist was bent backward and there were burns on her collarbone. They looked old. Moira frowned. "What are these burns from? I haven't seen them since you left your mother's house." She glanced at Emma. "That was five years ago."

Strawberry coughed, crying out in pain. She was so thin her bones looked like glass under her pale skin. "I don't—"

She broke off, falling into unconsciousness. Moira sobbed, dropping her forehead down to touch Strawberry's. Her long black hair shielded them from Emma.

Emma sat back on her heels, feeling confused and sad. Why had the wind pushed her here? What was the point? There was no evidence, no murderer to be found. Only another dead witch. It wasn't fair.

Lightning broke the sky in half. Rain poured over them in a pelting, angry deluge before Emma got ahold of herself. The rain stopped but they were already drenched. A warm mist lifted off the shingles. She squinted through the veil it made, wondering what she was looking at. Then it hit her, but too late.

The Sisters.

They coalesced in a circle around them, wreathed in deadly flowers and blood. They ignored Emma and Moira at first, reaching for Strawberry. The shingles iced, crackling like crumpled paper. The last of the rain misting the air turned to snow. Emma's fingers tingled with cold, her hair freezing into icicles. Below them, ice coated the street, wrapped frost-flowers around the iron lamps, and blackened the flowers growing in decorative urns.

The Sisters opened their mouths, an unnatural darkness held between their jaws. Their heads fell back like overblown flowers on the pale stems of their necks. They opened their mouths, sucking in the last of Strawberry's magic and ebbing life force. Her mouse tried to dart away but was caught by a vine of belladonna. It tightened around its neck, strangling. Fresh corresponding bruises formed on Strawberry's throat. She jerked violently then lay limp, chest barely rising. Ice crawled over her, hardening the mended rips on her dress, her shawl, and finally, shattering her cameo of a gargoyle hanging below her bruises. She went from pale to gray. Her hair glistened with frost.

"Leave her be!" Moira snarled, scattering blue and white powder from a pouch on her belt. A white horse formed out of the misty puff of the powder. The mare was wild, with one blue eye, but she wasn't enough, not while the Sisters were feeding.

"Bah, Keeper magic," Rosmerta spat.

Her glow intensified, pulsing brightly until Emma's eyes began to water. Rosmerta flicked her hand, her head still flung back, mouth open. A whip of dark amethyst-colored fire snapped around the mare's hooves, binding her. She screamed and there was something unnervingly human about the sound. The Sisters were already more powerful than they'd been just days ago.

Moira shivered, trying to reach a weapon, any weapon. Emma's teeth chattered so hard she bit the side of her tongue and tasted blood.

The Sisters paused.

Emma and Moira crawled closer to each other. Ice jabbed up like daggers between them, tearing through their sleeves, and peeling back the shingles. The Sisters floated together, approaching Emma as one.

"Yes." Magdalena smiled a disturbing smile.

Fear made Emma's throat spasm around a scream. She scattered salt and iron shavings. Strawberry's blood stuck to her, freezing to tiny crystals. Mrs. Sparrow would have reminded her that staying calm was her best defense.

Mrs. Sparrow likely hadn't been pinned to a rooftop by the spirits of three homicidal warlocks.

Emma could think of several better defenses but they all involved very sharp things, none of which she currently had in her possession. She barely had the strength to sit up. In fact, even as she tried to summon some sort of weather, she slumped over. They were draining her, not enough to kill her, at least not yet; but enough to shackle her in place.

Lark tried to stroke her hair. "Will you help me find my beloved?"

Moira inched away, all ice-burned cheeks and grim fury. Emma saw her flash a pointed glance at the gargoyle. Emma fumbled for her dagger with numb hands and flung it desperately. It sliced through Rosmerta, but since it wasn't made of iron, it left no damage whatsoever. But at least she had their attention. Their combined cold glares pinned her down. Moths and wasps buzzed around her.

Ice choked her lungs. Moira kept creeping toward the gargoyle, tiny perfect bat and bird bones bound in a ribbon clutched in her hand. She dropped the bundle between the gargoyle's stone feet. Shivering from head to toe, she tried to uncork the flask from her waistcoat pocket. Emma wheezed, her frozen antlers clacking on the roof when she rolled over. Her familiar glowed, pushing light through them. It had never fully materialized before. It made her feel even stranger inside.

A portal cracked open. The fissure of violet light wavered, stretching and shooting off sparks.

"I said not her!" Ewan stepped through the gate, swinging a spectral ax.

The Sisters turned, hissing. The white horse took advantage of their lapse in concentration to break free, placing herself between the Sisters and the girls. It was too late for Strawberry.

Behind them, Moira finally managed to get the flask open. She poured a stream of gold whiskey out onto the bones, stopping to take a generous mouthful for herself.

"She is ours to claim," Magdalena said, cold and calm in her hunger. "They all are."

Ewan shimmered into the shape of a white stag, hooves flashing silver. The roof cracked where he landed. The gate elongated and the ghostly outlines of the Sisters' dresses fluttered wildly. The portal pulled at them, sucking them in like a sinkhole. Rosmerta shrieked.

The white stag was a man again, fierce and foreboding.

"Stay here and be called back to the Underworld," he declared, purple sparks falling off his ax, as though he was sharpening it on a whetstone. "The Wild Hunt rides and they would love to harvest the Sisters three."

The gargoyle growled then, talons slicing through the cornices of the roof as it detached itself. Its leathery stone-colored wings flapped powerfully, sending another draft over the Sisters. They were sent closer to the portal, hissing. Magic seared the air.

Strawberry's body moved, pulled by invisible hands. Moira clutched at her desperately. Ewan dug in his heels, scrabbling for purchase.

The gargoyle snapped its jaws together, swallowing a swarm of spectral moths. Beetles and fire ants marched up Magdalena's hem for safety.

The white horse reared, bucking madly.

The Sisters flared once, blue as the heart of a flame, and then were gone.

The backdraft of energy from their sudden departure flung Strawberry like a rag doll. She was wrapped around the chimney, dangling dangerously.

"Wait!" Emma cried out as Ewan allowed himself to be pulled toward the portal. "Are you really my father?"

"You have my eyes." He glanced at her, almost smiling, as he was pulled through the gate. "And my antlers."

The gargoyle gave a rusty roar and crouched back on the ledge, scattering bits of broken stone onto the pavement below. The coachman stirred at the sound, waking from his stupor. He sat up, groaning and looking around, bemused.

Emma knew the exact moment the coachman looked up the side of the building to see her bending over the edge, her hands wet with blood, next to a dead girl.

"You!" he shouted, staring at Strawberry's body, curled around the chimney. "It was you!"

"No!" Emma darted toward the ladder. "Wait!"

The coachman had already leaped back onto the carriage bench, the reins in his hands. "Call the Order!" he bellowed to no one at all, urging the horses into a gallop.

"You'll never catch him," Moira said. "But they'll catch you."

"But I didn't do anything!"

"I'm a Madcap and you're a Lovegrove," she pointed out mercilessly. "Do you really think the truth matters?" She shook her head. "You'd better run. We'll split up, that way at least one of us will have a better chance." She looked dubiously at Emma's embroidered dress with the net overlay and the diamonds in her ears. "Can you handle yourself?"

Emma thought of the lightning, the ghouls, and the Fith-Fath spell.

"Yes," she said firmly. "I think I can, actually."

Chapter 45

Emma stole one of her father's horses.

Well, Lord Hightower's horses.

Technically she supposed he wasn't her real father. Did he know Theodora had been carrying someone else's baby? It seemed unlikely. He wasn't the type to lend his illustrious family name to a girl born on the wrong side of the blanket.

She rode all night, wrapped in the Fith-Fath glamour. She didn't just cover her antlers, but her entire body. She wouldn't be spotted by a Keeper or accosted by a highwayman who might be haunting the parks between London and the Lovegrove country house. She murmured the charm until her voice broke and her throat ached and there was no room to think about parents and secrets.

It was still dark when she reached the manor. The windows were closed up tight, reflecting the fading moonlight. She circled the house, until she found a partially open scullery window. She landed in the large sink and climbed out, catching her breath.

She released the Fith-Fath, exhausted. She needed every available ounce of magic left inside her to call the rain. The soft pitter-patter of water on the roof and the windows would hopefully mask the sound of her footsteps as she crept through the house. She stole up the stairs to open the door with the drooping flower handle.

Her mother was asleep in the wide uncurtained bed, hair tangled on her pillow, arms flung wide. Emma paused, watching her carefully. Her breathing stayed calm and deep and though her eyelids fluttered, they didn't open. It felt strange to be inside the house again, especially as an intruder. She didn't have the luxury of waiting. If the Order thought her responsible for Strawberry's death, they wouldn't stop until they found her. She had to link the clues together into a pattern, a constellation of stars that made sense when linked together.

She turned to the oak tree first. There was no doubt in her mind that it was key to the whole puzzle. According to Mrs. Peabody, her mother had instructed Aunt Bethany very carefully on the details and placement of the trees. Emma just knew if she could find the oak, she could find her mother's witch bottle, and release her from her prison. Emma, Penelope, and Gretchen had already claimed their powers and their family name, and Emma knew the truth about her father. There was no reason for her to suffer anymore.

She circled the room again, trying to find clues in the

placement of the painted trees. She didn't see any kind of pattern.

Not until she happened to glance up.

The whole room was a map, not just the oak tree and the red bird.

It was painted a deep blue with gilded paint along the edges and set throughout in a very precise pattern. She connected the gold dots easily, with an excited exhalation.

They formed star constellations.

The lion stalks the maiden fair, when the bear leaves his lair. But where the hunter goes, only the serpent knows.

The lion, the maiden, and the bear weren't familiars.

They were the spring constellations of Leo, Virgo, and Boötes.

Hydra was a kind of serpent, and another star pattern. Orion was the hunter. And the Hydra's head looked down.

Onto the oak tree and her mother's spell.

But only now, during the springtime, when the stars aligned properly. And according to the stars outside the window, the tree was south of the house in Windsor Forest, which she'd already guessed. But if she saw the whole room as a map, she knew it was also slightly to the west and tucked near a silver river.

That wasn't quite enough. There was another clue missing.

Gold is good but silver's better.

Both her mother and Ewan had spoken those words to her.

She paced the room softly, staring up at the painted ceiling. A silver circle crossed a gold circle. Was it meant to be an eclipse? The paintings were crudely done, like the red bird. Clearly they were an addition. She thought hard, but couldn't remember hearing of any eclipse expected this spring. She stared at them for a long time, until they blurred and looked like rings.

Rings.

People in love got married and had babies.

She looked around wildly until she saw the spellbox she'd left her mother. It was on the windowsill, under the moon and the shadow of the forest. But it was empty.

She stole to her mother's bedside. She was still wearing the silver ring, the bound antler dangling over her knuckle. Emma reached out to slip the ring free. Her mother clenched her fist and rolled over.

Emma went around to the other side of the bed, waiting until her mother began to snore softly. She moved with excruciating slowness, coaxing her mother's hand open, and then slipping the ring off as fast as she could, trying not to squeak with alarm. She examined it carefully, wiggling the iron nail back and forth, like a loose tooth. It finally pulled free and she could unwrap the thread. The two rings tumbled into her palm.

A thin trail of what looked like silver pollen sparkled out of the plain silver ring. A curl of gold powder did the same from the traditional gold wedding ring. It unfurled like a ribbon, toward her father's manor house next door. It must have been her mother's wedding ring.

The silver path whirled and danced like mist, snaking into the forest.

Gold is good but silver's better.

The silver ring was something else altogether.

She ran downstairs and followed it, palms damp and breaths shallow in her throat. It was cold outside, the grass heavy with dew. The stars shone, but the darkness was slowly going soft and gray, like rabbit fur.

The trail shimmered like stardust between the leaves, curling into tiny spirals along the edges. It led through the undergrowth and ferns and straight through the heart of a bluebell wood. It diverted around a willow tree to move alongside the river and finally wove around the roots of a giant oak tree, circling around and around the thick trunk to the fork of three giant branches.

Looking up, Emma saw the Hydra's starry eye looking straight back down at her.

"I found it," she whispered out loud, stunned.

It was the tree from Aunt Bethany's painting. She would have dug around the roots for her mother's witch bottle but the silver ribbon wound itself up into the crown of branches. She climbed gingerly, her shawl snagging. The first rays of watery light touched the crushed acorns in the grass and the pollen drifting on the wind.

The oak tree was full of nooks and crannies and spiders. The silver ribbon went into a crevice and faded away. Anticipation thrummed through her, almost painful in its intensity.

She was less impressed with the necessity of having to stick her hand in a hole full of beetles, spiders, and centipedes. Grimacing, she reached in warily. Years of leaves and acorns hoarded by squirrels and mice crumbled away. The smell of mold made her sneeze. Finally, her thumbnail grazed something smooth. She hooked her fingers around it and pulled it out, knuckles scraped raw.

It was a bundle of faded, moth-eaten velvet, green as spring leaves, as her father's eyes. She unfolded it carefully, heart pounding.

The bottle was smaller than she'd imagined, looking like an old silver perfume bottle more than a witch's spell. She could still smell the faint waft of roses. It was wound around with a ribbon of indistinct color, now mostly stained reddish brown with mud and leaves. When she tilted it, salt and rowan berries shifted inside.

And in the very center, a faint white glow pulsed, barely noticeable.

Emma jammed her nail under the edge of the stopper and tried to pop it open. The stopper was old and rusted and sealed tight. She couldn't even shatter it; the entire bottle was made of silver and clear faceted quartz. She tried again and again, until the splinter under her left thumb started to bleed, mingling with the blood of a dead girl on her dress.

Blood.

It was her blood that had unlocked the spell that gave her antlers.

Her blood that agitated the gate on the roof and called Ewan to save her from the old Greymalkin warlock.

Her blood when she'd shivered so violently on the rooftop next to Strawberry that she'd bitten her tongue. The glass of the bottle had sliced into her thumb right before the earthquake and Margaret.

Her mother had made Emma's blood the key to her binding spells and her witch's bottle.

She squeezed a drop from the small splinter wound, smearing it over the glass, the ribbon, and the blackened stopper.

When she tried to open it again, the lid popped right off.

The glow intensified, leaking out like spilled ink. It gathered into itself until it formed the shape of a small red bird with the crested head of a cardinal. It launched into the air, tearing through the leaves.

A glowing red feather drifted slowly down.

Emma watched it until it brushed her antlers, until it caught in her hair, until her eyes rolled back in her head and she fainted.

Part 3

UNCOVERED

Chapter 46

1796

Theodora and Bethany huddled in the hallway, each holding a candle, their bare toes curled on the cold floor. Their mother stepped out of the bedroom with a soft smile. "Nothing to worry about, girls," she said, as though their father hadn't just woken the entire household with his screaming. "It's just a nightmare."

"It's the Greymalkin," their father said hoarsely, stumbling to the door. His hair was disheveled, his nightshirt askew. He held an iron-wheel spoke tipped with jet and pearls in his hand. "They've set off the alarm. They're here."

"They're *not* here," their mother said sternly, catching his arm. "My love, that spell is decades old. It's gone faulty."

"I was a Keeper, wasn't I?" he barked. "I know when there's dark magic afoot."

Their mother closed the door firmly, looking tired. "Go on back to bed," she said. "Your father will want to check the wards."

"I can never sleep while Papa is working the wards," Bethany said. "It's like hot needles. Let's sit up until he's done," she suggested, ducking into a small parlor. It was cold and dark, the fire long since dead in the grate. "You can distract me by telling me where it is you go all day long."

Theodora took her candle to the window without replying. There was nothing but darkness and the reflection of the flame.

"You do that a lot," Bethany pointed out. "Who are you looking for?"

"No one." She turned hastily away.

Bethany didn't look convinced. "Theo, I know something's going on. I'm not bacon-brained. You never used to spend so much time in the woods. And just last summer you went into a fit because the sun gave you freckles on your nose that no one else could even see. Now you're dark as a hazelnut."

She knew she could trust her sister but she didn't want to share Ewan just yet. He was her delicious secret. And the longer she kept him that way the longer she could keep harsh reality at bay.

"Tell me this, at least," Bethany continued archly. "Is he handsome?"

"Yes."

"Not even a second's hesitation. He must be divine." Her smile was wry. "Not Alphonse, then?"

Theodora's only reply was a decidedly unladylike snort.

"He'll be devastated."

"He won't even notice."

"Our fathers will."

"I know, Beth."

"And he might—ouch!" Bethany winced. *"Papa's started."*

Theodora abandoned the window to curl up next to her sister. Bethany's familiar, a luminescent badger lying under her chaise, snarled. Magic prowled through the house, searching for holes in the wards, for residue of forbidden spells. It became a pressure in the temples, uncomfortable and irritating, but not truly painful.

Theodora slapped back at the magic when it poked around her, making her feel queasy. *"He hasn't been like this in months."*

"I wonder what set him off." Bethany pinched the bridge of her nose. The last time the wards were probed it had bled all over her favorite gown. The magic seemed more interested in Theodora this time, probably sensing she had secrets.

"He was distracted at supper," she said. *"But nothing like this."*

"I can't imagine seeing something so horrid it would give you nightmares almost forty years later." She shuddered. *"All those people drained and murdered."*

"Yes, but the Greymalkin have gone underground, if there are even any left. They were rather thoroughly banished."

"The Sisters could still be out there," Bethany pointed out. *"Perhaps Papa's right to be cautious."*

"Cautious, certainly." Theodora bit her bottom lip. *"But you don't think he's a little . . ."* she trailed off, searching for the kindest word. *"Excessive?"*

Bethany made a face. *"Sometimes."*

The flames of both their candles turned pink for a moment, flickering wildly. It was their mother's way of telling them to go to sleep. She'd been doing it since they were little girls. Theodora used to force herself to stay awake just to see the candle's pretty dance.

Her father paced the house for the rest of the night, his cat-familiar slinking by each doorway again and again. He was haggard by morning, his jaw set at a dangerous angle. He sent word to the Order, asking them to send Keepers to investigate the estate.

Theodora wasn't able to escape the manor; her father watched everyone too carefully. Three Keepers arrived later the next day, armed with iron and grim expressions. They disappeared with her father into the study and try as they might, Theodora and Bethany couldn't hear a single word of what was being said through the thick door.

They hid rowan berries and iron nails under all the furniture, where the servants wouldn't find them and ask awkward questions. Their father wore his sword everywhere, even in the house.

On the third day, Theodora hid at the top of the stairs and eavesdropped on the whispering in the hall below.

"There's definitely a trace," one of the Keepers said. "It's the Greymalkin signature but it's faint. I can't even follow it, it's like it's everywhere at once."

"I'll send the girls to London," her father declared immediately. He didn't know it, but she'd never go. She wouldn't leave Ewan. Disconcerted at the idea, she snuck down the back stairs. It might be her only chance to see him now that her father was so occupied with his mad warlock hunt. His fervor made her sad. It made him look old and sour, like a stranger.

Theodora moved through a gap in the hedges, staying hidden from the house. She ran as fast as she could until she broke through the line of trees of the edge of the forest. Ewan was waiting for her. She threw her arms around him, burying her nose in the side of his neck and inhaling his familiar woodsy scent.

"I was beginning to think they'd locked you away," he said into her hair.

"I missed you." She clung to him, feeling normal for the first time in days. *"My father's filled the house with Keepers."*

He eased back. *"Greybeards?"*

"He used to be one himself, a long time ago," she explained. *"He helped banish some of the Greymalkin when he was barely my age. And now he's convinced they're back."* She swiped at a tear. *"This obsession is eating away at him."*

"Father warned me," Ewan muttered, slapping at the long grass. *"How's it even possible? What trace could there be in your house?"*

Her eyes widened in surprise. *"Don't say you think the Greymalkin are back too?"*

Before he could answer there was a shout, a flash of light, and the pounding of horses' hooves. A short arrow with painted fletchings slammed into Ewan's shoulder. He jerked back, blood blooming on his sleeve. Someone screamed. Theodora thought it might be her, but she wasn't sure. Ewan tried to step in front of her.

The Keepers rode in, Theodora's father leading the charge. Theodora struggled to pull the arrow out but Ewan grunted in pain, his hand closing over hers. *"Leave it."*

"It's been spelled," she said frantically.

"I know," he said through gritted teeth, eyes rolling back in his head. Ghostly antlers rose from his head like smoke as his magic reacted to the danger.

"Get away from my daughter," her father roared, flinging an iron-spoke pendant. It hung from a long, thin rope like a lasso and it

looped around Ewan's neck. The smell of burning hair and flesh was acrid. The spectral antlers sizzled, laced with raw burns.

"Papa, no!" she yelled, leaping to stand over Ewan when he collapsed, struggling to fight the binding.

"He's one of them," her father barked. "We followed the magical traces here."

"He saved my life," she argued. "I love him."

"Stand down, Lady Theodora," one of the Keepers ordered as her father gaped at her, turning gray.

"Go to hell," she shot back.

"Theo, you don't know what you're saying," her father shouted. Spittle gathered at the corner of his lips. "He's one of them. He has you bewitched."

They flung salt and iron nails at her feet. She spat curses at them. Ewan moaned, sweat dampening his hair. He pushed into a crouch though it clearly cost him to do it. "Stand back," he said softly. There was blood smeared all over his arm.

Theodora glanced at him incredulously. "They'll hunt you."

"Trust me."

Muttering, she moved aside slightly. The horses circled them, carrying Keepers swinging iron-spoke pendants in their hands. Her familiar was locked inside her chest, prickling with fear. Her father threw an iron-binding chain. It struck Ewan across the face and would have flattened him if he hadn't already begun to shape-shift.

He lumbered to his feet, a giant white stag with shining antlers and blood dripping from an arrow embedded in his flesh above his right leg.

His fur was streaked red and his clothes lay in tatters around his hooves. He tossed his head, bellowing. The horses reared around them. One of the Keepers was thrown from his saddle. The grass caught fire, burning lavender and blue, and smelling like burned apples and fennel seeds.

Theodora didn't hesitate. She grabbed a handful of fur and flung herself onto the white stag's back. She held on tight, her teeth clattering together as he bounded over mounds of iron and salt. Her father was yelling behind her but she couldn't make out his words. The forest swallowed them. She knew the others would follow but they'd never find them, not if they beat the woods with a hundred hunting dogs and a hundred huntsmen. No one knew the forest like Ewan.

He crashed between the trees and Theodora shielded her eyes from the slap of branches and leaves. Her heels clamped around his sides, which pulsed like bellows. He pushed through pines growing so close together she had to slide to the ground, bruised and terrified, and walk behind him. He led them to a small clearing deep in the heart of the forest, that even the sunlight had a hard time finding.

The stag shimmered and shrank down, legs pulling in, hooves turning to fingers. Ewan fell and by the time he landed, he was himself again. Theodora dropped to her knees, gathering him close, heedless of the fact that he wore only his own blood. He was pale, his green eyes burning too bright. "Ewan," she said, frantically pulling the last of the iron-wheel pendants from around his neck. The others had snapped under the force of his shape-shifting. "I need to pull the arrow out."

He nodded, grinding his back teeth. "Don't pull it, push it all the way through or the arrowhead will hook into me."

"Are you sure?" When he nodded, she reached for the arrow with *trembling fingers. She took a deep breath and pushed as hard as she could. The arrowhead slid through flesh and muscle, scraped bone, and popped out the other side. He screamed hoarsely. Blood pooled under him. Shaking, Theodora sat back on her heels.*

He tried to smile. "Now all you have to do is snap the ends off and pull the wooden shaft clean out."

She wiped her eyes impatiently when her tears blurred her vision so that there were two arrows, each floating in a different direction. The snap of the arrowhead had Ewan jerking so violently she screamed for him. He fell back into the grass, panting heavily. She flung the pieces of broken arrow away, stifling a sob.

"You're going to be just fine," she said.

"I'm being banished," he said raspily.

"No," she snapped. "I'll have my father remove it."

"It's too late for that."

"Don't you give up, Ewan Greenwood. Do you hear me?" She clutched his good shoulder. "You're stronger than they are. And I won't have you wandering the Underworld unable to reach the Blessed Isles!"

"I need to tell you something," he said, wincing as the pain lanced down his shoulder and across his chest. The magic was draining him of his power, of his connection to the forest. It was stronger than any wheel-pendant. Before Theodora, he would have wanted to shift one last time, to die as a white stag. Now he dug into the last reserve of energy in his body to stay as he was.

"Another secret?" she whispered with a smile.

"I'm not who you think I am."

"Do you love me?"

"More than anything," he said fiercely.

"Then I don't care about the rest."

He grabbed her arm, holding her still. "You have to listen." She nodded, waiting for him to continue. The magic in the arrow spread through his veins, crawling under his skin like blue fire. He shivered even though he felt as though his blood was burning. "My mother never knew I survived. She was told I died and then she perished of the childbirth fever not long after. My father lied, to protect me."

"From your own mother?"

"Aye." He shuddered through another breath. "She was a Greymalkin, you see. My father only knew her as a pretty blacksmith's daughter. When he found out the truth, he took me and hid me in this forest, far from the mountains where I was born. I meant it when I said I wasn't good enough for you, Theodora."

She sat back on her heels, dumbfounded.

Her father had hunted Greymalkin all his life. She'd been raised on stories of their evil, of their blood taint.

But clearly Ewan wasn't tainted, whoever his mother had been.

He was beautiful and strong and kind. The Greymalkin name meant nothing to her now, not held up against the truth of Ewan Greenwood.

"Did you hear me?" Ewan asked.

"Yes, and I don't care." She smiled a little at his shock. "Because I need to tell you something too." She smoothed the tangled hair off his face. "You're not the only Greymalkin."

He didn't understand. She reached for his hand and pressed it to her belly. "Now I know why the wards broke that night," she explained.

"They knew I was pregnant before I did." She shook her head. "It all makes a strange sort of sense."

"You're . . . with child?" He stroked her belly wonderingly. "Are you sure?"

"I am now. So you have to get better, Ewan." Her mouth quirked. "Think of the scandal otherwise."

He smiled back, lines of pain etched around his lips. "I have something for you." He shifted, pulling the leather thong from around his neck. "I've been wearing it for days, waiting for you to come to me." He slid the silver ring free. It was simple and etched with oak leaves. "Will you marry me, Princess?"

"Only if you promise to survive this," she said, her cheeks wet but her smile wide. "I don't think I can get a priest to come this far into the forest."

"In the old days, they handfasted with a ribbon and a promise."

She pulled the ribbon from the collar of her dress. It was apple green and stained with his blood. They entwined fingers and she wound it around their wrists.

"With my body, I thee worship," he said huskily, slipping the ring onto her finger.

"With my body, I thee worship," she whispered back, kissing his cheeks, his forehead, his mouth. He kissed her back and she tasted the salt of his sweat and her tears.

"Protect our wee one," he said, green eyes glistening. "They'll come for the child."

"We'll protect the baby together." She kissed him again, hard. "You're not allowed to die."

"I wish I could stay, Princess."

The ground trembled beneath them. Violet light shot out of the grass. Theodora blinked, momentarily blinded. The light grew brighter, outlining Ewan's body. He pushed her away. She held onto the end of the ribbon, refusing to let go.

"No," she shouted at the portal, now causing the ground to heave so that the trees creaked ominously around them. Ewan half sank into the pool of burning light. She grabbed his fingers but her own were slippery with his blood. Ewan smiled gently.

"Let me go, Princess," he said softly, before releasing her hand.

"No!" She lunged for him but he was already being sucked back into the portal, his face bathed in that eerie purple light of poisonous monkshood flowers.

And then he was gone, without even leaving a body to mourn. The portal flashed like heat lightning before snuffing out. She smelled fire and blood. She stayed in the grass and wept until the sun sank behind the trees and her lips cracked.

She emerged from the forest later that night, her hair loose and tangled with leaves and blood. She cradled her belly protectively, and vowed that no child of hers would ever be at the mercy of the Order.

Part 4

UNBROKEN

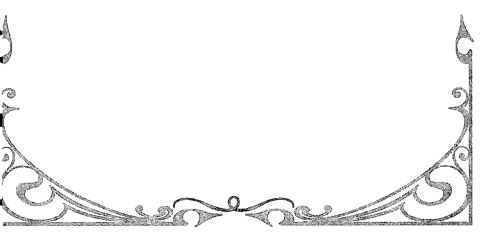

Chapter 47

Emma woke up flying.

No, not flying. Falling.

She clutched reflexively at the oak tree, disoriented and dizzy. Now she knew exactly why her blood was the key to her mother's spells. She wasn't just the daughter of a Lovegrove witch and an antlered man.

She was also a Greymalkin.

What did that even mean? Were warlocks born? Or made? Was evil a choice? Ewan, her father, hadn't seemed evil. He'd been kind and quiet. And he'd already saved her life twice.

Thoughts whirling, Emma wriggled out of the tree. She was unsteady on her feet when she landed, still covered in blood, dirt, and the detritus of her mother's witch bottle.

Her mother had willingly driven herself insane to protect her family, to make certain no one would ever know the secret behind Emma's birth and use it against her. She'd married the next-door neighbor's eldest son to protect Emma.

And in return Emma could count on one hand the number of times she had visited her mother.

Clouds raced across the sky as she stumbled through the forest. She'd thought that once she knew the secrets behind her mother's spell, she'd understand what was happening. Instead, she was more confused than ever. And poor Strawberry wasn't any less dead.

Emma was in the field, on the exact spot where Ewan was shot down with a cursed arrow, when her mother came racing out of the walled garden.

She was still wearing her white nightdress, her long black hair a tangle down her back. Her red bird flew happy circles over her, swooping down and around. Theodora paused in front of Emma, her feet bare and caked with mud. "How did you do it?" she asked, reaching for both her hands. Her smile was bright.

Emma smiled back through her tears. Her mother knew her. "I study the stars."

Theodora hugged her tightly. She touched the tip of one of Emma's tines. "You got these from your father."

"Apparently so."

"You must have found my spells." Theodora blinked, then shook her head sharply. "I haven't much time."

"What do you mean?" Rain swept over the field of wild columbines.

"I can feel the illness coming back."

"But I freed your familiar!"

"Some spells never fade completely." She rubbed her arms, chilled. "No more doctors," she said petulantly.

"*Maman?*" Emma murmured cautiously.

Theodora made a sound of frustration and the red spirit-bird lowered, disappearing into her chest. Her eyes cleared but Emma had no idea how long the lucidity would last.

"It's not fair," Emma said.

"More than fair," Theodora said easily. "My magic amplifies other magic and unfortunately it does the same to the repercussions. That's partly why my spell augmented your father's magic inside you." She nodded to the antlers.

"But why can't you be cured?"

"I'd do it again," she said fiercely. "As many times as it took to keep you safe. Gold is good but silver's better." She looked around, confused. "Why am I outside?"

Emma bit back tears, putting her arm around her mother's shoulders. She couldn't seem to make the rain stop. It was cold and constant, slapping at them. "Let's get you back to your room."

Theodora dug her heels in. "No."

"But you're getting wet."

"It doesn't matter. I'm not going back to that house. It's been too long since I've been in the forest."

"I don't think that's such a good idea. The Sisters are at large," Emma explained. "When I broke your spell, gates opened and they came through. And they keep finding me." She looked at her witch knot. "Now, I guess I know why. They must know I'm one of them."

"You are *not* one of *them*." Theodora fisted her hands. "You're a Greenwood. It's what your father called himself. Don't let the Keepers find you."

"Too late for that," Emma replied. "But my father . . . Ewan . . . he found me too."

"You've seen him?" Theodora sounded like the seventeen-year-old version of herself she'd trapped in the bottle. "Where? How? Tell me!"

"He saved me from hellhounds and the Greymalkin."

"He'd be able to, being one of their bloodline."

"Does that mean I'll be able to stop them as well?"

"My white stag," Theodora murmured. "My beloved."

"How do I stop them?" Emma asked sharply. Lightning tangled over the trees, flashing so bright there was a loud crash, followed by the smell of smoke.

Theodora twirled once, dancing with an invisible partner.

"*Maman.*"

"I'm Mrs. Greenwood," Theodora hissed angrily. Then she smiled again, all innocence. Emma ground her back teeth in frustrated worry. "And we're going to be together forever now."

"Please," Emma begged. "You have to concentrate." The rain froze in midair, turning to snow. The wind rolled the grass like white caps on a stormy sea. "*Please.*"

Theodora opened her hand slowly. Sitting on her scarred and scratched witch knot was the antler from the spellbox. It was just a small piece, like the inside of a cracked hazelnut. "I need to be where he was. Where he can find me. I won't go to the Blessed Isles without him, and I can't go back to not being able to remember him."

"What are you saying?"

"I need this, Emma. I need to be close to him. And this is the only way I know how."

Before Emma could stop her, she popped the antler in her mouth and swallowed it.

"A magic cloud I put on thee; From dog, from cat, from cow, from horse; From man, from woman, from young man, from maiden; And from little child. Till I again return."

It was the Fith-Fath spell.

Used for its original purpose.

"Tell him I'm waiting for him," she said fiercely. "When he comes looking for me. Tell him I'll *always* wait for him."

"Wait! You can't—"

But it was too late.

Theodora was already falling to her knees, her hands turning into hooves, delicate and strong. Her skin thickened to russet fur. Her hair lifted, re-formed into wide ears. Her eyes were huge and black. She rose on four slender legs, a graceful and elegant doe, a red bird perched on the ridge of her spine.

She'd used the Fith-Fath spell to turn herself into a deer. She was beautiful, a palpable kind of joy shining in her dark eyes. Emma didn't know if her mother could remember who she really was now that she was in the deer body, or it she was only able to think deer thoughts. It didn't seem to matter. Because she'd never known her mother to be more present in herself than she was in that moment, as a deer full of wildness and beauty and love.

The doe bounded away, leaping high over the grass, her white tail flashing. Emma ran after her into the complicated shadows of Windsor Forest. She followed her through the bluebell wood, racing until her legs ached. She might have the antlers of a deer, but she was still just a girl running in the woods. Branches slapped at her and the ground was uneven and unforgiving.

She finally found the deer, nibbling the leaves growing through the remains of a wooden hut built between two trees. A faded, crumbling gargoyle watched from a branch above her head.

Her mother was well and truly gone now.

But she was happy in the woods where she'd met her true love.

Chapter 48

When Cormac found the whirlwind of snow and rain in the middle of an otherwise fine spring morning, he knew he'd found Emma.

He bent his head down, his black hat torn away by the force of the wind, and tried to plow through the unnatural storm. It pelted him with hail and the wild foxgloves under his boots crackled with a thin coating of ice. Emma stumbled out of the woods, the weather raging around her.

Whatever invisible machinery had kept it going fell apart when Emma turned to look at him. The air was so still he could hear the crackling of the ice as it melted. Her reddish-brown hair gleamed like copper and snowflakes rested on her delicate antlers. He almost couldn't imagine her without them now. They were a part of her, made the world see her for how unique she truly was.

He crossed the field, closing the distance between them.

There was blood on her dress and an acorn tangled in a knotted lock of hair. "Are you hurt?"

Emma shook her head mutely. He gathered her in his arms because she looked ready to shatter. Water dripped from the trees and glistened in the tall grass. She finally shifted slightly.

"Don't you know hugging girls with antlers is a dangerous sport? You could lose an eye." She sniffled.

He pulled back. "What happened?"

"I broke the spell."

He sucked in a breath. "You freed your mother?"

"I freed her familiar but she's only half-cured. And now she's gone."

"Gone? What do you mean, gone?"

"She turned herself into a deer and ran off into the woods."

He blinked at her. "She did what?" He shook his head. "Never mind. We'll find her."

"She doesn't want to be found. At least not by us. I think she's finally happy." She smiled sadly, stepping out of the circle of his arms. "There's more."

He frowned, glancing over his shoulder. "You can tell me in the carriage."

"It can't wait."

"It has to," he said grimly. "The Order is searching for you. It won't be long before Keepers descend on the manor house, just in case you've taken up with your mother." He took her hand, tugging her firmly until she followed him. "I have a hired hack waiting in the lane. The coachman owes me a favor."

Emma stumbled after him. "Cormac——"

He broke into a run and she was too busy keeping up to say anything else. They were panting when he yanked open the carriage door and she clambered inside. He hadn't even sat down yet before the horses were breaking into a brisk trot, bouncing them down to the road.

"I didn't kill Strawberry."

He shot her an insulted glance. "I know that."

"It's important," she insisted.

"And it goes without saying."

Her eyes glistened dangerously. "Thank you," she said, her voice wobbling. She exhaled slowly, as if preparing herself for something unpleasant. "There was another memory in my mother's witch bottle. Ewan Greenwood isn't just my father. He's also a *Greymalkin*."

He sat back, stunned. "I beg your pardon?"

She wrapped her arms around herself. "My father called himself Ewan Greenwood but he was a Greymalkin, stolen away from his Greymalkin mother by his woodcutter father for his protection. His father didn't even know the woman he'd married was a Greymalkin, not until it was too late. So he took his son away and they lived in the forest, hiding away until the day Ewan met my mother. The Order didn't just kill Ewan, they banished him to the Underworld with a spelled arrow."

"How is it possible no one knew about this?" The Order wouldn't just bind her for this, they'd do so much worse. Fear made his veins icy.

"My mother's spell," she explained miserably. "And the fact

that Ewan's father raised him secretly and he wasn't from one of the aristocratic families."

"*That's* why your blood activated the gate when we tried to close it," he realized. "And why the Greymalkin warlock and the Sisters seek you out."

"Exactly," she said. "So you see? The Order will never believe I'm innocent."

"They can't ever find out," he said roughly.

"You may not want to help me now," she said softly.

He crouched in front of her, his hands closing over her shoulders. "Do you think me so cowardly?" His hands tightened. "If you were a man I'd call you out for that."

Her smile was fleeting. "Now you sound like Gretchen." She leaned forward slightly. "Why would you help me, Cormac?"

"Because you matter," he replied quietly. Her eyes were green as leaves, the shadow of her antlers like the shadow of bare branches on her face. "I let the Order come between us once. Never again. You matter more than the Order, more than anything. And I won't let them take you." He rose out of his crouch in one fluid motion, settling back onto the bench and dragging her with him. His mouth closed on hers. She kissed him back, fingers digging into his arms.

"I can't let you risk yourself for me," she murmured.

He narrowed his eyes. "And if I said those words to you?"

She wrinkled her nose. "I'd kick you," she admitted.

"And as I can't kick *you*," he returned, brushing his mouth along the side of her neck until she shivered, "I'll have to get my vengeance another way."

The kiss deepened, went wild and dark. Her wet dress clung to her waist and he followed the curves with his palm. Her tongue touched his and the kiss turned desperate. He was half-surprised steam didn't lift off them, and it might have if there'd been enough room between their bodies. When Emma pulled away slightly, gasping for breath, her lips were swollen and pink. He felt drunk on her. He could almost forget they had no idea how to prove her innocence. He could forget everything but the feel of her in his arms, the smell of rain on her skin.

He brushed his thumb over her cheek. "We'll find our way through this," he murmured.

She wished she felt as confident as he sounded. She sat back and tried to marshal her whirling thoughts. "Where can I possibly hide that the Order won't find me?" she asked.

"Moira's the one who told me you ran off, even before that coachman found a Keeper to tell about Strawberry. And I don't know anyone better suited to keep you hidden from the Order than a Madcap."

"Do you think she'll help me?"

His grin was crooked. "Will Moira help you thumb your nose at the Order? In fact, I think she'll insist."

"There is that." Her moment of smug triumph wilted. "What about Gretchen and Penelope? Are they in danger? Will the Order come for them as well?"

"Not yet," he said. "They may ask them questions, but they won't go before the magisters or the inquisitors. Not yet anyway."

"Can we send them a message? With your tabula perhaps, the way Olwen did when Moira needed you?"

"It's too risky." He shook his head. "Why do you think we're in a carriage instead of using the doorknob spell I gave your cousins that day in the goblin markets? Magic leaves a trace."

"How am I ever going to manage this without magic?"

"The same way I do," Cormac replied, with more than a hint of self-deprecation. His expression was mocking, that sardonic charm he used as a shield against the Order. "Creatively."

"I'm sorry, that's not what I meant." She took his hand. "You're stronger than they give you credit for," she said, feeling badly that he might have taken her comment in the wrong way. He was helping her at considerable cost to himself and she'd just added insult to injury. "They underestimate you. And they'll underestimate me." She lifted her chin, her smile decidedly savage. "And that's going to be our greatest weapon against them."

Chapter 49

It was nearly dark when they found Moira in the goblin markets. She was inside a striped tent cluttered with cameos and charms. A man in a worn hat puffed on a pipe whose bowl looked like it was stuffed with raspberries. The pink smoke took the shape of deer. The blue eye embroidered on his eye patch watched her.

"Emma?" Moira's eyebrows rose. "You're keeping bad company," she said, smirking at Cormac.

"We've come for your help."

She snorted. "Like I'd help a Greybeard."

"You'd help me if it meant crossing the Order, wouldn't you?" He was using that soft tone that made the back of Emma's knees weak.

Moira didn't seem impervious either. She cleared her throat. "Come again?"

"I need a place to hide," Emma explained, keeping to the

shadows, even inside the tent. "Will you lend me one of your rooftops?"

"The Order's after you, my pretty?" One-Eyed Joe shifted in his chair, the cameos on his hat tinkling together. "Bad luck to have you in my tent, inn't?" He plucked a cameo off the collar of his patched greatcoat. It was the soft blue of a lake at dawn but utterly blank. "Cover yourself up before they find ye."

"It's a glamour," Moira explained. "Joe's a dream-bringer. He works illusions," she elaborated when Emma just blinked. "That there will keep you hidden. For a while, anyway."

When Emma reached for it, Cormac stopped her. His fingers were firm around her wrist. "What's the cost?" he asked bluntly.

"It doesn't matter," she said. "I have money." Unless her father found out the truth and disowned her and then she'd be tossed out without a penny, without even a rooftop to her name like Moira.

"He doesn't want money," Cormac said darkly. "Do you, old man?"

One-Eyed Joe didn't lose his pleasant smile, but the smoke from his pipe turned to a creature with ridges and talons. "A lock of your hair," he said finally.

"Is that all?" she asked.

"Emma, don't," Cormac advised. He still hadn't let go of her wrist. "You don't know what he'll use it for."

She smiled wanly. "What else can happen to me today?" She disengaged herself gently from his hold and took the small brass scissors Moira gave her. She snipped off a lock of hair and handed it to One-Eyed Joe. He tossed her the cameo and she pinned it to her neckline.

"There now, such a fuss." He wrapped her hair lovingly in a square of white silk, slipping it into one of the hidden pockets inside his coat. Cormac's jaw clenched. "I can make you a proper cameo," he added, staring at her so intently she was half-sure he could see right into her secrets. "To hide the antlers, but I'll have to carve it in your likeness. Take some time, that will."

"Thank you," she said with a polite curtsy.

"Oh, I like her," he said to Moira. "What are they after you for?"

Emma swallowed. "Murder."

"She's the one they blamed for Strawberry," Moira explained quietly. "But Emma was on the ground. She didn't do it."

"I know that," he scoffed. "What do you take me for? An old man?" Though he had dark wrinkled skin and few teeth left, Moira wisely refrained from commenting. "Help her out, Moira. We don't often get fine ladies this side of the bridge."

"I need to tell my cousins I'm safe," Emma said. "Before Gretchen does something rash."

"I'll send word to Cedric," Moira promised. She cast a suspicious glance down the bridge. "Now come on, before the Greybeards infest this place like rats." She tilted her head at Cormac. "No offense."

"None taken," he replied wryly.

She led them out the door to the ordinary London streets and into the first alley on the right. After that it was a confusing warren of shadows, unfortunate smells, and the glint of eyes in the gathering dark. Cormac held her hand tightly and it helped her stay calm. Moira finally stopped behind a grocer. "Percy leaves the ladder out for the Madcaps," she explained, scaling it lightly. "And in return we keep his gargoyles happy." She disappeared over the top.

"I have to check in with the Order," Cormac murmured, adjusting Emma's hood so that her antlers were properly hidden. "If they suspect me, I won't be able to help you."

"I know." She smiled wearily. He leaned in to kiss her, slow and deep and soft. When he pulled away she felt warmer. As he left, she stayed hidden behind the ladder and the pile of turnip baskets, watching him tip his hat to the ladies on the street who giggled at him.

"Oi, are you coming or what?" Moira called, peering over the edge of the roof.

Emma climbed up the ladder, knotting her skirts to one side to make it easier. She understood perfectly why Moira only wore breeches. The roof was dusty and uncomfortable but it showed the stars as they glimmered through the darkening sky. A gargoyle perched on each corner but Moira had already left bowls of whiskey and honey for them and they stayed still and watchful.

With nowhere left to run and nothing to do but follow the patterns of the stars, Emma's thoughts feasted on her, like insects overtaking a ripe melon. They crawled and stung and bit.

So she'd focus on what she knew, start with the crumbs before eating the whole cake.

"We're going to find out who the Sisters are using to commit those murders. We're going to find out who killed Strawberry," she promised quietly. "Somehow."

Emma and Moira lay side by side for a long quiet moment as night dropped its last veil. The stars were bright as beads. "I always wondered what the shapes mean," Moira said. "Strawberry used to make up stories for them."

"Do you see that one over there? The one like a big spoon?"

"Aye."

"They call it the Plough."

"Strawberry always said it was a butter churn knocked over by pixies." There was a smile in her voice. "Show me another."

"That star there is the head of the Hydra." Emma pointed, dragging her finger carefully down. "And that line there is her body and tail. They say if you cut off the Hydra's head, two more grow back." She shifted, pointing again. "And that's Leo. From the story of Hercules." Moira just shrugged. "It's ancient Greek. He had twelve labors, one of which was killing the Nemean lion, after which it was put into the sky."

"You're lucky, you know," Moira said.

Emma turned her head to shoot her an incredulous glance. She smiled briefly. "I meant before all of this. I'm not allowed at the academy. And I always wanted to learn the way you can," she confessed. "And now I can't even get near the school without my feet prickling like the devil. They hurt to warn me away from danger."

Emma frowned thoughtfully. "So Rowanstone is dangerous now?"

"Aye," Moira said. "More so than Ironstone. Though to be fair, most of London isn't any better these days."

"You said you saw a white hem."

"I did."

"What kind of hem?"

She blinked. "A hem is a hem."

"Was it beaded?" Emma pressed for details, a hazy pattern forming in her head, unconnected stars suddenly forming a constellation. "Lace? Net overlay? Or was it homespun? Ragged?"

"Fine," she answered, thinking back. "It was very fine. And I did find some tiny silver beads afterward."

"So it's not just any girl," Emma concluded breathlessly. "It's a *debutante*."

"I knew the fancy were more trouble than they're worth," Moira said. "A bleedin' deb? Are you sure?"

Emma thought back to the Pickford ball, and the girl in the tree in Hyde Park. Daphne had been at each of those events, in her fine white gown with her gaggle of friends. And she was constantly throwing suspicion in Emma's direction.

"It's Daphne," she said, sitting straight up. "It has to be. She was there at each of the murders. You saw the hem of a white dress, and she always wears white."

"All debutantes wear white," Moira pointed out.

"Exactly!" Emma exclaimed. "That's why it's been *girls* getting drained. Not because girls are more vulnerable like the Order thinks." Moira made a face at that. "But because that's who *Daphne* would have access to. It's not about the *murdered*, it's about the *murderer.* She was at all those balls and soirees and in the park."

"You think she climbed a roof?" Moira asked doubtfully, also sitting up. "No offense, but I've seen how you and your cousins climb."

She worked through the scenario in her mind. "Daphne *could* have been there last night," she said slowly. "There was a masquerade on the same street. I saw the carriages waiting and Penelope was there. She can confirm it." Something close to excitement simmered in her belly. "I know I'm right about this."

Moira lay back down on the shingles. "Now all you have to do is prove it."

Chapter 50

"Daphne? Daphne Kent? Cormac stared at her. "As in the daughter of the First Legate?"

"Yes," Emma grumbled. She'd been hoping for a different reaction. Gretchen and Penelope stared at her as well.

"Actually, it makes a certain kind of sense," Gretchen finally allowed, nodding slowly. "I never did like her."

"I don't think that's a good enough reason to accuse someone of murder," Cormac pointed out.

"But I *really* don't like her."

They were in a cramped bedroom of an inn that smelled like smoke and boiled potatoes. There was a narrow table, two chairs, and a sooty grate piled with the crumbling coals of a dead fire. The bed was lumpy and when Penelope went to sit on it, something scurried in the sheets. She leaped off again and spent the rest of the time pressed to the wall.

It was the best temporary hiding place they could find as it had a window looking out to a maze of steps and landings that could be reached from the roof. Cormac paid for the room and Gretchen and Penelope had followed half an hour later. Moira and Emma came in through the window. Emma and her cousins had hugged so fiercely and for such a long time, Moira dropped into a chair, sighing impatiently.

"You have to admit it all sounds suspicious," Emma maintained.

Cormac inclined his head. "It does. But then you were at all those places as well and we know *you* didn't kill anyone."

She rubbed her face, frustrated. "Cormac, you're only seeing the side of her she wants you to see."

"Quite," Penelope agreed. "She's vicious with boiled beets."

"Even so," he insisted. "You can't accuse the daughter of the First Legate without serious, irrefutable proof. Especially you, Emma."

"I know," she sighed, sinking into the other chair. "I mean to get it."

"How?"

"I haven't exactly worked that out yet."

"We'll watch her while we're at the academy," Gretchen promised.

"They still let you go to lessons?" Moira asked.

"Yes," Penelope replied. "They probably think we'll let something slip, and lead them to Emma."

"What have they told my . . . father?" She stumbled over the word. She'd managed to give Gretchen and Penelope a very hurried account of her mother's secrets. Penelope said it was romantic. Gretchen said turning into a deer sounded itchy. They'd both made her smile.

"Nothing at all," Gretchen told her. "But they're watching your house."

"And ours as well," Penelope added. "I caught a Keeper staring at me from the bushes last night." She smiled smugly. "I set the dogs on him."

"The rumors are ridiculous." Gretchen rolled her eyes. "Apparently you've also gone on a criminal spree and have stolen several heirloom diamonds."

"Why in the world would I want diamonds?"

"I don't know." She shrugged. "But the younger girls have set up some sort of spirit board to commune with your spirit."

"But I'm not dead!"

"Presumably, that's why it's not working very well. You instructed them to crawl through the house at midnight bleating like sheep."

"*You* instructed them to do that." Penelope laughed. "She hid behind the door and whispered at them until they were terrified."

Gretchen folded her arms mutinously. "They made me angry."

Emma hugged her. "Thank you."

"I'll do it again when you're back at lessons so you can see them too," she promised. "I'll pretend to be some ghost or another."

"What did Mrs. Sparrow say?"

"Nothing, actually," Penelope replied. "And she didn't punish Gretchen for the sheep thing either."

"They'll start using soothsayers and the like to find you," Cormac said regretfully. "It won't be long now. So whatever you mean to do, we'd best do it quickly." He lifted the miniature iron-wheel pendant hooked to his cravat pin as it glowed in warning. "Very quickly."

He handed out bundles of banishing powder and other assorted amulets. "Take these," he said grimly. "I have a feeling we're going to need them."

Chapter 51

Emma was stretched out on the roof again counting stars when the breeze kicked up.

And up.

She clutched at the shingles but the wind was too strong.

The Sisters had found another victim.

Emma knew the force of the wind would toss her right over the side if she didn't get herself firmly planted on the ladder. She finally hit the ladder with her toe and let herself roll sideways until she could get a proper grip on it. It was rickety and not entirely sturdy. The wind didn't care. She lowered herself slowly, trying not to think about the fact that there was a girl dying somewhere at this very moment.

She finally made it to the ground but there was no moment to stop. The wind kept pushing at her, relentless and inexorable. Her hair whipped into her face, her skirts tangled around her legs. She let it push her, hoping she might finally catch Daphne in the act, save some poor witch, and exonerate herself in the process.

"Oi," someone shouted, confused. "What the bleedin' hell's going on over there?"

All it would take was for a single witch to see her and summon a Keeper. She'd be chained, her magic stuffed in a bottle, and left to run as mad as her mother. Rain pelted down for a cloud-thickened sky. She fumbled for the Feth-Fiada saltwater-soaked ribbon Cormac had pressed upon her. It was the same kind her Aunt Bethany had used. It felt like a hundred years ago. She could barely recognize herself in the lonely, uncomfortable girl she'd been then. She dropped the ribbon and when it hit the ground, a cloud of fog seeped into the street and over the pavement.

"Allo," the same voice said, more uncertainly this time.

The fog would cover her for a little while. Even through the haze she realized where she was going.

Rowanstone Academy.

"You can't be serious," Emma muttered, wrapping her hands desperately around the fencepost. It didn't help. The wind would not be denied. Until she plowed right into another person. They both squeaked, grabbing at each other for balance.

"You!" Emma cried out.

"You!" Daphne shot back.

They eyed each other warily and with a great deal of distaste.

"You have some nerve coming back here," Daphne finally said. "I'm calling for Mrs. Sparrow."

Before Emma could reply—or turn on her heel and run away—the wind returned. A sudden gust knocked them together. They fell against the side of a carriage, half-hidden in the thickening fog. The door creaked open and a hand fell limply out. The witch knot was bloody and unfurled.

Emma pushed her storm-knotted hair out of her face impatiently. "Who is that?" she whispered.

Daphne darted forward, going so pale so quickly Emma thought she might faint. Daphne yanked the carriage door open fully. There was just enough light falling through the fog to show Lilybeth sprawled on the cushions. Her blue eyes stared blankly. Daphne shook her shoulder desperately. "Wake up!" She shook again. "Wake up, I said!"

Lilybeth's curls escaped their pins from the violence of Daphne's grip, but she still didn't wake. Emma touched Daphne's arm. "She's not asleep."

Daphne made a strange sound and released her friend abruptly. "She can't be dead."

"She has the Greymalkin mark," Emma said gently. "What was she doing in there?" She swallowed, her throat tightening.

"She fell asleep in the carriage on the way back from the concert. We tried to wake her up but she's the worst after a nap. She sleeps like the dead." Daphne stifled a sob. "Sophie sent for a footman to carry her out but I was starting to worry."

"Where's the footman?" Emma asked. "Hello?" She called out loudly. It was hard to see through the fog. No one replied. Daphne looked furious. "Perhaps he's been injured?" Emma suggested.

"If not, he will be very soon."

"And where's the Keeper?" Emma pressed, glancing around nervously. "Shouldn't there be one on guard? How could this have happened?"

There were bruises on Lilybeth's throat and her dress hung oddly, as if something was poking out of her side. Emma frowned. "The Sisters don't usually leave marks like that, do they? I thought that as spirits they could only drain, not do direct physical violence."

Daphne followed her gaze, stupefied. "Lilybeth fell off a horse and broke that rib." Her brow furrowed. "When she was *six* years old."

"It doesn't make sense."

"I know. She got those bruises three years ago when . . . well, never mind. They're not recent, anyway."

As if to prove Daphne right, Lilybeth's sleek Siamese cat–familiar darted away, red as a burning ember in the white fog. Daphne reached out to touch her friend's hand, but stopped herself. She glanced at Emma, looking younger and more confused than Emma had ever seen her. She wasn't just a spoiled debutante with a sharp tongue. She was a girl who had lost a friend.

"I thought you were the murderer," she admitted, frowning.

"And I thought it was you," Emma returned, equally dumbfounded. She gave another wary glance around. The fog was still too thick to see much more than the outline of the school gates and the turret. A carriage rumbled by, wheels creaking and hooves echoing.

"You should go," Daphne said, surprising Emma. "Before I call for help."

"Will you be all right?"

"Of course I will. I'm not the one being chased by the Order."

"Daphne?" Emma paused at the gate. "Why are you helping me?"

"Because I saw you walking into the school. There's no blood on you and I saw you come through the gates so I know you didn't kill Lilybeth. But if the Order catches you and blames *you*, the real murderer will walk free." Her eyes glittered. "And that is not going to happen."

"Thank you," Emma said quietly. "And now we know why we've been at so many of the murders. I was mistaken about you, but I was right about one thing," she said when Daphne just stared at her. She nodded to the school looming in the misty shadows. "The murderer really *is* one of us."

Chapter 52

Emma planned to keep running until she was safely tucked into some dark corner where no Keeper would ever think to look for her.

She was doing just that when the first pigeon fell from the sky. It landed in front of her with such a thunk she shrieked and leaped out of the way. She wasn't sure what she was expecting; a ghoul, an iron dagger, another body. Not a dead bird with the Greymalkin knot blazed on its feathered chest, and its neck twisted at an unfortunate angle. She took a few more steps, staring at the sky and she tripped over a rat. His long tail was also twisted into an awful imitation of the Greymalkin mark.

And then someone seized her shoulder and yanked her into the alley.

She struggled, scratching and kicking and contorting herself to use her elbows as weapons. Her captor grunted, doubling over, but he didn't let go. He pressed her against the wall, securing her hands to the bricks.

This was it.

She was going to be taken back to the ship.

Dark eyes glowered at her from under the brim of a fine hat. A white cravat glowed in the dim light. She knew that jawline, that wicked mouth.

Cormac.

She bit him.

He snatched his hand off her mouth. "You bit me!"

"You scared me half to death," she said accusingly. "I thought you were a Keeper."

"I *am* a Keeper."

"Maybe," she allowed. "But you're not one of *them*."

"Now you sound like Moira," he said. He still had her pinned between the bricks and his body. "What are you doing out here? Shouldn't you be hiding behind a chimney pot somewhere?"

"I was dragged to the school by a whirlwind," she said. "Lilybeth."

"Damn it," he said harshly. "I wondered."

"Is that why you're here?"

"Someone sent up flares. But when I got there the place was full of Keepers. All muttering your name."

She winced. "Bollocks."

"Strangely, Daphne was most insistent that she didn't see you anywhere and that she was the one who found the body." He arched a brow.

"She's helping me," she admitted. "She thought I was to blame just as I thought she was to blame. Lilybeth was her friend."

Cormac scrubbed his face. "This is a right mess."

"It gets worse," she said, taking his hand. "Come with me." She led him to the mouth of the alley and pointed at the rat.

"Not again," he muttered. "We followed a trail of these to the academy just last week."

"So I'm right about the murderer being a student at least," Emma said. "Why else would it lead to the school?"

"We thought it was someone at Ironstone," he admitted. "The Order has been testing the lads ever since."

She peered down the sidewalk. "There, another bird," she said. "The Sisters must be on the run." She tried to dart out of the alley but he grabbed her arm and swung her back.

"What are you doing?"

"Following them!" She shook him off. "Come on, before we lose the trail."

"Are you completely insane? You've seen what they can do. And you know they must be searching for you now they've had a taste of your blood," he reminded her. With the last of her mother's spells fallen away, she was vulnerable.

"It doesn't matter," she insisted. "Do you really think we're likely to get another opportunity like this? Don't be a prat, Cormac." She hurried down the sidewalk, keeping her face concealed in her hood. The magic of the cameo was fading and she didn't want to be recognized, not as a Lovegrove, a Hightower, or a Greymalkin.

Cormac was at her side, muttering. "Did you just call me a prat?"

"Just help me look," she said, but she was smiling faintly.

They found another rat.

The trail took them through Mayfair, toward the dark shadow of Hyde Park. Candlelight glowed behind mullioned glass windows. Carriages, polished as new pennies, waited on the curb. There would be late suppers and balls tonight, or the theater on Drury Lane. There would be turtle soup and champagne and cucumber salads. She'd taken it all for granted. But even prowling through the dark in a ruined dress, cloak, and antlers instead of a proper bonnet, with Cormac beside her, it seemed worth it. Knowing was better than not knowing.

Even if what you knew broke your heart.

Cormac backed her against a lamppost just as she was wondering what she might have been doing right now if her life hadn't altered so dramatically. He lowered his head to shield her from view. "Keeper," he mouthed, before kissing her.

And since Emma Day, daughter of the Earl of Hightower and the infamous Theodora Lovegrove, wouldn't be kissing a Keeper out in the street for anyone to see, she kissed him back enthusiastically. She clung to him, finally feeling soft in a way that didn't infuriate her and strong in a way that didn't make her feel brittle. His tongue stroked hers and his hands clasped her close against his chest. She could see his pulse fluttering wildly in his throat. Someone gasped and she thought it might be her.

"We should go," she finally whispered, mostly because she

wanted nothing more in the world than to stay right where they were and continue doing exactly what they were doing.

Cormac kissed her again, so quickly and yet so tenderly she felt like crying for no good reason. He glanced left, then right. "He's gone," he murmured.

They went back to following the trail; two more pigeons, three mice, and a hawk later, Cormac came to an abrupt halt. They exchanged a grim glance before ducking into the shadows of the park.

"No," he said harshly. "Absolutely not. Do you have any idea how many Keepers are in this area?"

She nodded mutely, following his gaze across the street.

The trail of dead rats and birds had led them to Greymalkin House.

Chapter 53

They met in Hyde Park an hour later, after messages were sent out to summon them. Cormac carried a small chest under his arm. Emma, Gretchen, and Penelope sat together on the grass. Moira was perched on a low branch, the smoky light glinting off her cameos. "They've offered a reward for your capture," she said.

"Splendid." It wasn't exactly a surprise but it didn't improve her mood. It did, however, improve her determination. "I have an idea," she added, sounding more confident than she felt. "We need to close the last gate, that's obvious. And so we need to get into Greymalkin House to stop the Sisters."

"You're cracked." Moira whistled through her teeth. "No one goes in there. And how do you even know where the last gate is, if the Order doesn't?"

"Because we just followed a fresh trail," Emma replied

tightly. "And we only have until dawn before the gate closes itself up and opens somewhere else. We need to seal it. Now. Tonight." She rubbed her arms for warmth. "We need to find the real murderer. The Order insists it's a warlock, someone old and powerful. But Daphne and I both think it's a debutante."

Cormac raised his eyebrows. "I'm not entirely convinced, it has to be said. The Order thinks it's someone from Ironstone." The girls exchanged knowing glances.

"And that right there is why she will continue to get away with murder. Literally."

"So how is this lot meant to stop the Sisters if the Greybeards can't?" Moira finally asked.

"Because we can get inside the house," Emma replied. "When no one else can."

"But how are we supposed to defeat the Sisters without them?" Penelope asked. "We barely know what we're doing as it is."

"We just need to get in first, before they can stop us. Then we call for help and they can ride in on their bloody white horses and save us all if they'd like. But they'll never let us close enough to try unless we force them to."

"You're all mad," Moira sighed. "So how do we do this, then?"

"We'll have to take them by surprise." Cormac's smile was brief and crooked. "I can't imagine how we wouldn't, with a Madcap, a Keeper, two girls, and a fugitive." He unrolled a scrap of parchment, using the top of the chest as a table. He'd drawn out Greymalkin House and the surrounding area. "There are Keepers here, here, and here," he said as he pointed. "And likely a couple on the roof over there somewhere."

"Mine." Moira grinned savagely.

"Don't kill them."

"Spoilsport."

"We'll take them all out, give Emma a few moments, and then I'll send up the flare to summon the Order. And if we get caught," he added, "Emma and I will act as though I've captured her."

"Why?" Gretchen asked, suspiciously.

"Because if this doesn't work, we're going to need the Order to go on trusting Cormac," Emma explained. "We have to be practical about this." She nudged her cousin, smiling faintly. "So don't hit him too hard if it comes down to it."

"Why does she have to hit me at all?" Cormac asked.

"I have to make it look good," Gretchen replied primly.

"I already look good," he drawled.

Chapter 54

Fog hung between the houses, obscuring the gaslights so they flickered like fireflies. It drifted over the chimney pots, mingling with the scent of smoke. Moira listened to carriage wheels clattering on the cobblestones below. The soles of her feet practically caught fire the closer she got to Greymalkin House.

She leaped from roof to roof in her patched trousers. The fog was so thick, if Cormac hadn't told them exactly where the Keepers were lurking, they'd never have found any of them. As it was, she was seriously put out that one of them dared claim a rooftop. She crept closer, barely able to distinguish the outline of his beaver hat in the gloom. She crouched by a gargoyle so small it would have fit in the palm of her hand. It was attached to the very tip of an iron fence running around the entire roof. She bathed it in whiskey and murmured a few words in its stone ear. It flew into the air like a drunken bumblebee. Following orders, it flew around the Keeper's head.

"What the—" He covered his face as the tiny, vicious gargoyle attacked him. Miniature stone teeth tore through his shirt and his skin as it tried to get a bite of the Keeper's iron-wheel pendant. It darted in and out, coming away with hanks of hair, blood, and linen. The Keeper swung out again, toppling the gargoyle from its flight. It tumbled to the ground below, smashing into pieces.

Moira hit him on the back of the head with her hands clasped together. He stumbled against the fence, sliding into an unconscious heap.

Below, Gretchen sent her wolfhound-familiar tearing through the neighboring gardens. She kept him well away from the Keeper she knew was hiding behind the stable on the left, so he wouldn't become too suspicious. Her wolfhound leaped over fences, chased a carriage, and finally trotted happily away into the shadows. He was a very faint glow of light through the fog.

After a few moments, he whined.

Gretchen waited patiently behind a tree, reminding herself that the piteous noise was false. It still had her throat clogging with tears. The wolfhound whined again and again. The mournful sound splintered the fog.

The Keeper emerged from his position, frowning. He crept closer and closer to the whining dog, until he stood at the edge of a small root cellar. The wolfhound poked his glowing head out of the opening.

Gretchen slipped behind the Keeper and shoved him hard. He fell into the cellar, landing with a resounding crash. She shut the doors over him, pulling the lock tight. Her wolfhound bounded away, tongue lolling happily.

Across the street, Penelope ran straight to the Keeper pretending to admire one of the new gas lamps. She'd watched him walk the same round twice already. She let the tears flow, pretending she was Juliet weeping over the loss of Romeo.

"Oh thank Heaven, you're here!" she exclaimed. "I've seen the most horrid—" Her eyes rolled back in her head and she wilted slowly. The Keeper had no choice but to dart forward and catch her before she hit the pavement. She felt his arms go around her as he struggled to support her boneless weight. She waited until he'd carried her into the quiet lane adjacent to the road, intending perhaps to lay her down on a patch of grass to recover.

"Thank you," she said, right before she punched him directly in the throat. He gagged in pain and shock, dropping her. Her feet hit the ground and she straightened, elbowing him hard in the groin. He groaned, collapsing.

Carriages rumbled by, obscured by mists. She heard voices of passing pedestrians.

She hit him again. His lip split, and blood dripped onto his cravat. "Are you crazy?" he croaked.

Rendering a man unconscious was harder than it looked.

He was in too much pain to immediately retaliate but she knew he'd recover before long. She didn't know what to do. Spiders crawled over the grass. They scurried down trees and out from under beds of tulips and daffodils. She caught a glimpse of a particularly large one, nearly as big as a mouse.

She suppressed a shudder as she nudged him toward the Keeper, who was on his knees now. He'd be back on his feet in moments and summoning the Order. If they arrived too early, they'd ruin everything. The Keeper reached for a pouch of summoning powder.

The spider crawled up his knee. She knew the exact moment it reached his hand.

"He's poisonous, you know," Penelope said lightly, even though she was fairly certain there were no poisonous spiders in England. Still, it was big and hairy. "I had him brought over from India," she added. "But if you stay very still and quiet, I won't let him bite you."

He froze.

The spider meandered up his shirt.

"I really am sorry," Penelope said, before tying his hands tightly with the rope Cormac had given her. She used the fichu in the neckline of her gown to gag him. "You'll thank me later. Tonight is not a night for the faint of heart."

Chapter 55

The Greymalkin House loomed as desolate and sinister as it had the first time Emma had seen it.

She knew dark magic pulsed in its center and the wards and shields of the Order kept it invisible to ordinary eyes. People's gazes slid away from it, or saw only a patch of wild grass across from a deserted corner of the park. Unfortunately, she saw it all too clearly. The gates stood as strong and tall as they ever were and she had to crane her neck back to see where they met at the top. The black paint over the iron was peeling, the magpie sigil of the Greymalkin family silhouetted in the curlicues. There was no padlock, thick chains, or poisoned darts, but still the gates could not be breached.

Emma's heart thundered in her chest so hard her ribs nearly rattled. Adrenaline pumped through her, making her feel oddly disconnected to her own body. She took the knife out of the satchel strapped crosswise over her chest.

A little bit of her blood and this would all be over.

She jabbed the tip of the blade into her witch knot, dragging it across her palm until blood welled to the surface.

She took a deep breath and—"Emma?"—jumped a foot in the air, yelping.

She spun on her heel, dagger in hand. Sophie froze, palms out to show she was unarmed. Her white gloves glowed faintly in the moonlight. Emma lowered her weapon slowly. "Sophie?" she hissed, the back of her neck prickling painfully. "I could have killed you!"

A trio of gentlemen walked past them, barely glancing their way. Only one of them shuddered. "This corner gives me the shivers," he muttered. The fog swallowed him whole, rain dripping off the brim of his hat.

Emma just stared at her. 'This isn't a good time for a chat, Sophie."

"I know." She shivered delicately. "Those poor girls. And Lilybeth."

"Go back to the academy. Now," Emma said, impatient to get it over and done with, before her courage faltered.

Sophie followed her gaze. "You can't seriously be thinking of going inside!"

Emma ignored her. She had to get the gates open before the Order arrived to stop her, but with just enough time for them to get in and stop the Sisters. She couldn't afford to waste another second.

Gritting her teeth, she slapped the bleeding cut onto the magpie sigil, right in the center where the gate split the bird in two.

She waited, breath held. Sophie gasped beside her. The rain sliced through the mist.

The gates didn't open.

Emma blinked, sure that she was seeing wrong. The gates had to open. How else were they to get in and trap the Sisters? Her blood had unlocked all the other spells. It had to work. It had to.

"Emma," Cormac said from the wet shadows. "Keepers are on their way."

The mist hung veils between them. Her blood burned. She let her hand drop, disappointed.

"Let me heal your cut," Sophie said quietly, taking her by the hand.

The blood on the gate began to sizzle.

It smoked and burned but still the gates did not open.

They didn't have to.

Emma was sucked into darkness, dragging Sophie behind her.

Chapter 56

The inside of the Greymalkin House smelled like lemon balm, fennel seeds, and decades of accumulated dust. Light filtered through the cracks in the wooden shutters and the stained glass window in the turret above the front door. The chunk of jet Cormac had given her exploded before she was even fully aware of her surroundings.

The gates had opened after all.

She'd been sent through a portal linking them to the inside of the house. Emma grabbed the wall for support, blinking back flashes of violet light and waves of dizziness. She searched for Sophie, expecting to see her cowering somewhere, confused. She'd only meant to heal a little cut, after all, not travel through a portal into the darkest house in all of London, and possibly Britain.

Sophie didn't look the least bit concerned, actually.

She stood in the very center of the entrance hall, turning around slowly with a strange thrilled smile on her face. Emma's stomach dropped, recognizing danger before her brain fully caught on. Lightning flashed outside, searing glimpses of the room into stark relief. Rain dripped through the cracks in the ornate ceiling moldings.

"Finally," Sophie whispered. "I'm *home*. Do you hear that, Sisters?"

Emma backed up a step. That hadn't sounded like a taunt of revenge on Lilybeth's behalf.

It sounded like an invitation.

The front door, of course, was locked. Emma kept her back pressed to it, not taking her eyes off Sophie. "I don't understand," she said. "It was *you*?"

She nodded gently. "Of course, dear cousin."

Emma went cold. "*Cousin*?"

"Several times removed, but yes, essentially. Regrettably my own Greymalkin blood is too diluted. It's only enough to feed the Sisters, but not to open the garden gate myself to get inside."

"You killed Lilybeth. You killed all those girls!"

Sophie nodded sadly. "I had to. The Sisters needed me."

"Lilybeth was your friend," Emma said, mind whirling and belly nauseous. "And poor Strawberry."

"Who?" Sophie asked.

"The girl on the roof."

"Oh, the Madcap. Yes, I couldn't seem to get anyone alone at that ball next door. And then I saw her running along the roof. It was perfect. I told her I wanted to give her coins for her supper."

Emma's hands fisted of their own accord. Thunder was a long, deep growl, the sky turning beastly. "And Margaret York, the seamstress in the park."

"You're missing the point," Sophie said.

"I don't think I am, actually."

"How else are we to claim our birthright? And once the Sisters knew who you were, you went and got yourself accused and run to ground."

"I'm not all that keen to reclaim a birthright of murder," Emma pointed out. "Even my mad mother isn't that crazy."

"I'm not mad," Sophie snapped. "I'm inspired."

"You're cracked. Why in the world would you do this?"

"To have a family again," she replied savagely. "You don't know what it's like to be alone."

"Actually," Emma said, thinking of the big empty house and the man she'd thought was her father all these years. "I do. And it's no excuse."

"You had your cousins," she said, jealousy scraping through her voice. "I had *no one.*"

"You had all the Rowanstone girls!"

"It's not the same."

"Family is more than blood," Emma said, trying the door handle again. She had more than enough information. None of which would do her any good if she couldn't get *out* of here. "The Order is on its way."

"They won't get here before the Sisters," Sophie said. Emma's blood was still smeared on her hand. She wiped it over her heart and then traced a symbol at her feet. The chandelier rattled. Virulent violet sparks gathered in the air. "Sisters!"

"What are you doing?"

"Opening a gate, of course."

"But the gate's already *here*," Emma stammered. "It must be. Everyone says so."

"Everyone *assumes*," Sophie corrected her primly. "But don't you think if the Sisters could reclaim our ancestral house, they'd be here already? I had to leave that trail of marked birds for you to follow," she confessed, as though it were all a cheerful game. "I knew if I could get you there you'd do the rest yourself."

There was no gate.

She was risking everyone's lives for nothing.

It was a *trick*.

Wind pushed at the windows and howled through the slats. Lightning struck the locked shutters, exploding them into sparks and splinters. It flashed again, hurling a spear of light at Sophie.

The house swallowed the lightning before it could touch her. It sucked it into the violet sparks, bloating them into embers and strange licks of lavender flames. Emma remembered that purple fire, remembered the open gate releasing hellhounds and Greymalkin warlocks.

Sophie had tricked her to get her blood to open the gate. In the Greymalkin House, the Sisters could force it open indefinitely.

Emma reached for the storm again.

Thunder shook the dust off the rafters. A crystal drop came off the chandelier, shattering on the ground. Snow blew through the broken window.

"You can't hurt me, not in here. The Sisters told me which charms to make to use the house as a shield." She took a step toward Emma. "You've been as lonely as I have. I know it. Don't you want to be part of a real family?"

The rain stopped. The thunder retreated and even the mist blew apart, leaving the street clearer than any London street had ever been in recent memory. Too late.

The Sisters had found them.

Chapter 57

"Where the hell did she go?" Cormac demanded as Gretchen and Penelope closed in behind him. They stared at the dismal house.

"What just happened?" Penelope asked, stricken.

"Emma was right," Cormac replied grimly as she went through his arsenal of amulets. "Her blood was the key. Only it wasn't this gate she opened, but a hidden portal."

Emma's shout echoed clearly from the Greymalkin House. A storm gathered above their heads, raging with light and fire. Cormac launched himself at the gates.

The magical wards pulsed an angry acid green, flinging him off the way a dog flings water off its fur. He flew off his feet, landing hard on the edge of the pavement and tumbling into the road. He leaped into a crouch, barely avoiding a passing carriage. The horses nickered at him reproachfully. He pushed to his feet without a backward glance, even when they passed so close one of them took a swipe at his shoulder. His sleeve was torn and there was a bloody scratch on his cheek.

He didn't notice any of it.

He saw nothing but the gate and the house standing between him and Emma.

Gretchen and Penelope parted, scurrying out of his way. Pale glowing spiders crawled out from under Penelope's hem, clustering at the base of the gates. They flared that same virulent green and she winced, sweat beading on her brow. Real spiders began to congregate, coming out of the bushes, the nearby mews and walking in a line across the street from the shadowy edge of the park.

Cormac used his iron dagger to try to pry the gates open. He gritted his teeth against the pain shooting up his arm. The blade slipped, coming away red.

"Emma's blood," Gretchen said as it hissed and boiled. It had already eroded the metal, pockmarking the edge of the iron magpie's wings.

"That's my girl," he said softly.

"Let me try," Moira called down. She pointed to the immense gargoyle on the Greymalkin roof. She couldn't quite reach it, but the wards wouldn't have let her touch it anyway. "Where do you want him? Right on the gates?"

"Combined with Emma's blood, it might be enough to break them open," Cormac agreed.

Moira leaned over, trying to whisper in the gargoyle's ear. "I can't reach him. I need to lure him closer with another gargoyle." She looked around wildly, running over the roof until she found one attached to a rainspout.

"You'd better hurry," Gretchen encouraged from the mouth of the laneway. "Because cloaking glamour or not, we're starting to look suspicious."

Moira whispered in the gargoyle's ear. His wings were narrow and fluted. When they moved, they hardly made a sound at all. The rainspout creaked and then he was airborne. "Come on, little pip," she crooned, darting back to the other side. She took a small bundle of bat wings from her belt and poured whiskey over it from a flask in her pocket. The little gargoyle dipped down in front of her. She nodded to the Greymalkin House. "Go on."

The gargoyle flew too close to the wards and showered green sparks on the others waiting on the ground. The second time he circled around, the massive Greymalkin gargoyle growled. His eyes opened slowly, reptilian in their cold indifference.

Finally, after what felt like an excruciatingly slow eternity during which Cormac imagined hundreds of horrible deeds that could have made Emma scream, the Greymalkin gargoyle shifted.

His talons unclenched, dislodging dirt and debris. His stone wings turned a leathery gray and he pushed off the ornate parapet, snagged the wrought iron widow's walk below, snapping off the points. He flew slowly, erratically, and against all laws of physics. The Greymalkin magic anchored him to the protection of the house, but the pull of Madcap spells eroded the magical chains.

But only a little.

The gargoyle swung toward Moira, snarling. She swung out, dangerously close to falling, and tossed the whiskey-soaked bat wings and bird bones into his gaping mouth. He bit down reflexively, crunching through magic and marrow.

"To the gate!" she commanded.

The gargoyle descended with its own kind of grace, claws clutching the top of the gates and bending them. The sound of crushed metal made the hairs on the back of Cormac's neck stand straight up.

"Ha!" Moira shouted smugly. "Bloody Keepers couldn't do that!"

"That's because they didn't have Emma on their side," Cormac said with a grim smile, as her blood ate through the spells locking the gates together.

"Or a Madcap." She smirked.

"Or a Madcap," he agreed.

The gargoyle continued to tear at the gate, green fire searing his stony talons. At the very first crack, a large black spider slipped through. The gate peeled apart slowly, like the rind of an orange. Spiders scurried up the path.

Cormac used his dagger again, slipping it between the doors. Gretchen broke a branch off a nearby tree and joined him, using her entire body as leverage. The iron creaked and groaned. The gargoyle descended, forcing them to cover their heads.

Emma screamed again.

Cormac and Gretchen exchanged grim glances and doubled their efforts, pushing until the veins pulsed in their temples and their knuckles popped uncomfortably. The gap widened, just enough to let Marmalade slip through, leading a parade of glowing spiders. Wider and wider it opened, like the jaw of a beast with acid-green teeth. The gargoyle roared again and flew back to its perch.

The first spider scurried back toward them. Its glowing counterpart drifted free and raced up Penelope's ankle. She paled, eyes snapping open when she saw whatever the spider had seen.

"Hurry."

Chapter 58

There was nowhere to run.

Emma tried the door again but it held fast.

The Sisters drifted out of the portal hovering in midair, just under the chandelier. The purple light was as malignant as she remembered it. The stink of sulfur mingled with lemon balm. Ice clung to the banisters, creeping like ivy.

Sophie beamed at the Sisters in such a way that they might have been saints instead of warlocks. Lark looked as distracted and desolate as ever, but the blood dripping from her dress coalesced when it hit the cracked marble floor. The magic and life force of the murdered girls had fed them what they needed to stay anchored in this reality.

And now that they were in their own ancestral house, with not just one descendant but two, they were more powerful still. The Order might never get rid of them.

The lightning might not have stopped Sophie but it had at least broken the window open. The damp night breeze fluttered what was left of the curtains. Emma lunged for it. She was a whisper away, her fingertips brushing the wooden sill, when Sophie tackled her. She grabbed her ankles and Emma toppled, slamming into the floor hard enough to crack her teeth together. Her antlers scraped the wall. Dust lifted, choking her.

She kicked back and Sophie yelped when her finger got crushed, but she didn't let go. Emma struggled to turn over onto her back to get better traction. Her hand slipped when the cut on her palm opened up, bleeding more profusely than such a shallow cut warranted.

"The Sisters taught me how to work my magic fully," Sophie said. "I can work it backward and make every pain you've ever suffered come back worse than it was, right down to your very first aching tooth. That's how I trapped the girls so they couldn't fight back, so the Sisters could get stronger. And the footman who tried to protect poor Lilybeth. The Sisters can teach you too. And then one day we can join them."

Blood dripped down Emma's arm. Her palm pulsed with pain. She went limp, letting Sophie drag her backward, letting her get close enough for Emma to punch her in the eye. Sophie howled, shocked, her head snapping.

Ladies did not punch.

Ladies didn't have antlers either.

Emma swung her head, prepared to run the other girl through if she was forced to. She felt foolish but oddly vindicated. She was beginning to rather like her horns. Sophie slipped on Emma's blood as she scrambled to get out of the way. "We're family!" Sophie cried out.

"It's a trap," Emma yelled, hoping the others could hear her warning.

Suddenly, her scalp tightened, pain shooting into her skull. Every scraped knee and pinprick she'd ever suffered came rushing to the surface of her skin. Every bramble scratch, every bee sting, and bruise.

Her left wrist cracked loudly, snapping the way it had when she was nine years old and had fallen from a tree. It throbbed, full of hot needles. She and Sophie circled each other like two feral cats, all but hissing. Sophie had the audacity to look wounded, as though Emma had hurt her feelings.

The Sisters grew tired of waiting.

"Enough," Magdalena snapped. Death's-head moths fluttered out of her tangled hair. "We need you both for this."

Power snaked out in tendrils as the Sisters approached, slapping at Emma hard enough to make her stumble. Ice crept over the marble, glittered on the shards of glass, and froze the air hard enough to make her teeth hurt. Tendrils of deadly nightshade curled out from Rosmerta's belt, circling Emma's ankles and her sprained wrist, tightening agonizingly. Pain strangled her voice momentarily.

Magdalena lifted her hands. Her long hair fell down her back, hung with spiders and beetles. "Come," she called, her voice reverberating through the house. Wisps of violet light floated away on death's-head moth wings to lure the innocent to the house. "Come," she repeated as they drifted outside. The soft glow made them look like perfect jeweled butterflies.

"Don't struggle so," Lark said in a sweet, high voice when Emma pulled at her restraints. "We need to make you one of us. Then we'll be strong enough to find my beloved."

"He's dead," Emma spat, tearing frantically at the ghostly plants and the ropes of violet energy pinning her to the wall. Sophie smiled and the pain in her wrist flared, the cut on her palm went red and violent. "Go back to the Underworld if you miss him so much!"

"He's not there!" Lark screeched. Her voice scraped inside Emma's head, making her vision waver. Her ears were being stabbed with the awful sound. Her heart raced. "I looked everywhere, didn't I?" Maggots spilled out of her hands, squirming and wriggling until they turned to ice and shattered on the marble. "Didn't I?" Blood poured off her hem.

The lilac ropes dragged Emma up the wall. She hung there, struggling. Despite knowing it would do no good, lightning crackled and rain dripped from the ceiling. Wind whipped through the hall. Rosmerta smiled greedily, her poisonous vines flaring virulently green.

The portal burned brighter and brighter.

Emma felt their whispers. It was more than the sound of the Sisters, it was the way they prowled inside her head, in her bones and her belly. They pushed and poked at her magic, prodded her memories, pinned her inside herself. She fought them as long as she could. But how does one fight the water while drowning?

She was as substantial as mist and rain. It was a struggle to stay conscious. Only the fear of being even more helpless in front of the Sisters kept her lucid, but only barely. Her eyelids fluttered frantically.

The Sisters were more powerful than she was.

It took all of her effort just to turn her head. Her witch knot flared, going from the color of spilled tea to blood and rust. As they claimed her for their own, the points started to unfurl slowly, like a poisonous plant, like the mark of the Greymalkin.

Chapter 59

"Stay back!" Penelope called to the girl racing into the garden. There was a leather strap tied crosswise between her breasts. It bristled with iron daggers, nails, and various magical weapons.

"Where's Cormac?" she demanded instead of listening to Penelope's frantic order.

"Inside," Penelope replied. "Who are you?"

"I'm Cormac's sister, Colette. I saw the flares he sent up earlier."

"Is the Order with you?"

She shook her head and made a rude sound that perfectly explained how she felt about that. As she turned toward the house, giant moths flew out of the front door and the broken window. They were the size of robins, and gleaming and glittering the intense shade of mauve associated with the Underworld.

"What are those?" Gretchen asked.

"Will-o'-the-wisps," Colette replied. "They lure people into bogs and swamps and drown them."

"I don't feel the urge to follow them," Gretchen pointed out. "Do you?"

"They're not meant for you."

"Then who for?"

"Them."

She pointed to the small crowd of strangers wandering up the sidewalk, out of houses and carriages. They wore fine evening gowns, starched collar points, diamonds, and ostrich feathers; also nightcaps, aprons, and footman's livery. They came from sculleries and master's chambers and stables. They trailed after the violet moths as if nothing else mattered. Not even the fact that one of the ladies was still in her chemise and corset and nothing else.

Their pupils and irises were bleached out by magic, white eyes staring blankly. They were blind to everything except the path into the house. Penelope didn't know what was waiting for them inside, but she was sure it wasn't conducive to a long healthy life. She hopped down to the ground, trying to keep the gates closed but they kept coming. "I think the cloaking spell is definitely broken," she said, shoving back at insistent hands passing between the bars. She slapped at them. "Go home, you lunatics!"

"You figure that out," Colette said, dodging around them. "And I'll find Cormac."

"They're bewitched," Moira shouted, scrambling down the rainspout to help. "They're following the will-o'-the-wisps."

"How do we stop them?"

"I'm not sure we can."

A housemaid scaled the fence, her smile both besotted and drunk. She didn't notice the bleeding gashes on her palms from the wrought iron spikes. Several alley cats slipped between the bars. A large man who looked like he spent his time wrestling bears rattled the gates. Penelope was shoved across the flag-stones by the press of people, still clinging uselessly to the bars.

When the housemaid dropped to the ground next to Penelope, Penelope reared back and punched her. The girl slumped in the grass, dazed. Gretchen tossed her an approving, slightly vicious smile. They were reduced to tripping and shoving the people who tried to push past them. Moira dashed around to the back gardens, where three half-drunk gentlemen were attempting to scale the wall. She broke a branch of a tree and brandished it at them.

Despite the taint of dark magic, the gardens were coming back to life all around them. Green grass pushed up through the mire. Daffodils bloomed along the edge of the broken path. The foxgloves turned pink, and the ash's withered leaves unfurled thickly.

It wasn't just the garden. The house was also repairing itself. The shutters opened like flowers, and the cracks in the mortar faded away. The peeling paint smoothed out. The crumbled chimney mended itself, brick by brick.

The last of the wards and invisible spells fell away.

Chapter 60

The gates pulsed with dark magic, bleeding wider and wider like a wine stain on a white tablecloth. Dark residue oozed, leaving black scorch marks and deep fissures in the marble. It was the last unguarded gate left in London.

And it still wasn't the worst thing in the Greymalkin House.

Emma.

Her eyelids fluttered madly. The vines and magical ropes binding her were already leaving red scrapes and bruises. She was so pale she was nearly translucent. The room was utterly still. Cormac couldn't understand why she wasn't calling the wind, or blasting through her chains with lightning.

Unless she was no longer able to.

Ice traveled over her body, encasing her in frost. Icicles dripped from the ends of her antlers, like glittering needles. Her lips were turning blue.

"Emma!"

She tried to speak, her lips parting weakly. No sound emerged. The Sisters barely glanced at him, still congregating around her with greedy intense smiles. He wasn't a threat, even after having nearly banished them in the park. He had no magic. Sour fury scalded his throat.

He tossed a red bundle of banishing powder to the ground. The house shivered once, the tremor building under the cellar and traveling up the walls and through the floors. The chandelier rattled, dropping crystals. The portal widened farther.

The white horse who reared out of the powder was huge. The mare had flashing blue eyes and a mane that shot out showers of sparks. Sweet honey covered the stench of the house. She neighed and landed hard, her hooves cracking the charred marble into pieces.

But the Sisters still didn't abandon Emma. They didn't care that the horse had the power to drag them back to the Underworld. When the mare galloped at them, her hooves about to slash through them, she was stopped in mid-leap. He could hear the crack of the sudden cold, the snap of the hooves as they froze.

And then the ghostly mare shattered into pieces.

The very house had struck the blow, like a rock through a windowpane. The remaining threads of magic animating the horse were sucked into the portal, bloating it to dangerous proportions. It didn't widen low enough to be reachable; instead, it deepened like a tunnel. Cormac could hear the sounds of footsteps, hoofbeats, and wailing from the other side.

"You're too late," Sophie said, stepping out from behind one of the curved stairwells.

He stared at her. She looked like all the other debutantes in her white dress and carefully coiled hair. He half expected her to curtsy. "Sophie?"

She smiled demurely. "Hello, Cormac."

She clearly wasn't a prisoner. "What are you doing here?" He angled himself to keep an eye on the Sisters, his mind racing through possible plans.

"What I must." She flicked her fingers in his direction. "I'm sorry."

Old wounds long healed and long forgotten opened. Blood seeped through his shirt and down his leg. His trousers ripped at the knee under the force of an inner blow. He fell to his other knee, steeling himself against the unexpected pain. Emma needed him to survive this.

And fast.

Mottled bruises ran down to his ankle and spread up along his jaw. His little finger snapped like a dry twig. Multiple cuts opened like mouths on his arms and legs. The burns from the charms on the silver chain around his neck throbbed.

Sophie stood over him, sad but determined. She didn't see Colette arrive until it was too late. His sister flung one of her daggers, not bothering with spells or spirits. It slammed into Sophie's shoulder and she cried out, clutching at it in shock. Cormac kicked out at her feet and knocked her down. Her temple struck the floor. She blinked dizzily, diverting the magic she'd been pushing through him to heal herself. Blood seeped between her fingers.

"Get out of here," he groaned at Colette when she crouched next to him.

"Don't be stupid."

"Oh, look." Rosmerta glanced over her shoulder. "Another little lamb," she said. "Come for the slaughter."

"Leave her alone!" He coughed, spitting out the blood from a split lip he didn't even remember getting. He assumed he'd been fighting over a girl. Colette helped him up. His knee was a rusty hinge and there was a goose egg swelling on the back of his head. "We need to close the gate," he whispered, handing her a pouch prepared with rowan berries and nails.

"First things first." She stepped over the magic barrier and smiled darkly down at Sophie. "I don't think your kind of help is required," she said, grabbing her by the hair and cracking her head against the stones again. Her eyes rolled back in her head and she lost consciousness.

Sophie's magic fell away from Cormac. Still, his magical charms were no use in the house.

Finally, an advantage.

Not having magical abilities of his own meant he'd never been able to completely rely on them.

Emma whimpered. Her left hand was bent back at an awkward angle, the witch knot flaring. Light gathered into the lines, like lava. He saw the tips unfurling, the knot being forced into a mark of the Greymalkin family.

Over his dead body.

Quite literally, if it came to that.

He remembered Talia's cryptic dream from the night he'd

first encountered the Sisters. *Bottles break and knots undo but the only real binding is love that is true.*

He couldn't assume Emma loved him.

He only knew that he loved *her.*

It would have to be enough.

He had to get to Emma. *Now.* But he was going to need help, they all were. Before the gate was closed. He lifted his dagger. Her blood was still on the tip. He had to hope it would be enough to call her father out of the Underworld again, as it had before.

He turned and threw his knife, watching it spin blade over hilt until it whistled through the portal and something screamed on the other side.

Weaponless, he turned back to the Sisters.

Chapter 61

Cormac leaped into the cold coven of the Sisters.

The air was frigid and hard, stabbing into his lungs. His knee still throbbed, making him awkward. He knew he'd never make it past them. He remembered exactly how it felt to be drained by them, the cold seeping ache that made your bones hollow, that turned your heart into a lump of ice. It was just as awful as it was the first time.

Still, it was precisely what he'd wanted.

He'd aimed for Rosmerta. Her temper frayed the quickest and he wanted to be within her reach. Lark was so unbalanced she might kiss him or kill him, neither of which would help Emma.

Rosmerta grabbed him by the throat and flung him at the wall. The edge of the broken window dug into his shoulder. Vines of nightshade and belladonna draped all over her, crawled up to encircle his arms, thick as chains. They tightened until he felt prickles down his arms. "Wait your turn, boy," she scolded.

Beside him, Emma's eyes opened suddenly, the irises virulently, unnaturally violet.

Bottles break and knots undo but the only real binding is love that is true.

"Hold on," he murmured. "Don't give into them." Inch by slow, excruciating inch, he reached for her.

The Sisters were chanting, their hands raised, Greymalkin knots facing Emma. Their hair lifted in a breeze no one else felt, the ends tipped with lavender fire. The floor was completely frozen beneath them. They were still pale, but it was the pallor of skin kept from the sun, not the pearly gray translucence of spirits. They were nearly corporeal.

Alley cats slunk through the front door, batting at purple moths. Their breaths puffed into white clouds as they wound around the Sisters' ankles. They fell over almost instantly, frozen and drained.

A man followed, stumbling drunkenly after a will-o'-the-wisp. Before Colette could stop him, he'd grabbed the violet moth and collapsed. Cursing, she went back to building the small banishing salt-fire under the gate, using his body to block her from the Sisters' attention.

Cormac gritted his teeth against the same seductive weakness that stole over him. He was so cold. Fatigue dragged him down. He had to hold Emma's hand. He couldn't remember why, only knew that it was important. His joints creaked like rusty armor. His shoulder might as well have been a giant's war club for all he could lift it. He stretched his fingers out.

Nearly there.

He could see the magic flowing from the portal to the Sisters and from the Sisters to Emma. She was nearly completely possessed now. She waited obediently, strung up like a marionette.

Just a little farther.

He brushed against the side of her hand. It was frigid despite the blazing of her witch knot undoing itself. She twitched violently.

"You told me 'don't fight' was the worst advice you'd ever heard," he said hoarsely, ice clogging his throat. "Remember?" he begged. "So *fight*, Emma!"

"Drain him," Lark snapped. "He talks too much."

He could just make out the silhouette of antlers in the portal. He smiled.

Magdalena paused, instantly suspicious.

Too late.

Ewan strode out of the portal, swinging his spectral ax. His antlers were like a sweep of majestic oak branches. The Sisters sensed his arrival, turning one by one. Lark shrieked at him. "Blood traitor! You should be one of us!"

"I told you, you can't have her," he returned darkly. "My daughter's a Lovegrove, not a Greymalkin."

"Emma, can you hear me?" Cormac begged. Her eyes still blazed, like sunlight through an amethyst. Despite the pain in his shoulder and the toxic grasp of the vines, he was finally able to curl his fingers over her palm, gripping her tightly. He tightened his hold even when the fire of her marked palm seared into him.

The waves of magical energy linking her to the Sisters faltered. He felt it trying to sear through his hands, and his bones.

After a long grinding moment, the magic fell away, retracting with flickers and sparks. The connection was severed. Cormac smiled again, his split lip lined with frost, even as he and Emma tumbled off the wall, and landed in a heap. He curled over her, trying to shield her with his body.

She stirred, confused. "Cormac?" When she looked up at him, her green eyes glistened with tears. "What's happening?"

"Your father's here," he whispered, brushing the hair off her face. She turned her head sharply.

Ewan and the Sisters were facing off on either side of Emma, magic crackling acid-green all around them. The house grew brighter, drinking in the power. The torches and the candles in the tarnished candelabras burst into flame. Dust blew away and paintings of Greymalkin ancestors straightened on their hooks. Somewhere down the hall, the door to a cellar filled with warlock bones creaked open.

Cormac scrambled to his feet to help Emma when she rose. "I'm all right," she whispered.

A few feet away, Ewan's ax tumbled from his icy fingers. Chains of frozen snow had him lashed, winding around his arms and pinning them to his sides. The Sisters tossed ropes of ice into his antlers, driving him to his knees. He fought them as they tried to force his head to bow down.

"Can you walk?" Cormac asked, touching the small of her back. "We have to help your father. And the others."

"I can do more than walk," she promised, just before she called the lightning back.

It sizzled through the broken window, making her hair drift

around her as if she was underwater. The force of it slammed Cormac back into the wall. The shards of glass at his feet were slippery with ice and blood. Wind prowled through the hall and slammed doors on the second floor. Rain and snow hung suspended in the air, frozen in the same vitriolic shades of green and violet.

The wintry bindings melted off Ewan. He leaped back up, shaking melted ice out of his hair. When he swung his ax at the nearest Sister, Emma stopped him. Lightning arced between them. She was forcing the battle to a standstill but Cormac couldn't decipher the expression on her face. She'd released her father but she hadn't moved against the Sisters.

The ice coating the floor cracked. The banisters gleamed, newly polished. Colors seeped back into the rugs and tapestries and the dried flowers in tarnished silver bowls bloomed yellow and white.

When Emma lowered her hand, he saw her witch knot, unfurling even now.

Her eyes might have gone back to normal but she was still tainted by the Sisters' magic.

Bottles break and knots undo but the only real binding is love that is true.

There were different kinds of love.

And they would clearly need them all.

"Gretchen!" Cormac shouted. "Penelope!"

After all, Emma was a Lovegrove witch, not a Greymalkin warlock.

Whatever the Sisters might have to say about it.

Chapter 62

Emma felt the lightning go through her. It burned away all doubts, all fears, all questions of right and wrong. It was primal, beyond any judgment; it couldn't be contained, not even by the Order.

It was liberating.

It sliced through the magic gathered in the hall and seized it, both amplifying it and holding it in place. The Sisters were nearly flesh and bone now and even Ewan had lost that otherworldly glow, except for his antlers. Lightning wreathed her own tines, traveling to his, like spiderwebs linking branches in the woods. He looked kind, if weathered. Because of her mother's spell she knew more about him than she did about the man who'd actually raised her. She should probably care about that.

Right now she only cared about the storm. She pushed the

winds into every corner, sweeping the others away like litter. Colette and Sophie were shoved aside. Even Cormac. Especially Cormac when he reached for her.

Some small part of her was aware that she was being controlled, that the dark magic of the Sisters was tainting her.

But it was so much stronger than she was.

Icicles dropped from the ceiling, nearly stabbing Gretchen when she climbed in through the window. Cursing, she reached back to pull Penelope through after her. Both of them were wild-eyed.

"She needs you," Cormac grunted at them, pushing back at the wind that pressed him to the silk wallpaper. She couldn't hear what else he told them. There was too much magic and it was intoxicating. And it didn't matter, anyway. She didn't need them.

She was home.

She felt the house's pleasure. It was opulent and beautiful, nothing like the gray desolate building the Order had tried to burn to the ground. The walls were covered in silk, the chandeliers dripped crystals and diamonds. The marble fireplace was flanked with statues of winged Pegasus.

"Emma, stop it," Gretchen shouted. "You'll kill us all!"

"Don't interfere," Emma snapped.

"Then stop being such a termagant," Penelope snapped back.

"Shakespeare?" Gretchen muttered. "*Now?* Really?" She reached for Emma.

Ewan's antler dagger sliced Gretchen's hand, stopping her.

The second dagger nicked Penelope's finger, slicing it along the outside knuckle and pinning her sleeve to the window frame.

Cormac pulled her loose with a savage yank and sent her with a push to Gretchen.

"I'm on your side," Ewan told Emma.

But his aim had been careful.

He'd bought the cousins a moment in which to act and when they grabbed Emma's hand, their witch knots were slick with their own blood. She jerked away but it was too late. They held fast, tangling into a complicated labyrinth of fingers. Blood dripped to the floor. Light poured between their fingers.

The wind died abruptly.

Emma's head snapped back.

The combined magic of their Lovegrove lineage, their witch knots, and their own bonds of friendship, slapped the house with a violent flash of light. Ripples of energy spread out farther and farther, momentarily stunning the Sisters and sending them staggering back. The house trembled, struggling to absorb the sudden outpour of additional magic.

Emma's pupils flared purple again, then acid-green, and finally went back to their normal green of an oak leaf in summer. She blinked, orienting herself. "Bloody *hell*."

Gretchen's laugh was startled and grateful. "She's back."

Chapter 63

As Emma, Gretchen, and Penelope let go of one another's hands, a man dressed in finery fit for a ball entered the house, followed by a veiled woman and several Keepers. There were more in the garden, trying to hold back the bewitched following the will-o'-the-wisps.

The veiled woman didn't look around, didn't even pause as the vestiges of magic crackled and shot overhead. Veils frothed from the brim of her beaver hat, obscuring her features. Dozens of silver chains hung with pendants and baubles, rings, and bracelets adorned every inch of her. She set an earthenware jug down on the floor, unstoppering it. The gargoyle face stamped into its side leered.

The last of Magdalena's insects clung to her hair, too weak to fly. "You think to trap us, Lacrimarium?" she hissed. "And Lord Mabon." She laughed disdainfully. "You think the Order and its iron baubles can stop us now? Now that we've finally reclaimed our house?"

The Lacrimarium began to whisper some kind of a spell. Emma had never seen anyone more serene. "Who's that?" Penelope whispered.

"Bottle witch," Emma whispered back. "She can trap familiars."

The house shuddered in response. The shutters slammed, and the door locked with an audible snap. The torches blew out, one by one, until only the candle in Lord Mabon's iron lantern remained.

Ewan launched himself at the furious Sisters.

They retaliated with such force, the cold snapped one of his tines. It bled slowly, like tree sap.

Taking advantage of the distraction, Cormac flung an iron dagger to Colette, who had climbed up onto the balcony. She caught it easily, slicing through the rope used to lower the chandelier when the candles needed replacing. She jumped off the railing, swinging down with the heavy candelabra acting as a descending anchor. Her dagger dragged through the portal, before slamming into the small salt, rowan berry, and iron-nail fire she had started earlier.

The Sisters turned away from Ewan, shrieking. "You'll pay for that," Rosmerta promised darkly. "Slowly."

No one noticed Sophie stirring. Lark was on her knees, looking dazed. Ewan's last spell had felled her tenuous control. "Roman?" she wept. "Where are you, beloved?"

Ewan used Colette's abandoned dangling rope to steady

himself. The raw scrapes and ice burns on his arms shimmered with a sickly lavender hue. The scar from the arrow that had killed him blistered. He was seriously wounded but the sheer volume of magical energy in the house had nearly completed his reanimation. It recognized him as family. He was flesh and blood, a real man who might yet be reunited with her mother. Only his antlers were spirit, glowing and sparking silver and violet. The Underworld still had a hold on him, but not for long.

The gate flickered brightly, distended and misshaped around the line drawn by the dagger. It sizzled, greenish-black steam shooting out of the mended tear. The burned edges clung to each other. It was nearly closed. Emma held her breath.

Gretchen suddenly clapped her hands over her ears. "It's not enough," she said. "The spell needs something else."

"Hush." Magdalena snapped her fingers and Gretchen reared back, her lips stuck together. She made mewling sounds, trying to speak.

"Come here, little Whisperer," Rosmerta said, vines snapping out to grab her. Penelope tried to stomp on the tendrils as they rushed toward Gretchen's feet. Emma's lightning came from the ceiling this time, slashing through the vines. Rosmerta howled, a gash opening just under her rib cage.

Sophie dragged herself slowly toward the Lacrimarium who slumped over the witch bottle. Blood dripped unseen from her nose. The gate continued to leak the slightest traces of violet light.

"It will have to be closed from the inside as well," Ewan said, confirming Gretchen's opinion that the spell was incomplete.

"They'll try to stop me," he said, his voice barely a whisper. "That's when you get the hell out of this house. If I can't take them with me, they'll follow you, and you let the bloody Grey-beards finish this, do you hear me?" His eyes were hard on Lord Mabon. "Don't risk yourself for the Order, Emma," he added.

"You can't either!"

He laughed but there was no humor in it. "Not for them," he said. "Never for them. For *you*. For Theodora."

"But I just found you," she said. He was leaving her, just as her mother had left her.

"I know," he said gently. "But I'm so proud to call you my daughter, for however brief a moment."

"Then stay! There must be a spell to undo whatever the Order did to you."

"You know I can't. There's no time."

"But you'll be stuck there again."

He smiled sadly. "Tell Theodora I am waiting for her. However long it takes, we will be together again."

His ax was the first to return to mist. He leaped onto the banister, used to climbing trees as a boy, and to the agility of a spirit as a man. The temporary magical mending tore like paper.

And then he was on the other side, a silhouette of himself outlined against the crackling energy. He slashed down once with an antler-handled dagger and the portal began to properly seal itself. It was an ocean whirlpool sucking everything in its path to its dark mouth. The stairs shook, the chandelier beads lifted, and Emma was dragged across the slippery floor.

She didn't even have time to mourn her father's second death by magic.

The Sisters were dragged behind him, fighting the magic of the gate too desperately to be able to keep her or the others trapped inside the house. They howled, acid-green and violent purple energy flinging off them like elf darts. The floorboards began to peel away, popping nails.

She wouldn't let all of this be a waste, wouldn't let her father, or Strawberry and Lilybeth and the other girls die for nothing.

She wouldn't let the Sisters win. Not now. Not ever.

"We have to finish this," she said wearily.

"We can't," Cormac said savagely, staring at the slumped body of the veiled woman next to Sophie.

The Lacrimarium was dead.

Chapter 64

Emma dove out of the house and rolled down the steps, curled protectively around the Lacrimarium's bottle. Gretchen and Penelope dashed after, the silencing spell falling away from Gretchen once she was outside. Cormac and Colette dragged Sophie between them. Cormac was slipping a jet-inlaid iron-wheel pendant around her head, but too late. Emma knew Sophie had killed the Lacrimarium. She'd recognized the collection of odd small injuries on the woman's body, a result of Sophie's talent turned backward.

The garden was eerily quiet as the house shook with light. The drained and dead bodies of the innocent people the Sisters had lured to the house were scattered over the grass. Emma held the bottle in her hands carefully, standing between the gates, one of which hung crookedly off its hinges. This was a Threshold place. It was the best she could do. There wouldn't be a proper Threshold day until May Day and they couldn't afford to leave the Sisters loose until then. This was their last and only chance.

It had to be now.

And it had to be Emma.

She'd read everything she could find in the school library. She was as prepared as she could be. Never mind that the Lacrimarium had rare gifts and trained for years before attempting the kind of spell she was about to try. The Lacrimarium had prepared the bottle before she died. It was infused with the right magic, created on a Threshold day, under the three nights of the full moon and buried in salt and graveyard dirt for a year and a day.

And though Emma wasn't a Lacrimarium, she had an advantage they didn't have. Her connection to the Greymalkin gave her power over them. She could work the spell without the necessary training or talent.

In theory.

"I need hair from all three," she murmured to Cormac. "Or blood. Just in case my . . . in case Ewan doesn't succeed."

"I can help with that," Colette said, just as a hawk erupted from her chest, feathers bright as moonlight on water.

"Gather the horses," Lord Mabon ordered the Keepers who hadn't remained inside the house. "Circle the grounds so no one can escape." Within seconds, white horses appeared all around them, thick as fog. Their hooves shot sparks like falling stars. "Keep the Sisters contained if they fight the gate. We'll have to bind them until another Lacrimarium can be located." He snapped his finger at Emma. "Get back, little girl."

"I don't think so," she replied coldly. "You need me."

"You are still wanted by the Order."

"Even though she's the only reason you've gotten as close to the Sisters as you have tonight?" Gretchen pointed out acidly. "Closer than you have in decades, if I recall correctly." She smiled blandly. "And I know I do."

"Ewan Greenwood sacrificed himself to save us," Emma added, her voice shaking. "I won't let it be in vain. Now you can help me, or you can get the hell out of my way."

Several Keepers swung their heads to goggle at her. No one spoke to the Order that way. Especially not a young witch with a spotty family lineage. Lord Mabon looked taken aback. Cormac hid a grin.

"Here they come," Emma warned.

The Sisters floated out of the house, having already lost the weight of their bones to the battle and the magical wards. Sinister glee and fury rolled off them like steam from a kettle. Paint peeled off the doorframe.

Her father was gone. He'd managed to close the gate, but he'd lost the Sisters.

"Steady on," Cormac said softly as they approached.

The newly regrown garden began to wilt under a coating of ice and frost. A mouse darted out of the bushes and froze solid, burning with the Greymalkin mark.

Lord Mabon elbowed Emma back imperiously. "I can do this," she snapped at him when he showed every intention to ignore her plan. She shoved him back for good measure.

"Just like your mother," he muttered.

"You'd best hope so," she muttered back.

Colette's hawk had possessed a real hawk in the nearby park and it now swooped down with a vicious jab, flying away again with two strands of hair in its beak. When Rosmerta and Magdalena turned to fling a curse on it, Moira's gargoyle dove down between them. The dark magic cracked the stone. The hawk returned, sneaking in from behind and pulled one of Lark's tangled hairs out. She barely noticed.

Emma rubbed the cut on her palm until it opened up again, adding the drops to the bottle. The neck was long enough that she couldn't see what the Lacrimarium had placed inside it. By the smell of it, she probably didn't want to know.

Next, she added one of the hairs.

Fine tremors racked Rosmerta's body and her eyes rolled back in her head. Her familiar was a garden snake and it slithered out from under her hem. The magic of the bottle pulled it faster and faster, until it was sucked into the bottle. Rosmerta glowed brightly then fell apart into dozens of phosphorescent snakes, slinking into the shadows of the garden.

The white horses pressed closer and closer.

The next hair went in, long and auburn and tipped with blood. Lark faded away, her osprey-familiar sliding into the bottle without a struggle.

Magdalena smiled when the last hair joined the others.

Seeing the smile, Emma felt a premonition of cold dread, but it was too late.

Unsurprisingly, Magdalena's familiar was a moth. It landed on the lip of the bottle, folding up its wings and then dropping down the long clay neck. Magdalena turned to mist and drifted away. Sophie screamed. "No! Don't leave me! No, you promised!"

Emma hurried to cork the bottle but now that the spell had been activated, the clay jug froze, burning her hands. She struggled to hold onto it, skin sticking painfully. She felt a strange pull inside her, an uncomfortable severing that had her teeth chattering. The darkness paled to a pearly gray. It took her a splintered excruciating moment to realize she was looking at the witch bottle through her familiar. The luminous deer shape was being sucked into the bottle trap, along with the Sisters' familiars.

She made a strangled sound, unable to form actual words. Her hands blistered with cold, but a worse numbing chill had seized her insides. She knew she would never be warm again. She was being pulled apart and no one would be able to put her back together again. Cormac shouted something but it sounded as though he was speaking through water. She was shivering so violently she couldn't understand how she hadn't let go of the bottle. Her fingers were cramped around it. Her deer-familiar kicked its hooves, fighting the pull.

Cormac's hands closed around hers. His warmth sent needles of pain through her but it was anchoring. It reminded her of her body, dragged the deer back ever so slightly toward her.

"Let go," Cormac said while the Keepers watched, horrified. He peeled her fingers away. Her knuckles cracked, sounding like dry twigs. Her teeth were still chattering and she bit through the side of her tongue. The bottle shook in her grasp.

Cormac gave a hard yank, wrenching it from her.

Pain exploded through her. It scraped inside her skull and closed a jagged fist around her heart. She was scoured clean with it, like sand rubbing rust off an old kettle. She whimpered once before she could stop herself. Her familiar slammed back into her body so violently she was knocked off her feet. She landed on her tailbone in the grass. Gretchen and Penelope were at her side before she could finish catching her first breath.

"How did you do that?" Penelope asked Cormac.

"I have no magic," he replied. "Remember? So I was able to break the connection." He handed the jug to Lord Mabon. "Shall I restrain her, sir?"

"Which one?" He sighed, knocking the candle out of his iron lantern and slipping the bottle safely inside. A jet-inlaid wheel necklace was wrapped around it.

"Sophie was the culprit," Cormac replied without inflection. "But I can secure Lady Emma as well, should you wish it."

"I'd like to see you try." Gretchen bared her teeth. "Ungrateful, useless lot of you."

Before Lord Mabon could answer, the house flared once, shooting arrows of light between the shutters and under the mended door. The power behind it slapped into the garden, pushing everyone out so violently they left grooves in the dirt.

The Keepers flung up a line of shields and the others dropped to the ground, covering their heads.

The house's gates slammed together.

The magpie burned with such intense heat it fused, before fading to black scrollwork again.

The Greymalkin House was closed once more.

Epilogue

Emma stepped out of the carriage in front of the Rowanstone Academy for Young Ladies. She'd spent the last week at Penelope's house recuperating, answering questions from various Keepers and magisters, and eating as much cake as she could. Apparently, defeating warlocks made one hungry. Lord Mabon was commended for setting up the protocol to immediately bring a Lacrimarium to the Greymalkin House if flares were ever sent up in the vicinity. Cormac snuck up the servant staircase one night, disguised by a One-Eyed Joe cameo.

And none of it seemed nearly as daunting as returning to school.

Especially a school filled with several dozen witch debutantes. She could swear her evil-eye ring was warming up even now.

She'd been exonerated of the murders.

But she'd also been tricked into opening the Greymalkin House for the Sisters and their dark secrets.

The school loomed. The gargoyles peered over the corners, their shadows touching the foxgloves and tulips below. The sun gilded the walkway and the brass knocker in the shape of a lion's head. It was pretty and tidy and elegant.

And she couldn't help feeling like it was a trap.

She recited her new favorite constellation: *Leo, Virgo, Hydra.*

She was being ridiculous. She lifted her chin and forced herself to walk calmly into the school. Straight into Daphne.

Who was clinging to Cormac.

Blast.

"Welcome back, Lady Emma," Mrs. Sparrow spoke from the doorway to the parlor before Emma could decide how to react. "I trust you're recovered and ready for lessons?"

"Yes, Mrs. Sparrow."

"And you, Lord Blackburn. Shouldn't you be on Keeper business?"

"Of course. Ladies." Cormac bowed. He sauntered away without a backward glance. It took all of Emma's inner strength not to watch him go.

"Emma, if you could go into the back garden and clear up that thundercloud threatening our outdoor tea for the parents, I'd be most grateful."

"Yes, Mrs. Sparrow." It was a simple task and one she was glad to be given. It felt normal. The headmistress disappeared back into the parlor. Emma turned narrowed eyes on Daphne.

"What?" she whispered innocently. "You know as well as I

do that he can't afford to be seen with you." She smiled, flipping her hair off her shoulder. "But he can be seen with the daughter of the First Legate. In fact, it may just save his reputation, don't you think?"

Emma wished Daphne was wrong about that.

Behind them the staircase was filling up with curious girls. She thought of Ewan Greenwood sacrificing everything to protect her, and of her mother now wandering the forest as a deer. She released the glamour from her antlers and they instantly felt brighter, as if they'd been scrubbed clean of spiderwebs. One of the girls gasped. Several started to whisper loudly. Emma kept walking, heading to the garden.

"Oh go *on*," Daphne snapped at them. They jumped. "Don't gape at her. It's so common."

Emma couldn't help a smile as they scattered, terrified of Daphne. She wondered if they were the same girls Gretchen had convinced to bleat like sheep. All of a sudden she felt quite cheerful to be back at school.

And she felt even more cheerful when Cormac tugged her suddenly into the lilac bush.

"Why is one of us always lurking about in shrubbery?" She grinned. Tables were set up under striped tents, set with silver cake stands covered in delicacies made mostly of buttercream frosting. Silver urns of tea waited next to delicate china cups. The sun was making a valiant effort to shine through the clouds, but they were pewter-gray and plum-purple, and hung like overripe fruit, ready to burst.

"I've been hanging about for ages, waiting for you," Cormac

murmured against her throat. His lips were warm and wicked, trailing down to her collarbone. Her head tilted back of its own accord. "I've missed you," he whispered.

"Me too," she said, sliding her hands under his coat. He was warm and lean and smiling against her mouth.

"Does the Order suspect?"

"That I'd rather be kissing you than talking about them? No." He nipped at her lower lip.

"It's not over," she said, playing with the ends of his hair. She couldn't quite meet his gaze.

"I know." He lifted her chin. His eyes flared, piercing her. "But their hold over me *is*. I belong to *you*, Emma. Not the Order."

He kissed her with such promise, warm shivers chased down her spine. She pressed against him, kissing him back.

The storm clouds cleared.

Author's Note

The witchcraft in this book is purely literary. It is not intended to represent modern or ancient belief systems.